CW00690790

TREASONOUS

THE GABRIEL SERIES - BOOK ONE

DAVID HICKSON

AEON BOOKS

Copyright © 2021 by David Hickson

The moral right of David Hickson to be identified as the author of this work has been asserted by him in accordance with the Copyright, Designs and Patents Act 1988.

All the characters in this book are fictitious, and any resemblance to actual persons living of dead is purely coincidental.

All rights reserved.

No part of this book may be reproduced in any form or by any electronic or mechanical means, including information storage and retrieval systems, without written permission from the author, except for the use of brief quotations in a book review.

ONE

When the moment comes for my mortal remains to be identified I would like to be afforded the dignity of having it done by someone who knew me when I was alive. Someone who had liked me would be even better: someone who could replace the grey features of the dead with a memory of some lively expression, who could fill in a glint of the eyes, a not forgotten smile, something which spoke of joy or love. But failing that, someone who had at least known me.

Lukas Johansson was not afforded such a dignity. It had fallen to me to identify his dead body. I had barely known him, and what I had known I had not liked. His greasy blond hair had been combed by a mortuary worker in a bizarre attempt to soften the impact of death on his features. The effect was disconcerting because in life his hair had been a tangled mess like a bird's nest that he carried around behind his head. Even the photograph that went above his inflammatory and mostly untrue articles in *The Sun* had depicted him as an untidy and unconventional challenger of the traditional, a picture taken in his natural environment –

a bar with shelves of bottles behind him, a leering smile on his pale face, the eyes cold, the only colour on his cheeks provided by the consumption of the contents of too many of those bottles.

But now, dead, and lying on a trolley in the morgue, he was no longer that person. There was no leer, and the rosiness of the alcohol had faded. His hair had not been combed back in that way since his schooldays in the Swedish city of Gothenburg, over forty years ago. His thin face still displayed the deep creases of his hollow cheeks, but any other likeness to the living version had dissolved into the water of the Cape Town docks which had taken his life from him.

I confirmed his identity to the sergeant standing on the other side of the body. A sizeable man with a sad, droopy face, he had been watching me intently as he chewed the gum which he'd confided earlier helped him deal with the smell of this place. He accepted my confirmation, shifted the gum aside and explained that I would need to sign some papers. He signalled for the mortuary worker to take Johansson's remains back to their cold box.

He led the way out through a series of airtight doors which sighed reluctantly as we passed through them, allowing us into progressively brighter corridors until finally we gained the full colour of the autumnal day in the interview room. Outside the morgue a breeze was sweeping the leaves fallen from the oak trees lining the road. The sergeant pulled his standard issue blue coat tight about him as if the chill of the vault had been absorbed into his flesh. He indicated a chair for me to sit in, and shuffled through the papers as if they'd mysteriously been reordered while I'd been identifying Johansson's body.

"Your friend has no family?" he asked as I signed where his sausage-sized finger indicated.

"Not my friend," I said for the tenth time. "I honestly don't know about his family."

He nodded, but his look suggested he thought I was keeping something from him.

"Just work," he said.

"That's right."

"Journalism work."

We'd been through this before, but the sergeant was clearly of the school that believed in repetition.

"About the president," he said, making it sound absurd.

"He was doing background research. You know yourself the papers are full of stories about the president-elect."

"And you too?" asked the sergeant, as if this detail would prove I was responsible for Johansson's death. "You're also doing stories about the president?"

"I make video documentaries. Johansson asked me to confirm some details for him."

The sergeant nodded again and chewed his gum thoughtfully, trying to find the hole in my story.

"Gabriel?" he said.

"Ben Gabriel," I confirmed. I had written my name down for him in several places, but he wanted to be sure that it hadn't changed. "Like the angel," I said.

"Angel?"

"The Archangel Gabriel."

The sergeant chewed his gum.

"You always did that? Videos?"

"No," I said, because he would find out anyway. "I was with the military. British army."

The gum chewing stopped for a moment.

"British?" he asked.

"I grew up there and was a member of the British army. My mother was South African, and my father Canadian. He was in the diplomatic service, posted to the UK."

The sergeant didn't look as if this background alleviated his suspicions. He resumed the chewing.

"Normal army?" he asked. "You were a soldier?"

"Special ops."

"Special? How special?"

"Special Forces, like the SAS. I was originally a paratrooper. Not that special really."

"Why'd you stop?"

"I was discharged."

The sergeant nodded very slowly.

"Are you treating his death as suspicious?" I asked.

The sergeant rejected that notion with a sucking noise that might have been an attempt at clicking his tongue that was foiled by the wad of gum. They had pulled Johansson out of the docks with a blood-alcohol level that was so high, the sergeant had explained earlier, that he had clearly been unable to distinguish the paved walkways from the channels of water on the way back to his car.

"You work with this guy before?"

"No. First time. I did mention that earlier." I tried not to let any irritation show, but the sergeant's eyes narrowed with displeasure.

"What details?" he said, alighting suddenly on the aspect of my story that had been bothering him. "What details did he ask you to confirm for him?"

"Witnesses," I said. "To the fire. Johansson thought I might find him some." I regretted adding that last bit. Too much detail is a sure sign of a lie, and from the searching way the sergeant held my eyes I guessed that he'd been concentrating during that part of his training.

4

"The Khayelitsha fire?" he said.

I nodded. The new president-elect of South Africa, a man called Thulani Mbuyo, was referred to as 'The Phoenix' because of the way in which he had crawled out of a fire that had killed five fellow freedom fighters thirty years ago.

"And did you? Find witnesses?"

"No, I didn't."

"You were phoning to tell him that?"

"I was," I confirmed again.

Having pulled Johansson's body out of the water, the police had found a mobile phone on him, but no other means of identifying him. They had extracted the sim card, inserted it into another phone, then waited for it to ring. I was the first caller, almost eighteen hours after the discovery of the body.

They would have preferred a next of kin, or someone who could be more officially linked to the dead man, but when their other lines of enquiry turned up neither, they settled for me.

The sergeant collected his papers and studied each of my signatures for signs of forgery, then meticulously reached for the paper clip to bind them and tucked them safely into his battered document bag.

"We know where you live," he said ominously.

"Happy to help if you need anything."

He nodded sadly and chewed on his gum.

"We'll find his family," he said and sighed. "Sweden, you said?"

"I believe he grew up in Sweden," I said in a helpful way.

"Not many people liked him," he observed, drawing an inevitable conclusion from my earlier evasive answers about the character of Lukas Johansson. "You say he wrote a lot of shit about people?"

"You know *The Sun*. Not all fairy tales and happy endings."

"Think he made enemies?"

I shrugged. I would have thought Lukas Johansson had people lining up at the quayside to push him into the icy water, but it didn't seem like the right thing to say. The sergeant heaved himself to his feet with a sigh, and we made our way out of the building. He extended his hand to me when we parted ways beneath the oak trees and repeated his threat about knowing where I lived. I pretended to miss the subtlety and gave him encouraging smiles and shook his hand like an innocent man with a clean heart. Presumably he had decided, while watching me look upon the remains of Johansson, that I had not been the one to push him into the water. Or perhaps he was really convinced that no push had been required, and that Johansson's life had ended in a blur of alcoholic confusion between hard ground and deadly water.

I was not so convinced.

———

"Gabriel?" Johansson's voice had a sneering lilt that on other Swedes would have been a charming foreign accent.

"Who is this?"

"Lukas Johansson, *The Sun*. You're going to want to hear this."

"Hear what?"

"That's what I'm telling you, Gabriel. You the Gabriel that worked with Fehrson's crowd?"

"I stopped working there months ago."

"I know. And now you're doing the videos," he said with a triumphant sneer. Then, like the punchline to a joke: "I knew your girl."

That was a conversation stopper. The phone felt heavy in my hand. I had the sense it was radiating malice.

"What do you want to tell me?" I asked.

"We'll meet at the Fireman's," said Johansson as if he was reading a crystal ball. "In half an hour."

"Is this about Sandy?"

Johansson laughed in a way that made the hairs on the back of my neck stand up. "Nothing to do with your girl, Gabriel. I can't help you with that one. It's your friend Fehrson. He's in big trouble and he doesn't know it yet. You're going to help him out. Don't stand me up. You're buying."

The phone went dead before I could object. I placed it beside the laptop on which I was trying to compose some ideas about the Angolan bush war and gazed out of the window. Across the jumbled rooftops of Three Anchor Bay I could see a sliver of grey sea.

I knew of Johansson by reputation only, and that largely from the arms scandal that Sandy had worked on, which was probably why he claimed to have known her. Sandy had been one of a team of journalists who had uncovered the greatest abuse of political power to have happened in South Africa since apartheid, which was saying something: South Africa has an international reputation as a leader in political corruption. But Johansson's angle on the scandal had been the grimy underbelly, the infected bedsores of the monster. It had been his idea to ask the prostitutes what they remembered. The scantily clad sex workers had been in the background of every clandestine meeting, lounging on the furniture of the five-star resorts, decorating the golf courses, and floating in the swimming pools beyond the meeting tables.

It turned out they remembered a good deal, and Johansson enjoyed a moment of fame for providing information that proved critical to the exposure of the scandal. But his reputation among serious investigative journalists was not improved. They regarded him as someone who stirred up the nasty sludge that sank to the bottom of the pond to see what bubbled up to the surface, whether or not that proved beneficial. At least that was what Sandy had said. And she had considered herself to be on the serious side of the business – although sometimes I found it difficult to distinguish between the two approaches.

But Sandy wasn't around anymore to help me resolve the dilemma. She had chosen to find a different life, one that I sometimes hoped was a better one. On other days I felt less generous about her decision to disappear from my life. Because no matter how many carefully chosen words one might use, that was what she had done. One day she had been there, the next she hadn't. No goodbye, no tearful discussion about why things were not working. The police had rejected my missing person claim. There was no evidence of wrongdoing, and missing people do not take a small suitcase of clothes with them. 'Self-managed relocation' was the term the police officer used, with a sidelong glance at me as the probable motivation for the relocation. But that didn't change what she had done. She had arranged her own disappearance. Why not be real about it?

―――――

The Fireman's Arms was one of the oldest pubs in Cape Town, a squat brick building that an enterprising developer had added a steel extension onto in the nineties, thereby quadrupling the floor space and the profits. Johansson was sitting uncomfortably at a table in the large warehouse space created by the open steel girders. He sat alone, a buff-coloured paper folder on the table before him and a glass of rum beside it. The cramped space at the bar was more his style, but there were fewer people in this part of the pub and we could talk about things without worrying about what he described as 'waggling ears'. I recognised his thatch of unruly blond hair, the cold eyes and hollow cheeks, but was surprised by his height when he stood to shake my hand in greeting. A good few inches over six foot. He didn't stoop in the way many tall people do. He stood up straight and held his head back, pleased to be looking over my head, happy to let me know that he felt superior. His smile as he greeted me was a leer that implied he knew something about me that I'd be embarrassed to have generally known. He drained his glass as we sat down and waved at the barman to bring him another. I ordered mineral water. It was eleven in the morning, and something in Johansson's face made me feel that I would rather be sober when I heard what he had to say.

"You still not heard from her?" asked Johansson as an opening move, feigning something approaching a sympathetic tone.

He was talking about Sandy, and his arrogance solidified my initial wariness into a clear dislike for him.

"What is it you want to tell me?"

Johansson leaned back and worked at his teeth with a toothpick.

"Lindiwe Dlomo," he said and then waited as if expecting me to react. I didn't. Johansson paused as the barman placed the drinks on our table. Then watched the man withdraw to the bar area as if suspecting that he might try to eavesdrop.

"Know who she was?" asked Johansson.

"Why don't you tell me?"

"You think the new Top Dog is above board?" he asked, and leered a little wider in order to get the toothpick at the molars.

"I haven't thought much about it," I said. The president-elect was due to take office in six weeks, much to the relief of the populace, who had endured a difficult struggle over several years to rid themselves of the previous incumbent. "He seems more above board than the previous bunch."

"You ever discuss him with Fehrson?"

"I stopped working there almost a year ago."

"And started making your little movies ... yes, yes I know about that. But Big T came up in conversation at the weekly piss-up?"

"No," I said. "Big T never came up."

"No jokes about how you know if Scarface is smiling? Or how to recognise a true hero?"

Thulani Mbuyo, president-to-be, was widely regarded as a hero of the people, an idea supported by the scar tissue that distorted most of his face, a legacy of the fire he'd escaped from with his life, less than a third of his face intact, and a smile that operated only from a corner of his mouth.

"Because Fehrson and his crew know all about what Big T did to Lindiwe Dlomo." Johansson cracked the toothpick in two with long, thin fingers and leered at my obvious confusion. He reached for another toothpick and peeled back the plastic wrapper, which he tossed onto the floor. "And I'm guessing that kind of cover-up takes a team effort."

"I think you have the wrong Fehrson," I said, and meant it. Don Fehrson was a stalwart of the South African Security Service, a man who had been a rising star in the last years of apartheid, had survived the regime change, and then continued his career working for the 'other side', the new rulers of the country, whom he liked to joke had been his previous enemies. Although it was not so much a joke as it was the truth. In recent years his star had faded as he approached retirement, but the concept that he might be hiding a dark secret about the future leader of the country was laughable.

"I heard that she just up and left. Your girl, Sandy. Made it look like she disappeared. Is that how it played?"

I sipped my mineral water. Johansson fiddled with the cover of the buff folder as if he was resisting the temptation to open it and display the contents.

"Not so much as a goodbye kiss. That's what I heard." He abandoned the game with the folder and looked up at me to see how I was taking it. "She was a tough cookie your Sandy, I always knew it. Had style, I'll give her that. You must be asking yourself whether she did it to get away from you. Or is she in some trouble? Is she waiting for you to ride in on your white horse and rescue her? You've been trying to find her, that's what I heard."

Johansson grabbed at his glass as if it had been trying to get away from him and threw the contents into his mouth, ice blocks and all. Then he made as if he was rinsing his mouth for a while, and cracked the ice with his teeth.

"You called because you want to discuss my love life, or because of some fairy tale about Fehrson?"

Johansson finished his mouthwash routine and swallowed the rum, which caused his eyes to water slightly. He inserted the toothpick again and spoke through it like a cowboy.

"I have evidence of what Big T did. A witness. Fehrson

and his happy band of swindlers think they can stop this from blowing up in their faces," he said. "But they cannot."

"Why not go straight to him?"

"You and me know each other. Fehrson wouldn't be here buying me drinks, would he?" He waved at the barman again.

"If you thought I would jump to Fehrson's defence you're in for a disappointment. Publish your story for all I care."

"It's like a ship though isn't it?" Johansson's voice dropped abruptly to a threatening whisper. "All hands go down with the captain."

"Go ahead and publish it," I said, and finished my mineral water to indicate that the conversation was over. "I jumped that ship a long time ago."

"Who said anything about publishing?" said Johansson as the barman delivered another drink. We sat in silence and his cold eyes laughed at me as the realisation of what we were doing here dawned on me. I said nothing as we waited for the barman to retreat, and Johansson switched to an all-business voice.

"You're sitting there with your ears flapping like a damn elephant but you're not hearing me," he said. "I don't want to publish anything. When you find the mother of all gold veins, do you tell the world? Not me, buddy. I just want a few of the filings that fall to the factory floor."

"You want to blackmail Fehrson?"

"Not Fehrson, he's just the nerve-ending. It's the whole damn system behind him that's at stake. Fehrson's just our way in. He knows how some guy without an education and nothing to offer but a lot of scar tissue is about to become the most powerful man in the country. Fehrson's the keeper of the secrets, isn't he?" He scanned the bar as if the mention of that word might cause some of the sad early morning imbibers to cast off their soiled overcoats and reveal their hidden recording devices.

"And you've discovered one of his secrets?"

Johansson raised an offensively delicate white hand. "If you want to play the innocent," he said, "that's okay by me. But your man Fehrson is in up to his eyeballs."

"Fehrson is not in anything," I said. "Not up to any part of his anatomy. He's long overdue for retirement and is just hanging in there because his pension won't cover more than a couple of loaves of bread each month. There's no covering up of secrets. And certainly no big haul."

Johansson smiled with the joy of having made me angry.

"I'm here to help you, Gabriel. Don't you see that?"

"By telling me dirty secrets about the president-elect's past?"

Johansson took the toothpick out and smiled to show me what a splendid joke he thought that was.

"Your life has fallen apart, Gabriel. I've done my research. The Brit army don't want you anymore. What happened there? You kill too many people? Kill the wrong people? They wouldn't let me see your files, you know that? And then your girl up and left. You haven't made one of your little videos for months."

"Nevertheless," I said. "I'm not interested in your blackmail schemes."

"Just ask Fehrson about Lindiwe Dlomo. That's all you need to do."

"Where are you getting this bullshit? Did you dream it up?"

"Fuck you," said Johansson, and he tilted his chair back onto its hind legs to see how I would take that. When I didn't respond he let the chair right itself, propelling him back to the table where his hand found his glass with practised ease, and he grinned widely as if to quell my offence.

"No, no … that's where I get it from: 'fuck … you'. It's a Xhosa clan name. You know the Xhosa tribe have clans? You wouldn't understand – you're a foreigner."

I didn't bother pointing out that he was no less a foreigner. And I didn't want to encourage him by discussing Xhosa clan names.

"You talk to Fehrson," he said magnanimously. "Tell him I'm not the vindictive sort. We can work something out."

"Talk to him yourself," I said and stood up to leave.

Johansson nodded as if he approved of that move on my part.

"If you like," he said. "But I thought that you might want to know where this was taken." He placed a hand like a long-legged spider onto the buff folder, pushed it across the table towards me and swivelled it around so I could open it with ease. I didn't open it. His eyes were gleaming with an extraordinary malice.

He opened the folder, and despite myself, I glanced down.

It was a photograph. What I'd heard Sandy call a 'four by six'. A good quality matte colour print, taken with a telephoto lens. The subject in clear focus, and the background blurred. A professional job because at that range the depth of field would have been only a few inches.

It was Sandy. Her dark hair was pulled back, and she was looking over her shoulder as if she was running from someone, or more likely because she was about to cross a road and was simply turning to look at oncoming traffic. Her face looked pale and drawn, lighter than the creamy toffee of my memory, as if she was stressed or unwell. Her face had the look I remembered, of vulnerable misery. Her large eyes were liquid, as if she might be about to burst into tears, and her lips compressed for fear that they would spill everything she had bottled up inside. But this was an illusion. There was a strength within her that was at odds with the fragility of her face. The impression that she was miserable was a conspiracy of her physical features, and the moment she smiled it vanished. But in this photograph there was no smile, and the tension in her face was all too clear.

I sat down. Johansson had been talking, and now he repeated himself.

"It's recent," he said and reached out a thin finger with knobbly joints to point at the foot of the photograph. A date was burned into the image. Two weeks ago.

"Dates can be faked," I said.

"Sure they can," he admitted and shrugged like a man who wouldn't be bothered to do something so foolish. "My buddy took that picture. There are more where that came from." He closed the folder and pulled it back across the table. I was still looking at it, transfixed. I raised my eyes to his. There was a glint of triumph there. He smiled, revealing a row of even and very white teeth. Were they false, or was he simply a good example of the standard of Swedish dentistry? They were out of place in his battered face.

"My buddy was on a job. Human trafficking. Nasty business."

"I'm not interested in what happened to Sandy. I've moved on."

"Words, that's all those are, Gabriel. Meaningless words. I'm thinking you want to know how your girl ended up there. Voluntary or involuntary? Is she waiting for you to

15

save her?" He showed me his teeth again. "Tell you what. Give me an address, and when you've spoken with your old boss, I'll send these over."

He pushed the folder back across the table and produced a pen.

"I'm not interested in your holiday snaps," I said, but my voice didn't come out quite as strongly as I intended.

"We make this a win-win," he said in a friendly tone and handed me the pen.

I wrote an address – not my own address because I have learned to be circumspect about these things.

"Dlomo. Lindiwe," he said. "Remember the name. Then phone me."

"I am not peddling your shit to Fehrson." I said more firmly.

Johansson allowed the smile to drop off his face like someone had cut the strings. He reached for another toothpick and peeled it. "Forty-eight hours enough?" he said.

I stood up, considered a parting shot, decided against it, and instead turned to leave.

"Ask the barman for another, will you? When you're paying."

I ignored him and strode away.

"Forty-eight hours," he called after me.

But he didn't get to see those forty-eight hours through. Johansson was pulled out of the Atlantic Ocean a mere thirty-six hours later. The thing that bothered me as I left his chilled body in the morgue and walked away like a man without a conscience was whether he had ended up in the ocean because of me.

TWO

Four hours after I had left Johansson to finish his drink and think his greedy thoughts, I arrived at the Warehouse. Thirty-two hours before they would pull his body from the sea.

"Hail, the conquering hero," said Khanyisile. "Or should I welcome back the prodigal son?"

"There isn't a lot I've conquered recently, Khanyi, so don't think flattery will get you anywhere. It'll just make me bitter."

"It never took much," she said with a laugh that sounded like a row of bells on a chilly morning.

Khanyisile was a Zulu from the north, as she reminded anyone who made the mistake of thinking she came from the sleepy Cape. Her people were warriors, and she demonstrated her ancestral tendencies in a fierce ambition. She had started at the Department with a secretarial qualification and a mediocre typing speed, and had lost no time in dusting off a piece of legislation that provided for educational funding for staff members. In five years she had armed herself with two university degrees, and leap-frogged everyone else so that by the time I had joined the team she had become Fehrson's right-hand woman. And, it was rumoured, the highest-paid person on the ninth floor. So strong was her ambition that envious colleagues claimed she dedicated all of her free time to her betterment and had not enjoyed a single social engagement since swearing to the Official Secrets Act. Such self-control baffled the many men and occasional woman who found that her Masai-warrior body, tightly plaited hair, and perfectly symmetrical features inspired in them a curiosity to discover what might lie beneath her dramatic sense of office dress. Today she was wearing a demure two piece in blue suede. It stretched in all the right places and looked as if some buttons had popped.

"Father was so surprised you called, he asked me to check that we'd paid all your expenses," said Khanyi as the lift hauled us with great effort towards the ninth floor. 'Father' because Fehrson had started his military career as an army chaplain.

"And you found that you hadn't?" I said.

Khanyi handed me a tight-lipped smile. "All approved expenses were paid," she said primly.

"I just need a quiet word with Fehrson alone. I won't bring up the unpaid expenses."

"We will be alone," said Khanyi, demonstrating the strength of her position in the Department.

The lift jerked abruptly to a stop, as if noticing too late that we'd reached the ninth floor. Fehrson's small Department of State Security occupied a handful of rooms on the upper floors of the Warehouse. A relic of the eighteenth century, the building was an opulent trader's warehouse on Greenmarket Square in the centre of Cape Town. A new face had been put onto it in a moment of Baroque optimism many years ago, but behind that ornate front was the same old crumbly building with wrought-iron staircases, creaky wooden floors, and rooms that could have accommodated giants if it hadn't been for the doorways that were made for midgets. There were ten rambling storeys, and to this day I'm convinced there are some rooms that haven't been opened for over a century, so labyrinthine is the design of it. The old building provided premises for the sort of things that burly security guards discourage one from looking into too closely. Here Fehrson had spun his web, appropriately distant from any official state offices, and had trapped his handful of employees with the efficient assistance of Khanyi.

I had worked with the Department for less than a year, employed initially because Fehrson wanted me to bring my military experience to bear upon the work that they were doing. But my experience had proved too extreme for him. Too much of the less salubrious aspects of military life, the fuel of nightmares that wake you up in the small hours of the morning. Fehrson had smiled bravely in the face of this realisation, and had told me many times he didn't like the word 'breakdown', because many retired soldiers had issues that they needed to resolve. And the fact I'd been discharged – who cares whether it was honourable? – and that I had spent time working through these issues with various psychologists did not mean that I was in any way 'broken'.

———

'Father' Fehrson arrived at the small chrome and glass meeting room that Khanyi had organised for our little talk looking like an English gentleman called in from a pheasant shooting weekend. A tweed jacket with understated tie, corduroy trousers, and shoes that were smart enough for the cocktails, yet would handle the muddy fields. It was an inappropriate image because Fehrson was an Afrikaner of German descent, without a drop of English blood in him. But it was an image he fostered, having astutely surmised that an Englishman in the South African security service was more likely to survive the turbulent transition of the country from pariah state to rainbow nation than would an Afrikaner. Whether that accounted for his persistence in the service after so many years, I wasn't sure. He was certainly one of very few old hands who still roamed the corridors of secret power.

He stood at the door and opened both arms as if he was inviting a large audience to share in his wonderment.

"Look at you," he said, and took another moment to do just that. Then to Khanyi, "Didn't I tell you he'd be back?"

"You did, Father," she said demurely, a kitten in the presence of her master.

"Press that button, Khanyisile," he said as he greeted me with a handshake that felt more like a judo grip, my hand grasped in both of his, and he studied my face for damage. "We'll get some coffee."

Khanyi pressed the button on the intercom box on the table. It squawked in response.

"Ask her for the real stuff," said Fehrson. "It's not every day we get to welcome back one of our own."

The box didn't seem to like the idea of the real stuff, and Fehrson sighed as it expressed that dislike in a high-pitched stream of squawks. He relinquished my hand, and we took our places at the table, with Fehrson and Khanyi facing me, their backs to the window so that the light was in my eyes and it could become an interrogation in a moment if things went that way.

The light turned Fehrson's neatly combed white hair into a halo, although a few sections tried to break away from the rest and turn him into a crazy old man, which is pretty much what he was, being a good five years past retirement. But the moment anyone made the mistake of thinking that Fehrson was a doddery old man, his clear blue eyes would flash and he would give a glimpse of the qualities that had earned him his original nickname, 'Fearsome'.

"Secrets?" said Fehrson incredulously after I'd presented the first part of my pitch. I'd been careful to avoid any details, and had only gently hinted at a vague suspicion, but Fehrson was too sharp to miss the main thrust of the thing. "Your friend is suggesting that someone from our department is covering up dark secrets about the new leader?" His incredulity turned into indignation. "That's preposterous."

"Which is what I told him," I said. "He's not my friend, I met him for the first time this morning."

"But he does the same ..." Fehrson searched for a word that might describe the lowly work I'd been engaged in since leaving the Department. "The same sort of ... would you call it journalism?" he suggested as if that was a dirty word.

"He writes for a disreputable newspaper. Not really the same thing."

"*The Sun*?" asked Khanyi.

"*The Sun*. Yes," I said. There didn't seem much point in denying it, and although it wasn't the only disreputable newspaper in the Cape, it was the worst one. "I thought I should let you know these rumours are circulating, just in case you'd like to do anything about them."

"Do anything?" said Fehrson, the note of incredulity still ringing strong. "What would you expect me to do?

Laugh about it? Or were you thinking of something more action oriented?"

I honestly hadn't any idea what I expected them to do about it. I had left the Fireman's Arms in a fuming rage, determined to forget the unpleasant encounter with Johansson as quickly as I could. But a couple of hours staring blankly at my computer screen, a few listless phone calls to people who were not interested in discussing their experiences in the Angolan war, several cups of coffee, and then a determined walk through the blustery rain of an early autumn afternoon for a late lunch at Giovanni's, had done nothing to remove the image of Sandy's face from my mind. I had struggled back through the wind and damp leaves to my apartment and wondered what harm there would be in picking up the phone and calling the Department. But that was about as far as my planning had gone.

I didn't think Johansson would tell me where that photograph had been taken, no matter what I did. He was that kind of person. But sitting here talking to Fehrson seemed like a better thing to do than stare at a computer screen until my forehead started bleeding.

Khanyi and Fehrson were looking at me as if expecting me to say something. I realised my mind had wandered.

"Or is it supposed to be just a blanket 'sins of the past' kind of secret?" asked Fehrson.

"There was a name mentioned," I said. "He implied it had something to do with a woman."

"Doesn't it always," said Khanyi with a dose of bitterness.

"Well, let's have it then," said Fehrson, pretending to gird himself up for a bombshell. "What dalliance is coming back to haunt our new leader?"

I searched my mind for the name that Johansson had

thrown at me. I hadn't stopped to have him write it down and felt foolish for having rushed out without at least clarifying some details. Then it came back in a rush. "Lindiwe. That was it. Lindiwe someone or other."

Fehrson didn't react. His face remained still as if he had not heard what I'd said, but I could have sworn his eyes did something. It was as if the pupils suddenly dilated. I'd been paying attention when they taught us that the pupils dilate when you get a sudden shock. I'd even seen it firsthand in the field. But this was not an interrogation, and I wasn't looking for it, so I dismissed it as a figment of my imagination. At that moment the door opened, and Belinda waddled in with a tray of coffee. Fehrson looked away and focused on the coffee and the six dry biscuits she had arranged symmetrically around the plate to make it seem as if it was full.

"This the real stuff?" asked Fehrson with feigned bonhomie, taking a deep sniff an inch above the ruinous milky brown liquid.

"It is not, Mr Fehrson," said the spherical Belinda, who steadfastly refused to call him Father because, as she pointed out whenever she had an opportunity, she was almost his age, and she already had someone she called Father. It was generally accepted that someone was part of the Holy Trinity, because Belinda was Presbyterian.

"Besides, Mr Fehrson," said Belinda as she withdrew from the room. "That nasty machine you bought last year has stopped working. I did tell you about that."

Before Fehrson could respond, she closed the door.

"It's because she tried to get it to produce coffee without filling the water tank," confided Fehrson as he reached for a biscuit. "Two each," he said in case our mathematics wasn't up to the challenge. "Unless you're not biscuit-ing today, Khanyi?"

Khanyi indicated that she was not biscuit-ing, and when I bit into one of them I realised why. It would have been more tasty to have taken slices out of the wooden floorboards.

"Dlomo," I said, as the full name came back to me. "Lindiwe Dlomo was what he said."

"Ah yes?" asked Fehrson casually as he tried to wash some biscuit down with what Belinda called coffee.

"That's the one," I said. "Lindiwe Dlomo. This journalist implied that it all had something to do with her."

Fehrson didn't respond but looked down at his biscuit as if suspecting that it wasn't edible after all.

"Do we know a Lindiwe Dlomo?" asked Khanyi.

Fehrson shook his head and put the biscuit back onto the plate. "You don't, my dear," he said. "There was a Lindiwe Dlomo who did something for us a very long time ago. Back in the eighties. More than thirty years ago." He glared at the plate of biscuits, wondering whether he'd been unlucky with his.

"There is a connection then?" said Khanyi. "I mean this journalist isn't spouting absolute nonsense. The woman exists, and she had a connection with the Department."

No, no," said Fehrson, uttering the two words like the beating of a rhythm on a drum. He looked up at me, reluctantly giving up on the biscuits and focusing instead on our conversation. "She died many years ago. I doubt you'd find anyone here who even remembers her."

Apart, of course, from Fehrson. I didn't say that, but glanced at Khanyi and imagined I could detect the same thought tiptoeing its way across her mind.

"We could pull her file and see if anything floats to the surface," suggested Khanyi.

Fehrson shook his head. "Those old files all went over to the archives when we moved here from that old Woodstock dungeon. All that Truth and Reconciliation nonsense. Before your time, you wouldn't remember it." Fehrson sniffed.

The Truth and Reconciliation 'nonsense' had been a commission established after the fall of the apartheid regime to sift through the troubled past of the country and expose the truth behind politically motivated crimes and military actions, then attempt to achieve reconciliation within a complex collection of cultures who had until recently been at war with one another. Fehrson was correct in saying that I didn't remember it, because it hadn't been big news at the grammar school I was attending at the time in Dorset, but I certainly did know of it. I also knew that it was Fehrson's shortest fuse. It was well established among the Department staff that the quickest way to rouse Father's temper was to mention the TRC.

"If it was with the TRC files she must have been more than a person of interest," said Khanyi. "It would have been operational."

"No, no," said Fehrson again. "It was the time of the great collapse. The war was over and everything we had was ripped out from our carefully concealed hiding places and put up on the shelves like god-awful library books for everyone to read. Operational, personnel, even the office expense sheets were taken from us. You could go over to those archive people and ask for the files, I suppose. If they can find them."

"It hardly seems worth it," said Khanyi. "You don't remember what this woman did for us, Father?"

Fehrson shook his head and adopted the look of a man struggling to recall his youth. "She was a bit-part player," he said. "Just a pigeon; carried messages back and forth, if I recall. I was not directly involved, but she told us about things happening on the ground – that fire, that sort of thing."

"That fire?" said Khanyi. "The Khayelitsha Massacre fire?"

"Amongst other things," said Fehrson.

"They call the president-elect the Phoenix because he survived that fire," she said. "That would be a connection between them."

"I doubt it. She was a carrier pigeon, that was all. Don't complicate things unnecessarily, Khanyisile."

Khanyi turned to me. "Was that all this journalist said? Just a name?"

"That was it. A woman called Lindiwe, and someone from the Department 'covering up' for the new president."

"And why did he come to you?" asked Khanyi. "Why didn't he ring our doorbell and come up for some tea?"

I wanted to ask Khanyi whether she had seen the size of the men who answered their doorbell, but instead I shrugged. "He thought I might have more influence with you."

"Influence with us?" asked Fehrson. "Why would he think that? Are you part of some club of people who do this sort of thing? Go around stirring up nonsense from the past," He gave a faint shiver of horror. "He wants a statement from us to stop him publishing this ridiculous nonsense?"

"I rather think he is not planning on publishing anything," I said.

"Well, of all the ludicrous ... What on earth is he planning on doing?"

"He wants hush money, doesn't he?" asked Khanyi.

"I think so."

"And you came to us expecting we would agree?" asked Khanyi, her eyes lighting up with anger.

"I came here because I thought you should know someone was going around spreading this rubbish. I wasn't going to mention any money."

Khanyi narrowed her eyes to slits as if she could see my flaws better that way.

"Of course you weren't," said Fehrson. "We're all friends here, Khanyisile. Don't be ridiculous."

Khanyi flashed a perfect white smile at me. "I know that, Father," she said, and shared her smile with him.

"My advice, young Ben," said Fehrson as he pushed his coffee away in case he accidentally took another sip. "My advice is that you go back to this journalist friend of yours and tell him he's got his knickers all in a twist, and that there is no story."

"And there is no money," said Khanyi.

"That is my intention," I said. "Has been all along. I thought it would be rude not to mention it to you though."

"For which we are very grateful, my dear boy," said Fehrson. "Khanyi can take some action as you suggest. A small statement perhaps? Just in case your friend decides to go ahead and publish when we refuse to pay. We'll go through what paperwork we have and play an open hand. Come back in a couple of days and we'll show you what we've got. You can go back to your friend and tell him with your hand on your heart that there is no dark secret. My goodness," he produced a hearty laugh. "The sheer absurdity of it. Now you help yourself to a few of those biscuits. It's not every day Belinda is so generous."

———

"It's that Swedish jerk, isn't it?" asked Khanyi as we descended in the lift together. "He's the kind who would dream up some nonsense from thirty years ago and then try to extort money from us."

I didn't answer, but dug around in the pockets of my jacket for some cigarettes. I found a pack of Gauloises and pulled one out.

"Never liked the rubbish he wrote," continued Khanyi. "He picks on the vulnerable and then crushes them. Aren't journalists meant to do things the other way round?"

"Is the Department vulnerable?" I searched for some matches.

"You can't smoke that in here you know," said Khanyi. "I thought you'd given up."

"I had," I said, and held the matchbox in my hand as the lift lurched downward in small discreet steps. "But what are we going to do when this lift gets stuck and they have to call the firemen to cut us out?"

Khanyi sighed.

"Of course we're vulnerable," she said. "You know how they're always trying to push Father out. He's a dinosaur, an embarrassment for Pretoria. We're fighting for our lives here, Gabriel, you know that. It was the same when you were here."

I did know it, and for the last few floors we descended in silence. There had been a time, before I understood the subtlety of the situation, when I'd thought Khanyi would have welcomed Fehrson's downfall. As the high priestess of the Department, she would have stepped into his shoes and achieved the ultimate accolade: her own department. But Johansson's comparison with a ship came back to me. Like a ship that has travelled too far off course, if the captain went down the ship would be doomed. None of the crew knew the way back.

———

Two days later, after identifying Johansson's remains, I returned to my apartment and took a shower to clean off the lingering smell of death. Then I stood on the balcony and watched a cold front approach over the sea as the evening light faded. I lit the cigarette I'd been toying with the past couple of days and wondered how much time you would need to plan to push someone off a waterfront quay. There had been about eight hours since the time I left the Warehouse and the time that Johansson discovered just how cold the Atlantic gets in late autumn. That would have been enough time. But surely Fehrson didn't still engage in that sort of messy activity. Or did Khanyi handle it all for him?

The sun found its way under the bank of clouds but then collapsed into a molten pool which oozed into the Atlantic. I found no answers out to sea, but the gathering storm did provide me with some resolve. I might not have liked Johansson, but the least I could do was find out what sordid intrigue might have ended his life.

THREE

Cape Town swims through the Atlantic like a jellyfish alongside the whale that is the African continent. Behind it trails a single knobbly sting, the Cape Peninsula that keeps the Atlantic and the Indian Ocean from getting together too soon. There are two strings of suburbs, one on each side of the peninsula. On the east you find the suburbs for serious types who commute into work and like to pretend that they're not living in a holiday camp. On the western side of the peninsula are the more frivolous suburbs that squeeze onto the steep slope between the sea and a row of mountain peaks called the Twelve Apostles. These people are well aware that they live in a holiday camp. It's why they're here, after all. This is where all the big money resides, where the international pop stars live incognito behind their sunglasses, sipping gin on terraces overlooking the sea, waving coyly at the yachts that drift past.

If you drive down the road that winds along this coast you eventually leave behind all the glitz and glamour, and arrive at Hout Bay, one of the most beautiful bays on the peninsula. It has a small harbour for yachts and fishing boats, a few real old fishermen, and houses that yearn to be little farms, each with their own plot for growing vegetables and orchards of fruit trees.

Bill Pinter had a house one road up from the shoreline, so that when the genuine oak French doors were open one could hear the sea below and smell the ozone. It was an old building, a touch of Provençal France, and one wall was still the original stone wall that had been part of the farm building that stood here before Bill came along and modernised it. Terracotta tiles with underfloor heating paved the way onto the terrace with vines growing over the trellis. From here one could survey the fruit trees, and beyond them the sea. Bill insisted that his trees were on a plot: apparently gardens are the things with flowers. Plots are much more serious.

"You've got nothing more than her name?" asked Bill as he topped up my glass. "The name of a woman who died thirty years ago? That's going to be a tough one." He was wearing an apron stretched across his ample stomach, because my unexpected visit had inspired him to indulge in his favourite pastime, and he was 'whipping up' something in the kitchen while I admired the view.

"She had a file with the NIA," I said.

"Oh no, Gabriel," Bill paused in pouring the wine as if not sure that I deserved any more. "You're not working with those government goons again are you?"

Bill had never approved of the Department. He didn't approve of anything related to government and had made his position on the matter abundantly clear when Sandy had introduced us. Theirs was a friendship of many years, one that I had been fortunate to inherit when Sandy 'took me on' as Bill liked to say.

"Back then just about everyone had a file with the NIA," I said.

"But now they've misplaced it, and they've asked you to sweep the remains under the carpet?"

"They haven't asked me anything. A journalist suggested that she was a stain on Mbuyo's past. I'm intrigued, that's all."

I didn't mention that the journalist was now lying in a morgue.

"Why don't you take a look at the NIA file?"

"I don't think they have it. They transferred those old files to the archives after the TRC hearings."

Bill nodded, a movement that involved most of his upper body. He had always been Sandy's 'secret source'. A lecturer in contemporary history at the University of Cape Town, he was a walking and talking reference on everything that had happened in the country in the past fifty years. At least Sandy had always claimed so. When she needed to know something she had turned to Bill first and was rarely disappointed. Which was why I was now sampling Bill's fine collection of Chardonnay and was preparing to enjoy his famous veal cordon bleu. It was rumoured he had perfected the dish by testing it upon a series of young and flirtatious female students, of whom he seemed to have an endless supply. Bill was like the Pied Piper of the History department. He was a junior lecturer and tutor, but most people were surprised when they discovered that he wasn't the professor in charge. This probably had something to do with the way his voice would boom down the corridor, causing secretaries and other minions to flutter about with nervous anticipation whenever he paid one of his sporadic visits to his shoe-box office.

"Thirty years ago is my speciality. Not much I don't know about that time."

"She was probably no more than a messenger. Hardly headline material."

Bill harrumphed and finished topping up my wine. Bill is large. I would like to find a kinder way of saying it, but there isn't one really. He is tall, and big boned no doubt, but there is a substantial amount of flesh on those bones. He has several chins, and hands that look as if they've been inflated, but his largeness is not merely a matter of being fat. He has a presence that would be enough for two normal mortals. He dresses with refined taste in oversize clothes, usually in strong colours, and is hard to miss in a crowd, not that he ever hangs out in crowds. At the opera, Bill always sits in the balcony where he reserves two seats, one for each half of himself.

"It's not a name that rings any bells," said Bill as he returned to the kitchen.

"It was worth a shot," I said. "Sandy always claimed you were the best place to start."

"You should go direct to the archives," he called back as he shook the pan and a wall of flame reached up to the ceiling. "Those old NIA files are in the Gold Archives now."

The Gold Archives had been established by the South African Gold Mining Conglomerate, and were really just a big publicity stunt in which Riaan Breytenbach, the chairman of the conglomerate, stood around smiling in front of pictures of shelves of dusty files, and explained that he was using a microscopic portion of the blood money he and his cronies had made from their gold mines, in order to preserve the rich heritage of the country. Heritage in the form of the written history and archive material. It was too late to preserve the heritage in the form of the gold which had all been sold, or was stored somewhere safe and now mostly belonged to Breytenbach and his cronies, and certainly too late to preserve the heritage in the form of the thousands of lives lost in the mines. But everyone smiled for the cameras and Sandy had told me I was being a cynical bastard, which was probably true. That was when the Gold Archives were opened – before Sandy left. And she said that I was prejudiced, which was also true. It was during a posting to Breytenbach's gold mine in northern Uganda that my military career had come to an end. He had needed help dealing with a terrorist problem, and the British government had been most obliging.

"And this Lindiwe had something to do with Mbuyo?" asked Bill as he brought the food out to the terrace.

"There's a possible connection with the fire," I said.

"The Khayelitsha fire?"

"The Khayelitsha massacre was what my erstwhile employer said."

"Well, well. That's an interesting connection." Bill tucked a napkin beneath his chins and raised his cutlery as if about to perform a ritual slaughter. "I've got some old photographs and news clippings and the like. If you're up to some nostalgia we could go through my slides after dinner. But have yourself some veal before it gets cold."

Bill's Veal Cordon Bleu was worth the wait. "That's Dutch cheese, the genuine stuff, made down the road from here," he said, and I believed him. I'd seen the cows on my way up.

"It's very good," I said. "And that's an understatement."

Bill shook his head, and grimaced. "Too tough," he said.

"Nonsense, I hardly need the knife."

"The point about cooking is to make each dish better

than the last time. And this isn't. An honest critic would tell me that."

I was about to say that he hadn't cooked this dish for me before when I remembered that he had. On the last occasion that Sandy and I had eaten with him. Bill saw the memory bubble up to the surface.

"I should have chosen a different dish," he said. "I would have, if you'd called."

"My fault," I said, and we both drank some wine and sat in silence for a moment. Sometimes I forgot how Sandy's disappearance had affected her friends, I was so blinded by my own sense of betrayal.

———

Bill's slides were a collection of photographs and news clippings that he had compiled years before for a lecture about the many ways in which South Africans had killed each other during the apartheid years. He'd prepared the lecture in the days when things were done the old-fashioned way with light projected through plastic.

"I've got a lot of pictures here that have nothing to do with Mbuyo and the Khayelitsha Massacre, but we'll skip ahead to the important stuff," said Bill. "It's all a bit nasty," he added, and it certainly was. Khayelitsha is a township about thirty kilometres from Cape Town which developed from the humble beginnings of squatter camps in the area. These camps sprang up in the apartheid years wherever migrant workers found empty spaces on which they could build shacks out of iron roofing sheets, old shopping carts and cardboard boxes. The government etched dusty roads between the tin shacks, and built simple brick buildings to make them official. Mangy dogs roamed the streets which turned into mud streams whenever it rained, which was often. Or whenever the open sewers overflowed, which was even more often. At the height of the violence in South Africa, before the country changed its face, Khayelitsha was a place of death, poverty, and near civil war. Troops patrolled the streets when they dared in huge armoured vehicles called Casspirs, and everywhere shacks burned, and people died. The Khayelitsha Massacre was one such fire, in which five people had been killed when a small shack in Khayelitsha burned to the ground, early one morning. The sole survivor of the fire was the man who would be taking the helm of the country a few weeks from now.

"One wonders how it could possibly have been five of them, in such a small shack," said Bill, "but when you see the photographs, you'll understand. There were two rooms to the shack, and people were sleeping everywhere."

Bill had found his old slide projector, so we cleared some pictures of Audrey Hepburn off one wall, and turned down the lights.

"There was a small media stir about it. At first everyone thought it was just an accidental fire. There were so many of them in those days. But when the names of the dead came in, it was obvious that it had not been an accident. Five members of an ANC resistance cell seemed like too much of a coincidence. But remember this was in a time of military rule. There was a national state of emergency. The newspapers couldn't publish anything political, particularly not violence like this, so effectively the whole thing was kept quiet. It's hard to imagine nowadays with the proliferation of news and media, but in those days if the papers didn't print it, it didn't happen. How else would you know something had occurred? The papers used to print blank columns, sometimes whole pages were empty in protest of the censorship. This massacre featured overseas for as long as it made big news, but it soon got replaced by bigger and better things."

"Let's see what we have here ..." A black and white blur jumped onto the wall. "Oh damn." Bill fiddled with a knob and the blur did aerobics against the wall. "Now what's happened to that ...?" Suddenly the blur disappeared, to be replaced by another brighter, bigger blur which had a bit of colour in it.

"How's that?" Bill asked hopefully.

"Not quite there yet," I said.

Something clicked loudly, and a dead body appeared in place of the blur. It was face down with one arm underneath it, the other flung back and around as if it was giving itself a last embrace. Several large, uneven wounds had attracted flies. The body lay on a surface of compacted dirt, and in the top corner of the picture a shoe was visible, and beyond it a lifeless foot.

"Oh dear," said Bill, "looks like they're out of order. That's the brother, Wandile. Let me see." The slide machine swallowed Wandile and presented us with the image of a corrugated iron shack hanging suspended from a thin sliver of ground. Some people stood around on their heads.

"That's upside down," said Bill. There were more slide machine noises.

"Ah!" The shack, or what was left of it, was the right way up now. It was one of a row of shacks and all that was left were some charred wooden poles and warped corrugated iron sheeting. A group of people stood around the shack, all looking at the desolation, their backs to camera. "Newspaper photograph," said Bill, "This is where it happened, and now here ..." Wandile appeared on the wall, but now he too was upside down.

"Oh dear ... Well, never mind. This is Wandile Mbuyo. Brother of Thulani. Did you know his brother was killed in the fire?"

"I didn't even know he had a brother," I said.

"Few people do. He never mentions him. Bad blood in the family."

The next slide appeared – the same shack, but this was obviously later in the day. A group of soldiers in army browns stood around the shack clutching their Denel R4s nervously to their chests. The crowd had grown larger.

"Things got volatile. There was some stone throwing, that sort of thing. Nobody else was killed, but then news leaked out that someone had survived."

The next picture was from further away. An even larger crowd, and towering over them a bright yellow Casspir.

"That's from the Swedish," said Bill. "None of this was reported in the local papers because of the censorship. But you can see the names clearly enough. There's Thulani ... Wandile ... No Lindiwe though."

Bill moved on to the next slide, a photograph of a necklace killing, popular around that time according to Bill. "They would force a car tyre over the victim's head, pinning their arms to their side. Douse them with petrol and set them alight." Bill changed the slide.

We looked at several more slides, some of which Bill managed to get the right way up and in focus. Some were rather attractive blurs of colour that pulsated as Bill cursed and fiddled with the knobs, and they were really the best ones. The others were too graphic for my tastes. A few of them included written articles which discussed the massacre. But not one of those had the name Lindiwe Dlomo.

––––––

Bill made coffee after the slide show and we sat on the terrace trying to rid ourselves of the haunting images.

"That cold front's going to hit tomorrow," said Bill and swirled his coffee about, looking into it as if he could read the future there. Bill liked milky coffee, even at this time of day. Mine was short and black. Below us the masts of the yacht club swayed back and forth like a field of wheat being disturbed by giant moles.

"The quiet before the storm," I said and Bill looked at me as if he had many things to say, but was struggling to get past the inanities. He probably did have many things to say. Certainly, he and Sandy would have talked deep into the night in the relaxed way that old friends don't notice the passing of time. My friendship with Bill had never graduated to that level, perhaps because Sandy was a constant presence between us, like a spectre that rose up whenever the conversation hit a lull. I wanted to tell Bill about Johansson's photograph, but I knew that it would only upset him. I wondered about it now as we gazed into the dark night. I didn't suppose that I would ever discover where it had come from, with Johansson lying in a fridge, and the police crawling over his meagre possessions. I thought of saying something to Bill about the fact that I had written his address on Johansson's folder, but he was watching the masts performing their silent jig, and had sunk into a trance as if their swinging motion had hypnotised him.

Bill had been a good friend to Sandy, and I had inherited some of the good will, but if I started discussing my reasons for providing his address to Johansson, I guessed that it would only stir up his suspicions about my history, and the narrow crack through which I tried to engender our friendship would close. It was bad enough that I'd had a career in the military, an institution of which he was highly suspicious. Then to have worked – albeit briefly – for state security rendered me even less desirable as a friend. If I was to start picking at the scab of the wound caused by Sandy's disappearance that might have been the last straw. So I drank my coffee and gazed out to sea, in companionable silence.

Bill slurped at his coffee noisily and regarded me over the brim of the cup.

"There's a man I interviewed for that book I worked on," he said suddenly. "He was on Robben Island at the same time as Mbuyo. I could ask him if the name rings any bells."

"Don't stick your neck out," I said. "It could be that Lindiwe Dlomo isn't a very popular name in those circles."

"Leave it to me," said Bill, and he slurped his coffee.

FOUR

At ten minutes after nine the next morning, I found myself sitting at one of Giuseppe's dingy back tables. A heart attack special was popping its full cream foam in front of me, and I was fiddling with the first of a fresh pack of those filthy French things, telling myself that I wouldn't light it until I was outside. Members of the leisure class of Cape Town, from indolent artists to the toy boys of the rich, surrounded me and chatted while looking over each other's shoulders to see who else was featuring today. Beyond them Greenmarket Square was warming up to its day's activity, with stall owners laying out their wares, and the pickpockets exploring the escape routes they'd be using. Greenmarket Square is an old, cobbled space in the heart of Cape Town enclosed by a stern Methodist Church, a five-star hotel, some Parisian pavement cafes, and the most expensive African curio shops to be found on the continent. For forty years the square has played host to a flea market, a constantly swelling collection of stalls which occupy it like an arrogant hippie camp during the day, and then disappear by nightfall to allow the tourist limos some space to manoeuvre. Giuseppe's presented a narrow doorway onto the cobbled square which provided me with a good enough view to be sure I wasn't being watched. I also had the chance to admire from afar the old Warehouse where Fehrson and Khanyi were waiting for me with the little information they had been able to find about Lindiwe.

I noticed Khanyi when she was about halfway across the square, bearing down on me like an Olympic walker nearing the home straight. She was disguised as a leopard – an extraordinary suit of imitation leopard skin which comprised a jacket that looked like it had lost its bottom half, and a skirt which the tailor hadn't been able to finish because he'd run out of leopard. It pretty much made it below the crotch line, but one didn't want to look too care-fully. Black stockings were Khanyi's only compromise with the impending winter, and I've got to say I can understand why she left it at that. With legs like hers, it would have been a shame to wear anything over those stockings.

Giuseppe greeted her like she was a long-lost sister, kissed her very thoroughly, and only with great reluctance let her go so she could make her way into the shadows at the back to find me.

"I smelt the smoke from across the square," she said, standing silhouetted in the light, with a hand on her hip, and one leg bent so a shaft could paint her shadow on the floor. "Father is furious."

"Father doesn't even know I'm trying to give up."

Khanyi pulled an I'm-not-in-the-mood face.

"We're waiting in the attic for you. Father says when you've had enough coffee, you should feel free to join us. We said nine o'clock."

I said I'd be right along and blew into the froth of my

cappuccino to show how keen I was. Khanyi sighed. "He means now," she said.

"I'm certainly not crossing that square with you, Khanyi. Any self-respecting game ranger would gun me down on the spot."

Khanyi looked up to the ceiling for spiritual guidance. "We'll wait until you sound the all-clear," she said. "Just don't make it all day." She turned sharply on her heels like a ballet dancer and made it out the front door before Giuseppe could show any more of his Mediterranean appreciation.

Khanyi was a desk person. For all her brilliance at office politics, she handled people like she handled numbers on a computer. For her the old-fashioned practices of exercising caution, making sure one wasn't being followed and all that boy scout stuff, were just bad habits us old fogeys were clinging onto purely to irritate her. I watched the leopard skin sway elegantly back across the square. I shouldn't have said that about the game ranger. It was bound to make trouble for me later.

I finished my cappuccino at a pace that would have made any Capetonian proud. One doesn't rush the good things in this place. It was all very well for Khanyi to mock my caution. She had nothing to worry about. Desk people seldom woke up with nightmares. I allowed myself a satisfying moment of gratitude for being one of the few who had managed to change the course of my life and avoided thinking too deeply about why I'd been sitting in a back corner of Giuseppe's for an hour.

———

"Giuseppe hasn't lost his touch, has he?" asked Fehrson with genuine concern when I arrived in the Attic. He looked at me with the envy of someone who didn't have time for luxuries. "In fact," he reached out to the neat plastic box sunk into the oak table, and pressed its red button, "I think we'll organise some coffee for ourselves."

The black box on the table squawked back at Fehrson.

"Belinda," he said, ladling all the charm he could onto that one word. He released the button, and after a brief pause the box squawked again with an extra note of impatience.

"Belinda, we were thinking about coffee," he said. The box said something, and Fehrson said, "Not that bilge Belinda, my dear. We were thinking of some real coffee." He looked up at me with a conspiratorial smile. It looked like he would win this one. He released the button, and the box launched into an angry retort. Fehrson sighed.

"Alright, dear, just an idea," he said in a placatory tone. He released the button with a snap and coughed as he shuffled some papers around on the table in front of him.

The Attic spanned the entire top floor of the warehouse. Its ceiling was lost in the shadows of the exposed rafters, from which hung the lights with their flying saucer shades, like the ones spilling pools of light over gangsters in the movies. An oak table provided enough space for twenty barbarians to feast, but the only ones there today were Fehrson, Khanyi and myself.

"We'll proceed without coffee," said Fehrson as if he'd reached that decision of his own volition. He forced a grim smile. "It's for the best as we are running a little late." His penetrating gaze lingered on me, as he wondered whether a reprimand was in order.

"There's been a problem with the journalist I spoke

about," I said, tiring of his games. "The whole thing is beginning to smell bad, and on the slight chance that the stench is
not emanating from this office, I felt that caution was
advisable."

"What kind of problem?" asked Father.

"The worst kind. He's lying in a fridge in the Pinelands
morgue."

"Your doing?" asked Khanyi in a gentle tone to indicate
that she wouldn't hold it against me.

"Of course it's not my doing."

"There's no need to shout about it, Ben." Fehrson stood
suddenly and moved over to the large arched windows. He
was a man who liked to think on his feet, or liked people to
think he was that kind of man. "We understand you're
upset, but let's take this one step at a time shall we? This
man's death explains your late arrival?"

"I chose tardiness over foolishness. I wanted to be sure
that whatever happened to the journalist didn't happen
to me."

"You wanted to establish whether you were being
followed?"

"I was being cautious. It would have been hard to miss
the leopard, though."

"Don't blame Khanyi," said Fehrson, "it was my idea to
send her out to fetch you. Are you being followed?"

"No."

"But you are suspicious about the circumstances of your
friend's death." He turned to look out of the arched
windows. "You could have indicated those suspicions to us
We would have been more careful about letting the wildlife
out." I couldn't see his face, but from the way Khanyi gave
me both barrels over her notepad, I suspected that she had
shared my earlier ill-considered comments.

"My suspicions have formed since we last spoke," I said.

"Fair enough," said Fehrson. "What makes you think this man's death has anything to do with you? Or with us?"

"He was asking some pretty hefty questions. Perhaps I'm a cynic. I'm not a big believer in coincidence."

Fehrson gazed out of the window like a hunchback trapped in a bell tower.

"We have a clean conscience, Ben," he said. "In all of this. No dark secrets, no dirty business involving slanderous journalists."

"Not that it was any concern of his," said Khanyi applying her golden voice which made her sound like a late-night radio disc jockey. "We were happy to discuss what we know about this woman in order to refute the malicious suggestions of that journalist. But if he is dead, why are we here? Gabriel no longer works here. This is none of your business."

"Your objection is duly noted," I said.

"Alright you two," said Fehrson coming back to the table and holding up his hands as if trying to quieten a rowdy crowd. "We know the context, Khanyisile. It's a valid question. Is it worth spending any time going through this?"

"You mean now that the journalist is dead?"

"I do," said Fehrson. "Would it be churlish to point out that there is no longer a need for you to convince him that there are no nasty secrets?" He ran his hand through his fractious white hair and then clamped it over his mouth as if to stop himself from saying any more.

"It might," I said.

Fehrson's eyes were pale blue pools of intensity. They gazed at me as his mouth produced a polite smile. "But it has piqued your interest," he said. "And we have nothing to hide. So we will continue. I think we're done with the opening comments. Let's get some coffee," he said, brightening at the idea, although it took only a moment for him to remember the failure of his earlier attempt along those lines. "Khanyi, how about you be a dear and get over to Giuseppe's for some takeaways?"

Khanyi was not really the sort of employee who fetches coffee, and I thought she was going to explain that, but perhaps she suspected that Fehrson had ulterior motives, and so she went off with as much dignity as she could muster.

"Let's start with a clean slate here," said Fehrson when the sound of Khanyi's high heels had faded. He swept his hand over the table as if he was clearing it of imaginary objects.

"I want you to know that I remember Lindiwe well. Very well."

"I see," I said because he seemed to be waiting for a response.

"When you mentioned her name, it gave me quite a turn. I will tell you what I remember about what Lindiwe did for us, we'll show you what paperwork we have, and then I ask that you let this thing rest. Despite the allegations of your late friend, there is nothing worth digging up here, I would like you to understand that, Ben."

Fehrson paused, so I said I understood. He sat back in his chair and adopted the pose of a man about to recall the distant past. A glaze to the eyes, and a blank gaze at the ceiling.

"She was a bright spark, Lindiwe. A few years older than my son. You know my son? I don't mean know him, because I doubt that you've met him, but you know that I have a son?"

"I do," I said. Fehrson's son was one of the first things

explained to any new member of staff, in hushed tones while waiting for the kettle to boil in the kitchen. He was the reason that Fehrson's hair was so white. The reason that Fehrson's marriage had not lasted. The reason, it was said, for the lengthy pauses in Fehrson's conversation, for the times that he would gaze out of windows or stare blankly at ceilings. The son had been released from prison several years ago when the murder charge was dropped, but no one was sure that he had stopped the drugs.

"Well, just a few years older," said Fehrson, and looked at me with damp blue eyes.

"I see," I said. "And she worked with the Department?"

"She was very young," said Fehrson. "Very young. Didn't work with us, but was involved in an operation with us thirty years ago. Not the Department as we know it now. But the Service as it was then."

"You mentioned she was just a messenger."

"She was more than that," said Fehrson and he sniffed. "My memory served me badly on that front. It was an operation, one that went horribly wrong from our side, and was buried as a result. I wasn't directly involved. The files were locked away, and we all did our best to forget about it."

Fehrson paused and so I gave another prod to keep the ball rolling. "What was the failed operation she was involved in?"

Fehrson fiddled with the papers on the table and pushed them back into a folder as if he'd decided not to share their contents after all.

"There were personal reasons I was not involved. Family reasons. I wanted you to know that." Another damp blue stare.

"I see," I said.

"We'll wait for Khanyisile to get back before we discuss

the operation," he said. "She's been reading up about it since you called."

We sat in silence for a moment and I wondered what Fehrson had wanted to say out of Khanyi's hearing, or whether his desire for coffee was the only reason he had sent her off.

"Lindiwe was what we used to call a free spirit," he said suddenly. "Dynamic, bright as they come, with a future that had no bounds. She worked *with* us, but never *for* us." Fehrson gazed down at the closed folder on the table before him, as if he was peering into a deep well. "She was her own person. Had that sense of completeness that is so irresistible. She needed no one, but everyone needed her." Fehrson looked up at me, "you know the kind of person I mean."

It was a statement, but I nodded in response to the question he hadn't asked.

"She came from the dust pits of the squatter camps," he continued, "but she had an education that was strictly the reserve of white people in those days. Her mother worked as a domestic servant, and her employer used to insist that Lindiwe sit at the table and do the homework her own child was doing. She even provided extra textbooks for her, and the two children grew up like siblings. At least that is what she used to say. Her mind was like a sponge, and she had dreams of getting herself a university degree, which was by no means impossible in those days. Difficult, but not impossible. She had a bright future and was fired up by the kind of indignation that comes from actually understanding the history she'd read. She was going to right the wrongs of the world."

"And she chose to do that by working with the

apartheid government?" I asked with barely concealed incredulity.

Fehrson shook his head. "No, no, no," he said as if the idea was absurd. The sound of Khanyi's heels rang out on the steel steps that climbed into the Attic, and Fehrson added another couple of no's for good measure as she distributed the coffees.

"Latte for you, Father," she said as she passed Fehrson an impressively large cup and several sugar packets, "and short black for our conquering hero." She handed me the toy replica of Fehrson's cup. "No sugar ... bitter as it comes," she said.

"No, no," continued Fehrson as if he hadn't noticed Khanyi's return. "She was a woman trapped between two worlds. White on the inside, black on the outside. She was a ... what is that term they use? For that kind of thing."

"A coconut?" suggested Khanyi, not without an edge of disdain.

"That's it. A coconut! What an absurd term. Practically raised by a white family, so she was white on the inside, they would say. At least, she identified with what they call the 'European culture' today."

"And she was black on the outside," explained Khanyi.

"Such an absurd term," said Fehrson who had noticed Khanyi's tone of voice.

"Not to mention insulting," said Khanyi who had no doubt been called a coconut many times.

"Of course, of course," said Fehrson who took sustenance from his latte, only to realise that he had not added sugar. "Not a term we use nowadays. Not at all." He smiled at Khanyi, who did not return the gesture. She sipped her cappuccino noisily.

"Botanical comparisons aside," I said, "could you tell me about the operation she was involved in?"

"I'm just explaining to Ben here that we don't have much to say about the woman."

Fehrson started tearing off the tops of the sugar packets one at a time and pouring the contents into his latte with great care as if he was counting the grains.

"Almost nothing at all," said Khanyi obediently. "It was so many years ago." She peered at me over her cappuccino, ready to duck down behind it if I started throwing things. I guessed that they'd reached the scripted part of the performance.

"We can tell you what we know about the operation she was involved in," said Fehrson studying the plastic stirrer that Giuseppe had provided and wondering which end he should use. "But honestly, Ben, I wouldn't want you jumping to any erroneous conclusions." He realised both ends were the same and started stirring.

"Conclusions?" I said. "About what?"

"We wouldn't want you joining the imaginary dots. I'm sure all this film stuff you do is very interesting, but you must long for something with more ... what is the word?"

When I didn't suggest any solutions to his puzzle, Fehrson looked down and gingerly extracted the stirrer from his coffee. He raised the cup to his lips and tested a micro-drop of it.

"Meaning," he said. "That's what I was thinking. These ..." he looked at me blankly as he tried to find a suitable word.

"Documentaries," supplied Khanyi.

"Exactly," said Fehrson as if Khanyi had proved his point. "These documentaries you do now are all very well, but you need to get back on your feet my boy, and I would not want you to start charging at windmills just to find a little more meaning in your life."

"By joining imaginary dots and drawing conclusions?"

"No need to get touchy," said Fehrson. "I'm merely suggesting that you tread carefully. Khanyisile, why don't you tell Ben what we know?"

"Of course," said Khanyi, returning to the script with a bump. "We pulled the register for you. There is a connection between Ms Dlomo and Mr Mbuyo, but as Father says, it is not one that is likely to lead anywhere."

Fehrson pushed the folder of papers across the table. It contained a few typed pages, a list of subject lines and reference numbers with dates. A form of indexing system that the National Intelligence Agency had used to simplify their case files and which was referred to as the register.

"You can keep that," said Fehrson. "Get hold of the files for yourself if you choose." When I didn't react he added, "We made that copy for you." The two of them sat there as if waiting for me to leap over the table and embrace them as thanks for their boundless generosity. I disappointed them.

"Why don't you just tell me about it?" I suggested.

"Father's memory of the whole thing is very vague," said Khanyi.

"Very," affirmed Fehrson. He nodded sadly and did his best to look like a confused old man. "I was not personally involved. But I can provide you with the background if that helps."

I said it would. Fehrson tested a little more of his coffee, then drew a deep breath. "Lindiwe came to us when things were going badly. Very badly. We were licking our wounds after losing some of our ground crawlers. What we called our people on the ground, the ones out in the field. The rebellious students who would work their way into the youth leagues, chant the slogans, lead the marches and shout about freedom for the people, then come and tell us all about it. We lost a string of them and were wondering what we could do next. The Americans and Brits were coming up with fresh ideas but none of them worked here. The Cold War was shifting, the landscape changing around the world. We tried a few of their tricks, but what works in the First World rarely translates well here in Africa, as you know."

"This was the time of the resistance cells in the squatter camps?"

"It was. Our enemy were scattered throughout those squatter camps. There was a state of emergency, big meetings were banned. The sort of stupid political decision that made our work even harder. Instead of large groups we could easily watch, there were now small clusters of them spread all over the informal settlements. We needed to find a way to infiltrate them, which is when Lindiwe got involved.

"She had a boyfriend who was getting chummy with some of the people who'd been sent off to Moscow, and then smuggled back into the country through Angola, or Mozambique. In Moscow they'd been subjected to the kind of training that would make you cringe, but they knew which end of a gun the bullet came out of, and the talk everywhere was the big R word. There was going to be a Revolution. The communists were behind it, and they were all slapping each other on the back, and drinking the vodka they'd brought back from Moscow. The revolutionaries didn't like the idea of communism, but they liked the idea of toppling the apartheid government more than they disliked communism, so no one worried too much about the details."

"And Lindiwe came to you? She wanted to assist the regime? Join ranks with the apartheid security police?"

"That's the problem with the history books," said Fehrson in response to my tone of incredulity. He got to his feet again and took his latte over to the window. "It's all so black and white, good and evil. You were on one side or the other. It wasn't like that. How can I explain? When you're in something, swimming in it as it were, it isn't so easy to put things into their neat boxes and stick a label onto them. I don't think Lindiwe was helping the 'regime' as you like to call it. She found herself in a situation that presented an opportunity that furthered her ends, and those of her boyfriend, and probably the plight of her people as she saw it, although honestly that is the kind of neat nonsense that writers of history books espouse. She took the opportunity because it was in her nature. She was probably against your 'regime', adamantly against it I would imagine. But I believe that she took exception with the way that her boyfriend and his chums were doing things."

"They set up an operation," said Khanyi. "Called 'Spieël',"

"Afrikaans," said Fehrson. "Mirror to you Brits."

I didn't remind him that my mother had been Afrikaans and that my understanding of the language stretched to household furniture.

"I don't remember why Spieël – could have been a play on words, or one of those meaningless code names. In those days everything was double entendre and nudge-nudge wink-wink, but in any case. The plan was simple enough. Her boyfriend was very chummy with some of the big play-ers. He was always a rung below them as I remember, the boyfriend was. He was the one sent out to buy cigarettes when they were having adult conversation, that kind of thing. It rankled, and he passed his dissatisfaction down to Lindiwe, where it built up like steam in a pressure cooker. He was better than an office boy, she said."

"So the boyfriend passed things on to Lindiwe who brought them back to you."

"Not directly of course, they met up with one of the surviving ground crawlers." Fehrson gazed out of the window at the building rain clouds. "The information was reliable, if a little dull. Low-level stuff really. They planned civil disruption, sabotage, that kind of thing. Useful but not earth shattering. Of course the Pretoria boys wanted us to expand, build a network. They were megalomaniacs with visions of grander things. Empire builders. A man called Du Toit came down from Pretoria and took himself a desk. This was when we were in that awful block in Woodstock. He told us we were doing it all wrong. Said that we'd lost control. Although as a sponge operation there didn't seem much about it that needed controlling."

"Sponge?"

"Information gathering only, no action. We had young Breytenbach collating it all, and he was doing a good job."

"Breytenbach?"

"The Gold man. The Breytenbach gold mining family. The son, Riaan. Of course, he's heading up the family business now."

"He worked for the Department?"

"Not the Department. Not back then. We were just a small division of military intelligence. He was with us for his national service. His family wouldn't take the risk of having him posted to the border where he could step on a mine or get shot. They secured him a cushy posting far away from the action. He was a weakling, and the family knew it. He rather resented it, I think. His father insisted that he do the full four years instead of the two years with annual camps. So he spent some time with us. He proved himself to be reliable."

"He handled Lindiwe's operation?"

"No, no. Operation is too grand a term for it. And he certainly wasn't 'handling' it. There wouldn't have been any contact between them. There was someone on the ground as a contact for them, who passed on their reports which he compiled and presented to us. Not very complicated."

"But the man from Pretoria said you were doing it all wrong?"

"Du Toit, a conspiracy theorist of note. Said we had none of the necessary checks in place, and he was right about that. But it was too late by the time we realised it."

"Too late?"

Fehrson sipped at his latte and gazed out at the darkening clouds.

"Du Toit said it would just be a matter of time before the whole house of cards came down. Of course, I wasn't the one responsible for it, by any means. I was up and coming, as they say. Still naïve and optimistic."

Fehrson sipped at his latte modestly.

"But things did go wrong?"

"Oh yes, things unravelled fast."

Fehrson paused as if he'd lost his way in his memories. "It's going to rain," he said and turned away from the window, looking at me as if expecting I would deny it. "First winter rains."

"Things unravelled?" I said.

"They did. There was something big being discussed by the boyfriend's little gang. A power station, if I remember correctly. They were going to cripple the Peninsula, bring the Cape to its knees, all that nonsense."

Fehrson stopped talking and sat down at the table as if he'd finished his story.

"That is when it happened," said Khanyi.

Fehrson nodded slowly as his mind pulled itself back to the present. "Oh yes, it did that. Five of them, trapped like lobsters in a shack that was burned to the ground. And a pregnant woman was injured, lost her child, which got the media doing back flips for weeks. The international media that is, the local media were censored."

"The Khayelitsha Massacre?"

"That's what the media called it. But there was no evidence it was anything but an accident. The whole of Khayelitsha was a death trap in those days. Shacks built of wood and corrugated iron, ten or fifteen people crammed into a shack half the size of this room. And everything done with paraffin. Lights, cooking. You knocked a paraffin lamp over, and the shack would turn into a gas oven in moments. The iron would expand and you couldn't open a door to get out. It was nothing short of horrific."

"But not an accident in this case?"

"It was absurd to think it could have been, despite the lack of evidence. Five leading African National Congress revolutionaries all having a sleep-over party? You think they were all so fast asleep in there they didn't notice the tin box they were in was on fire? No, as I remember, no one tried to push the idea of it being an accident. The fact that five revolutionaries died was not generally regarded as a tragedy among the tax-paying class of the time. There were blank columns in the papers, their way of protesting the censorship. There was a story, but they couldn't print it, was what they were saying. And a few weeks later it all blew over. No one had taken clippings of the blank columns to put into their scrapbooks. Some politicians shook their heads and bemoaned the health risks posed by the influx of illegal immigrants who had created the squatter camps. Then they turned the conversation to topics that made them look like the protectors of the people they liked to pretend they were. Protectors of the white people, of course. The fact that five members of the *swart gevaar* – the 'black danger', for you Brits – had suffered an unfortunate cooking accident was downplayed."

"And it had something to do with Lindiwe?" I suggested when Fehrson seemed on the verge of sinking into another trance.

"Her boyfriend was one of the five. Did I mention that? It was her boyfriend's little revolutionary cell. All of them. The mirror was broken. Seven years of bad luck for us. And she wasn't giving any standing ovations. She blamed the Service. Du Toit got himself nominated for an award and received pats on the back, Freemason handshakes and the like. He flew home to Pretoria, blaming the wet air that came from the docks for his failing health."

"The fire was Du Toit's idea?"

"He denied it. But it was obvious to us he'd planned the entire thing. From our perspective, the fire had snuffed out any hope we had of an entry into the enemy camp. When you have that kind of opportunity you don't put them in a tin pot and roast them to death. You keep them alive, at the very least. But Pretoria hailed it as a glorious success. The elimination of an entire terrorist cell. The greatest irony of all was that the principal target – because there was a target, despite all the protestations to the contrary – that target crawled out of the ashes."

"Thulani Mbuyo."

"The big one, the boy whose photograph the Pretoria boys had been using as a dartboard. The reason Pretoria was involved in the first place. Recently returned from Moscow, being groomed as leader of the pack. I believe he was the only one Du Toit and his cronies were really interested in and Pretoria probably considered him worth the collateral damage. It was worth losing all the possibilities provided by *Spieël* if they could eliminate Mbuyo."

"But Du Toit failed. If Mbuyo survived."

"Survived might be the wrong word. We didn't describe him as having survived at the time. He was discovered alive, but the fire had taken most of his skin off. He spent months in a hospital bed being rebuilt, then was put behind bars. He was 'discounted' by Pretoria. Spirit broken, no chance of a return to the fighting was the official story. They were wrong about that, of course, but it was years later that anyone realised."

Fehrson dried up and Khanyi picked up the story.

"Which is why Du Toit returned to Pretoria a hero," she said and reached over the table to turn the pages of the register they had printed for me. "There was a debrief of course. The register shows the entries."

A long-nailed finger pointed to them.

"Reports of the debrief," she said. "The conclusion was that Du Toit had stepped in and taken advantage of Dlomo's inside line on the group. He had single-handedly destroyed the best thing the Cape branch had going for it, and failed to kill the targeted revolutionary."

"The scope of the debacle was just beginning to emerge," said Fehrson. "And I don't imagine that Lindiwe had anything good to say at that debrief. Her boyfriend was dead, it had all been personal for her in any case, not some big political quest. They kept the debriefing closed. All hushed up. But she had never been one to hold her tongue. A few months after that the file was closed."

"With her boyfriend dead, I don't suppose she had anything else to offer," I said.

"There was that," said Khanyi. "But it was more ... definitive." Khanyi's glitter-polished nail pointed to the written comment beneath the red-lettered stamp that marked the file as closed. "Subject deceased."

"Lindiwe deceased? Does it explain how?"

"Not in the register," said Khanyi.

Fehrson had subsided into a silent heap. Khanyi glanced at him like they were actors about to take a bow, but he didn't respond.

"Nevertheless," said Khanyi. "File closed. The story ends there."

Fehrson nodded regretfully, and they both looked at me.

"It certainly provides a link between the woman and our president-to-be," I said.

"There you go jumping to conclusions," said Fehrson. "Didn't I tell you he'd do that?" he asked Khanyi.

"You did," said Khanyi, and she looked at me dispassionately. I'd proved a disappointment by fulfilling Fehrson's worst predictions. Fehrson got to his feet and returned to the window to gaze down upon the populace.

"That's what we have for you, Ben," he said with resignation. "That's all we have. Yes, there's a connection between Lindiwe and Mbuyo. But she's been dead for thirty years. Why would she be of any interest to him now? Your friend probably stumbled upon one of those old files while browsing the archives and let his imagination get the better of him."

The thought of Johansson stumbling upon an old file in the archives was an unlikely one, but I said nothing. Johansson had not been the sort of person to hang out where there were dusty books and minimal liquid refreshment.

"I'm sure you're right," I said. "Just a flight of the imagination."

There was a lengthy silence as everyone tried to work out whose responsibility it was to bring the curtain down. "I've been wasting your time," I said eventually.

Fehrson turned back from the window, and the mood lifted as if the sun had managed to poke its way through the heavy rain clouds.

Khanyi rewarded me with a smile, and Fehrson came back to the table in preparation for the farewell scene.

"I doubt that Thulani Mbuyo would remember her name," said Khanyi as I closed the folder. "The fire was not connected to the *Spieël* operation, which was in any case buried under a pile of other failed operations. I doubt very much he ever discovered that someone had been talking out of turn, let alone that they provided the tenuous link to the people who lit the matches that started the fire."

"So there's not really anything I can say in the eulogy at the journalist's funeral?"

"Oh, you wouldn't want to do that," said Fehrson with alarm. "Ah, of course. Always the clown. One day someone will take you seriously, Ben." He wagged a scolding finger at me.

"Would Riaan Breytenbach be worth speaking to?" I asked.

The clouds returned, and the mood darkened.

"About what?" asked Fehrson.

"A final confirmation. That there is nothing to worry about."

"Already done," said Fehrson. "He was the first person I called after you mentioned that journalist's absurd suggestion. He agrees with me: no nasty secrets. But the point here, Ben," Fehrson raised his hands again to calm the troubled crowd, "the point is that the tragic death of your friend can have nothing to do with the story of Lindiwe Dlomo. Now that you know her story you can see the absurdity of the idea that anyone from the Department would be covering up any dark secrets involving her. In any case, the absurd allegations that your journalist made are not the sort of thing that befits the attention of our office."

Fehrson waved vaguely to indicate the echoing space we were huddled in as if that demonstrated the extraordinary importance of his office. The truth fell a little short, as I well knew. Fehrson and his small team were relegated to dusty offices that offered a view of an internal courtyard and the aroma of the plumbing pipes.

It was only later, after Fehrson and Khanyi had said their goodbyes, and after they had scurried back to their smelly offices, that I realised what bothered me. I took the stairs down, and emerged into the uncertain autumn morning. I lit the Gauloise I'd been avoiding all morning and wondered about Fehrson's personal reasons for having been kept away from an operation involving Lindiwe Dlomo. A woman who had died shortly after the massacre that had nearly killed Thulani Mbuyo. What kind of personal reasons had they been? And why had he made sure that Khanyi was out of the room before revealing that minor detail? I regretted the Gauloise, stubbed it out, and threw the pack away for good measure.

―――――

The rain that had been toying with the Cape Peninsula all morning chose lunchtime for the onslaught. This gave me the chance to gather my thoughts as I drove through the disaster movie set that the unpolished edges of Cape Town turn into whenever it rains – cars stopped haphazardly in the streets; their emergency lights blinked through the darkened twilight of the rainstorm, while the cars still able to move crawled around them as if the survivors didn't dare stop to see what the trouble was.

I've been called paranoid, but I would always rather take the taunts than find myself floating face down in the Atlantic. And things were not making sense. I phoned the archives.

"I'm sorry, Mr Johans," said the archivist after I'd waited on hold for five minutes. "We have no files at all for a Lindiwe Dlomo."

"They were old NIA files," I said. "National Intelligence Agency. I can provide you with reference numbers."

I provided the numbers from Khanyi's generously printed register, and waited a further five minutes, as the rain did its best to break through the rusted roof of my car.

"I am truly very sorry Mr Johans," said the archivist, who had written Johansson's name when I'd provided it, but struggled with including all three syllables. "We don't have any of those files. If you would like to leave your number, I'll ask the director to give you a call."

I assured her it wasn't important and ended the call.

Bill had left a message while I was on hold, but I had another call to make first. I dialled the archives again and asked whether Mr Riaan Breytenbach had an office there. I was treated to a minute of music, and then the smooth voice of a woman told me I had the pleasure of speaking with his private secretary, but that regrettably Mr Breytenbach had no times free on his busy calendar. Not today, not next week, nor for the foreseeable future. I explained that it was a private, sensitive matter that I wished to discuss, and that Father Don Fehrson had insisted. I was placed on hold again. It took Mr Breytenbach only a minute to find time on his busy calendar for the private and sensitive matter. Mr Breytenbach would squeeze me in before his lunch. He would do that for a man of the church. Of course he would. He was that kind of man.

I called Bill back.

"Remember the brother?" he said.

"Wandile?"

"She was his girlfriend."

"Lindiwe?"

"What are you? A poet? Stop with the word games, Gabriel. Yes, the woman you're looking for was the girl-friend of the big guy's brother. Thulani Mbuyo's brother was her boyfriend."

So much for Khanyi's suggestion that Thulani Mbuyo wouldn't recognise her name.

"I called Matlala," said Bill with enough volume to make the use of the phone seem superfluous. "The guy who was on the island same time as Mbuyo. He helped me when I was researching Prison Island. You know I did a section of that book?"

I did know. "Good book," I said.

Bill was taken aback. "Sandy force it on you?"

"Just the blurb on the back," I said, although I had read the full book, and not because Sandy had forced it on me.

"Well anyway, Matlala knew the name. The woman's name. And there's more. You are not going to believe it. Very odd. Very odd, all of it. You free now?"

"Believe what?" I asked.

"Come around here, we'll go see Matlala and he can tell you all about it."

FIVE

Jacob Matlala lived in a house nestled between the vineyards of Constantia. The rain was trickling to a stop when Bill and I arrived, and a few shafts of sunlight poked down to highlight some of the best vines. For a moment we were trapped in a picture calendar, the buttress slopes of the wrong side of Table Mountain providing the ominous backdrop to the glistening vineyards.

"I chose money over power," said Jacob Matlala after we had squeezed hands and Bill had explained that I was doing research for a documentary video. "There were others," he said, "who chose power over money, but I was never one for the limelight. I prefer the quiet life."

The quiet life had not been disappointing. Matlala's business endeavours – aided, a sceptic might suggest by the government requirement that South African businesses have management with a racial balance more representative of the country's population – had proven to be lucrative. Having an ex-freedom fighter on the board, particularly one who had served time in the political prison on Robben Island, was worth at least two non-political dark-skinned members, and Matlala had taken full advantage. We were sitting in the lounge of Matlala's Cape Dutch homestead, a room that was large enough to accommodate my entire apartment. The wooden floors had been recently polished, and several Persian carpets were needed to improve the acoustics. An open fireplace crackled its way through logs that would have required two people to carry in from the wood store beside the stables that housed Matlala's champion racehorses.

"We're preparing him for the Durban July," explained Matlala as we watched 'Beast of the Night' follow his stable hand out to the exercise track. A diminutive jockey trailed behind them carrying a saddle and a handful of riding accessories, like a child who has just had a tantrum and doesn't want to walk with the adults. "Three sessions every day, rain or no rain. Can't let the weather get in our way."

Matlala's wife Rose brought us a tray of tea and biscuits. A round, cheerful woman, she smiled at us in a sympathetic way. "Don't let my Jacob go on too much about those horses," she said. "He'll never stop, and we'll have to bring you something stronger than this tea."

"They need alcohol," said Matlala, "not that colonial piss."

Rose smiled and shook her head regretfully. "Better stick with the tea. Jacob has an important meeting, and he should arrive sober." She gave us each a hard glare to ensure we understood who was in charge. Matlala didn't press the point.

"You're asking questions," said Matlala when we had divided the 'colonial piss' into three equal portions and made a start on the chocolate biscuits. "Questions about Thulani," he added with a touch of indignation.

"My friend is filling in some background," said Bill

soothingly. "Background on President Mbuyo."

Matlala nodded and bit into his biscuit. He was a powerfully built man who had allowed his good fortune to abuse his waistline. His bald head was supported upon extra rolls of fat around his neck, but the impression of a cheerful clown was deceptive. His eyes glittered with a hard intelligence.

"It's what everyone is asking about now, isn't it?" he said through a mouthful of crumbs. "Where did the big man come from? He came from the cold stone cells of Robben Island, that's where he came from. Those little rooms with the twenty square centimetres of barred openings. That's where he came from. There's nothing I can add."

"He chose power over money?" I asked.

Matlala's bright eyes swung onto me like the headlights of a war machine.

"No, no," he said, and a chuckle bubbled to the surface. "He chose nothing. Thulani had it all thrust upon him. Power and money. It was always the way it was going to be, from the day he arrived on the island, pink and delicate like a newly made person. He'd been in the hospital for months, and they'd made him all new. The scar tissue was fresh, and he wasn't black anymore. That's what we used to say. He was a whole new race. Pink." Matlala chuckled some more and helped himself to another biscuit.

"He didn't choose any of it," he continued, "but what could he do? People saw him and said to themselves: This man, he is special. He's the one. He has to be, he's pink." Another hearty chuckle. "And he didn't want any of it. We could see that. He hid away in his new pink shell and wanted none of it. If they'd let him out, he would have faded into the background and the country would never have heard of him. That's what they didn't see. Those old

Nationalist fools. Their prisons were no more than training centres, meeting rooms, incubation units where they reared their enemies."

"But he'd been a revolutionary leader," I said. "Before prison, before the fire. He'd been to Moscow, formed his own resistance cell. He had a reputation."

Matlala shook his head and took a gulp of tea, then winced at the taste of it. "That might be," he said, "but that fire burned it all out of him. It broke him. He wasn't interested in any of it. Couldn't bring himself to talk with the men he'd known from before the fire. Just shut himself up in his new pink shell. They said the effort to survive took all he had; there was nothing left for anything beyond that."

"He recovered though," I said. "Got that energy back again. Look where it's brought him."

"Not recovered," said Matlala. "Over the years he grew into the new skin. He found his passion, but he found it in the way someone discovers something new. It was not a recovery of the old, but a new passion that was thrust onto him."

A rattling on the windows announced another cloudburst, and we looked out to where the jockey was remonstrating with an elderly man under an umbrella. The horse stamped its feet, and the stable hand finished tightening the straps of the saddle. The haze of falling rain moved away and across the field beyond them, and the jockey reluctantly held out a hand to confirm it had passed.

"She runs like a beauty that one," said Matlala. "Poetry in motion, you'll see. When they get the midget up onto her." He laughed at his political incorrectness and repeated the word "midget" to show he had no regrets.

"Ben here is interested in the woman, Lindiwe Dlomo," said Bill to get the conversation back on track.

"You told me that," said Matlala accusingly, still gazing out at his horse. "What is it that Ben-here wants to know about the woman?"

"What the connection was with the president-elect," I said.

Matlala turned his gaze onto me again. "You're digging for dirt aren't you?" he said in a voice that didn't hold any resentment. "Dragging the skeletons out of the closet."

I didn't deny it.

"Well," said Matlala with a dismissive laugh, "this isn't one of them. She was Wandile's girl. His brother's girl. Came to see Thulani. I told you that, Bill. Came to see him on the island."

"You did," said Bill.

"That was unusual?" I asked.

"Unusual? It was flat-out unheard of. They weren't running a holiday camp there. We didn't have all our girls coming round for tea." Matlala's attention returned to the horse, and his face softened as we watched the jockey being helped up. "Goddamn midget," he muttered.

"They were close? The president-elect and the woman?" I asked. "If she was his brother's girlfriend."

"Can we drop the 'president' shit?" asked Matlala. "He's Thulani to me, so let's just call him that. You know what Thulani means? The Quiet One. That's him. Quiet."

The horse started pacing in a stiff-legged way, like it was taking part in a military parade. "There she goes," said Matlala. "Now you'll see."

"And Thulani and the woman were close?" I persisted.

"Like hell they were." Matlala looked at me accusingly. "He hated his brother. Hated him. You think he liked the brother's girl?"

"If she visited him," I suggested.

"No, no. That wasn't a lovey-dovey holding hands and crying about the dead brother kind of visit. They weren't running guided tours. It was something the pigs dreamed up."

"And Thulani talked to you about it?"

"The hell he did." Matlala was still watching the horse, which had turned its stiff walk into an anxious pacing. He reached for another biscuit, keeping his eyes on the horse. "Never spoke about it, not a word. We knew it happened because one of the guards told us."

"But not a reason for the visit? The guard didn't mention that?"

Matlala spared me a momentary glance. "Those guards dealt in facts. They weren't big on conjecture," he said, and turned back to where the jockey looked as if he was giving the man under the umbrella a salute with a stubby whip which he tapped on the peak of his helmet. Then in a motion that was like fluid pouring from a spout, the horse lengthened and accelerated away from us across the field. The sound of the hooves came afterwards like an experiment to measure the speed of sound. Matlala had stopped chewing his biscuit, and he breathed heavily through his mouth as the horse disappeared in a flurry of wet spray.

"Didn't I tell you?" he asked in a voice hoarse with emotion. "Poetry in motion, just a thing of beauty."

"Extraordinary," said Bill, and he looked as if he meant it. We sat in silence for a minute, watching the horse loop out across the field and sprint along the fence at the far end.

"You tell me," said Matlala, "why the pigs would send in the girlfriend of a hated brother. To visit a man who was becoming a leader of the resistance. You think she came in with flowers and chocolates?"

"They wanted information," I said.

"Damn right they did. Wouldn't have got it though. They'd read the situation all wrong."

"He was angry? Thulani was angry about that?"

"No, not angry. Not the Quiet One. He was never angry. Just quiet. Said nothing, went quieter than ever. For weeks after. Weeks. Months, maybe. Mind you, that's not a long time on the island. Not when you're there for years. Twelve years I did there. Twelve years of my life in a little stone room with bars."

"And they didn't try again?" I asked after a suitable pause during which we reflected upon the twelve years.

Matlala shook his head and reached for the last biscuit. "No point. Must have realised their mistake. Discovered how much he'd hated the brother, so there was no point."

"Did he talk about that? Why he hated his brother?"

"He brought it up in our group therapy sessions," said Matlala, then allowed another chuckle to rise to the surface. "Your friend Ben-here is good entertainment value, Bill. He has unusual ideas about what it was like on the island."

"Why don't you tell me?" I said, trying not to sound as if I'd taken offence.

"Sure, I'll tell you," said Matlala, and the clown was gone. The brittle core was showing now. "When you're thrown into the back of a truck with bars on it, and the stench of the vomit and blood of the previous occupants. Kicked and beaten with those long quirts and called every name their limited minds can come up with. Taken away from your family and your friends. Stood up in front of a room full of people who speak the oppressor's language, with someone to beat you when you don't give the right answers. Then locked up in a concrete room, forced to break rocks in the quarry all day, every day." Matlala held his hands up and studied them as if looking for damage.

"When you live with the realisation that you will never get off the island except in a box without breathing holes, when you hear months after the fact that your family members have died, or that they have given you up for dead. When that is your life, you don't sit around and discuss the reasons you're feeling angry." Matlala watched his horse as it sprinted past the trainer and stable boy, and the sight gave him a lift.

"Thulani's little brother had always been weak," he continued. "He'd been the little puppy you want to hurt just to see how long it will be before he cries for his mommy. That's what they said, the ones who'd known Thulani before. I hadn't known him. Met him on the island, didn't I? And Thulani had done just that. Hurt him until he cried. Often."

The trainer turned from the fence and raised a finger to the sky, looking at the large window we were sitting behind. He added a second finger, then turned back again. Matlala raised a hand to acknowledge the gesture, but I doubt the trainer could have seen him even if he had waited for a response. The window would have been reflecting the wet vineyards and exercise fields.

"Second best time," said Matlala with satisfaction. "That's good, isn't it?" Then without waiting for a reply he resumed his story. "Except that the little brother didn't cry. That's what they said. Would just take it. More and more of it. They used to say that he'd started the fire, you know that?"

"What did Thulani say to that?"

Matlala chuckled again. "Did I not tell you what his name means? He didn't say nothing. No thing. Just kept quiet about it. But he wasn't crying a whole lot over his dead brother."

Matlala turned to Bill. "It's in the cabinet over there, beside the fire," he said. "Glasses on the shelf above. Ice in the fridge. The dark green bottle, that's the good stuff."

Bill heaved himself out of the armchair and lumbered over to the fireplace. Matlala turned to me.

"You didn't bring your camera," he said. It was not a question.

"Just research at this stage," I said.

"When I helped your friend Bill with his research, he had notebooks and pencils. Even a tape recorder." Matlala's beady eyes regarded me with suspicion.

"I'm not sure there's a story here. All of that will come later."

Matlala nodded as he considered this. "Bill wrote a book," he said, putting to shame the inadequate approach that I was taking. "Prison Island."

"I contributed," Bill called over from the drinks cabinet, "Didn't write the whole thing."

"I helped him with that book," said Matlala, ignoring Bill's modesty, "because something good came of it. You going to be doing something good with this? Or are you just combing the shit to see what falls out?"

"I'm doing nothing with it," I said. "I'm looking for the truth, which surely cannot be a bad thing."

"That all depends which truth you choose," said Matlala. "There are so many of them these days. All different." He gave an unamused chuckle. "This journalism," he said. "What did you do before?"

"I was with the army. British army."

Matlala nodded as if that confirmed his suspicions. "Posted out here?" he said.

"I did a tour on the mines."

"And you stayed."

73

I didn't embellish. Bill returned with three glasses on a tray. They clinked merrily as he handed them to us.

"Ben was special forces, but he's left all that behind now," he said. "Makes documentary videos."

Matlala didn't react to that but kept watching me as if he was trying to remember something.

"Glenlivet," said Bill and raised his glass in a toast. "Here's to old stories, estranged brothers and long-lost girlfriends."

I raised my glass and took a sip, trying not to feel disconcerted at the way Matlala was watching me. Then he smiled broadly and consumed his whisky in a single gulp.

"We'll go and see him now," he said. "You've been wasting your time talking to me about all this. Big T will answer your questions better than me." He reached a large hand into his Armani brushed-silk jacket and extracted a tiny mobile phone. I didn't look at Bill, who had become very still in his chair.

"That's not necessary," I said. "I'm sure he's too busy to be bothered with discussing his late brother's girlfriend."

"No, no," said Matlala, and his cold eyes brimmed with suspicion. "No. Let's do this the right way. I'm meeting with him. Didn't Rose mention it? He's doing the second round of interviews for Cabinet. I'm sure he'd be happy to spend a few minutes talking with you two clowns."

"He has better things to do," said Bill.

"Like choosing his Cabinet?" Matlala laughed. "He's got weeks for that. This is just the early rounds. He's going to like me bringing you two in. And while he handles the press, I'll get to work the room. Get myself a cure for this damned sobriety. Get us one for the road, Bill, and I'll let him know you're coming."

SIX

"I asked if the name meant anything to him," said Bill as we followed Matlala's latest series BMW over Constantia Nek through the saddle between the mountains and towards the coastal road that would take us to the Waterfront where Matlala was intending to present us as hunting trophies to the future leader of the country. Rose was driving Matlala's car. Her approach was governed by the principle that right of way was determined by size of car. She expected the drivers of smaller cars than hers to make sure they were not occupying the same part of the road as her as she progressed along the windy mountain pass with her foot pressing the accelerator all the way to the floor. All the other cars on the road were smaller than hers, and so far it had worked out fairly well, although there had been some worrying moments. We rushed behind her like ambulance chasers because Matlala had warned us we wouldn't be able to get into the private quay without him.

"That's all, I swear," said Bill. "Thought I was doing you a favour. I honestly had no idea he would rush us off to see the man himself."

"Don't worry about it," I said. "What is wrong with asking after his late brother's girlfriend?"

"I don't like it," said Bill for the fifth time. "Don't like any of this confrontational stuff. Give me a phone or an email, not this nonsense."

"Why don't you wait in the car?" I suggested.

"I'm the only reason you'll get out of there alive. I'm legitimate, an historian. Try not to look so damned military, can you? You're meant to be a documentary video maker."

"I am a documentary video maker," I said. "Don't I look like one?"

Bill did not reply.

We arrived in record time at the entrance to the private quay, a couple of kilometres before the public entrance to the sprawling collection of shops, hotels, bars and restaurants that made up the Victoria & Alfred Waterfront complex. There we could have bumped over a few circles and been sitting behind a cold draught beer within minutes. But the entrance to the private quay didn't work like that. Here there was a three-metre wall, topped with electric fencing and additional broken glass set into the cement just in case the two-thousand-volt shock was not deterrent enough. The huge steel gates did not open for Rose despite her aggressive approach. Instead, a smaller pedestrian gate to the side opened and a man wearing a black paramilitary uniform strolled over to the driver's window at a pace slow enough to ensure that we realised that any haste on our part was not something that he felt obliged to prioritise. He was paid to keep people out, not let them in.

It took Rose a few minutes to fill in the details on the clipboard, and then the security guard checked her spelling without haste. He strolled back through the pedestrian gate which closed with a loud clang behind him. I wondered aloud whether things were going to turn nasty and they would open fire on us.

"I should have known you'd be nurturing military fantasies," said Bill.

"It was a joke," I said, but Bill didn't look convinced. "Sandy told me you never stopped thinking like that," he said, gazing ahead steadfastly through the windscreen. "She said it had scarred you for life."

"Not scarred," I said. "When you form habits that your life depends upon, I wouldn't call them scars."

That had sounded defensive, so I stopped right there. I knew Bill's feelings about the military. There were some people who were impressed by the idea that I had endured one of the toughest military training processes in the world. Some people who felt respect, even awe at the thought that I had been a member of one of the world's most elite platoons. Others who felt their own manhood threatened and would strut about like roosters to show how much more manly than I they were. Others who were disappointed that I wouldn't tell them what it felt like to kill another human being, and others who were appalled that it was something I could tell them. But Bill was none of these. He was dismissive and vaguely irritated by the fact that a good friend of his had chosen a man such as me. Not that he felt she should have chosen him. But I was a disappointing choice: she could have done better. And although he never said it, I knew that he blamed me in some indefinable way for the fact that he had lost her. For the fact that we had all lost her. But as we sat there in silence waiting for some unseen person to approve our entry into this fortress on the sea, it occurred to me that the simple fact he had mentioned her indicated some softening of his resentment.

"It's my fault," said Bill. "I should have known Matlala

wasn't going to invite us around for a cup of tea. He's a cunning little bulldog, that one. And they're all like this with Mbuyo. I should have known."

"All like what?"

"Like a pack of lion cubs. They bring their day's kill back to him so that he can approve. He's like the big alpha male lion who lies under the tree all day licking his paws and smiling for the cameras, while they're out hunting. Then in the dark of the night they drag their kills back to camp."

"You don't approve of him," I said.

Bill turned to me with a deadpan expression.

"I didn't say that. I don't ask myself whether I approve of him or whether I don't. I don't express opinions about political leaders. That's the quickest way to end your career in this country."

Bill removed a large handkerchief from the pocket of his linen jacket and blew his nose loudly.

"Got caught in the rain," he said as if the few drops that had fallen on him might have brought on a man-sized cold. "You'd do well to remember that about this country," he continued. "Things are different in the civilised First World countries of your birth and upbringing."

"My mother was South African," I reminded him. "She instilled in me a healthy wariness of political leaders."

"Of course she was – Sandy told me that. I keep seeing you as a weird British-Canadian mix."

"I'm even weirder than that."

The gates before Rose's car swung open silently, and Rose nudged her way inside the complex. Just when I thought we could sneak in behind her, the security guard emerged with a hand held up to the sky and stood squarely in front of my rusty old Fiat. He looked at the car with disdain and waited until I had turned off the engine before lowering his hand and coming around to the window.

"We're with Mr and Mrs Matlala," I said, indicating the gates as they closed on the sight of Rose reaching maximum acceleration on the way to her allotted parking space fifty metres ahead.

"Is that the truth?" asked the guard, with the rolling r's of the West Coast. He was an elderly man with a neat white moustache that had been stained by the nicotine of a thousand cigarettes, above which were a pair of sad, droopy eyes. It was a rhetorical question. He shoved his clipboard at me.

"We'll need your underpants size nonetheless," he said. "Have some important guests here today, don't we?"

———

By the time security had found a parking space where my decrepit car would not embarrass the patrons or infect their glossy luxury vehicles, Matlala was dealing with his sobriety problem, and Rose was sipping orange juice on the terrace. Bill and I stood in the reception area of what turned out to be a private club, feeling under-dressed and unprepared. Well, I cannot speak for Bill, whose rich orange linen jacket made him glow like a traffic beacon at night, but I felt under-dressed in my jeans and camera jacket. The girl at the reception desk was also under-dressed, although the clothes she did have on were of the highest quality, with sparkling sequins and elegant lace details. It's just that there wasn't very much of them. She explained that we weren't on any list, and therefore couldn't proceed further, and spoke urgently into a phone while smiling uncertainly, the kind of smile that could be denied if things turned nasty. Through sliding glass doors we could see an open-plan bar area, all glass, chrome and mirrors, with subtle down-lighting over deep marble bar counters. Beyond the small clusters of men standing about with drinks and cheerful faces, the wooden-decked terrace stretched out over the sea, designed to look like we were floating on a luxury cruise liner.

The glass doors emitted a subtle hiss, like portals to another world, and Matlala appeared, beaming and holding out his hands for an embrace as if our presence was an unexpected surprise.

"It's okay, Lulu," he said to the receptionist. "These are my guests. The big guy knows about it."

The receptionist's forced smile relaxed, and she pulled her shoulders back in a way that demonstrated the efficacy of the straps that defied science by holding the top part of her clothing in place. Matlala beamed with pleasure, and Bill and I smiled to show there were no hard feelings, and with that we were ushered, a hand of Matlala's on a shoulder each, into the exalted domain.

Thulani Mbuyo, president-to-be and hero of the people, was standing in the centre of the room, with a small crowd of men clustered around him. Matlala had timed his approach well because as we neared him there was a burst of laughter and the crowd shifted as a natural break in the conversation occurred. President-elect Mbuyo was a tall man and as the lopsided smile on his face subsided, he looked over the heads of the men around him and his eyes settled on our incongruous trio. His bright intelligent eyes focused on mine, and although the smile on his face was slipping, there was amusement still in his eyes. The repair work that had been done to his face had been hasty and not a good example of the abilities of the medical profession at the time. They were only patching him up in order to shove him into jail, after all. And there, they had reasoned, it wouldn't matter if he had less than a quarter of a face. At least that was the way the press liked to explain it. And now, when it did matter, he wore his scars with pride. Physical evidence if you needed any that he was a true hero of the people, in the mould of Nelson Mandela, and not the power-hungry charlatans that had followed him. Nevertheless, the sight of his scarred face was a shock.

Matlala introduced me as 'that journalist I told you about', and Bill as 'the writer'. The president-elect held my hand for quite a long time after we'd exchanged a complex sequence of shuffling handshakes, twisted the corner of his mouth and told me to just call him Thulani after I'd addressed him as 'Mister President', feeling like Marilyn Monroe. I did so in the hopes that he would release my hand, and it wasn't long before he did. He gave Bill the same treatment, and for a moment we all stood around like idol worshippers drinking in the presence of the supreme being.

"You had some questions about my brother," said just-call-me-Thulani, and he smiled to show that he didn't mind.

"About Lindiwe Dlomo," I said. There seemed little point in beating about the bush, although Bill's face twitched as if he had a nervous tic.

"Lindiwe Dlomo," he repeated, as if trying to get his tongue around the letters for the first time. Somewhere between the D and L he produced a sound as if he'd knocked two pieces of wood together. "It's been many years since I heard that name."

"She was your brother's girlfriend?"

"She was. Many, many years ago. But, like my brother,

she is now long gone." He said it with no regret, and his bright eyes held mine as he took a sip of his sparkling mineral water. "I'm surprised anyone remembers her. Or my brother." Thulani's eyes made that into a question.

"A journalist," I said, "A newspaper journalist asked me about her. Mr Matlala gave us a little background."

Thulani turned to look at Matlala, not entirely with pleasure it seemed to me.

"And this journalist. Where is he now?" asked Thulani.

"Travelling," I said.

"Of course," said Thulani in a way that made me wonder whether he knew that Johansson would not be returning from his travels. "This becomes more intriguing. First the mention of my late brother, then a woman who died many years ago, and now a journalist who is travelling."

"I knew you would want to know," said Matlala suddenly, feeling perhaps that the conversation was not going in a direction that would reap him the rewards he had hoped.

Thulani swung his beneficent gaze onto him and the corner of his mouth that still had some muscle attached curled upwards.

"You were right about that, Jake," he said, and Matlala glowed. Thulani turned back to me. "The thing that surprises me," he said with a warm tone so it didn't come across as threatening, "is that anyone would have any interest in my brother. Or his girlfriend." He paused, and I opened my mouth to speak, but he raised a scarred hand and continued. "Particularly considering that they both died thirty years ago. My brother was not someone worth speaking about when he was alive. Why speak about him now?"

"He was an informer," said Matlala with a sudden burst of acrimony. "He deserved to burn."

A slight flash of what I mistook for anger passed behind Thulani's eyes, but when he turned to Matlala, he spoke gently.

"Now, Jake," he said. "You weren't there." Matlala looked contrite and sipped at his sobriety cure like an enthusiastic devotee flagellating himself after overstepping the mark. "My brother was a weak man, that is true," said Thulani, turning back to me. "But not a man that was worth holding any resentment over. I never have. Resented him."

He looked at me as if suggesting that I doubted this assertion.

"What were the questions that your travelling journalist had?" he asked.

For a moment I thought of Johansson lying in the refrigerator and wondered whether he did have any questions about Lindiwe Dlomo. Was her name just one that he had stumbled upon while catching up on his reading in the archives as Fehrson suggested? Was it all just a ploy to have me stir up trouble hoping some loose change would be shaken out to fall into his pocket? Perhaps he was lying in the refrigerator now because he'd had one drink too many and hadn't been given the time to explain his elaborate joke.

"He suggested," I said cautiously, "that she might have been an informer." There was no reaction from Thulani. "And that you and your comrades were betrayed by her," I added in the hope that made the whole thing sound convincing.

Thulani didn't respond for a moment, and it felt as if there was a pause in time. Or as if everyone in the room was holding their breath, which was absurd because others around us were talking and laughing. Thulani took a deep breath. His mouth attempted another smile.

"For many years," he said, "others have pointed fingers. They have accused everyone they can think of for the fire that killed my friends. That killed my brother. That nearly killed me." Thulani turned to Matlala. "You know it, Jake. The only people who have not been accused are the people who had the good fortune to die before it happened. Such as my father. And my mother. No one has suggested they started the fire because they had been dead for many years by the time the match was struck. God rest their souls."

Thulani laughed, perhaps in an effort to lighten the mood, because we were all looking pretty glum. At least Bill and Matlala were not looking as if they were finding much to amuse them.

"You know what I always say to these accusations, Jake?"

Matlala nodded. "That it is not important," he said obediently.

"That it is not important," repeated Thulani. "Because it isn't. The fire happened. I know that better than anyone. And knowing who started it will not change that. Everyone else seems to want to know. I am happy not to."

Thulani looked to each of us as if to ensure that we were hearing him. I was beginning to understand how he had risen to the position he had. There was something of the religious teacher in his rhetoric.

"Or perhaps I would rather not know. Because if I did know, the anger within me would be so great that I would do something more unforgivable than the crime they are guilty of. To kill for vengeance is truly unforgivable."

Thulani sipped at his mineral water, and Matlala said,

"So true, Big T. So true," in a low whisper. Bill and I kept silent lest the thing turn into a religious gathering.

"Which is why the question of whether Lindiwe Dlomo was an informer is not a question worth asking," said Thulani. "You can tell your journalist that, and he can focus on more interesting subjects."

"There was the suggestion," I said. "That information about Lindiwe Dlomo might be used against you."

"Information? What information?"

I opened my mouth to answer that but was saved by Matlala who said, "She had no information. Big T gave her nothing."

Thulani nodded. "That's right Jake," he said, and turned to me. "You can tell your journalist that there is no story."

"Not so much information from Lindiwe Dlomo," I said. "More, information about what happened to her. There was the suggestion that might be used against you."

Thulani didn't react. His eyes regarded me from behind the mask of scar tissue. His tongue came out and ran along the ridge that served as an upper lip.

"Was there?" he said after a pause that had seemed a little too long. "How extraordinary."

"Which is why," said Bill, for whom that awkward pause had been too much to bear, "we thought we should follow up on this."

"Of course," said Thulani. "Of course you should."

"On the other hand," I said, "she came to see you. On Robben Island. Is it possible that something you said might have fallen into the wrong hands?"

"Ah," said Thulani, and he put up another smile as his composure returned. "Your journalist is suggesting that I became an informer myself. That when my late brother's girlfriend came to the Island I was so overcome with emotion that I gave her all the names I could think of, and that she carried that information back to her apartheid masters. That is very good. Very amusing."

A youthful man with glasses and a receding hairline appeared beside Matlala. "Mr President sir," he said in a breathless voice. "I am sorry to disturb you." He glanced at us dismissively. "We have the room prepared. You can begin as soon as you are ready."

"We shouldn't keep the people waiting," said Thulani solemnly, and he passed his glass of water to the callow man and held out a hand to me. I took the hand, but instead of shaking it, he held my hand between his. "You should tell your journalist when he returns from his travels that he has nothing to fear. None of us have anything to fear," he added magnanimously, raising a hand from mine and using it to indicate the occupants of the room, "because it would be a mistake to think that any information could be used against me. Let me state clearly for the record. I did not betray my people thirty years ago to the girlfriend of my late brother. The truth is not to be feared because, as we know from the Good Book, it will set us free."

"It might make us miserable first though," I said.

"Ah!" the corner of his mouth curled up, and he squeezed my hand a little harder in appreciation. "You quote a president to a president! You journalists are not all bad, although I think Jake is mistaken in thinking you are one." Thulani turned to Matlala. "You hear that? He quoted an American president to me. A dead American president. He doesn't smell like a journalist to me." Then back to me, "Tell your journalist friend that I would be very interested in hearing his information, even if it does make me a little miserable before setting me free. There is nothing to be feared in the truth, but sometimes carrying it can become a burden, and your friend should share that burden." Thulani released my hand and took Bill's hand in his. "There was nothing bad in Lindiwe," he said as if trying to convince Bill of it. "Nothing at all. Not her fault that the man who adopted her was a policeman. Nor was she responsible for what happened between my brother and her. No," he turned back to me. "There is nothing about Lindiwe that could hurt me, so you tell him that."

With that Thulani moved away from us, and like a ship leading an armada, the others followed. The callow man held the half empty glass of mineral water like a holy relic and looked at us sternly as our cue to depart.

———

"History in the making," said Bill as we walked back to the car. "The politicians and the people with the money."

The wind was picking up again, and it started tugging at Bill's orange jacket. He pulled it tighter about him and glanced up at the sky anxiously. The clouds were lowering again, and we rushed to get to the car before the rain started.

"I guess your journalist friend was wrong," said Bill as I nursed the car into action. "No dirty secrets."

"Looks like it," I said. The engine finally caught on the fourth attempt.

We made our way out of the parking lot, past the moustachioed security guard now sporting a large sheet of clear plastic over his uniform to protect it against the rain. He was remonstrating with a man in sunglasses who had parked his Lamborghini in the disabled bay and was refusing to move it.

"You must be relieved," said Bill, unconvinced by my response. "You're going to drop the whole thing?"

"Yes, of course."

I knew how stressful Bill had found this direct challenge of authority. He was someone who liked to stay within the lines, no matter how much he complained. Sometimes I envied people like him because once you stray outside the lines it can be hard to get back in.

SEVEN

The entrance hall of The Gold Mining Conglomerate of South Africa Archives, or Gold Archives, was what the architect had managed to remember about Gothic churches without having to look it up in a book. There was a lot of genuine marble worn smooth by the feet of the proletariat. The extensive security desks, tables and benches looked like they were authentic Anton Anreith church pews which had only been slightly chopped up and glued back together again. The vaulted ceiling echoed the reverent tones of the security guards behind the x-ray machine and the clicking shoes of a woman on her way out. I felt sure that if I listened carefully enough, I would hear the echo of my own breathing. The security team were serious about protecting the history of our nation. Or perhaps they were serious about the kind of people they allowed in to view that history. They went to great lengths to prevent me from entering the building, subjecting me to a pat-down because the fact that the x-ray machines refused to beep was clearly an error: I was the kind of man who looked as if he carried a weapon. They reluctantly allowed me through but held me in no man's land until the honey-voiced, long-limbed private secretary to Mr Riaan Breytenbach appeared in person to escort me into the presence of the master.

Riaan "BB" Breytenbach remained seated as I settled into the low-slung chair at the visitor's end of his mahogany desk, and he waited patiently as I declined the offer of sustenance from his private secretary. He kept the friendly face up for as long as it took the secretary to leave us alone, and then he allowed the suspicion to return to his eyes.

BB showed no glimmer of recognition, which did not surprise me. The encounter we had shared had been several years ago, and I had been in uniform, covered in the mud of the Ugandan rainforest and the blood of men whose existence he denied. I recognised him though. All five feet and six inches of him, the tan you get from spending more time on the golf course than in an office, and the wavy dark hair peppered with grey at the temples and carefully coiffed in order to give him more height than his genes and early nutrition had provided. His face was familiar to most South Africans. The dark eyes, black hair and strong nose implied an Italian ancestry, and he was often touted in the pulp media as the country's most eligible bachelor with his film-star good looks and oodles of money. But it was a particularly familiar face to me. I did my best to conceal the shiver of revulsion that I felt on seeing him and gave a brave smile to match his suspicion.

"They call him Father now?" asked BB. "In my day it was Fearsome."

"I think he prefers Father," I said.

"I told him there was nothing to worry about. Why all this anxiety?"

"Being thorough. If there are nasty secrets lurking in the

background, I am sure everyone would rather know about them now, before they take us by surprise."

"Us?" said BB, but then without waiting to hear who we were, said, "The journalist is dead."

There was no question in that statement, but I took it upon myself to provide an answer.

"The concern is others he might have spoken to, and of course the source of his information."

BB grunted and studied me carefully. I wondered whether some recognition was beginning to form behind his cold steel eyes.

"Don't know why you're here," he said. "Nothing I can say about it. Doesn't matter a damn what he did to that woman, does it? She's been dead for thirty years. Who cares? Your Fearsome Father might mourn her and worry like an old woman about it, but no one else gives a damn."

"We wouldn't want someone suggesting that the president-elect was responsible for her death."

BB shrugged, a gesture that was European in its manner. I remembered how he liked to model himself as the refined descendant of an elite European culture, although that was a very thin layer which barely covered the ugly, brutal nature that lay beneath.

"Why would he have killed her?" he asked.

"If he discovered what she and her boyfriend were doing."

"Doing?" BB loaded each word he uttered with aggression. He used his short manner of speaking as a means of attack rather than communication.

"They were passing information to the security police. It was your operation as I understand it. *Spieël* ... or have I got it wrong?"

BB's face lifted a little, as if amusement had replaced

the suspicion. His eyes almost twinkled.

"The information they passed was nothing," he said. "A silly game they played. What would have made him angry was realising that she and his little brother were the ones who tried to kill him. But he never figured that one out, or if he did, she was long gone before he could do anything about it."

"It was them who started the fire?"

"How the hell would I know?" The defences went up again, and the suspicion returned.

"You handled the reports they sent in. Didn't you know that was the plan? To get rid of them all?"

"Like hell it was. That maniac Du Toit put it in their heads. If you're looking for someone to blame, it would be him. That girl and her boyfriend had a grudge, and Du Toit told them it was payback time."

BB leaned back in his chair and gave a nasty smile.

"Du Toit ran it as his own operation?"

"Du Toit wanted a piece of the action, thought he could muscle in on our territory. I was young, doing my national service, and he didn't like the fact that they allowed me to handle secret documents. There was nothing secret in them. I just laughed at him. Old, cranky arsehole. Then the whole thing blew up in his face. Served him right." BB's tanned face twitched, and he made an effort at a sneering laugh.

"Looks like we're in the clear then," I said, "in terms of Lindiwe Dlomo being a dark secret in the president-elect's past. If the whole thing was a botched operation from Pretoria. You don't think the president-elect would have figured out a connection between the fire and Lindiwe?"

BB smiled at the absurdity of that suggestion. "In the clear," he confirmed, with a satisfied smirk. "She is well and truly forgotten. And even if, in his dying moments, the brother confessed to their crimes, what could he have done about it? He was lying in a hospital bed for weeks. Then maximum security on Robben Island. He was a terrorist, wasn't he? So what if he was seething with rage? Planning his revenge. What could he do? It's not like he could slip a note to someone who would go out and wreak that revenge. They weren't having piss-ups with their hoodlums on the outside. There is really nothing that can be pinned on him."

"Although he did receive one visitor."

BB's eyes had strayed to a point above my head, a habit of his that I remembered from the debriefings in Uganda. A little device of his to show his superiority, as if he were not speaking to me, but some more important audience beyond me. His eyes jumped back to me now.

"On Robben Island?" he said.

"Lindiwe visited him there. Wasn't she sent in by the service?"

"Visited him? What the hell you talking about?" BB shook his head. "Prisoners on Robben Island didn't get visitors."

"Perhaps it was arranged by Du Toit?"

BB shook his head again. "Du Toit was out of the picture by then."

"Perhaps there would be something about it in the files?"

"There aren't any files."

"Fehrson's office said they had been moved here, to your archives."

BB shook his head regretfully, but there was no regret in his voice. "Lost in the transfer. It was thirty years ago. Those bits of paper were in a dreadful mess. A good many of them were simply thrown away."

"This facility doesn't seem the kind of place where papers go missing."

"Nothing wrong with the facility. I checked myself, after your Fearsome Father called."

"I thought these archives were considered one of the better storage facilities."

"State-of-the-art," said BB with a bully's tone. "We've invested heavily in this place. I've invested personally. There isn't a safer place on the whole of this continent."

He waited for me to express some admiration. I didn't.

"It's like an iceberg," said BB. "We drilled down beneath it, it's what we do. Mining is in my blood. We have levels and levels below ground. There isn't a safer place on the continent."

"I'll tell Fehrson we're in the clear then."

"You tell your Fearsome Father there is nothing to worry about. That journalist was just peddling horseshit. He dreamed the whole thing up. The new boy is clean as a whistle. You can take it from me. Forget the whole thing."

I climbed out of the low-slung chair, and considered offering my hand in farewell, but BB remained crouched behind his desk and didn't look in the mood for physical contact. I gave him a nod instead, and his eyes narrowed.

"I remember you now," he said. His voice had an awed quality. "Thought there was something familiar. You were with that team of killers they sent us. To the mine – my gold mine in Uganda."

"I served in the 14th squad. That's correct, they posted us to your mine."

"14th squad? But you guys were no ordinary squad, were you? I thought they were sending me a team of soldiers. But you guys ... you guys weren't soldiers."

"22nd Special Forces Regiment, G squadron, 14th squad."

"Yes, yes," said BB. "But you were like the phantom squad, weren't you? They only told me after. You guys were the killers. You weren't the real deal soldiers. You were the outcasts, the ones they'd pushed too far in the training, the ones they could rely on to do what no self-respecting soldier would do. That's who you are."

I turned back to the door and stepped towards it.

"Didn't one of you guys get himself killed at that plane crash? It was an ambush, wasn't it? And you numbskulls just walked straight into it."

"It was a mine," I said, turning back to BB. "He stepped on a mine. They booby-trapped the dying civilians with mines."

BB smiled. "Well, that's too bad. One less killer in the world."

I smiled in agreement and didn't say that the killer who had stepped on the mine had been a friend. A good friend.

"And now you're an office boy for the Fearsome Father?" said BB, with the note of a taunt. "No more killing?"

I said nothing. Memories of our mission on the mine in the northern reaches of Uganda were coming back to me and making me feel queasy.

"Never thought I'd bump into one of you again." He regarded me as one might consider an interesting curiosity. "You guys did an outstanding job, I'll give you that. Killing was clearly your game."

My agreeable smile was still in place. I took it down, nodded and left the room. It had occurred to me there was one other person who might know what had happened to Lindiwe Dlomo.

EIGHT

South Africa is a country where the elderly are cared for by their children, are revered by their grandchildren, and are given pride of place at the head of the table when the family convenes. Their stories are listened to with interest and enthusiasm, and their wisdom is passed down through the generations. But this is not true for the elderly white people, who invest their life savings in order to stay in euphemistically named retirement villages, which are one step up from hospitals, one step down from hotels, and not far from the morgue.

Andre du Toit was withering away in one of these retirement villages to the north of Pretoria. A two-hour flight, and an hour in a hired car had brought me to the place he had chosen to die. It had been built around a golf course and inmates were encouraged to play the game for as long as their medical plans could keep them fit enough. After which they could sit on the balconies of their clustered bungalows, breathe oxygen from the provided canisters, and dwell alone on what memories they retained, while they waited to die – or worse: simply faded away from lack of interest. I had made the journey here because, despite Fehrson's assurances that I would not find anyone who remembered Lindiwe Dlomo, and BB's confidence that she was forgotten, it turned out that the villain of their version of events was still alive. Although as I approached the terrace of Du Toit's bungalow and made out his huddled form under a blanket with an oxygen tank at his side, I wondered whether there would be much memory left. He reached up a shaky arm from his wheelchair and allowed me to grasp his birdlike hand for a moment. His eyes were clear above the oxygen mask, but there was a confusion in them, as if he knew that he should challenge strangers who came asking questions but had forgotten why that was.

"Don't tire him out now," said the cheerful nurse who had shown me the way. "He cannot talk for too long. Ten minutes, or he'll not make it to dinner. Too many cigarettes, wasn't it, Major Du Toit?" she said loudly at him.

"What's that?" he asked in a surprisingly forceful voice and looked up at her as if suspecting that she was saying nasty things about him.

"You smoked too many of those cigarettes, didn't you Major Du Toit?"

"Bullshit," he retorted. "Gave them up years ago." And he gave a scoffing laugh with a wheeze that turned into a cough.

Du Toit was the wrong end of his eighties, and the once tall and domineering man I'd seen in photographs had shrivelled into an old man.

"He gets a bit cranky," the nurse said to me. "It's the pain. Never takes his pills, and then this is what happens. Take it easy with him."

"She's a tricky one," said Du Toit as he watched the nurse's large rear end retreat. "Always fussing about." He removed the oxygen mask and looked over at the tray of drinks the nurse had brought with her. Two glasses with generous tots of rum, a bottle in case we needed more, and two cans of Coca-Cola.

"May I?" I asked, realising that we were not likely to get past the pleasantries until Du Toit had one of the glasses in his hand.

"Not too much Coke," he said. "I have to be careful with sugar."

"Don Fehrson sends his regards," I said. Du Toit's eyes flickered up from monitoring the proportion of Coke to rum to show that he knew I was lying about that.

"You work with him?" he asked.

"In the new building on Greenmarket Square," I said as I handed him his drink. "The Department moved out of Woodstock."

"I heard he was running his own little circus," said Du Toit.

"Just a small team."

"That's what I heard. A small team. They're cutting him out, aren't they? He was never any good at reading the writing on the wall." There was an element of smug satisfaction in his voice.

"He survived all the changes," I said, and immediately regretted it. Du Toit had not come through those changes smelling of roses. His stellar career in the National Intelligence Agency had been reduced by the Truth and Reconciliation process to a series of brutal crimes as his victims' families had taken to the stand and wept. Du Toit had emerged as a cruel and unrepentant abuser of the power the former government had given him. He took a sip of his rum and Coke and looked out over the links with an irritated pursing of the lips.

"But you're right," I said. "He is being moved sideways. I think they're treading water until he retires."

That seemed to lift Du Toit's spirits.

"It was that fire you wanted to know about? And that woman with the boyfriend."

"Some files have gone missing. We're tying up a few loose ends."

"Gone missing? What kind of 'gone missing'?"

"They've been transferred to the archives, and it's all a bit of a mess."

Du Toit nodded as if it was to be expected. A golf cart rolled onto the green before his bungalow, and two elderly couples clambered out with stiff legs, and looked around as if choosing a picnic spot. One of the men raised his hand in greeting to Du Toit, who pushed his lower lip out and scowled.

"It's because of that new Zulu chieftain they're putting in, is it?" said Du Toit. "He wants to read the files and see if there's anyone else they can hang from the rafters. Anyone they didn't get the first time round."

"Is that what happened? They hanged people from the rafters?"

"Course they did. What did you imagine they were doing on Robben Island?"

"There's no record of what happened, with the files all gone."

"As soon as they'd cut his tongue loose from where it had welded into the roof of his mouth he sent them out after her, you can be sure of that. She was a marked woman, I told them that. Fehrson and his incompetent crew. But did they care?"

The four golfers were standing around like party-goers who realise they've got the venue wrong. Then a second golf cart rolled onto the green with two young caddies and a bunch of golf bags. The caddies set about handing out clubs like they were organising a children's party.

"How was she killed?" I asked.

Du Toit turned to me, and for a moment his eyes shone with something other than the dull glow of pain. "You don't know?" he said.

"It's not mentioned in the register, and there's no reference to it."

"Of course there isn't. There wouldn't be. The file was closed. The spring had run dry. When that Zulu survived they flipped sides didn't they? Found a scapegoat to blame: that's me. Have they told you the whole thing was my fault?" Du Toit didn't wait for the answer to that. "They let the Zulu kill the girl so he could get his rocks off and turned a blind eye so they could be best buddies afterwards."

Du Toit looked out at the golfers, who were preparing to putt. The man who had waved at Du Toit was pacing about the green, tapping it with his putter, and stooping down occasionally to rearrange the blades of grass.

"Scapegoat?" I said. "Are you telling me it wasn't your plan to set fire to that hut?"

"My plan?" Du Toit sprayed spittle and splashed rum over me in his anger. "I was the one who warned them it would go wrong. They had that limp rich kid on it. Homosexual piece of shit."

"Breytenbach?"

"That's the one. He had no idea what he was doing. There was some ground contact who used to meet with them and give him the reports. Someone whose identity nobody was allowed to know, except of course the fucking homo. I smelt a rat from the beginning. I knew there was something wrong."

Du Toit watched the golfer he had spurned taking his putt. The ball missed by a few centimetres and his fellow golfers oohed and aahed. A satisfied look settled onto Du Toit's features.

"Something wrong with the ground contact?"

"Homicidal maniac. He's the one the Zulu should have killed."

"If you weren't allowed to know the ground contact, how do you know he was a maniac?"

Du Toit moved his eyes to me like a chameleon looking for its prey.

"She told me, didn't she?"

"Lindiwe?"

"Of course Lindiwe, you idiot. The night of the fire, she told me."

"That it was their ground contact that did it?"

"No, she did it alright. She started the fire. But he set her up for it."

Du Toit took a sip of his rum, lowering his lip to the glass, and then lifting it slowly so that the liquid reached his waiting tongue.

"The night after the fire she told me," he said. "Late that night. Very late, two or three in the morning. The place had been in chaos all day, we'd all been running around like headless chickens. At first it was the way it always was after something big goes down. Like after a bomb hits. Silence all about, everything goes still. Then the whoosh of hot air, and we were all running. They clamped down on the news, and it was impossible to know what was going on. We had ears on the ground, but not nearly as many as we should. Like a bunch of amateurs caught with their pants down. We had photographers in there, but they were the enemy as far as those army guys were concerned, so they couldn't get clear shots. I'll have a little more of that." He waved his empty glass at me. I poured him another drink.

The spurned golfer was being cheerful about his missed putt. He noticed us watching him and raised his hand again in greeting. Du Toit didn't respond.

"And you saw Lindiwe?"

"It looked bad," said Du Toit, and he swirled his rum about to make sure there wasn't too much Coke mixed in with it. "The whole shack was gone, nothing but twisted metal and smoke. And of course the bodies. We wanted close shots so we could identify them, but the idiots went for the arty nonsense where you can't make out shit." Du Toit repeated his painstaking drinking action and licked his lips, savouring every drop.

"We got an emergency meet request. Breytenbach was busy panicking, couldn't get hold of the ground contact. I wasn't going to send him in to see her. That prick of a priest had been kept out of it because of 'personal' reasons, and so I went down there. Train station, end of the platform, and she was all peace and quiet. I thought she'd lost her mind. Back in the office everyone's running around feeling a bit sick. But also maybe good. You wouldn't know what it feels like. The vermin were dead, but you feel sick in your stomach. You wouldn't understand." Du Toit paused and watched as the third golfer dropped the ball into the hole on a long putt from the far end of the green. The other three cheered, and the caddies applauded obediently. I didn't bother telling Du Toit that I understood only too well.

"Anyway," he said with a sigh, "when I got to her it was

like she'd had some religious experience. Found God. I said to her, 'What's eaten your goat?' and she laughed. Laughed! Said it was all good. I didn't want to burst her bubble, but I could count, and we had six dead bodies. That meant her boyfriend was one of them. I said something about trying to identify the bodies, and it didn't look altogether good. She just smiled and said it was okay, he'd survived. That's when I realised it was the shock. It does that, turns people upside down. They go from hysterical to zombie just like that."

The golfers were moving on to the next hole. They handed their clubs to the caddies and climbed into their golf cart. The friendly one waved again at Du Toit.

"Arsehole. Does that every day," said Du Toit, glaring after the cart.

"She said he'd survived?" I prompted. "Mbuyo?"

"Some paramedic told her he would live. It was the first we heard of it. Our reports said all dead, but it turned out the one cockroach lived. We went through our photos, but they all looked good and dead to us. Turns out the guy lay there some time before anyone bothered checking the pulse."

"And she was pleased about that? That Mbuyo survived?"

"Pleased, oh yes. But she had the wrong Mbuyo, didn't she? That was the joke. Thought it was her lover lying there in the mud with his clothes all melted into his skin. Guess it was hard to tell."

"When did she realise her mistake?"

"About Mbuyo? A couple of days, I guess. Not such a religious experience after all. She found God, but not in the way she'd expected. Considering as she'd been the one to kill him."

"She told you that? That she'd started the fire?"

Du Toit nodded and stuck his lower lip out. "That same night. I said if we got our hands on the cocksucker who'd done it we'd throttle him and shove his balls down his throat, and she said she didn't have any balls. And maybe her boyfriend didn't anymore because they'd been burned off."

"She and her boyfriend? They did it together?"

Du Toit repeated the painstaking process with his rum.

"Their ground contact cooked the whole thing up. That's what she said. Orders from above. She and the boyfriend didn't object. Had a big grudge against the brother. I told her they had duped her. She was a murderer, not a political activist. Told Breytenbach to haul the ground contact in, get him to explain himself."

"What did he say?"

"Said he couldn't do that. Ground contact had disappeared. Said she made it all up. Said she was unstable. But by then they were covering their arses. Put me in a back room and told me they'd call me when they needed me. Four days I sat there getting myself pneumonia from all that sea air, while they drank tea and made up their bullshit stories."

"They didn't bring the contact in?"

"He went AWOL. No contact. Puff of smoke."

"But you thought she was telling you the truth?"

"Listen, sonny boy," said Du Toit with a return of the bitterness the rum had only temporarily assuaged. "I might be getting on, but I'm not losing my mind. They've filled you with their lies. But I know what happened. As soon as they figured out which Zulu was lying in that hospital bed they decided to help him deal with her. Kill two birds with one stone. Make a new friend, and get rid of the woman. He did her in as soon as his tongue could get itself around all those clicks. You can be sure he put the finger on her, and his compatriots went out and dealt with her. I told them that night: she's a marked woman. Doesn't stand a chance. They'll be putting a tyre around her shoulders and lighting the night up with it. You see if I'm not right."

"But why send her to Robben Island to speak to him?"

Du Toit uttered a cackling laugh which became a hacking cough.

"They didn't send her to Robben Island," he said, and did the chameleon eyes again.

"She went to the island," I said.

"Of course she did," said Du Toit. "I sent her there."

He wheezed and coughed again at my surprise, then tipped another few drops of rum into his mouth.

"Weeks after the bonfire, she called me. Head office in Pretoria. She called from a phone box, remember those? No security, nothing. But she'd given up on it all, lost her heart, hadn't she? We all knew that. I said you're lucky to be alive, that Zulu is going to get his buddies to give you what's coming to you. And she agreed. Said she wanted to talk to him. I laughed, but she begged me." He gave a wheezing cough that might have been intended as a laugh. "She knew she was good as dead, said they were already after her. Wanted to go and see him. Beg him to spare her. Went on and on. I put the phone down on her."

"But she called back?"

"Every day. Started making threats. I don't think she had anything that hadn't been blown already, but still she made them." Du Toit's tongue emerged for more rum.

"You took pity on her?"

"Wasn't difficult. Said we needed direct contact with the Zulu. They'd just about finished putting his face back on, and he was in isolation anyway. No harm in it. We owed her that much, at least."

"But it didn't work?"

Du Toit shrugged. "Doesn't look that way, does it? I guess she didn't plead hard enough, wasn't as convincing as she hoped to be. She was a looker she was, tight little body, had all the right tools, but that was not enough."

"What did she say about it?"

"Say? She said nothing. I called that priest of yours a couple weeks later: Fehrson, I said, what's become of your girl? Put me on hold. That baby-faced homo came on the line. Said the file had been closed, like it was something that had happened accidentally. Like they'd dropped it by mistake, and it was out of their hands. My help wasn't needed he said. I hadn't been intending to help. Told him that, little homo."

"You never heard from her?"

"My next trip down to the Cape I asked around. She was gone, presumed dead. Told me to keep my nose out of their business. Suited me. That sea air did it for my lungs." He gave a wheezing cough to prove it. "I got the hell out of there, never went back."

I poured Du Toit a third rum with not too much Coke. The nurse returned to move me along and threatened to confiscate Du Toit's glass because she suspected that he had already had enough. Du Toit faced this threat by downing the drink and handing her the glass. As I made to leave, he grabbed the sleeve of my jacket and held me back.

"You young upstarts," he said, breathing rotten teeth and rum all over me. "You think we did it all wrong, don't you? Think we should all be locked away or put out of our misery."

I started to deny it, but Du Toit would not be stopped.

"We were fighting a war, that's what none of you cock-suckers gets," he spat angrily. "Yes, we killed a lot of gooks. Others died too, like that girl. But it was a war. The ANC was a terrorist organisation. And not just because we said so. They were declared terrorists by the United fucking Nations. Amnesty wouldn't step up for that darkie in prison, you know that?"

"Darkie in prison?"

"Mandela."

"Mandela?" I tried to hide my surprise. There weren't many people who would have described Nelson Mandela in those terms. Du Toit spat as if to rid his mouth of a foul taste.

"When that darkie came out he became an instant saint, and now that he's dead he's sitting up there with the Holy Trinity. But he was a terrorist before he became a saint. He killed people. Not with his bare hands, but with his bombs. Amnesty wouldn't fight for his release. You go check your facts, you little upstart. And when you go back to your new Zulu leader, you remember that. He killed that woman because she fought on the other side. On our side. That was her right, but he killed her for it. And that's war crimes. Hell, not just war crimes, that's murder. You tell him that." His claw-like hand clutched at my sleeve and his eyes swam in a sea of rum and bitter memories. "So don't you come snooping round here thinking you'll find someone else to pin that one on. Her blood's on his hands. Get the file with my report, it's all in there. But you'll need to get yourself a crowbar and maybe a gun. 'Cos they're not going to show you the files. 'Cos they helped him do it. And while you're at it, go back to your priest, Father Don fucking Fehrson, and ask him why he was kept at a distance. That's a question worth asking. But watch your step, sonny. They'll not think twice about smoking anyone who starts stirring this shit up. So worry about that before you come back here throwing the shit at me."

Du Toit's anger culminated in a wrenching coughing fit. I extracted my arm from his grasp and wiped the spittle from it.

I thanked Major Du Toit for his time. The nurse helped him get the oxygen mask in place, and I wished her luck as I made my way out.

————

I sat in the hired car and looked out over the purple carpet of fallen petals beneath the jacaranda trees while the half tot of rum I'd consumed chased some confused thoughts round my mind. Behind all the brittle anger and spite that came from Du Toit, his story was the only one that had the slightest ring of truth to it. I thought about his suggestion that I get myself a gun and take the file with his report in it for myself. Sometimes the only path to the truth was a little crooked. I knew that.

Khanyi answered her phone with a sigh.

"Tell me you're not calling about that dead woman," she said. "Father's been quite upset about the whole thing."

"Could you tell me which of those files includes a report by Du Toit?"

"I would imagine all of them. You heard what Father said: Du Toit had his fingers all over it."

"It should say on the summary sheet," I said. "The night of the fire."

Khanyi sighed again, and I heard the shuffling of papers.

"I thought you were going to drop this whole thing,

Gabriel. Mister Breytenbach complained that we sent you snooping around there. Father said that if I heard from you, I should remind you that you are no longer employed by the Department. And that claiming you are is illegal. He said it amounts to a criminal action."

"Do you know what his personal reasons were? The reasons Fehrson was kept away from the operation?"

"Are you listening to what I'm saying?"

"Criminal actions, yes. You can tell him I will do my best to keep it legal."

"You should do your best not to do anything," said Khanyi and sighed once again for good measure. "Here we are. Du Toit's name comes up twice. Two of the files reference him."

"Is either of them a report by him?"

Khanyi gave me the number of the file that included mention of a report by Du Toit.

"It was family reasons," she said. "He told you, there were family reasons that kept him out of it."

"But he didn't say what family reasons?"

"It's none of your business, Gabriel, but it was about that time his marriage fell apart. And his son started with the drugs and killed that person not long after. You know all that."

I remembered Fehrson telling me that Lindiwe Dlomo had been about the same age as his son and wondered whether there had been more to the connection than a similarity of age.

"Mister Breytenbach said those files aren't available," said Khanyi. "We've already spoken to him about it. Don't even think of going back to him and asking for that file. Father would lay charges if you did."

"I wouldn't think of it," I said.

As I started the car and listened to the gentle popping of the carpet of purple flowers as I rolled over them I wondered how difficult it would be to walk into the archives and see for myself whether the file was missing. And if it wasn't, on Du Toit's advice, how difficult would it be to get a crowbar and a gun and take the file for myself?

NINE

I found another pack of cigarettes in the kitchen cupboard, and lit myself one that evening, watching the moon meet its grisly end on my small patch of sea. I hadn't liked Johansson, and what did I care if the new president of the country had killed someone thirty years ago? I am sure some people would argue that a murderer should not be allowed to lead a country and would ask why Mbuyo was not paying for his sins. But I was the wrong person to ask that question, let alone answer it. Yet the thought of Johansson's body lying in a fridge lurked at the back of my mind like an insistent regret. And why was everyone going to so much trouble to lie to me? Because despite all the assurances and placatory smiles, I knew that there had been scant truth in anything that either Fehrson or BB had said, and probably little more in what Du Toit had said.

My thoughts returned to BB. Meeting with him had been a mistake. Memories I had been running from for years were bubbling to the surface again. Inevitable memories. I lit another cigarette.

I recalled BB at our briefing, wearing his tailored suit in

the air-conditioned meeting room at the top of the mine complex, behind him the expansive view over the African bush, his conceited grimace of regret, as he told the lies that condemned so many men to their death.

We were at the Kigesi Gold Mining complex in northern Uganda, not too far from the border with the Democratic Republic of Congo. Some of the gold from the mine had gone missing. Lord Eversham, BB's partner and joint investor in the mining operation, had not been pleased to discover that some of their gold bars had been replaced by bars of worthless tungsten with only a thin veneer of gold. Lord Eversham was a member of the British aristocracy. He had political connections in the British government and a hotline to Special Forces. He started asking why it was that not all the gold they pulled from the ground and passed through the refinery was ending up where it should – in a vault in London, where it could line his back pocket.

It hadn't taken them long to figure out that there were a few rotten apples among the transport drivers. But BB and Lord Eversham were not content with simply firing them. BB was a man who believed in a more conclusive form of punishment. A more terminal punishment. That was where we came in. Lord Eversham pointed out to BB that his political contacts could arrange for that kind of punishment, but only if there was a bit of a political angle.

Fortunately for them the ADF, or Allied Democratic Forces, were a terrorist group active in the area, mainly over the border in the Democratic Republic of Congo. The idea that the men BB wanted to punish had a connection to that terrorist group was spurious, if not a downright lie. Their crime was not political, but they had offended BB and Lord Eversham by daring to think that they could steal from them. And that was a crime that carried a more severe punishment than any act of political rebellion.

So they assigned the blame to the convenient neighbourhood terrorist group. It took only a few phone calls from BB's noble partner to ensure that the best interests of highly positioned British aristocrats were protected from the criminal activities of the foreign terrorists.

And they sent our squad.

We were a special squad. BB had been correct about that. Not a phantom squad by any means, but we had special talents. And we were not known for asking questions, so we should have been the perfect solution. But they had not accounted for the fact that, well trained as we were, we did have a few questions about our posting. We were probably tired; we had just finished a long tour in Afghanistan, and our weariness manifested in some self-doubt. They had also not accounted for our captain, Steven Chandler. He was a leader who listened to his men and took it upon himself to answer some of the more basic questions that we started asking. Such as 'why are we in Uganda?' And 'why are we dealing with terrorists who are in no way endangering the lives of our countrymen?' And 'are these people even terrorists?'

We set about our lethal task and started the hunt. Our job did not involve speaking with the enemy, it was a shoot first, ask questions later job. But speak with them we did.

The first conversation was held in the slovenly mud hut where our victim had taken shelter. Even our translator refused to believe the story he told, which was too incredible to be true. Nothing but a fantasy, our captain declared. Certainly not something that would stand in the way of the fulfilment of our task.

But it was a fantasy that was repeated by others.

113

We started to believe that the men they had sent us to kill were not terrorists. They were simple locals, too weak, too stupid, or just too poor to meet the minimum requirements of employment at the mine. After failing to gain employment, they had each been offered special work. Dangerous work. Work on the mines, shoulder to shoulder with the lucky ones who had been accepted. What made their work dangerous was that they were diverting a tiny proportion of the valuable metal to a different destination.

It seemed absurd, but the absurdity was repeated over and over. The contact was made after they failed in their application to work at the mine. Just as they were contemplating a bleak future, a member of their community would make an approach. Someone from their village, or the distant cousin of a friend. A different someone each time. Someone who explained the alternate rules, the role they needed to play, each of them a minor piece in a complex game.

We kept quiet about the fantasy we were glimpsing. Captain Chandler was determined about that, and when he spoke we obeyed. No questions there.

And besides, the reason for keeping quiet became obvious to us: it had to do with where the stolen gold was taken and why. The missing gold was stored in an underground vault. Nothing unusual about it being underground. But it was an underground vault in South Africa, which seemed a little unusual, given the greater police presence in South Africa. Most unusual of all was the suggestion that the vault belonged to a man that our victims knew well. A Mr. Riaan Breytenbach, chairman of the mine.

We found ourselves in a difficult situation. There was no point in us speaking to our local contact for the operation, who happened to be the same man. Captain Chandler appealed to our masters for a review of our operation. But he made the appeal too late. Too late to start arguing the morality of our orders. We were highly trained men. We had our orders. It was our duty to do what we were told. And so we did.

Our tour was extended, and still there was no review. And extended again. And still we obeyed. Until the day that a plane carrying tourists was shot down in the nearby region of Kivu and our orders were changed. We were the nearest people capable of parachuting in to see if there were any survivors. There were, and we managed to get some of them out. Not all of them. And not all of us.

The image of BB's smug grimace came back to me often, usually in the middle of the night, the darkest hours before dawn. The smirk on his face, the cold eyes that said he didn't care what we knew. His smug confidence that we would do his killing for him, no matter what we knew to be the truth. And there were times that I wondered whether BB would not rather have done the killing himself.

That smirking man was now one of the people telling me yet again to turn away. That there was no story. That I should not worry about a journalist who fell into the sea. That the president-elect was clean as a whistle.

I reminded myself that I am not political, that I hadn't even liked Johansson and that I honestly didn't care whether Thulani Mbuyo, president-elect of South Africa ever paid for his sins. But as I poured myself a whisky and lit a third cigarette, it occurred to me that I knew just the person who could help me get a crowbar and maybe even a gun.

TEN

Captain Steven Chandler stood at the window that stretched the entire width of the house and reached from the floor up to the ceiling two storeys above us. Like a vast screen the window provided me with an intimate close-up of the Atlantic, which was thrashing about under the constant pouring rain. The room had nothing to make it feel homely. It was more an architectural experiment, a large space defined by the sea on the one side, and raw concrete on the other, with wooden detailing to render the stark interior. It was the sort of building that architects are proud to demonstrate developed from a squiggle drawn on a restaurant napkin. It was also about as friendly to live in as a squiggle on a restaurant napkin, although the double glazing and under-floor heating kept us warm. I was sitting on one of the chrome and canvas sculptures that served poorly as chairs. Chandler was taking a while to settle, prowling back and forth like a caged animal.

"You had difficulty finding me?" asked Chandler. Then without waiting for a reply added, "I've developed the need for caution." Although he was looking out to sea, I had the feeling that he was watching me. He had all the wariness of a wild animal in that moment that it looks up after an alarm call. He turned back to face me and it occurred to me that, with the window going right down to the floor, it looked as if he was walking on water. Tall, lean and muscular, in his early sixties, his face was lined as if from rivers of tears that had run from his eyes and gouged out his cheeks. His white crew cut was distinguished and military, his tall forehead austere, and his bearing was cold. But his eyes gave him away. They were grey and cold to match the mask he wore, but they were the kindest eyes I've ever looked into, exposing a soul that was rich and human. Or was that merely my projection? Because of the number of times I'd looked into those eyes and been surprised by the kindness I had found there.

"A drink, perhaps?" he asked.

"Something soft." I said.

His grey eyes twinkled just slightly, as if he found that amusing and unexpected. "I heard you'd changed," he said. "A metamorphosis was what they said. Put down your gun and taken up a camera. I could hardly credit it."

"It's true," I said.

"You're not doing the press monkey thing, surely?"

"Video documentaries, that kind of thing. Battle histories, wars."

"Of course. Never fades, does it? The fascination with war."

"There's no fascination. It just happened to be a subject I understood. The soldiers I interview find it easy to talk to me. We have something in common."

"And all for love," said Chandler. "Who would have thought it possible? She must be some woman."

"She is," I said, and his eyes twinkled to let me know that he knew about Sandy.

He moved away from the window to get the drinks. He was dressed in paramilitary clothes. A tight black top that showed the outline of every muscle group, and black pants that were tucked into the top of boots that one could use to climb glass walls. Beneath the wooden spiral staircase that led up to the mezzanine deck was a bar area. Chandler approached it with a precision that looked like he was about to perform a tactical manoeuvre. He reached for two Cokes with both hands, cracked them open simultaneously and poured them, one from each hand, into glasses that were standing to attention on the sideboard.

He handed me a glass and perched himself on a bar stool, keeping his legs sprung so it didn't look as if the seat was taking any weight. He was still built like a machine and kept his body tuned like a lovingly maintained instrument. He took in my diminished physical condition and said nothing, but I could feel the disappointment. I guessed that he still rose at four-thirty and exercised like a demon, then meditated as the sun rose, by which time I was hitting the snooze button for the third time and trying to forget that there was a better way of living.

"I could hardly bring myself to believe the message was from you," said Chandler. "You've been a stranger." He raised a hand as if to stop my protests, although I was making none. "I know, it's not easy. I understand. You're putting it behind you, after that mess with Starck." The smile had gone now, and he pushed past the mention of Brian Starck before it dragged him down. "And you've got your new woman now, a whole new career ..." He dried up at that. The mention of Brian had caught him despite his efforts to be light and breezy.

"Damn," he said, "how many years has it been?" And he held the back of a wrist against his nose as if to block a sneeze. The moment passed, and he washed it away with a sip of Coke, then kept talking in case it caught up with him again. "You're here with your camera, are you? A new project? The personal angle ... people behind the uniforms, that kind of thing? I saw that one you did about Zimbabwe. Very good, real heart."

"No camera," I said, and Chandler avoided looking at me by turning to look out to the sea. The rain had lifted slightly, but the heavy clouds still brought an untimely darkness and from the grey shifting blur between the sky and the sea some lights were twinkling at us: a ship was making slow progress around the tricky coast. The lights danced across the window as runnels of rainwater caught and twisted them.

"I'm interested in getting my hands on a file in the archives," I said, "and wanted to ask your advice."

"A file?"

"An old intelligence operation. Potentially sensitive information involving our new president."

"You worked with those shifty people for a while," he said, still contemplating the lights of the ship. "Heard about that. The desk-wallahs. You did a bit of that government work is what I heard. Did it suit you?"

"It got me out of the house," I said. "Something to do that didn't require a classical education or a private trust fund."

Chandler stepped away from his barstool in a fluid movement as if he hadn't been resting any weight on it at all. He returned to the window and stared out at the angry sea. "Tell me you're not here for those spook-chasers," he said, "we could keep discussing the weather and old times and get all emotional about fallen comrades. I've got a fridge full of Coca-Cola, but let's get straight to the difficult stuff shall we? It's those snivelling government white-washers who sent you to find me, is it?"

"I came here under my own steam. Nothing to do with them."

"They need something done and cannot face the thought of getting their hands dirty. That sums it up, does it?"

"They want me keeping my nose out of their business. But there's a nasty smell coming from the basement and I'm thinking of going to see what's decomposing down there."

Chandler turned to face me and looked at me as if continuing the conversation by telepathy. "And you want my help with that?" he asked eventually.

"I do."

I was finding this harder than I had expected. There had been a time when Chandler had been like an older brother to me, or perhaps even a father. He'd certainly been more of a father to me than the Canadian diplomat who would forget to pick me up from the station when I had a break from military training. But now I was finding it impossible to get back inside the shell, find my way back into the cosy dugout we'd shared for several years. Until Brian's death. Brian's death had been a watershed moment that had changed everything. I was different now, Chandler was different, and we were like strangers with little more than a vague memory of a shared past life.

"You're not going to sing Rule Britannia?" he said. "Or ask me to give the toast at mess tonight?"

"Rule Britannia would be inappropriate. This is more of a personal project."

"I don't do any of that now, Gabriel. None of it, not for

the governments of this world, nor for sacks of gold. I consult now. I talk, others listen, and we all go home and get to bed early and keep our noses clean."

"Consulting is all I'm asking for. You don't need to dirty any noses."

Chandler uttered a scoffing laugh. "Beware strangers seeking consultation."

"I'm hardly a stranger."

"Aren't you, Gabriel? You might not have been one, but you have become one, haven't you? Ever since that business in Kivu. And now that you have new friends – frankly rather shady and untrustworthy friends – you think you can walk in here and rope me into some job you're doing for the security service? Or have you come back here to get vengeance for your friend?"

"Brian disobeyed orders," I said. "He blatantly disobeyed your orders."

Chandler flinched as if I'd slapped him in the face, and he turned back to the sea. The ship that had been making its way across the bay seemed to have got into difficulty. It had turned and drifted closer in to shore, and I could see the crew leaning over the side and trying to catch something floating beside it with long grappling poles.

"Bastards," said Chandler. "They take the chance in weather like this. The inspectors will be too lazy to come out of their huts, so they know they'll get away with it. Lobster for dinner all round." I could see now that the thing they were trying to catch was some netting that was folded to make a basket and floating with it was a man in a diving suit. They weren't in trouble at all.

"Starck did not disobey orders, Gabriel," said Chandler, his voice as hard as steel. "You know it as well as me. I live with my demons, and you should learn to live with yours. You should know better than to play that cheap card."

I shook my head and found myself getting to my feet. I placed the Coke on the bar top. This had been a mistake. Then came the rushing sensation. The onset of a panic attack. It felt as if the room had started to spin, and I held onto the edge of the bar counter. "Turn around, Corporal Gabriel," said Chandler, but he was shouting now. I turned and looked up to meet his eyes. He glared at me, and his eyes pinned me against the aeroplane's buckled hull. He was shouting something else at me, and there was blood on his face. Not his own. Brian's blood, little bits of Brian's bones glistening white. The bodies had been booby-trapped.

"It's OK," said Chandler, and his hand gripped my forearm. He was no longer standing at the window but was beside me at the bar counter. Both his hands gripped me now and I thought for a moment he was going to shake me, but instead he smiled. Not the tight, reluctant line of his usual smiles, but a genuine opening of the mouth, flash of the teeth. "Does that happen to you often?" he asked, and there was genuine concern in his voice. "You should see someone. You know you should."

"I'll be fine," I said, "it's all the sugar in that Coke."

Chandler nodded as if he believed me.

"And I did see someone," I added. "You know that."

"Look at us," said Chandler, and he laughed. "Like a couple of school kids. I'll fix us a proper drink, and you tell me about this caper of yours."

The proper drink was an espresso coffee with a shot of aniseed liqueur. "Caffé corretto" Chandler called it, a trick he'd learned from an Italian he'd been with in the 44 Pathfinders. Coffee's a great drink, but sometimes you need to correct it a little. I had finished making my pitch and Chandler had said hardly a word. He added a splash more aniseed to his cup and swilled it around to clean off the remains of the coffee and threw it down his throat.

"Your problem, Gabriel," he said, "is that you haven't found your tribe. You haven't looked into the mirror while shaving that ugly mug of yours and admitted to yourself that you're not one of them."

"One of them?"

"The people you hang out with. Your crowd of desk-wallahs and happy, contented people."

"This has something to do with trying to get a file out of the archives?"

"It does. Because I understand now why you've come to see me. You've been a good citizen, driving between the lines, doing the right thing. You've asked them nicely and they've stonewalled you. You're frustrated because you're getting nowhere. I understand that. I've always understood that. Which is why you've come to me. What I don't get is why you think I'd share your interest in some old file."

"I thought you might have some interest because the file is in the Gold Archives."

"Why is that interesting?"

"Because the man who is claiming the file doesn't exist is an old friend of ours."

"An old friend?"

"He boasted that those archives are the best place on the continent to hide something of value."

Chandler poured more aniseed liqueur into his cup and

swirled it around. His eyes seemed to go right through mine, and they bounced off the back of my skull, the way they always had in the days we served beside each other. The dark days I'd been trying to put out of mind for some years.

"Of value?" he said.

"Best on the continent."

"Underground?"

"Many levels. He has a background in mining."

Chandler stood and walked to the window as if he'd seen something out to sea, but there was only the inky black water being whipped to a frenzy by the foul weather.

"There's a name for what you're suggesting," he said.

"Penance? Is it time our friend BB paid his penance? That was how Brian described it, remember? How he said we should find the underground vault and make BB pay his penance."

"Incitement. It's a punishable offence to incite others to commit a crime."

Chandler came back to the seat beside me and settled his frame upon it in the same sprung manner, ready to leap at a moment's notice.

"Because let's be clear," he said. "You're not talking about the kind of thing we used to get up to in the name of God and Queen."

"Was that who we did it for?"

"You're crossing the line, Gabriel, and I don't know that you're ready for that. Stay on your side of the line; it works for you. Look at you: you've been employed, you've created a better life for yourself, a good woman, gainful employment, you've made it work."

"You know very well the extent of my success."

"Perhaps those desk-wallahs are your tribe, Gabriel.

The good people fighting for the rights of the regular citizens, the ones who make sure the flock sleep well at night."

"I have only one tribe," I said, "and you know it, captain."

Chandler got to his feet again. "Alright then, Corporal Gabriel. We'll ask them again for that file. Ask them nicely and see what they say." He held out his hand to me and helped me out of the chair, although honestly it wasn't necessary, I'm not that out of condition. But then he held my hand tight and pulled me into him so that our faces were almost touching. His eyes burned holes in mine, then he nodded and gave a small smile. "Alright then," he said. "Had to be sure. And it's Colonel now," he said. "They call me the Colonel. Let's go and ask those archive people for your file."

ELEVEN

"Always such a pleasure to welcome a foreign power to our little library. And an ally at that, colleagues in arms," said Anton Lategan in accented but precise English, as he strode across the Persian carpet towards us, his hand outstretched. Blond hair brushed back, and a polite smile pinned within a thin transparent beard. He timed his welcome speech to culminate beneath the ornate chandelier that hung in the centre of his office so that the lighting optimally presented him against the backdrop of the teak desk with inlaid ruby leather, and incongruous iMac. His office was on the twelfth floor of the Gold Archives, and floated high above the canopy of the Company's Gardens oak trees that, framed by the window behind the teak desk, provided an artistic touch of green to contrast the rich reds of the room.

"Lategan," he said as he took Chandler's hand in his.

"Templeton," said Chandler, "Captain. And this is Corporal Morris," he indicated me. Lategan held the hand that I offered with a soft grasp that was less a handshake than a gentle caress. His smile was a stretched but closed mouth. He turned back to Chandler, his nearly invisible eyebrows arching upwards as if he was about to ask a question.

"Tea," he said. "I arranged for tea."

He indicated the two leather armchairs which faced the desk, and seated himself and his stomach behind it, allowing the late afternoon sun to shine in our eyes as if he was about to run the intimidation routine. The tea was already poured, and we each took a fine porcelain cup, and sipped it, while adjusting to the strong backlight and trying to make out Lategan's face.

"Such a privilege," he said, seeing me gaze out of the window. "A humble man such as myself with a view like this." He didn't turn to look out of the window and so to clarify that he was not referring to his view of Chandler and me, he added, "My chair swivels."

"Marvellous," said Chandler. Then sensing that the introduction phase was over, he said, "Thank you for accommodating our request at such short notice."

"If there is something we can do for the British Marines," said Lategan, "we are only too pleased. You never know, do you? When you might need a marine."

Chandler gave a confused nod. "It's a few pension issues. The marines recruited here in the 90's, as you probably know. We've been to the state archives of course, but there were a few they couldn't help with."

"Does that surprise me?" asked Lategan and paused for long enough to make us wonder whether it was rhetorical. He shook his head sadly and his mouth kept a secret joke trapped behind his beard. "They are in complete confusion. I don't want to point fingers," he said, doing so with a freckled hand, "but they have no organisation. Which is why we have taken on so much of the burden."

Chandler nodded, and we assumed expressions that showed how impressed we were at the burden they were carrying. "I confess that has confused us," said Chandler. "The division of the archive material between yourselves and the state archives."

Lategan nodded and looked as if he wanted to reward Chandler for asking such a good question. "We take on anything and everything of any significance," he said, and raised a hand with a question of his own. "Who is to say what is significant?" His mouth stretched into another smug smile. We were getting the feel for the rhythm of his speech and sat waiting for the answer which he provided all by himself. "Me," he said, and the smile grew so that he resembled a toad. "Of course I am joking," he added when neither of us had burst into laughter. "I have a team. Wonderful girls, all of them." I had always imagined that some archivists are men, but I suspected Anton Lategan preferred to focus more on the women, particularly the younger ones.

"Well," said Chandler, who didn't want to go too far down that conversational path, "I'm not sure that any of our recruits were what we might call significant. We're talking a long time ago."

"Even quite ordinary people could be considered significant," admitted Lategan. "Although perhaps not through their own actions, but through circumstances, or people they knew, or the simple act of having been recruited by the notorious – can I say notorious? – no, perhaps impressive would be a better choice. The impressive Marines."

"They earned themselves pensions," said Chandler, choosing not to help resolve the linguistic dilemma. "And we need to make sure that there aren't family members left behind who are not on our files but are entitled to compensation. Many of the names we have on the original files are no longer traceable."

"If they can be found, it will be here that you find them," said Lategan. "When you have finished your tea I'll take you through to the Reading Room, where you can do your business." The way he said business made it sound like a dirty activity. Chandler and I obediently finished our tea, and we all rose to our feet.

"You have impressive security," said Chandler, "and I believe that there are underground vaults."

"I'll give you a quick tour of the facilities if it would interest you," said Lategan. "The Reading Room is at the other end of the building."

Chandler said that would interest us very much.

———

The yellow afternoon sun formed pools like melted butter on the marble floors of the long corridor that led from Lategan's office to the lift.

"Offices," said Lategan dismissing the closed doors that faced onto the corridor. "My top girls up here."

We looked at the closed doors, and Chandler made an impressed sound.

"We are the proud keepers of our nation's history here at the Gold Archives," Lategan announced as if he was launching into a prepared speech. "Gold standard, and of course funded by the Gold Mining Conglomerate of South Africa, but who wants to go around saying The Gold Mining Conglomerate of South Africa Archives?" Another pause that seemed to invite a response. I shook my head because I certainly didn't want to go around saying that.

"Easier to call us the 'Gold Archives'. And we don't

mind," he said magnanimously as we entered the lift. He reached past Chandler, who was inconveniently blocking the buttons, and held his finger against a fingerprint reader. It emitted a satisfied beep. "Just show you a paper vault, then I'll let you get on with it."

The paper vaults were where all the original paperwork was stored, explained Lategan as the lift dropped. "Of course, most of it we digitise and destroy. You are probably wondering why we even need these rooms." Another lengthy pause while we showed the extent of our wondering. "Still working our way through it, that's why. Think how many sheets of paper would be needed to describe the history of your life, multiply that by forty million, and you have one generation. We might be a new country, but we've got a good fifteen generations under our belt. Work it out."

Chandler looked as if he was doing the math but was saved by the ping the lift emitted as it arrived at the subterranean floor. "That's a lot of paper," he said because Lategan was looking as if he needed an answer.

"Don't you know it," said Lategan as he led the way down a gleaming corridor.

"All your vaults hold paper?" asked Chandler. "Or do you store other goods here?"

Lategan did his toad face. "We hold all manner of goods here, Captain Templeton. All manner."

Steel rails ran along the wall at waist height as if we might need something to hold on to, and on our left the wall comprised steel sections like over-sized links of a watch strap. Cold blue-white light dripped in pools every few metres, creating perfect circles on the spotless white floor.

"There's Anna," said Lategan. "One of my girls," he added just in case her ownership might come into question. At the far end of the corridor a tall Xhosa woman with long plaited hair was standing at a console set into the wall. I expected her to be wearing a lab coat at the very least, if not a full space suit, but she was wearing casual street clothes, jeans one size too tight and a blouse which didn't have as many buttons as it could have. "This will interest you," said Lategan. "In case you thought we had enough space down here to store the paper in bookshelves," he laughed like an irritated donkey. "Shelves need space for the humans to get in between them, and space is just what we don't have here. Watch out there!"

He held up a hand to stop us from passing and held us back against the rail. In a moment we saw why. The steel wall to our left was moving, the humming noise was a nearly silent motor that was moving the wall a single panel at a time. A gap appeared between two panels, and with a few desultory clicks the motor whined away to nothing. Anna's heels clicked along the corridor as she approached us. "All robotic," said Lategan like a magician showing us that the locks were real. "Now watch this." Anna flashed us a big-toothed smile as she joined us beside the gap in the steel panels, and she tapped something into another console mounted in the panel. She applied a finger to the reader. A whirring sound came from the gap, and above the console a blurred picture appeared. The whirring slowed, stopped, and the picture showed us a section of a futuristic book-shelf. Anna tapped something, the screen went dark, and a series of hydraulic sounds announced the passage of a file from the shelving to a hatch in the panel which Anna opened. The file itself was buff coloured and looked like the kind of file I kept my unpaid bills in.

Lategan introduced us to Anna once the performance was complete and then invited her to walk before us as we returned down the corridor towards the lift.

"Very impressive," said Chandler, although I think he was referring to the equipment rather than Anna's rear end, which seemed to be occupying Lategan's attention.

"No expense has been spared; we're state of the art here. Temperature control, humidity, fire protection, insects."

"You wouldn't want paper moths moving in."

"We would not!" exclaimed Lategan, and he laughed like a donkey as we squeezed into the lift with Anna and her file. Anna held her finger on the fingerprint reader in a way that had Lategan licking his lips like an overheated lizard. Then she pressed a button, and we all smiled at each other.

"You have a similar system in the vaults that don't hold paper?" asked Chandler as the lift dropped another few floors. The doors opened, and Anna stepped out. We were afforded a glimpse of a very different style of corridor. Raw concrete and dim light bulbs hanging from the ceiling. There were no robotic shelves here, but a sliding door of bulletproof glass with a fingerprint reader beside it, and beyond that a worn wooden counter with more bulletproof glass and a microphone to speak into. Anna applied a long finger to the reader.

"Similar, yes," said Lategan, and he pressed the button several times in an attempt to close the doors. "We shouldn't be down here," he said, a little flustered. "These levels are strictly out of bounds."

"This is where you keep the dangerous secrets," said Chandler.

"Not dangerous," said Lategan, and he gave the button another few pokes.

"Higher value, perhaps," suggested Chandler.

Lategan nodded anxiously, and we stood in silence for a

few moments before he realised that he hadn't satisfied the fingerprint reader. He did so, and the doors closed.

"Let's take you to the Reading Room," he said. "Then you can get to work."

———

The Reading Room was where the architect had taken the 'no expense spared' concept to heart. It was a room that reached up three storeys and had been inspired by the great libraries of the world with an emphasis on Gothic. Bookshelves lined the walls and narrow iron balconies ran around the second and third floors, with twisted railing supports that imitated ivy.

Movable wooden ladders from the private libraries of eccentric billionaires were placed haphazardly about. The reading tables had low lights with gleaming brass shades, and green leather desktops, only two of which were occupied.

Lategan moved across the marble floor like a cat, ensuring that his footsteps didn't make a noise. We reached a central desk built like an island from which the chief librarian could fend off invasions from all sides. She had the look of someone who had just switched screens away from a solitaire game and was trying to appear busy despite the fact that there was nothing on the desktop. She gave a regulation business-only smile when Lategan introduced us. Her earrings, which were gold hoops the size of small dinner plates, bobbed up and down enthusiastically in time with the extra rolls of chin.

Meghan would retrieve files for us if we would be so kind as to provide her with as many details as we could. We indicated that we would. The more information we could provide, the easier it would be for Meghan to deliver the gold standard in service that was their promise to the good people of South Africa. Or the United Kingdom, as the case might be.

Lategan fussed about us as we settled at a table, and Chandler opened his steel-framed case that looked as if it should have been handcuffed to his wrist. He removed a thin sheaf of paper from the case and snapped it shut again with more noise than Lategan seemed to feel was necessary, but he kept his smile in place until Chandler had provided details for our first candidate to Meghan, who wrote them down like a waitress taking our order. Chandler suggested she take the sheet, and she waddled back to her island and started frowning at the computer like she was trying to remember what all the icons meant.

"Most advanced search algorithm in the world," declared Lategan. "Based on Google's original engine, but developed far beyond that of course."

Beyond Meghan was a large gilt-framed portrait of a familiar man in hunting gear with a pack of dogs at his heels.

"That's Riaan Breytenbach, isn't it?" asked Chandler.

"It most certainly is," said Lategan. "Our benefactor and founder. Mr Breytenbach is the chairman of the Gold Mining Conglomerate of South Africa, and we have him to thank for all of this." Lategan looked up at the portrait like a supplicant witnessing the second coming. It portrayed Breytenbach as a handsome man, a firm jaw, piercing blue eyes and black hair with some peppering about the temples. He was taller and more impressive than in the flesh. What the portrait did best was to express the way in which he was imbued with power. He looked as if he was about to leap out of the frame. And it wasn't just a physical energy. It was a power derived from the confidence that settles upon people who have access to unlimited amounts of money. A confidence that comes in part from knowing that there is nothing he cannot have.

"Yes," said Chandler, "I've had the pleasure of meeting him." I'm sure that he hadn't meant to sound sarcastic, but I couldn't help glancing at him. He was not looking at the painting but at me. Deadpan expression.

"Did some work for him on one of his mines," said Chandler, then put his hand up to his face as if to adopt a thinking pose, but I knew he regretted bringing up Breytenbach and the gesture was an effort to keep his mouth closed. Always say the truth, had been what the Welsh captain had said in the training sessions, always the truth, but don't make it a truth that is so specific it can be traced.

But Lategan didn't seem to have heard. "Still takes a keen interest," he said. "Comes in every few weeks, spends a few days in his office. Floor above mine. This is not just an investment project for him. Oh, no. It's something that means a lot to him." Lategan turned to Chandler. "A lot," he repeated and did his toad face again until Meghan arrived back at our table.

"I've got something on this one. It'll just take a few minutes," she said, and fluttered our page at us, on which she had pencilled several long strings of numbers.

"I don't suppose that you have anything on the history of this building?" Chandler asked Meghan. "Your boss has been kind enough to give us a tour. It must have a fascinating history."

Meghan shuffled her weight from one leg to the other. She glanced at Lategan.

"The building?" asked Lategan.

"I have a dilettante's interest in architecture," said Chandler.

"We'd have the plans," said Meghan. "Nothing else really."

"Fascinating," said Chandler. "For an enthusiast like me, even the dull lines of an architectural plan tell a story. Thank you, Meghan, I would be so grateful."

Meghan blushed and padded softly over to the lift.

"Well," said Lategan, who looked as if he had a few reservations about sharing architectural plans but struggled to find a way of expressing them. "I'll leave you to it then." He held out a fleshy hand which we took turns at shaking, then he crept silently back to the lift.

———

The first six names went really well. Meghan seemed to be getting the hang of all those icons and we settled into an efficient rhythm of pretending to write important things while she searched for the next lucky pension winner, then with a flutter of her pencilled notes would leave us to it, as Lategan would have said, and she descended to the paper vaults to retrieve the file.

She also managed to find extensive architectural plans which delighted Captain Templeton, and his enthusiasm pushed her to greater efforts. She produced cross-sections, isometric views and even wiring diagrams, which particularly pleased Captain Templeton.

When she was gone we kept our heads down and I doodled a bit on a pad of paper, while Chandler pretended that he was not taking photographs of the details of the building plans. We had both seen the security cameras mounted high in the ceiling like little bubble eyes and I wondered whether Lategan was keeping an eye out while he enjoyed his afternoon doughnut, or whether he left it all to a team in an underground room where no expense had been spared on technical gadgetry.

"Impressive place," said Chandler as if he'd been reading my mind. He looked up at me. "A lot of security. For archives."

"Protectors of the country's proud history," I said and Chandler forced himself not to smile at my imitation of Lategan's precise English.

It was on the seventh name that things went wrong. Meghan spent a good deal longer gazing into the depths of her iMac, and she even muttered to herself when she started encountering the red flags, or blank screens or whatever the clever people who had advanced Google's algorithms had dreamed up to indicate no-go areas. Chandler and I didn't look up. Meghan's rubber-soled shoes made little squeaks on the marble as she came over to us.

"This one doesn't seem right," she said. I looked up, but Chandler finished writing something down before allowing himself to be distracted.

"Could we have the ID number wrong?" I suggested.

"No, I've found her. We have severals files for her. But that's the thing, it's a woman. Wouldn't your recruits be men?"

"Not necessarily," said Chandler. "We have women in our ranks. Have done for years."

"Well ..." Meghan fanned herself a little with the page as if this was causing her to overheat. "There must be a mistake. Do you want to check the details?"

"But of course," said Chandler in his soothe-the-anxious-children voice. He took the paper back from Meghan and opened his steel case to consult a bunch of typed pages he'd collected from a copy shop's paper recycling bin on our way over. He started paging through them nonchalantly.

"We've been lucky with the weather today," I said to distract Meghan, who was staring intensely at the pile of pages and would not take long to realise they had nothing to do with the British Marines. She looked at me as if I'd tried to communicate in a language unknown to her. Meghan was not really a weather person. "The rain seems to have held off," I said, "although I guess that doesn't bother you, parking underground."

"Oh no, I park in the street. Only some upper floor girls get the parking," said Meghan. "There's only one floor of parking, the rest are all high security storage." She turned back to Chandler as he returned the papers to his case and snapped the locks closed again. He gave her a broad smile and handed back the page that caused the trouble.

"All correct," he said regretfully. "Why don't we come back to it? The next is the last one anyway."

Meghan's large rear end bounced back to the island, the page fanning her growing discontent. Number eight gave no problems and Chandler was folding up the blueprints when Lategan appeared again. By now Meghan had taken to staring blankly at her screens and shaking her head in confusion. Lategan padded over to her and they held a whispered conversation. Lategan then glided over to us. He placed the offending piece of paper on the table and opened his hands as if inviting us to join him in prayer.

"Still a few cracks," he said and shook his head sadly. "Some people fall into them, and there's nothing we can we do. This ..." he picked up the paper and scowled at it, "... L. Dlomo has no records that we can find."

"Ah well," said Chandler, and he smiled. I said nothing,

manfully resisting the temptation to suggest that Lategan should have checked with Meghan before coming up with his own version of the story. "Such a shame," said Chandler, "because that one is a substantial pension amount. You're not able to find anything at all?"

"We are not," said Lategan, who had used up all his excuses and didn't feel like talking about it anymore.

"She fell through the cracks?" I asked.

Lategan smiled and got half a laugh out. "Her records, not her." He finished the laugh without conviction. "The files we get from the state archives have many of these gaps. We work hard to fill them. But," he added as if suddenly spotting the silver lining, "Meghan tells me she was able to help with all the others."

"She was wonderful," said Chandler as we rose to leave, having taken the subtle hint from the way in which Lategan had shuffled to the side so as not to block our exit. Meghan squeezed out a bright smile, although she was pretending not to listen.

"The British Marines thank you," said Chandler, and we pressed our hands together again and walked like satisfied men to the lift that would get us out of there. As the doors opened, I turned back and raised a hand in farewell. Meghan and Lategan were standing there like wax dummies, but their smiles had expired, and I noticed Meghan's hand resting on the files she had retrieved for us. They'd be going through them, I had no doubt. Fortunately, Chandler's contact at the Marines knew what he was doing, and they were all genuine names. Except for Lindiwe Dlomo. That one would prove to be a problem.

TWELVE

"The secret to our future lies in the secrets of our past," said Chandler raising his espresso cup in a toast. A cafe corretto should only be considered in the morning or after lunch. But special occasions brought special demands.

"And they will not be sharing that secret," I said.

"Let's clear up the conflict of interest, shall we?" said Chandler as he sipped at his corrected espresso.

"Conflict?"

"You're a manipulative bastard, Gabriel, I've always known it. Don't think I don't know you planned this. The moment you walked in here, I guessed this was where we'd end up. But you knew I'd not be interested in some old file, and the sad demise of a woman thirty years ago, so you dangled BB's underground vaults before me. I know you well enough by now."

"There is no conflict, Captain. This is a mutually beneficial opportunity."

"If we do this, Gabriel, there is no us and them. We can do our best to get your file and also lighten BB's load a little.

But they are one and the same. I won't have you flying your flag of moral rectitude while I do the dirty work."

"When have I ever done that, Captain? There is nothing morally right about what I want to do. Perhaps we should have a good laugh about our play-acting, I will apologise for taking up your time, we can shake hands on it, and I will walk out of your door and not bother you again."

"Bravo," said Chandler in his soft voice. "But that's bullshit, isn't it?"

I poured myself a little more aniseed. Who needed the coffee anyway?

"You're in trouble aren't you, Gabriel?" said Chandler. "I heard what happened with that woman of yours. She ran away. And the job with the desk-wallahs didn't last. I've been keeping my eye on you, just as you've been watching me. It's all falling apart, isn't it?"

"Not at all," I said.

Chandler looked up to the ceiling and used a hand to drag his cheeks down and test the closeness of his shave.

"Let's laugh about it then," he said. "I'll accept your apology, and we'll shake hands."

He stood up, and I did the same. He held my hand firmly and looked into my eyes. I looked back.

"There are five levels of underground vaults," he said, still holding my hand.

"I saw that," I said. "Just like those men in Uganda said."

Chandler released my hand and walked over to the window where he gazed out at the grey expanse of sea and cloud.

"We'll need others," he said to the window.

"Of course," I said.

141

"Your friend's widow," said Chandler. "Why don't you go see her?"

"Robyn?" I said with surprise. Robyn and Brian had been engaged to be married, and so she was not strictly his widow, but this seemed like a change of subject. Robyn was surely not someone we would need. I knew that she had a history of struggling to stay on the right side of the law, but that had been years ago. Chandler turned back to me and I was surprised to see indignation in his eyes.

"Yes, Robyn. Why do you never see her? She asks me every time we get together. She wants to know what you're doing, when you're going to be ready."

I said nothing, and Chandler's voice rose. "How the fuck should I know, Robyn? That's what I tell her. Brian's death affected us all differently, and I'm not holding a candle for that little Gabriel creep. You are! That's what I tell her."

"I should see her," I said.

"She's struggling, really struggling. Been hitting the bottle and making new friends who are no good for her."

"I will go and see her," I said.

"She could do with something to keep her sober for a week or two, and better she does that kind of thing with friends. Starck wouldn't hold it against you, Gabriel, you know that. He would want her cared for, and you would have been the top of his list if he'd been pushed."

"I'll call her," I said.

Clearly there were things I didn't know about Robyn, but Chandler was on a roll. He turned back to the sea as if it was luring him in.

"Fat-Boy is the perfect snoop man," he said. "He's a lunatic, but the best ones are."

Then he turned back to me like he was coming to attention on parade. He smiled. Lips in a straight line that you had to know him well to realise was a smile and not a nervous tic. There was a light in his eyes that I remembered from some time back.

"Trust you, Gabriel, to come up with something like this. It would have made Brian laugh."

THIRTEEN

I stood wrapped in a long coat to keep warm as I watched workmen throwing sparks over an old whale of a ship in the dry dock. Other workers huddled in little groups on scaffolding, reaching up with tall poles to stroke on fresh paint. Beyond the dry dock the sea lapped gently, calmed by two outer basins. The rain had stopped, but the sea was still feeling pretty angry about the whole thing.

Robyn had not answered my call. I hadn't expected her to, not after three years. And when she finally answered on my fourth attempt, I could hear the hesitation in her voice. We agreed to meet on neutral territory. The wind buffeted me and caught a strand of sparks from the welder closest to me, trying to string them between us and set fire to my coat. I turned to look out to sea and found Robyn standing by my side. Her elfin face was floating on a huge red scarf, her eyes hiding behind wide-screen dark glasses, and she allowed herself the glimmer of a smile when I caught her watching me. She hesitated a moment, then stepped closer and committed to the embrace. Her arms came up and squeezed me.

"Oh, Ben," she said and held onto me like I was her last chance. Her body was thinner and more frail than I remembered. "We fucked it up, didn't we?" She let go and grabbed my arms to hold me at the right distance to see my face. Her brown eyes were so dark as to seem black, and they were ever so slightly off balance so they seemed to be doing that subtle curling in movement that eyes do as a girl leans in to kiss you, holding your eyes for every last moment. Her dark hair was cut in a straight fringe, like a forties actress, but it gave up on being organised around her ears, and ended a little above her red scarf. A narrow nose and thin raised eyebrows gave her a teasing look that told you she didn't take you or anything else very seriously.

"Should have stayed in touch," I said.

"We'll promise now," she said. "We won't be strangers. Never again."

"It's a deal."

"And you found your soul mate. The Colonel told me."

"And lost her," I said without having meant for it to sound pathetic.

"He told me that too," she said, and tucked an arm into mine and leaned against me as we walked along the edge of the dock. "He's been keeping tabs on you, you know. Like a proud father. And he's been kind to me, so kind."

"He feels responsible," I said.

"No," she stopped and pulled me around to face her so she could make her point. "Not responsible." Her eyes were a little bloodshot at the edges. "He's over that, Ben. And it's right that he is. What happened on that last trip to the mines ..." she searched for a word, and blinked, "... well it was what it was." She laughed lightly at herself and used the back of her hand in a familiar gesture to wipe away her tears. It was a child's gesture, not the sort of thing you'd expect from an elegant woman. "I'm no good with words, you know that. I mean it happened, and it's over. The Colonel doesn't see me only because of what happened in the Congo. And neither should you, Ben."

"You're right," I said. "And what's with the 'Colonel'? He's only a Captain."

Robyn gave a coy smile. "Just what I call him," she said. "And no, it's not what you're thinking. There's none of that going on." She slapped my chest playfully and leaned against me. We continued down the quayside. A whistle sounded and the workers on the ship in the dry dock put down their tools, pulled off gloves, and started clambering down the steel steps that ran up the scaffolding.

"Lunch," said Robyn. "You will treat me to the best meal out I've had in years and tell me all about this thing you've got going."

———

We found a table on the balcony of the Hildebrand, where it reaches a point like the prow of a ship in an architectural fantasy that is considered quaint, and allows diners to feel as if they're heading out to sea, but can enjoy the rich *spaghetti al vongole* without the inconvenience of having the deck move with the swell. Our maître d' was a tall Zulu man with a polished bald head. He brought the spaghetti to our table personally in order to get a closer look at Robyn, who had that effect on all men. He took a few extra moments as our spaghetti cooled to explain that he was descended from the warrior who had led the victory at Isandlwana, enjoying Robyn's rapt attention, and embellishing the story so as to linger in her gaze.

Robyn's beauty was of the kind that attracted men, and

women at times, like a magician's spell. To strangers she was unreachable, like a goddess on another plane, but the moment she looked at you and smiled you were drawn in. Brian had complained that he'd fallen victim to an African voodoo spell when he met her on the week's break we were given after the first operation on the gold mines. "I can't breathe right," he'd said in his strong north country accent, holding a hand on his chest as if to demonstrate this. "She's done something to me Benny, I'm done for aren't I? Put me out of my misery now, I cannot be falling for a felon. What are the old wrinklies going to be saying if I take her back home with me?"

But as it happened Brian didn't take Robyn back home to meet his parents. They stayed on in Cape Town, where their whirlwind romance spread itself over breaks in Brian's tours of duty, and the journey to the north country to show her off to his parents never came about because it was scheduled after the final tour to reclaim the Kigesi gold mine from the Allied Democratic Forces of the Congo. The operation that Brian didn't return from.

Describing Robyn as a felon was accurate, but faintly absurd at the same time. Watching her now as she smiled demurely and focused on the Zulu warrior, it was hard to believe that she had spent three years behind bars. A predecessor of Brian's – "We don't mention ex-boyfriends," he'd told me, "She's moving up the scale and we don't like to look back" – had been killed in a shoot-out with police when the two of them had tried walking out of a bank in the small town of Montague, a couple of hours drive from Cape Town, with a large burlap sack of the bank's cash. The burlap sack had been Robyn's idea and the defence lawyer had argued in the juvenile court – because Robyn was a few weeks short of her eighteenth birthday – that with that bag in her hands Robyn couldn't have handled a gun and was therefore not involved in the shooting. He had obviously never seen Robyn handle a gun and encountered some difficulty explaining the number of holsters strapped to her body when they arrested her. But he won over on the sympathy vote, explaining why Robyn had left home at the age of fourteen: escaping an abusive stepfather, but glossing over the fact that she stole the abusive stepfather's Glock 35, and spent months perfecting her skills on photographs of him stuck to the shooting range targets.

Having heard about the way in which our Zulu warrior's ancestor had fought to the bitter end from a cave above the battlefield of Isandlwana, and shared for a moment in the glorious thought that the British army had suffered its most crushing defeat in history, "Every single officer killed?" repeated Robyn as if she refused to believe it, and a moment of silence for the one thousand seven hundred British soldiers who had died that day, Robyn turned to me and as her eyes focused, I remembered Brian's claim that she possessed a witch's magic.

"I meet the strangest people when I'm with you, Ben," she said.

"I'm not sure I can claim responsibility for the shift management here."

Robyn laughed and rested her hand on mine as if to enjoy gazing at this conjurer of strange people.

"Is your little project above board?" she asked as we tackled the spaghetti. "I mean it's nothing official, surely, because you wouldn't be coming to me. We don't do official jobs."

"It's extra-curricular," I said, wondering for a moment who 'we' was. "I'm no longer employed by any of those government officials. And no, the project is not entirely above board."

Robyn's eyes twinkled. "Would Brian have approved?"

"It was Brian's idea. But he would have locked you in a cage and cut the phone lines to prevent me from talking to you about it."

Robyn focused on her spaghetti for a few minutes and then reached for her sparkling water. "No wine over lunch?" she asked. "Or champagne? Isn't this a celebration? A reunion such as this deserves something sparkling."

"I was thinking of a dry white with the lobster," I said. "But if you want champagne …"

She shook her head and sipped at the sparkling water like she was doing the close-up in the seduction scene. "I'm kidding with you," she said. "I can stay sober if I need to, and this is a moment I'll enjoy for some time. Seeing how the mighty have fallen."

"The mighty?"

Robyn's laugh was a pebble skipping across a country stream. "The defenders of our moral integrity are crawling under the floorboards, and I think I'm entitled to enjoy that. Don't get me wrong, Ben. I was proud of Brian, and of you. And Colonel, your whole unit. But sometimes the glare from your halos was a little blinding. You were fighting on the side of right and that puffed out your chests and gave you the right to strut about the farmyard. Sometimes us lowly rodents found you all a bit overbearing." She turned to look out over the sea, which was throwing itself with abandon onto the pier beneath the prow of our ship, and she blinked. For a moment I wondered about the burden she carried with her; the shadow of her youthful mistakes. The whispering behind her back because she was a jailbird, the silence that would fall across a table when someone mentioned robbery, or even dropped an accidental 'bank' or 'shoot-out' into the conversation. Robyn turned back to me.

"So, we're crossing over to the other side," she said and tossed another pebble of a laugh. "I'm okay with that, Ben. Where you go I will follow, you know that."

"I'm the one doing the following," I said. "Chandler gave me a speech about crossing a line, and I'm not so naïve as to think that you and he are following my lead."

Robyn sucked up a strand of spaghetti and looked at me with big innocent eyes.

"In any case," I said. "We didn't have any halos. You know the kind of soldiers we were."

Robyn made a sympathetic noise as if I was a cute puppy that needed help climbing out of my cardboard box. She reached a hand to my cheek. "The nasty kind," she said. "I know that. But you've still got that bayonet stuck up your arse, haven't you, Ben? Shoulders back, chest out, fighting for what is right." She stroked my cheek and looked into my eyes. She opened her mouth to say something else when she realised that our Zulu warrior was hovering and trying not to destroy the romantic moment of the day.

I realised, as he placed the lobster before us, and Robyn sympathised over the tragedy that was the Battle of Rorke's Drift in which the British turned the tables on his ancestors, that I'd been wrong to feel any pity for her. I was wrong about the whole thing. She had not lived under a shadow of shame for all these years. She didn't regret any youthful mistakes. I saw the tough woman of stone that lay behind her beauty as she looked at me to share the outrage of the treatment the British had dealt the Zulus. "She's a tough cookie," Brian had said when I asked about her act of felony one night, "the toughest I've met." He had turned to look at her sleeping in the back of the car. "She has no regrets. I'll say that."

The lobster was followed by a tiramisu because the Hildebrand considered itself a cross-cultural establishment. After a couple of short coffees we walked back along the quay. The clouds were finally delivering upon their threat, and Robyn pulled her scarf up into a red hood.

"Brian would have been okay with this," she said as she embraced me like I was leaving on a long journey from which I might not return. She pulled away but held on with an arm and looked over the water at a brightly coloured fishing boat that had been restored and fitted with windows for the tourists to enjoy the view even when it was raining. The boat was heading out of port and I could hear the loudspeaker on its roof announcing that the trip to Robben Island would take half an hour, and that they would be starting at the graveyard for the people who had died from leprosy in the days when it had been a leper colony before becoming a prison.

"This is such a beautiful place," said Robyn, "but there is something that happens here, isn't there? They might have sent the lepers out to that island, but all the rest of the flotsam of life ended up collecting here, at the bottom of the continent. We're all outcasts, aren't we? We live here because all this beauty makes it possible, despite who we are."

I said nothing.

"I'll be there tomorrow," she said. "With my toothbrush and sleeping bag." Her eyes glistened with a laugh. "And I'll leave the bottles at home."

FOURTEEN

Chandler's lunatic of a snoop man was called Stanley, although he suggested I call him Fat-Boy because, as he pointed out, he was. He told me he was of Xhosa origin, while we shared a cigarette on the fire escape stairs outside what Chandler called mission headquarters.

"We're the soft ones," he said. "The forgiving ones. Not like those Zulu bastards who stride around like they can't get their legs past their over-sized cocks, because some distant ancestor called himself a warrior. Warrior!" he scoffed, then made a sound like a trumpeter warming up his lips. "Weren't warriors, nothing but savages who set out to kill anyone who got in their way. You know they came south because they'd killed so many people up north they couldn't sleep up there for all the wailing from the women? They'd left the women alive. Some of them." Fat-Boy spoke with a strange mixture of American and African pidgin English syntax, with the accent wandering between the two.

I had never heard that version of the history of the Zulu people and told him so, but Fat-Boy insisted. "S'true," he said. His pear-shaped face had heavy cheeks that pulled his mouth into a natural expression of deep sadness, and his left eye was lazy, so it kept drooping as if he'd been hit on the head and was struggling to remain conscious. "So that's why," he said and sucked desperately on his cigarette. I realised that the history lesson was all background to his weight problems. "Mandela was one, is why he was so forgiving. Xhosa. Soft people."

Fat-Boy covered his lazy eye with a hand while he exhaled a cloud of smoke as if he had just noticed there was something wrong with the eye. Then he moved his hand to the other eye and turned his head gently. Like he was performing some kind of alignment.

"I thought you'd given up," said Chandler when we went back in.

"I had," I said, and we left it at that. Chandler went back to laying out notebooks on three school desks that he had arranged in the room.

Robyn arrived as promised with her toothbrush, and a small bag that might have contained a sleeping bag, although from the weight of it I suspected it was more likely to contain her favourite handguns and enough ammunition to mean she wouldn't have to do anything as insecure as going out to stock up. She was wearing dungarees that looked a couple of sizes too big, with baggy trouser legs and straps that looked like they might slip off her narrow shoulders. Fat-Boy seemed to notice that aspect of her attire and revealed his sexual persuasion with a momentary raising of his eyebrows and a twitch of his left eye as it overcame its laziness. Even in baggy overalls Robyn exuded a sexual energy made all the more appealing by her apparent lack of awareness of it.

"When you're quite done gawking at each other, we have work to do," said Chandler.

———

The space Chandler had rented for the purpose of preparing us for the task ahead was the first of a series of conversions in an old brick warehouse that had been a match factory in its youth. The new conversions consisted of inserting vertical and horizontal planes to divide the big warehouse space into a large puzzle of interlocking cubes. Steel staircases linked the spaces, and new balconies thrust themselves out to take advantage of the fashionable view of the foreshore area of Cape Town, a view that had been considered ugly a hundred years ago.

"We're on a photo shoot," said Chandler. "Remember that, if anyone asks. Not that I expect them to. Builders have been sent away while they work out what went wrong with the budget, so we have the place to ourselves."

Chandler was walking up the centre of the room, starting his briefing from a position of power behind us. We were all seated on straight-backed chairs at small tables like overgrown school children.

"All above board," he said. "Paid for, cash in advance, we're taking some nice pictures of Robyn. Or of Fat-Boy as far as I could care. But nice pictures. Clothes on, nothing anyone could point a finger at. We like the unfinished concrete look."

He reached the front of the room where Fat-Boy and I had placed a portable blackboard, and several easels on which were mounted large printouts of the architectural plans of the Gold Archives. He did the parade ground pivot and faced us.

"Corporal Gabriel," he said, switching to the business side of things, "for reasons known best to himself would like to read the contents of an ancient file which is to be found here." Chandler had armed himself with a snooker cue which he now used to strike the architectural plans. It produced a satisfying bang. We jumped a little at the sound, and so Chandler whacked the plans again for good measure.

"The Gold Mining Conglomerate of South Africa Archives," he announced. "It's a fortress, crawling with security, fingerprint scanners, cameras galore. And we also suspect that there is something of a little more interest in there to us non-readers."

"Gold," said Fat-Boy, breaking Chandler's flow. "Big fucking blocks of it." He grinned.

"Gold," agreed Chandler. It wasn't the climax he had intended, but we all looked impressed about it. "Big blocks as Fat-Boy says. What they call Good Delivery bars. Four hundred ounces, twelve kilograms per bar."

"What are they doing in an archive building?" asked Robyn.

"Good question," said Chandler, and he rewarded her with a thin-line smile. "Those bars belong in a vault. They should be sitting in the Bank of England, but Mister Riaan – 'BB' to his friends – Breytenbach took offence when the London Gold Bullion Association refused to accept him as a member and insisted that he deal with them through an agent. An agent BB didn't like. Which is when he had the idea to substitute a cheaper metal that has a similar density into a few of the bars he was sending them."

"Tungsten," said Robyn, then added sharply, "Colonel," like a cadet in an army training movie showing her discipline.

"Tungsten indeed," said Chandler, wondering if she

might be teasing him. It was a feeling that Robyn often aroused in men, perhaps because her eyes always seemed to be laughing, even when she was serious.

"Tungsten weighs the same as gold," he explained to the slower members of the class. "But is a fraction of the value. Add to this the fact that BB discovered a weakness in the antiquated physical gold bullion system. The inspection of his gold would happen at source, it would then be transported to the Bank Of England by trustworthy bullion couriers and locked away in their vault. There were no repeat inspections, apart from simple weight checks. If he substituted a few of the bars with gold-plated tungsten after the initial inspection, they would pass all the follow-up checks. He wouldn't substitute all the bars, that would be too obvious. Just a bar here and another there."

"This man BB a friend of yours?" asked Fat-Boy suspiciously.

Chandler looked at Fat-Boy as if wondering whether he was strong enough to hear the truth.

"Not a friend, Fat-Boy," he said with restraint. "No. Not a friend."

There was a regretful silence.

"The tungsten bars are sitting in the vault at the Bank of England?" said Robyn.

"We have reason to believe so," said Chandler. "The Bank of England never discovered the deception. BB's business partner, Lord Eversham, found out, but was not aware of the extent of the crime, and kept quiet about it to protect himself. The bars that might be sitting four levels below ground here ..." Another satisfying whack of the snooker cue. "Are the original bars. Ninety-nine point nine-five percent gold. Our great benefactor Riaan 'BB' Breytenbach has taken his revenge on the condescending members of the

London Gold Bullion Association by slipping them the fake bars. It is probably a crime that sits heavily upon him." Chandler paused and avoided my eyes lest I challenge his portrayal of BB as a man with any kind of conscience. "It is our intention to lighten his load a little."

Robyn gave a nod of approval, gazing at Chandler with the attention a precocious girl at the front of class lavishes on her university lecturer.

Fat-Boy looked disgruntled.

"Might be, Colonel?" he said. "What's might be? You don't know it's there?"

"That," said Chandler, and he pointed the snooker cue at Fat-Boy's forehead, "is where you come in Fat-Boy. You need to get eyes and ears in there. Your equipment arrives this afternoon. The Angel Gabriel will give you a hand."

"Angel?" said Fat-Boy.

"The Archangel Gabriel," said Chandler. "You don't know your angels? He's one of the big ones."

Fat-Boy pushed a lower lip out, studied me with some disdain, and shook his head.

"He ain't no angel, Colonel. Bubbles is better."

"Bubbles?"

"Them big bubbles he's got in front of his eyes." Fat-Boy indicated the glasses I was wearing because I hadn't bothered with my contact lenses.

"Bubbles it is then," said Chandler, "You okay with that, Gabriel?"

I said I was okay with that and was rewarded for being such a good team player by one of Robyn's smiles. She has a way of lowering her face when she smiles so that you get the full effect of the eyes included. It was pretty powerful.

"A very old file?" said Robyn as she marked the positions of the fingerprint readers with a red highlighter. The large-scale printouts from the photographs Chandler had taken in the Reading Room of the archives were blurred in places, and so we were using coloured marker pens and straight rules to tidy them up and get a better idea of the layout of the building.

"It's an old military intelligence file," I said.

"You told me there was nothing official about this."

"There isn't. I'm doing it to satisfy my own curiosity. For a friend who died."

Robyn stepped back from the plan we were working on and tilted her head like an artist considering her work. I thought about explaining that Johansson had not actually been a friend, but let it go.

"Colonel said you worked for them. For military intelligence."

"For a short while."

"Isn't it true what they say? Once a spy, always a spy."

"I was never a spy. I was on the other end of it."

"Managing the spies? Running the agents in the field?"

"Something like that."

Robyn spotted another fingerprint reader and swooped on it with her red marker.

"And this file," she said, with her focus all on the plan, "is so important that you need to break into the archives to steal it?"

She turned to me and I felt the force of her gaze, her eyes dark as coal.

"It's to do with the president-elect," I said.

"I know. Colonel told us. A woman that he killed."

"And there's a journalist who has died, after asking questions about that woman."

"Your friend?" asked Robyn.

"My friend." I agreed, finally adopting the nasty Johansson posthumously.

Robyn selected a green-coloured marker and turned her attention back to the plan.

"I think I understand it now," she said. "I couldn't figure out why you were doing this, but now it makes sense."

"What do you mean?" I found the air-conditioning layout for the floor we were working on and set about marking the positions of the vents. I remembered this about Robyn. The way she would make leaps of logic and seem to divine the truth by intuition. I used to wonder whether she had known how I felt about her in the days that Brian had wanted the three of us to party together. Her dark eyes had scrutinised me as I made my excuses and suggested that they leave me out of it, and her mocking gaze told me she knew. Knew that my attraction to her was something I was struggling to control, was something that shook the foundations of my friendship with Brian. Or had she known it? I watched her now as she concentrated on the fire escape routes and wondered again whether I had misinterpreted her serious glances, her casual smiles. Sometimes the thing we dread is the thing we hope for the most, even if that thing could destroy us.

"You didn't go to your militarily intelligent mates with this problem because you think they're part of the problem, don't you?"

"I haven't ruled that out," I said.

Robyn laughed, the skipping pebble laugh. "It's not just a matter of the president killing a woman," she said with a teasing tone. "It's a secret government plot." She placed a hand on my arm. "I love your intensity, Ben, you're so earnest. You know that? I really love it."

I smiled and said I knew it. A sensible smile, nothing inappropriate. Robyn removed her hand from my arm and turned back to the fire escapes.

"I've loved that about you since Brian first told me about his serious friend. The thinking one – you know he called you that? He said you'd change the world one day." Another light laugh and a glance to be sure I didn't take that too seriously. "He said you would be the one to pay the debts to society, for all of you."

"Debts to society?"

"I know what you and Brian did. What your unit did. He told me you were not a normal squad."

"I see."

Robyn turned back to her fire escapes again. I remembered Brian's broad grin, the bottle of whisky he'd brought for us to share because he needed to tell me how strongly he felt about Robyn. And discuss with me the inconceivable idea that he should ask her to spend the rest of her life with him. His complete trust in me. He had not guessed how I felt, not even suspected it. Or had he? Right at the end, when the tripwire on the Claymore mine had latched, clicked, and he'd turned to look at me. Had he known then?

———

Fat-Boy enjoyed complaining. Most of what he said was prefaced by a complaint of one kind or another, with a pout of his lips that dragged his cheeks down and showed you just how sad the whole thing made him feel. His boxes arrived that first afternoon, and he stood on the empty concrete floor of the ground level of our building like a man trying to build a castle from cardboard boxes.

"What the fuck am I meant to do with these?" he asked

me when I went down to give him a hand after Chandler pointed out that it had been over half an hour since the delivery.

"Plug them in?" I suggested. "That's normally the mistake I make with these kinds of things." Fat-Boy didn't think that was funny. He told me so several times as we heaved the boxes up the five flights of steel staircase. He enlisted my help in what he called 'the mounting'. After setting up the frames, we mounted all eight monitors in two rows. Then he connected the box, "water cooled this baby, super silent" because he explained that you couldn't have that humming shit going on when you needed to work. He fired it up and then fiddled about getting hooked up to a wireless modem and downloading software. It was mid-afternoon by the time we found ourselves on the roof of our match factory, bouncing a cigarette between us because I wasn't buying packs.

"C-276," said Fat-Boy as he pulled a miniature satellite dish out of the bubble-wrap. "Can't go wrong with these."

I did my best to look impressed, but frankly if I'd found it in my cupboard I'd probably have been eating my breakfast cereal out of it. It was about the right size to give you a great start to the day.

Fat-Boy mounted the little dish onto the tripod stand that we'd bolted into the flat roof, allowing it to poke up above the low parapet.

"How do you know where to point it?" I asked. "Or does that not matter?"

Fat-Boy shook his head. It hadn't taken him long to discover the extraordinary depth of my ignorance, but it continued to disappoint him.

"Tomorrow my brother, we'll do that tomorrow. For

now, we wrap her up in this," he brandished a roll of tinfoil, "and let her cook."

As Fat-Boy wrapped the dish in tinfoil, I finished the cigarette and gazed out over the view of the City Bowl and foreshore area. I could make out the corridor of green where the Company's Gardens ran up the spine of the city, and the jumbled tops of the buildings that marched alongside them.

"You and the Colonel are tight," said Fat-Boy as he smoothed the tinfoil to get rid of the wrinkles. It wasn't a question.

"I guess so," I said vaguely.

"You were with him in the army," said Fat-Boy, and he gave me an accusatory glare. I nodded. "We been told not to talk to you about the jobs we've done with him," he continued. "He thinks there's something special about you because you were in the army together, and he's gone all baby-talk and let's pretend." Fat-Boy regarded me critically and failed to observe anything that marked me as special, so he continued. "It fucked him up good and proper, the army," he said and pulled another cigarette from his pack. "He don't talk about it, but I heard enough from what others say. They say his squad were all killed."

"They do?"

"They do," said Fat-Boy and his eyes narrowed in a challenge for me to deny it. "He went nuts after that. Lost it completely. Rampage," he said, adding in some extra 'a's for dramatic effect. He gazed at me through an exhalation of smoke, expecting a confirmation or denial.

"I expect those rumours are exaggerated."

"Hmmph," said Fat-Boy, leaving me in no doubt that I had confirmed his wildest suspicions.

"At any rate, he was never a Colonel. He was a Captain, and that's as far as it went."

"Colonel's his *name*," said Fat-Boy as if I just didn't get it.

"If you like," I said and put up a friendly smile.

"I do like," said Fat-Boy with intensity. "Colonel is one of a kind. You don't get them like that anymore."

"Like that?"

"If Colonel asked me to walk into a furnace and close the door behind me I'd do it," said Fat-Boy. "Like that."

I was about to suggest that it was a good thing in that case that he was one of a kind, but Fat-Boy didn't seem in the mood for flippancy. Besides, I wondered whether I would do the same, and I was hoping Fat-Boy would share the last cigarette.

———

"I thought you'd end up here at the arse end of Africa," said Chandler. "Going back to Dorset was never going to be your thing, and with your mother being from here ... They say South Africans always find their way home."

"Even half South Africans," I said. Chandler lit the gas ring with a pop and watched as the flame settled. He gave a nod of approval. Our field kitchen was nearly complete. The fridge hummed quietly in the corner, the trestle table had fresh chopping boards and racks of knives, a portable cupboard unit was filled with dry goods, and a photo-flood light reflected an even glow off the concrete ceiling, powered by the diesel generator we'd set up in the basement.

"That doesn't explain why *you* stayed on here," I said. "There's no South African blood in you."

"Oh, you know," Chandler shrugged. "Sun, the healthy climate ... happy memories."

"No relatives? Friends?"

"Associates," he said. "You know how it goes ... join the army, travel to distant places, meet new and interesting people ..."

He paused and lit the other gas plate, which popped and fizzed.

"... and then kill them." I provided the punchline to the old joke. He rewarded me with a tight smile.

"There were a few that we didn't kill, weren't there?"

"I like to think so," I said.

"So do I," said Chandler, "so do I." Then he told me about the menu he had planned for the week that we would be spending at the match factory. Chandler had always loved fine food and had dedicated himself in recent years to perfecting his culinary skills. I said it all sounded good, and he told me I would have to step onto the balcony if I wanted to light Fat-Boy's last cigarette and so I did that.

It was late afternoon, but the skies were ominously dark with some trouble brewing on the horizon. Chandler joined me a few minutes later.

"This is going to be fine," said Chandler as if I'd expressed some concern. "We'll make a good team. Very good."

Chandler showed his nerves by constantly repeating the affirmation that everything would be fine. He'd always done it. I'd thought it was his idea of boosting morale, but I soon realised that he did it for himself and his own morale, no one else's.

"Fat-Boy has encouraging things to say about your leadership," I said.

Chandler smiled. "But he gave you a hard time? Did he complain about the cattle?"

"He didn't mention any cattle."

"Then you have a treat in store. Ask him about the cattle massacre of 1800-and-something. It was all our fault. The British people. He has a few screws loose, I told you that. But he's good. The best."

That seemed like the perfect opening for me to ask Chandler about the years that had passed since the helicopters had dropped us into North Kivu. With Brian, and our optimistic futures. The head shrinkers who had examined me afterwards with their toy magnifying glasses had told me life would return to normal, just as it had for my Captain Chandler. But I discovered later that Chandler's life had not returned to normal. He had lasted only three weeks with the psychologists. Then he'd packed his bags, thrown their blue and yellow pills in their faces and walked out. He'd boarded a plane the next day. At least that's what I'd heard. Not from the blue and yellow pill people of course; they had told me all along that Chandler was doing just fine, and why couldn't I do more like him?

Perhaps in the end I had done like him. As different as we were, our stars were inexorably crossed, and here I was again blowing the smoke of my cigarette downwind from him as he gazed up at the sky as if he was waiting for the stars to come out so he could navigate a way out of all this. Brian might have been my closest friend, but he had been like a son to Chandler. And so instead of asking Chandler how he'd started working with the lunatic snoop-man Fat-Boy, or how he and Robyn had started their criminal careers, or how he'd got into this whole game, I said simply, "I'll ask him about the cattle then."

Chandler nodded with approval. "You do that," he said

and gave me the tight-lipped smile that had always made me think everything would turn out okay. Then it occurred to me that his insistence that we cloister ourselves in this isolated space as we prepared for the task ahead was largely for my benefit. He wanted to watch me. Despite years of serving together, Chandler was still not certain he could trust me. I would have to prove that he could.

FIFTEEN

That evening we carried a folding table and chairs up to the roof, and Fat-Boy fetched pizza and beer because our gourmet dining would only start the next day. We sat up there with Fat-Boy's mini satellite dish catching moments of the sunset which oozed under the clouds, an amateur artist exploring the range of oranges and slashing them in great angry brush strokes until the low cloud base finally got the better of him. Behind us loomed the flat-topped Table Mountain, to the left the lights of the city, and to the right the great plain of the Cape Flats over which the flickering lights of airliners etched their arrival routes like aliens staging an invasion.

"Royal Guards. That's where I served," said Fat-Boy, who was brooding over our earlier discussion and clearly wanted to draw Chandler out on the subject of the military.

None of us responded, and so he elaborated. "Fucked me up."

"I didn't think they accepted Xhosas," I said.

"Fuck you, Bubbles. Gave me my own horse."

"A big one?" enquired Chandler politely.

"Yeah, a big one," said Fat-Boy.

"Not the Swedish Royal Guard then," said Chandler. "The Queen's Guard?"

"That was us," said Fat-Boy. "Protecting the old lady. Up and down on our horses."

"You're a lunatic. Have I ever told you that, Stanley?"

Fat-Boy glared at Chandler over the thick end of his beer bottle as he finished it.

"You're not here because of your military service, as remarkable as I'm sure that was," said Chandler. "So you can stop making up stories. All we need from you right now is to get that little bird singing." He indicated the dish in its tinfoil wrapping.

"She'll sing alright, Colonel."

"You're certain they have a patch bay on the roof?"

"What's certain, Colonel? What does that mean? You think I'm psychic? They'll have one somewhere up there. We've been over the wiring diagrams, and I've installed enough of those doozies to know. You don't run hard lines to all those cameras. There'll be a patch bay. Tomorrow I'll locate it. Easy peasy."

"You'll do it, Fat-Boy," said Robyn who had rigged an extra camp chair to form a couch, and was reclining like a cat, her legs resting on my lap. "You've never let us down," she said, and blew out a cloud of smoke. Her eyes were half closed, whether from the smoke or exhaustion, I wasn't sure. There was a moment's silence as the implications of the fact that Fat-Boy hadn't let us down before whirled about in the smoke. Robyn bit her lip and gave me a coy smile. Strictly speaking she hadn't broken Chandler's rule about them discussing previous jobs.

"Besides," said Fat-Boy, who had not noticed Robyn's slip. "I'll have the war hero with me." He gave me a glum look to show me how little he was looking forward to it.

"You and the Angel Gabriel will do just fine," said Chandler.

"Sure," said Fat-Boy without enthusiasm. I didn't deny his ironic war hero epithet, but there was very little heroic that I could remember of my life as a soldier, particularly in the later years. I'd been a square peg trying to fit myself into the round hole that the army cut out for me – until I joined Chandler's squad and realised I was not the only one who didn't fit. We had been a squad of misfits. Nothing that we did was in any way heroic.

"You want that last piece of pizza, Colonel?" Of all of us, I suspected that Fat-Boy was the only one not standing with one foot in the past.

"You go ahead Fat-Boy, I've had my share."

"Too right you have," said Fat-Boy helping himself, and opening another beer. "'Cos you're a lion, Colonel, that's what you are. You guys ready for a bit of Xhosa culture?"

Robyn rolled her head to see Fat-Boy better. "Hit us, Fat-Boy," she said.

Fat-Boy took a deep slug of beer.

"So there was this lion, his buddy the wolf and a sneaky fox," said Fat-Boy, indicating each of us in turn with the neck of his beer bottle. "They went out hunting together and got themselves a good haul. A nice juicy buffalo, a fat zebra and a little rabbit for afters. Later, while the wolf is getting the fire going, the lion comes up to him and says 'Mr Wolf, would you be so kind as to divide the meat for us today?' The wolf says, 'I think it best, your royal highness that you should have the buffalo and my friend the fox

169

should take the rabbit.'" Fat-Boy took a bite of pizza and chewed it noisily. Behind him the silent flickering light of an airliner banked for final approach over Tygerberg. "'Me,' says the wolf, 'I shall be most content with that zebra.' On hearing this, the lion was furious. He raised his mighty paw and struck the wolf on the head." Fat-Boy demonstrated and splashed beer over the table. "The wolf fell to the ground and died. His skull had been cracked by that blow. The fox says nothing, and the lion, he pads quietly over to the fox, and says to him, 'Now Mr Fox, you should be so kind as to try and divide our meal better.' The fox was frightened, of course, but he didn't show it. He spoke quietly and solemnly. 'The buffalo will be your midday dinner, sir, the zebra will be your Majesty's supper and the rabbit will be your breakfast tomorrow morning.' The lion is much pleased by this, also surprised. He asks the fox, 'When did you gain so much wisdom?' The fox replies, 'Your Royal Highness, when I heard the wolf's skull cracking."

"That's not a Xhosa story," said Robyn.

"It is too," said Fat-Boy. "Baked into our culture it is."

"When I heard the wolf's skull cracking," said Chandler, and he bared his teeth. "That's a good one. Very good." And he laughed. It was one of only a handful of times I have ever heard Chandler laugh.

———

We parked the white panel van before oh seven hundred hours, and Fat-Boy grumbled as we sat in the back and drank the espresso shots Chandler had provided in a flask. He looked into his plastic mug and then across to mine.

"Where's the rest of it?" he asked.

"Espresso. It comes in small servings."

He looked unconvinced but threw his shot back and pulled a face at the bitterness of it. I guessed that Chandler had only sent the flask because I'd made a fuss about the early hour. It wasn't the kind of kit that he normally sent Fat-Boy out with.

"Couldn't they have found one my size, for fuck's sake?" said Fat-Boy as he tried to squeeze the shirt together over his belly where a button had popped.

"When did you see a Telkom guy in a suit that fitted?" I said to make him feel better about it, but he poked at his flesh despondently as if he might be able to squeeze it back in.

"You and sex bomb an item?" he said.

"No."

Fat-Boy delivered a side-looking sneer. "Don't get me wrong. I'm not interested. Not my league," he said. "Besides, she's a skinny bitch. I prefer something to hold on to. Stick insects don't do it for me. Anyway, Colonel wouldn't approve."

"You worked much with him?" I asked casually.

Fat-Boy allowed his lazy eye to droop as he gazed out at the desolate street and considered that. "Never," he said. "Never worked with him before."

I left it at that. We had an hour to kill before the curtain went up, but if he didn't want to talk about Chandler, I would respect that.

"You often dream these things?" asked Fat-Boy.

"What things?"

"Where you need to get yourself a file out the archives. All desperate like, and you need a genius like me and a screwball like sex bomb to do it for you."

"Not often," I said.

"Don't like dreams," said Fat-Boy. "I told the Colonel that but he said the yellow metal we're pulling out'll be good for my health. What I don't get is why he's getting us twisted up in your shit. Get the gold, no problems, but why bother with your bits of paper? Where's the benefit? Is what I say. When the Colonel said it was paper you were after I said that was okay. I can do paper, so long as it's wrapped in bundles and fits nicely into my top pocket. Then he says you gonna bring down the new president with your paper. Why the fuck you wanna do that?"

"It's about exposing the truth," I said. "Not bringing anyone down."

"So what if he killed some bitch?" said Fat-Boy. "Colonel said you wanna bring him down for that."

"You don't think that's a problem?"

"Problem?" said Fat-Boy, and he opened his lazy eye to project his scorn. "You all tried to kill *him*, didn't you?"

"I don't think that the blame for the fire he survived can be laid at my feet."

"Sure it can. That's the point, isn't it? He's the Phoenix, our president is. You all tried to kill him. Why shouldn't he kill a few bitches in return? I said to Colonel: what makes Bubbles so special he thinks he can bring the Phoenix down?"

"And what did he say?"

"Said I didn't know you as well as he did."

Fat-Boy's cheeks sagged, and he pouted his lips as he searched my face for some redeeming quality that might explain it. He didn't find one. "I told him I don't like the Brits," he said as if proving a point.

"Even though he is one?"

"I like him for other reasons," said Fat-Boy.

"And when he told you I wasn't a Brit?"

"I like the Yanks less than I like the Brits," said Fat-Boy.

"My father was Canadian. Yanks are from the United States."

"Same thing," said Fat-Boy.

"In the same way that the Xhosas and Zulus are the same?"

Fat-Boy focused his lazy eye on me. He knew I was taunting him, but he rose to it anyway.

"Ain't nothing the same," he said. "'Cept maybe the colour pencil you use in your kiddie books. Actually ... no, even our colours is different. You seen those brothers from the Sudan? They're blue man, nothing black about them. We're all different, even one clan to the other is different."

"Clan?"

"I'm Khumalo. The Khumalo clan is the most trustworthy. AmaXhosa have clans. Your clan is your people. You don't marry your clan, they're like your family. Same ancestors, aren't they?"

"Is there a clan that sounds like 'fuck you'?" I asked with Johansson's sneering voice sounding an echo in my mind.

Fat-Boy looked at me to be sure I was not mocking him. He nodded.

"Far-coo," he said. "F-A-K-U, Faku. Khumalo are better though."

We watched some early risers making their way proudly down the road with the skip in their step that people get when they've got the best parking spot.

"The Colonel says any case you not doing this 'cos of the new president, he says you don't give a shit."

"Sounds about right," I said.

"He said you doing it 'cos you got problems, personal problems."

Fat-Boy's good eye matched the droop of the lazy one so he could better see my problems. I gave him a smile to show I didn't hold it against him or his Colonel. A drizzle started to fall, and the early risers picked up their pace as they realised they'd left their umbrellas at home.

"Sex bomb Robs says it has to do with your past," said Fat-Boy, making it clear that he hadn't fallen for that one. "Something you did together in the army. Some boyfriend of hers who died. That's why you doing it, and that's why the Colonel's helping you. She says you've got big issues, and he's doing it because of your shared past or some shit. She's a real psychologist that one."

———

At oh eight hundred hours sharp Fat-Boy clambered out of the panel van and placed the metal trestles to form a protective square around the junction box. I stayed in the back of the van because the Telkom technicians usually went solo. Fat-Boy pulled the metal handle with the square socket out of his pocket and inserted it into the front panel of the box. The lever was stiff, but after a bit of jiggling and an extra effort that had his cheeks pop out like a jazz trumpeter it gave way and the panel swung open, revealing about a thousand coloured wires scrambled like a Pollock painting. Fat-Boy seemed undeterred, and if I hadn't known what the plan was, I would have thrown in the towel at the thought of finding the correct wires in that jumbled mess. I passed Fat-Boy his little folding stool, and he sat down in front of the panel and unrolled the canvas bag of tools on the ground.

He pulled his cap lower against the light drizzle. "Ready?" I asked.

"Give me a moment to get in the zone," he said. "Hang on while I find my mandala." He glared at me. "Of course I'm fucking ready, what the fuck do you think?"

I dialled the number on the cheap phone Chandler had given me the night before. It rang three times and was answered. Gold standard service that was. "How may I direct your call?" asked the receptionist. I ended the call.

"OK, go," I said.

Fat-Boy used a large screwdriver and a pair of pliers to detach the entire top section of the junction box. It came away like the innards of a mechanical animal, trailing wires and metal spikes. Over a hundred phone lines died without a whimper. He turned to me and nodded. I hit the redial button. Three rings and an answer. I let the receptionist complete the greeting. "Sorry," I said. "Wrong number." I shook my head and Fat-Boy inserted the panel again, careful to line up all the metal spikes. He fastened the screws and then moved on to the next one.

It was on the fifth section of eight that the Gold Archives stopped answering. Fat-Boy stood up and grabbed a long torch from the back of the van, as well as a case with cables and another of his favourite breakfast dishes inside. He gave me a nod.

"Call the sex-bomb," he said, and pulled a canvas tarpaulin over the disembowelled junction box to protect it from the rain and prying eyes, then started the three-minute walk to the archives.

I called Robyn, who told me that she was standing by, although I'd seen her carry the duvet up to the roof when we left, and so I knew there wasn't a lot of standing going on.

She had the binoculars and was watching the roof we'd agreed was the correct one yesterday. As soon as Fat-Boy had convinced the Gold archive staff that he needed to get onto their roof in order to fix their phone lines she'd be ready to provide the signal for him to orientate the transmission dish. Then I could reconnect the lines at the same time that Fat-Boy was connecting his breakfast dish into their patch-bay.

There was nothing for me to do but wait. I searched the van and ended up sitting glumly in the back making sure that no one was taking too much interest in the exposed junction box. I cursed Fat-Boy for taking his cigarettes with him.

Robyn called back twelve minutes later. Fat-Boy had appeared on the roof in the company of a security guard who had helped him bolt the dish onto the parapet. We were all set. And the Colonel wanted us to buy bread rolls on our way back. We were having vegetable soup for lunch.

I sat in the rain and reconnected the panel in the box. Pedestrians hurried past with their coat collars pulled up, and umbrellas sprouted from the underground parking ramps like an invasion of black mushrooms. It occurred to me when I'd closed the box and returned the tools to the back of the van that I hadn't checked the glove compartment. But Fat-Boy hadn't left any cigarettes there either. I cursed him afresh.

———

We gathered in front of the monitors just before lunch like a bunch of excited schoolchildren. Fat-Boy had been wielding the mouse and tapping on the keyboard since our return, but now the screens were dark for added effect. We said we were ready, and all eight screens sprang to life. Bird's-eye views of the rooms and corridors of the Gold Archive arranged in a cubist pattern across all eight monitors.

Robyn gave a small Hollywood gasp and clapped her hands.

"It's a thing of beauty," said Chandler. "Now let's get to work."

SIXTEEN

The next three days were spent in front of those monitors. We took it in turns to watch the comings and goings of the foreshortened figures as they moved through the complex puzzle of bird's-eye views.

The archivists, researchers and office workers lived dreary lives, arriving in the morning in their suits and skirts, applying their fingers to the scanners in the entrance hall, waving at the security, waiting at the lifts, then spreading through the building to their cubicle offices, emerging at lunchtime and reversing the process in order to leave the building and forage for food. The afternoons were shorter and more weary. By early evening only the most dedicated survived, and they were soon replaced by a team of stooped cleaners who worked their way through the building with mops and vacuum cleaners.

Robyn wanted to be a cleaner, but we agreed that the security team provided us with our best opportunity. Their fingerprints allowed them to move freely throughout the building whereas the cleaners had limitations.

"BB's little army," said Chandler as he looked over my shoulder and warmed his hands on his third mug of coffee.

"Not so little anymore," I said. Breytenbach had always taken security seriously. His gold mines were protected by security teams that were recruited locally, then sent away for training by retired military experts. By the time they returned from their training they had surpassed any level normally associated with your run-of-the-mill security guard and were more like an army of over-trained and dangerously under-utilised soldiers.

"We'll get ourselves kitted out in their fancy dress," said Chandler, referring to the black uniforms the guards wore. Like military fatigues with more straps and pockets than any soldier would need, but which projected a sense of preparedness to anyone who might be foolish enough to think of challenging the wearer. "How are you doing with their schedule, Fat-Boy?"

"Almost there, Colonel," said Fat-Boy who had built himself a satellite station with two laptops, a large plate of doughnuts, and a flask of instant coffee that Robyn was under instruction to keep filled. The guards were on rotating shifts, and Chandler's plan was for us to find a way of substituting ourselves into one of those shifts. "Watch this guy," said Fat-Boy. "Redhead coming in now."

To the side of the floating island on the marble-floored expanse on the ground-floor hall that was the visitor's reception desk, was a channel used by security staff. A security guard we had come to recognise from his bright red hair was stuck at the gate, applying his finger to the reader with frustrated jabs. A guard behind the desk was suggesting that he wipe his finger and try again, a suggestion that wasn't being well received by the redhead.

"What have you done?" asked Chandler.

"Wiped his fingerprint file, haven't I?" said Fat-Boy with a smug smile.

"It's how we'll get in," said Robyn who was curled up on a chair like a cat beside me. "Watch what they do. Fats tried this earlier."

Redhead produced a plastic card from his wallet, and the guard behind the desk scanned it. Then Redhead applied each of his fingers to the reader. Less than a minute later the gate swung open, and he pushed through.

"It cannot be that easy," said Chandler.

"Nothing easy about it," said Fat-Boy. "It takes genius to wipe those files."

"And all they do is scan the fingerprints again," said Robyn.

"But we need to present one of those ID cards?" said Chandler.

Fat-Boy spun one of his laptops around to show us a mock-up of an ID card with the surly face of a man with bright red hair, a name and a strip of bar-code.

"What d'you think I've been doing all this time, Colonel?" Fat-Boy stuck his lower lip forward in a childlike pout. "Lot of good it'll do us though," he mumbled, returning to his favourite theme. "Nothing but a bunch of old paper in there."

"We need to be patient," said Chandler. It was not the first time he had said it, and his voice was beginning to show the strain of bolstering the team's faltering motivation. Long hours of watching the screens and seeing no sign of anything remotely gold-like were taking their toll. We all looked at the dimly glowing box that was the security station on the fourth underground level. Two security guards immobile in their bleak white world. White walls, white floors, and a white door that never opened. One guard standing, the other seated at a desk with a phone and a small control box.

"It's in there," said Chandler. "I know it is."

"But they never open it," complained Fat-Boy. "You don't know nothing, Colonel, 'cos you ain't seen nothing. Besides, if that door never opens, how are we gonna get the gold out of there?"

"We'll find a way," said Chandler with as much positivity as he could muster. "It won't take long." Fat-Boy blew a disparaging riff on his lips, but as it happened we didn't have long to wait at all.

———

"Who are those two characters?" asked Robyn an hour later. It was her turn in the big chair, the one that tilted back and swivelled on its hydraulic base so that we didn't have to suffer from neck cramp during our vigil.

Fat-Boy and I were working on our ID cards, and Chandler was filling the place with the smell of frying onions from the lower level where he was getting the lunch started.

Two black-suited guards we hadn't seen before had appeared in the white stretch of corridor on the fourth level below ground. They followed the portly figure of Lategan, who looked as if he was giving them a guided tour, gesturing around the empty space with his fleshy hands. One of the guards had short blond hair like a tight cap, and down the side of his face we caught the glimpse of a bright red scar. The other guard walked a pace behind him, a narrow bony skull and ebony skin. When he turned his face to look up at the camera, there was hardly any flesh on it, just a gaunt skull with hollow cheeks.

We watched as they reached the blank white door,

Lategan completed a jig with his hands, and flourished towards the guard seated at the controls. Like magic, the door smoothly retracted into the wall beside it, moving slowly as befitted the kind of door that would withstand any and all efforts to be breached. The space beyond the door was brightly lit. We could see a polished concrete floor, a corridor that extended beyond our view, flanked by steel cages. Each steel cage was about the size of a rabbit hutch, and they were piled on top of one another. Each cage had layers of neatly stacked bars which shone with a golden light, like tightly wrapped bars of chocolate.

"Fuck me," said Fat-Boy, and his lazy eye jumped to see it better.

"I think you should take a look at this, Colonel," called Robyn without taking her eyes from the screen. There was something hypnotic about that golden glow, and when Chandler joined us a few minutes later we were all still staring at it in complete silence.

"Well, what do you know?" said Chandler. "There it is."

"Fuck me," said Fat-Boy again. "There's a lot of that shit. How the hell we supposed to get it out of there?"

"We're not greedy. We'll just take a little," said Chandler. "Can you tell me who those two clowns are with the big guy?"

Fat-Boy turned back to his laptop and took less than a minute to find them.

"That's fucked up," he said. "The guy with the scar is down here as a Captain, and the thin dude is a first lieutenant. But their postings aren't listed, and when I go to view their history it's denied."

Chandler nodded. "They're here for a reason. Keep an

eye on them. My guess is they're BB's version of special ops. His personal team."

"What do you think they're doing?" asked Robyn. "You think they know we're watching them?"

Chandler shook his head. "They'd cut the cable if they knew that. But something is afoot. Those two are not doing a sightseeing tour. Let's eat lunch and discuss speeding things up a little."

———

It was agreed over lunch that we needed to poke the beast and see how Breytenbach's private army responded to stressful situations. And so Robyn tied her hair up, put on a skirt and some heels and we watched the top of her head as she signed the visitors' book and was ushered into the lobby on her way to the public Reading Room.

In the Reading Room the ever-helpful Meghan provided Robyn with the last remaining copy of an obscure book about the language of the *Strandloper* people, and Robyn paged through it, and gazed up at the cameras in the ceiling as if she thought someone might be watching her. Fat-Boy told her she was being irresponsible, and she laughed. The laugh echoed around our concrete box because Fat-Boy had his phone connected to the speakers. It looked as if Robyn stuck her tongue out, but then Fat-Boy's laptop showed him that an archivist from the fifth floor had returned from lunch and was waiting for a lift to carry him up to his office. Robyn abandoned her book, entered the lift lobby and ignored the sign indicating which lifts were reserved for staff only. Chandler had identified a weakness in the fingerprint control of the lift system: catching a ride with the owner of an authorised finger rendered it ineffective. Very few of the archive workers were likely to challenge anyone who climbed into a lift and travelled to the same floor as them. Particularly if that person looked like Robyn.

Her timing was perfect. We watched as a lift door opened, revealing the feet of the archivist on his way up to the fifth floor. Robyn stepped into the lift and I imagined the smile and demure downturn of the eyes which would deter the archivist from questioning her right to be travelling with him.

We had chosen the fifth floor because one of the corridor cameras was out of order. Fat-Boy had argued we would betray our presence to their security by choosing a corridor without a camera, but Chandler made ominous noises about the two clowns in the vault and said that in his opinion time was running out anyway.

Robyn emerged from the lift behind the archivist and walked slowly down the corridor as if her skirt was limiting her stride. She turned the corner and disappeared from view. Her voice called out the numbers of the office doors she was passing, and Fat-Boy chose one that he knew was empty.

"Start the timer," said Robyn, and then came the slow intake of breath as she prepared to pick the lock. I'd watched her demonstrate her skill to Fat-Boy the day before. She had turned towards me, leaned her ear up against the door with a seductive gesture, opening her mouth slightly, her eyes closed. The tension bar was inserted into the lock, the spring was worked gently in and out. And her tongue moved inside her mouth as if it was mapping the position of the pins.

"Done," said Robyn. It had taken her twelve seconds. We heard the beeping of the office alarm demanding a fingerprint. But Robyn closed the door again and her breathing quickened as she moved down the corridor to the fire escape.

"No running now," said Fat-Boy.

"You don't think?" said Robyn and the sound of the crash bar on the fire escape door came to us, then the clatter of her feet down the escape stairs. She ended the call.

The alarm was on a thirty second delay, and Robyn had just emerged into the entrance lobby when it must have sounded. We heard nothing, but it was obvious from the synchronous lifting of heads on the screens before us, and the slightly delayed emergence of office workers into the corridors.

Chandler made notes and Fat-Boy called out times. The security response was fast but predictable. All guard stations in the building were double-manned, and from each station one of the two guards moved to an advance position while the other remained where they were. Three guards were dispatched to the fifth floor and drew their weapons as they moved down the corridor.

"Shoot first, ask questions later," I said and Chandler grunted.

It took fifteen minutes for them to stand everyone down.

"We'll need something more," said Chandler.

"Fire," suggested Fat-Boy, "we start a fire. That'll keep them busy."

Chandler considered that and nodded. But his eyes were on the screen with the vault. Scarface and his sidekick had not paid the slightest attention to the alarm. They were standing over a metal device which looked as if it belonged in a supermarket. A hand-pushed hydraulic loader of the sort used by the drivers of delivery trucks to enable them to move their heavy boxes from the truck into the storerooms.

Chandler stood up abruptly. "They're moving it," he said. "That's what they're doing. They never expected to move it, so now they're trying to figure out how to do it. The bastards are moving it." He turned to us and his eyes were jumping with excitement or anger, it was difficult to tell which. "When our girl gets back, we go operational. We're going in tomorrow."

———

"We're not ready," said Fat-Boy, and he did the sulky child thing with his lips.

Chandler nodded. He turned to Robyn.

"What do you think, Robyn? Are we ready?"

"No," said Robyn, and her eyes glowed as if the coals were alight. She had changed out of her skirt and heels and was back in her fatigues. That was all the time Chandler had given her before he started the ops meeting. We had been working on the plan for three hours, and there were still holes and unanswered questions.

"But when are we ever ready?" said Robyn.

Chandler nodded. "If we hit the evening shift change, we will have the full day to collect the uniforms, get ourselves a delivery truck and all the accessories." He looked at the screens where Scarface and Sidekick were now testing loads. They had failed to lift an entire cage between four of them and Chandler had laughed at their comedy routine as they discovered just how heavy a cage loaded with Good Delivery bars was. "Looks like they've figured it out," he said now. "How many bars is that?"

"Twenty-four," said Fats. "Two-hundred-eighty-eight kilos."

A guard had provided them with a stack of closed

plastic crates. Scarface had opened up a cage, and they had been testing their hydraulic loader up and down the corridor, presumably trying to work out how many bars could be pushed.

"It's getting too late for them to start now," said Chandler. "That truck still closed up?"

"Driver left it there," said Fat-Boy. "He buggered off again." An hour earlier an unmarked armoured vehicle of the sort used by banks to transfer cash had parked in one of the delivery bays near the lift two floors above the vault. It was still there. Chandler's guess that Scarface and Sidekick were going to be moving the gold looked like a good one.

"It's tomorrow or never," said Chandler. "If we wait any longer, there won't be anything left. Do the A-B-C's, Robyn."

"A-B-C's?" I said.

"There's a limit to how much planning we can do," said Robyn. "But every situation has three possible outcomes. Best case is A, Worst case is C. And B is how we twist the worst case in our favour. When we have our A-B-C's we're ready. Because it usually comes down to what we do in the moment. When we do what we do best, which is to improvise."

The idea of improvising didn't sound appealing to me, but Chandler nodded. For a moment I wondered whether that had been the plan when Robyn and her boyfriend walked into the country bank with their burlap sack and enough weapons to shoot their way out of trouble. Had their plan been to improvise? I tried to ignore the slipping sensation I was getting. That feeling when you look around at your teammates before the big match and wonder whether you can actually play the game.

"We can get in," continued Robyn. "Getting in is the

easy part. It's the exit that's hard. That's where the A-B-C's come in. Give me the A-plan, Fat-Boy."

"Nothing hard about it," said Fat-Boy. "I turn the key in that delivery truck, and drive on outta there."

"Fat-Boy's our A-plan man," said Robyn. "But if something goes wrong, we're stuck in there like a school of goldfish in a bowl full of piranhas."

"Piranhas?" said Fat-Boy.

"The fish with sharp teeth," said Robyn.

"And what do goldfish do when they're trapped by piranhas?" said Chandler.

"They get eaten." I suggested.

"They get eaten," agreed Chandler. "And downstream their broken scales and traces of their blood wash up on the shore. That's the C-plan."

"Do fish have blood?" asked Fat-Boy.

"There are three ways we get out of that building," said Chandler. He counted them off on his fingers. "We drive our delivery truck out." Another finger came up. "Or we come out with our hands cuffed behind us because the archive people call the police."

"They'll never call the cops," said Fat-Boy, pulling his mind away from the circulatory systems of fish. "They've got their own army in there."

"Or we come out in a hearse," said Robyn.

"Not a hearse," said Chandler. "Who calls a hearse?"

"They call an ambulance," said Robyn. "Which is our B-plan."

"I don't like it," said Fat-Boy. "How do we get them to call an ambulance?"

"They'll call an ambulance when one of us gets shot."

Fat-Boy puffed out his cheeks with exasperation. "You wanna ask them to shoot us?"

Robyn shook her head. "We do the shooting."

"Like fuck I'm gonna let you shoot me," said Fat-Boy. "I know how this will work. It'll be the black guy who gets shot, won't it?"

"It might," said Chandler. "But we'll be shooting blanks. We'll get blood bags for the effect. It's our best fall-back."

He got to his feet and went to stand before the monitors. Scarface and Sidekick had completed their tests, and the vault was closing up again.

"We have a plan, don't we?" said Chandler. He turned back to face us. "What do you say, Robyn?"

"I say we do it," said Robyn.

"Fat-Boy?"

Fat-Boy took a moment, but then nodded. "We do it, Colonel."

"Angel?"

"Let's do it," I said.

Chandler gave a curt nod. I felt a shiver run down my spine. The thing about being a part of a team of madmen is that you keep thinking surely one of you should be sensible and should provide an anchor of sanity. But the others didn't seem to worry about that. Robyn noticed me watching her and held my look with eyes as hard as steel. There was more to Robyn than the struggling, bereaved alcoholic. I'd always known it, I suppose, but seemed to keep forgetting.

———

I watched the sun give up on the day from the roof terrace. A blanket of smog smothered the city and glowed with the dying golden light. Chandler joined me as I was finishing my cigarette.

"You have your file all worked out?" he asked.

"Fat-Boy tells me it's on the second floor down. The floor Lategan didn't want to show us. It's been tagged for no withdrawal, but if you could make a phone call at an appropriate time... Fat-Boy has the number."

"He's good that Fat-Boy," said Chandler, and he drew a deep breath as if he was about to start his Swedish exercises. "Very good with the computers, and all the technical stuff. But you need to watch over him tomorrow. His nerves get the better of him."

"I will," I assured him.

"Let Robyn do the shooting. She's got a talent for it, one of the coolest heads I've come across. So long as she stays off the sauce."

"Are they all blanks that she's carrying?"

"Not all blanks, no. If she needs to do some real damage she can."

"But if we start shooting at them we're unlikely to get out of there."

"Which is why we leave the shooting to Robyn."

Chandler gazed out over the smog. A light wind was starting to tear at the edges. I could tell from his silence that there was something on his mind.

"You think they're expecting us, don't you?" I said.

"Certain of it," said Chandler, and he turned to face me. "It's why they're moving the gold."

"Then why not cancel?"

"Because that's what everyone has done in the history of that man BB's life. It's what gives him his power, isn't it? Anyone who dares to think of challenging him ends up cancelling, pulling out, or giving up. Am I wrong?"

"Or dying," I said.

"That's right. Or dying. As we know. How many men was it, Gabriel?"

In all the years I had known Chandler, we had never spoken directly of the men we had killed.

"For BB ... thirteen," I said. "There were thirteen of them."

Chandler blinked and nodded. He knew the number as well as I did.

"Thirteen," he agreed, and turned to look out at the smog again. "What Robyn says is true. We can improvise. It's only a bit of yellow metal, for goodness' sake. We're not starting a war. We'll show BB that he is not untouchable. You get your file, expose what they're doing in protecting that new president. And if we get a few gold bars into the bargain, all the better. It's time someone showed that man that his wealth and his power have limits."

Chandler went quiet, and I lit another cigarette.

"It surprised me," he said after a few minutes of silence. "When you came to me. I could see the change in you. Was he a good friend, that journalist who died?"

"I met him once, and didn't like him," I said.

Chandler laughed. "But you're doing the right thing by him. After all these years you've turned out okay. I can still hardly believe it."

"I'm going soft," I said.

"No, Gabriel, you're not. You're doing what no one else will do. There will be no way back for you, and you know it. No one will like you, least of all Breytenbach and his government cronies. You're messing with the most powerful people in the land. That's not going soft, Gabriel. Not soft at all."

SEVENTEEN

"It's a matter of accountability," said Robyn. "Our leaders should be accountable to us. The most powerful man in the land cannot be hiding secrets from his people. If he killed someone he cannot expect to assume a position of power."

"My leader killed people," said Fat-Boy. "And I don't care. You did kill people, didn't you, Colonel?"

"It was our job to protect," said Chandler, "not to kill."

It was after midnight and we were up on the roof. I'd been asked by Fat-Boy to explain my 'bit of paper'. Chandler was presiding over the dinner that he'd prepared as we 'cleaned house'. Everything was gone. The empty spaces of our match factory were echoing and dusty as they had been when we arrived. Not a paper clip, thumb tack or wad of chewing gum could be seen. The monitors were gone, extension cables rolled up, furniture loaded into the panel van in the basement. The only things that remained were for what Fat-Boy insisted on calling our 'Last Supper'. And we were doing it in style. Balloon wine-glasses, wooden pepper grinders and Chinese lanterns dangling from the one remaining power cable, bouncing back and forth as the wind built up its strength for the onslaught it was planning for the next day. The news had been full of anxious anticipation of the historic – once in a generation – storm that was expected. Chandler had said the storm would work in our favour, and we were holding onto that idea.

"Bubbles is playing with fire is all I'm saying," said Fat-Boy. "He should forget his lousy file, focus on the important stuff."

"The information in that file is important to Bubbles," said Chandler as he finished pouring the wine, and lifted his glass as if that was a toast. "We'll leave it at that." He sipped the wine, sloshed it around a bit in a puckered mouth and then sat back with satisfaction.

Fat-Boy pushed his lower lip forward and glowered.

"You doing the usual Fat-Boy?" asked Robyn.

"What do you think, baby? Bit of white sand, azure sea. Catch myself a tan, pick up a few plump bitches. A couple skinny bitches for variety. You wanna join me?"

Robyn laughed and shook her head. "I've got my own plans," she said.

"You could be skinny bitch number one," said Fat-Boy, "but it'd make Bubbles jealous."

"Of course it wouldn't," I said. "Go ahead and be Fat-Boy's skinny bitch."

"Oh, I love it." Fat-Boy pretended to be incapacitated by a laugh that shook his frame but made no sound. "Look at him. So jealous."

I pulled a face at Fat-Boy.

"Bubbles is spoken for," said Robyn, presumably because she thought that would end the discussion, but she had misjudged her audience.

"I know baby, I know all about that," said Fat-Boy.

"Fetch me a box of tissues. The coloured chick who went AWOL. Know all about it." Fat-Boy looked at me with dispassionate interest to see whether he'd get a rise out of me. I gave him a blank look in return.

"Seriously AWOL?" asked Fat-Boy, who liked the bit where you twist the blade the most. "I mean she just upped and left, or did she find herself another man, and give you the heave-ho?"

"Seriously AWOL," I said, keeping it light.

Fat-Boy was encouraged by this.

"You woke up one morning and her bags were packed. She's at the foot of the bed blubbing and telling you it'll never work?"

I almost said that was the way it was, and how did Fat-Boy know? But they say that's not healthy. Honesty is healthy, that's what they say.

"I woke up one morning and there were no bags. No blubbing either."

Fat-Boy whistled softly. The other two kept their heads down, but Fat-Boy liked this stuff, and was going in deeper.

"Overnight?" he asked. "The night before, she slipped you a pill after her third orgasm? Or you slept so hard 'cause you banged her so hard? She called her mates with the removal van and they shifted everything out?"

"There wasn't much to shift," I said.

"That's harsh, brother." He shook his head like he was feeling my pain, and took a deep draught of wine, mistaking it perhaps for his usual beer.

"She was a journalist?" asked Robyn.

"She was."

"Bubbles put down his gun for her," said Chandler. "Never thought I'd see that day."

I didn't point out that he hadn't seen that day because it

happened long after I'd sworn I'd never set eyes on him again. But arguing about it would only have encouraged the group therapy session. In any case Fat-Boy had tired of discussing my regrettable history.

"The point," said Fat-Boy, "is that you can be my skinny bitch, Robsy. Bubbles can go cry into his pillow, but there ain't nothing to stop us having fun."

"I'll pack my bikini," said Robyn and gave him the full smile.

"The Angel tells me you haven't given him the cattle story," said Chandler.

Fat-Boy stopped wiggling his tongue at Robyn and looked at Chandler as if he had just given him awful news. He shook his head and turned to me.

"You said you were a Yank." He turned to Chandler. "He said he was a Yank," he complained. "And if he's a Yank, then it's all on you, Colonel. The Yanks were still dealing with their own native problem, can't push the blame onto them."

"I'd hardly call him a Yank. He was born in Toronto, and spent his school years in the UK, isn't that so, Gabriel? There's nothing Yank about him."

"I'm a citizen of the world," I said. "But if there's blame going around, I'll be the other one."

"You're a freaking mess is what you are," said Fat-Boy. "Figure out whose side you're on first and then I'll tell you about the cattle."

"The story changes according to who is hearing it, would be my guess," said Chandler.

"Only too right," said Fat-Boy, and we waited as he finished his wine. "1856," he said as Chandler refilled the glass. "My people were destroyed. That's what happened."

"Destroyed because of the cattle?" I said.

"Cattle were our wealth. They were all we had, but we had a lot of them. The Xhosa people were powerful and wealthy. Then in 1856 a teenage girl called *Nongqawuse*, but don't worry about the name – you whities will never be able to say it right – she had a vision. She met a man who said the Xhosa people would become the most powerful in the land and would force the white people back into the sea where they came from. This sounded good to the girl, but the way it needed to be done, said the man, was that every single cow had to be killed."

"Surely nobody believed the girl," said Robyn.

"She was the daughter of a great prophet. That's why she was believed."

"So they killed the cattle?" I asked.

Fat-Boy nodded his sad face. "It took them over a year. By the end of 1857, most of the cattle were gone. They destroyed crops as well. My people were broken. Forty thousand amaXhosa died. They had nothing, their wealth was gone, they had no food. Nothing. And the white people didn't go back to the sea."

"But what does this have to do with the British people?" I asked.

"Who do you think was the man that appeared to *Nongqawuse* in her vision?"

"That's an unfounded allegation," said Chandler. "The British administrators in the Cape did what they could to stop the massacre of the cattle and support the Xhosa people. I read up on it after you told me the story."

"That's why I don't like the Brits," said Fat-Boy, and he glared at me.

We settled into a comfortable silence. Chandler sipped again at his wine as if he was trying to make the glass last all night. He looked at each of us in turn and I resisted the impression that he was taking mental snapshots as someone does when they know they might not see that person again.

A gust of wind caught our Chinese lanterns and twirled them on their strings. The stars over the sea were being smothered one by one as a bank of cloud approached the city. "It's starting," said Chandler, and Robyn gave a shiver as if it had grown suddenly cold, although the air being pushed ahead of the storm was warm like the tantalising promise of a return of summer.

———

We cleared up after dinner and carried the table and all but two of the chairs down to the panel van. Chandler allowed Robyn and me to sit up with a bottle of wine for me, mineral water for Robyn, and a couple of cigarettes before sleeping. Robyn wrapped herself up in a duvet and gazed out at the approaching storm.

"It makes sense," she said. "That you're Canadian. It explains so many things."

"Half Canadian," I corrected her.

"And what? Half South African?"

"That's about it. What does it explain?"

"But grew up in the UK?"

"What does it explain?"

"It explains your problem, Ben. You're not quite anything. South Africans think you're English, the English think you're South African and god knows what the Canadians think."

"It allows me to stay neutral."

"But don't you see, Ben? That's the problem. You're always neutral, always the outsider. It's never you, always the other guy. Always the best man, never the groom. Can't you see that?"

"I've had my fair share of the action."

"Now I've upset you. I didn't mean to." She reached over with a finger and ran it down my cheekbone. "You can be so stubborn sometimes it makes me want to slap you," she said. "You let Fat-Boy ride rough shod all over you, and he just needs to be told it's none of his fucking business."

The wind picked up again and spun the Chinese lanterns in a frenetic dance. Robyn blew smoke into the wind and turned to me. There was something bothering her.

"I should just keep my mouth shut, shouldn't I?" she said. "Who would want to hear advice from an old soak like me?"

"Advice?" I said. "I must have missed that part."

"Criticism then. I was getting to the advice part, but I think I'll just shut up now."

She sat quietly, and we watched the lanterns throw themselves with abandon off the building only to bounce back when the cable caught them. Perhaps she wasn't bothered, maybe it was simply her nerves. We were all feeling the tension.

"You're not an old soak anyway," I said.

Robyn turned to me and finished her glass of mineral water as if making a point.

"I am, Ben. There are many types of soak, and I'm the other one. You don't know what it's like. The feeling that builds up. The desperation, and then days later the shame and the disgust, and it all starts over. It's an endless cycle. You have no idea."

The wind had built up to the point that it seemed likely the Chinese lanterns would make a break for it and scatter themselves over the neighbouring buildings, and that would not make Chandler happy. I got up from my chair beside Robyn and took them down and wound up the cable.

"That girl of yours really just disappear like that?" asked Robyn.

"Pretty much," I said. "Cleared her clothes out a few days after she left on a work trip."

"You don't want to talk about it."

"Not really."

Robyn flicked the stub of her cigarette away with an irritated gesture. I still had the feeling there was something she wanted to say but couldn't find a way of saying it.

"We've known each other for years, Ben," she said with the irritation showing. "But you talk to me like a speak-your-weight machine. I wish sometimes that you would let me in. That you would talk to me. What do you feel? About her, about me. Say something, for god's sake."

I didn't say anything. Her eyes held mine, and I thought of all the things I wanted to say, but they all seemed wrong. They were the kind of thing I could never say to her. They were disrespectful to the memory of Brian. They made a mockery of the alleged friendship she spoke of between us. The wind was buffeting us now, and Robyn's hair was being caught up in handfuls and being used to flay the back of the camping chair.

"We should probably go down," I said. "Big day tomorrow."

Robyn's face clouded over. "That's you right there, Ben," she said. A sudden spark of anger flared behind her eyes. "You open the doors but then slam them closed before anyone can get in."

"It's not that, Robyn. It's late."

"Bullshit. There I was thinking for a moment that we

have a connection, but you slap me in the face. Like you always have. Your problem, Ben, is that you're a cold fish, a man without a heart. There's just nothing in there."

It occurred to me that recently many people had been gifted with the ability to identify my flaws. I said nothing, but Robyn had seen the shadow of the thought behind my eyes.

"Don't say it," she said, and stood up with her back to the wind so that it caught her words and threw them at me. "Always a flippant comment, always the sarcastic arsehole. You wouldn't know a friend if you tripped over one. You're a bastard, Ben, you know that?"

"Luckily I have friends to remind me when I forget it," I said. It was one of my less impressive moments.

Robyn shook her head, then gathered the duvet up into a big ball. She grabbed my untouched bottle of wine like she wanted to punish me, and took it with her to the door that opened onto the stairs. She paused there a moment.

"Colonel thinks this whole thing has nothing to do with the new president, or your old intelligence outfit. You know that? He thinks you've just dreamed up the presidential secrets stuff because you're lonely and sad and consumed with guilt. He thinks this is all about you finding a way to get over that girl who probably made the best choice of her life when she walked out your front door."

She slammed the door behind her. The camp chairs started skittering across the roof in the wind, so I ran after them and folded them up. The storm was still several hours away. It was going to be a big one.

EIGHTEEN

The storm delivered fully upon its promise of the night before, which made things a little easier for us. We gathered everything we needed under cover of the morning's rain and high velocity winds, which turned out to be no more than a warmup. By the time we were eating a light lunch, the main act had started. Telephone poles were ripped out of the ground and streets in the city were flooded in a remarkable demonstration of violence. In the late afternoon the storm reluctantly subsided, the winds were all blown out, and only the rain continued as a last effort to keep the party going.

Chandler gave us a final briefing at sixteen thirty hours. We went through the process that Scarface and Sidekick had established the day before. Sidekick, stationed at the lower level, had supervised a guard as he loaded bars into crates in the vault. A second guard pushed the loader down the corridor to the lift. He emerged three floors up to be watched by Scarface as he heaved the box into the back of the armoured carrier. We had a small window of opportunity, but Chandler was optimistic that we could load a full crate in the fifteen minutes we would have available to us after Robyn triggered the alarm and detonated the smoke bomb. He warned us again that it was one load only.

"It has to be fast. No going back for second helpings."

Fat-Boy was disappointed that it would only be one load, but then he did the numbers in his head and whistled. Chandler said he shouldn't count our chickens before they hatched.

Fat-Boy climbed into his delivery truck at seventeen fifteen hours. He was wearing baggy overalls but complained that the bulletproof vest was preventing him from breathing normally. Chandler told him it was just his nerves and that he would be fine. Fat-Boy said he wasn't nervous and made a sound that was intended to prove that, but which failed. He then gave me a series of complex handshakes and squeezed Robyn so hard I thought she might pop. Then he told me not to fuck it up, reminded Robyn not to shoot him under any circumstances, and he drove off.

Robyn and I rode with Chandler in the ambulance, in the back with the drips and life support machines. Robyn's eyes were a little red, and she'd had a slightly glazed expression all day. I hadn't mentioned the bottle of wine to Chandler, and it worried me now. She had her cleaner's outfit on because her first role was playing at being a cleaner. It was only later that she would change into the security guard outfit that she carried in a plastic shopping bag. She was still angry with me and avoided looking at me as we rattled through the heavy afternoon traffic.

I walked the last few blocks and at eighteen oh one hours stood on the edge of the pavement across the road from the Gold Archives. That extra minute bothered me. A minute is all it takes to pump a little extra adrenalin into the system.

Cars rushed through the early evening, their lights slipping ahead on the wet road. It was still coming down pretty heavily, and the rain was drawing a veil over the end of the day. I could barely see across the street to where the Gold Archives were looking all streaky and dark, and not in a forgiving sort of mood. Deep windows punched into the stone wall, a feeble orange light trickling from them into the miserable evening. Low cloud came down to swallow the top floor.

I found a gap in the traffic and splashed across the road, took the revolving doors by surprise and passed the point at which I could turn back.

———

The eyebrows of the guard at the front desk climbed with surprise as I dripped all over his lovely floor. He said I was not the first one to have a problem with the fingerprints. A cleaner ahead of me had also had the fingerprint problem. But she had been less wet. I said that she had taken my umbrella, but he didn't believe that and gave a big laugh. I could see Robyn stepping into a lift on her way to the fifth floor, and wondered fleetingly what her secret power was, that a momentary glimpse of her in drab cleaner's garb could take my breath away. I also wondered whether she would do what was required when it counted. I should have told Chandler about the bottle of wine.

The fingerprint scanner liked my fingers even though I was wet, and it occurred to me as I waited for the lift that this was really a building that had always wanted to be a church, what with its vaulted ceiling, the muted tones, the hard marble floor. A church to the religion of secrecy perhaps, the high priest Lategan conducting the services, and I was a sinner about to blaspheme at the altar.

———

At the second basement level an old man watched me with resentment as I applied my finger to the scanner. The machine flashed green and the glass door emitted an inviting beep. The old man tutted as I approached him, his lips twitching with annoyance.

"Know the time?" he asked me and shook his head as if I'd ruined his evening, although it looked like it was already going badly. He was standing beside a steel trolley of the kind they use to dispense medicine in hospitals. It was piled high with haphazardly discarded file boxes and he had been scratching his head wondering how to rearrange them so he could fit them through the small door that provided access to the storage room to which these files should be returned.

"Look at them," he said with dismay. "Do they ever read the notice?" Above the tottering pile was a faded sheet with the printed words "Stack returned files neetly", with the first 'e' of 'neetly' crossed out with ballpoint pen and an 'a' scratched above it.

"Perhaps the spelling distracts from the message," I said.

"You're too late," he said. "We don't issue files after six."

I was a little late. I knew that every day it took him or one of his colleagues about ten minutes to rearrange the returned files and wheel them into the back, but I had arrived before he'd managed to do that, so I was on time.

"I'm the guy they sent down to check the number on that file," I said. "There was a problem with it? A security breach. Someone requested a tagged file?"

The man nodded without enthusiasm and walked down a short corridor to a side door into the back room where the secrets were kept. He appeared ten seconds later behind the thick bulletproof glass and peered out at me as if to check that I was still there. The file in question was in his hands.

"They can't take it," he said with grim satisfaction through the bulletproof glass. "It's tagged. See?" He held the box up to demonstrate. I leaned up to the glass and squinted as if I was trying to read the fine print. He brought the box closer to the glass, but it didn't help. I shook my head.

"Let me check that number," I said, and he opened his mouth to deny me that opportunity when the alarms sounded. He froze with the file box held tantalisingly in the air just a couple of feet from me. My timing was out, I should have had that file in my hands by now.

"What the hell is that?" he asked as if it was yet another problem I was throwing at him.

"It's a fire alarm," I said. "Shall I come back later?"

"There is no later ... I'm going home, sonny."

"Let me check the number," I said again, holding out my hand for the file.

He handed it to me through the narrow slot below the bulletproof glass.

I ran my finger along the line of numbers and squinted as if my glasses were not providing the focus I needed. It was then that the phone in the back room rang. The old man looked at me as if expecting that I might answer the call myself. For a moment we were suspended in time as he realised that I was standing with a forbidden file in my hands, and he searched his mind for what the rulebook had to say about the recommended action. His watery eyes stared at me and flickered down to the file in my hands. It was then I realised that my uniform was still wet, and I was dripping onto the floor. He looked up, and our eyes met. I could see him sizing up the risk, but he stepped back and ducked into the safety of the back room.

I had only twenty seconds before his suspicious eyes appeared behind the bulletproof glass again. But that was enough. He seemed almost surprised to see me still standing there, the file in my hands.

"No can do," he said to me as a summary of the discussion on the phone, and he held out his hand for the file. I gave it to him and shrugged.

"You told them I checked the number?" I asked because to have said nothing would only have raised suspicion.

The old man nodded and verified the number on the box to be sure I hadn't switched it. Then he opened it and made sure there were still papers inside.

"Have a good evening," I said in a cheerful way, but he wasn't in the mood for returning the gesture. I felt his steady gaze on my back all the way out of the room.

The emergency stairs clattered under my feet as I ran down to the fourth level. I tucked the file under the straps of my bulletproof vest and arrived out of breath at the fire escape door to the lowest level. The old man might discover the empty file box on his pile of returns, but I intended to be well clear of the building before then. The alarm started up again, a wailing, melancholy sound. I was on time.

———

Sidekick was less menacing in real life than he had appeared on camera. His cheeks were hollow, and his face was like a skull with a thin coating of skin. But his eyes were visible, which revealed some life, although a primitive and not very friendly form of life. Both of the guards that had been posted to the lower level had moved away when the alarm sounded. Sidekick was standing motionless beside the loader as if he'd experienced a mechanical breakdown and was waiting for roadside assistance. His wary eyes swung onto me as I came through the fire escape and his hand moved toward his holster. But the sight of my uniform put him at ease.

"Fire alarm," I said. "They sent me down to help out."

"Who sent you down?" asked Sidekick in a whining, high-pitched voice.

I shrugged. "The boss on level four," I said.

Sidekick stood motionless as he processed this. Finally, he gave a nod. I stepped up to the loader and gave it a shove. It didn't budge. I put my head down between my arms and applied all my strength. The loader started to creep forward. Sidekick watched me, his mouth twisting up into a sneer. I resisted the temptation to point out that I'd seen him fail at moving the three hundred kilogram load the day before. He reached for the radio strapped to his shoulder and said something into it. There was a pause as I heaved at the loader and gradually gained speed. His radio crackled a confirmation and Sidekick leaned back against the wall to enjoy the sight of my struggle.

It took me almost three minutes to travel the length of the corridor to the lifts. Fat-Boy was dead on time, but the lift announced its arrival before I'd had a chance to pretend to press the call button. I felt a shiver run up my spine in the echoing silence following the triumphant ping, because I felt sure that would have betrayed us and imagined that Sidekick would be pointing his Beretta at me. But a glance back as I brought the loader to a halt and started to turn it towards the lift doors revealed that Sidekick was still leaning back against the wall watching me with the remnants of the sneer. The early arrival of the lift had not bothered him.

The doors opened to reveal Fat-Boy, his eyes as wide as saucers. I recognised the signs of panic. His breathing was too fast, his shoulders rising and falling with each breath.

"Take it easy," I whispered as the doors closed behind us. I should have taken a moment to calm him, but we had work to do. I pressed the button for the eleventh floor and applied my finger to the scanner.

Fat-Boy had the refrigerated box on his loader open, and we worked fast to transfer the bars, moving one at a time. They were heavy and slippery in my hands. Fat-Boy dropped one and cursed, but as the lift doors opened onto the eleventh floor, we sealed the empty crate. I helped Fat-Boy push his loader out and pressed the button for the parking level. Fat-Boy watched me with his wide, panicked eyes as the doors slid closed. I knew that I should have taken a few seconds to calm him. But it was too late, the lift was already dropping, and we had only a few minutes left.

———

If Sidekick had been a disappointment, Scarface more than made up for it. His physical presence was so menacing it struck me like a blow to the gut. He was not albino, but there was so little colour in his face that he appeared to be. It was the contrast provided by the bright red scar that made the rest of his face seem particularly pale. It was a raised keloid scar which ran the length of his cheekbone and down to his jaw. It gave the impression that he was gritting his teeth and causing his jaw muscles to pop. His eyes were a cool blue and fiercely intelligent. They watched me coldly as I struggled to push the loader out of the lift, and up to the back of the armoured carrier.

"Who are you?" he asked.

"Fire alarm," I said. "They sent me down to help."

I pumped the hydraulic handle to raise the crate so I could push it into the carrier. Scarface kept watching me, and his eyes narrowed. The fire escape door beside the lifts opened and footsteps approached.

"You know this joker?" Scarface asked the newcomer.

"No, sir," said Robyn. "Don't know him. But I'm new here."

Scarface watched me as I kept pumping. The crate reached the level of the back of the armoured carrier and I started to heave at it to push it in.

"Hold it," said Scarface, his voice taut with suspicion.

It was sheer bad luck that the lift bearing Fat-Boy chose that moment to arrive. The arrival ping burst into the tense silence. The doors slid open to reveal a wide-eyed, sweaty Fat-Boy.

Scarface and Robyn turned to face Fat-Boy, who stood frozen to the spot. I willed him to push forward and behave normally. He was a delivery man with an empty refrigerated box returning to his vehicle.

But Fat-Boy didn't move. He stared at us, and guilt seemed to wash over him. The lift announced with a female voice that the doors were closing, and still Fat-Boy stood rooted to the spot. He swallowed.

Scarface moved swiftly. He pulled his 9mm Beretta from its holster and stepped up to the lift in one smooth action. He levelled the gun at Fat-Boy and jammed his foot between the closing doors. The doors opened again and Fat-Boy raised his hands.

Robyn didn't hesitate. She raised her own Beretta,

pointed it at my chest, her eyes on mine. For a fleeting moment I wondered whether she had been sober when she loaded her magazine. Was the first bullet a blank? She squeezed the trigger. The sound of the shot deafened me. I dropped to the floor and pulled the cord on the blood bag. Scarface spun back around, and Robyn turned and fired at Fat-Boy. He slumped down behind the refrigerated box and I was hoping he had remembered to pull the cord on his blood bag when a searing pain ripped through my body and I heard the delayed bang of Scarface's gun.

Robyn swung back to see me as the wave of pain threw a black veil over the world. I could see her eyes fasten on Scarface as she assessed whether to use one of her real bullets on him. But he lowered his gun and gave her a nod of approval.

"Good job," he said.

I tried to identify the source of the pain. It was in my lower abdomen, just below the bulletproof vest as far as I could tell. The fact I could feel it was encouraging. I could still feel my legs and so my spinal cord was probably intact, although the nerves can take some time to fade. What other damage had been done I couldn't tell. I didn't move lest Scarface decided to finish the job.

Another wave of pain and then Robyn's knees were beside my cheek. Her hands were pulling on my shirt, ripping at it without moving my body. The sharp intake of breath when she saw the wound, and her eyes held mine as the only comfort she could give. The file had been ripped free when she lifted my shirt, and it lay flapping in the pool of blood, taunting me with my failure.

"We'll need an ambulance," she called out, and I wanted to say that they should send for a genuine one, not the fake one driven by my crazy ex-captain. But Scarface was already on his radio, and I saw Robyn press the call button on her phone. She took an extra three seconds to rest a hand on my cheek. I was grateful for that. Then another wave of pain came to push me into unconsciousness.

———

I struggled back above the surface to find Scarface kicking at me with his boot. I was lying on my back and could see a nightmarish red light painting the ceiling above him. On the other side of me stood Lategan, a phone pressed to his ear.

"You Gabriel?" he shouted, as if I was lying at the bottom of a deep well. I didn't respond, and so Scarface kicked me again. "Johansson's friend Gabriel?" shouted Lategan, and when I still didn't respond Lategan turned away from me and said something into his phone about the man bleeding all over his parking lot. Scarface gave me another kick and then I felt myself floating upwards and heard Chandler's voice saying "Gently now" and hoped that he'd stayed out of sight of Lategan. I found his face, and he had a mask and full personal protection on. Lategan wouldn't have recognised him. Chandler pushed my stretcher into the back of the ambulance where Fat-Boy was sitting with a drip and looking as if he too had been wounded. His face was drooping, almost blue in colour, and shining with sweat.

There was an altercation at the door. I heard Chandler say only one guard could ride with us, and she was already sitting up front. The door slammed closed and the grotesque skull of Sidekick settled beside me as the ambulance lurched forward.

———

Engines throbbed and echoed around us as we waited to leave the underground parking. Then we accelerated and the drumming of rain sounded on the roof. I focused hard on pushing the pain to the back of my mind. I needed to hold onto the thin thread of consciousness. Sidekick's skull face was looming over me as if he was trying to say something. I breathed the acrid smell of his breath. Then his face moved away from me and I realised that he had turned to Fat-Boy. I twisted my head to see what he was doing as the ambulance turned abruptly onto the road and the siren moaned itself up into key, and we accelerated. Sidekick stumbled against my stretcher, and I saw the flash of the long blade in his hand.

A burst of adrenalin surged through me, riding a wave of unstoppable rage. I found the strength to roll onto my feet and grabbed the bony hand that held the knife. The skull face turned back to me in shock, and I twisted the hand and felt the bones crack. Sidekick screamed, but still held the knife in his crippled hand. The ambulance jerked to the side as Chandler mounted a pavement, and I felt the long blade penetrate my side with a fresh burst of pain. The skull face grimaced and he tried to twist the knife, but I had my elbow up and struck his exposed windpipe. He gasped and fell back into Fat-Boy. I considered using the knife for a moment, but the energy the rage had produced was beginning to drain and knew that killing him with a knife would take too long. I turned away from him and kicked at the back door of the ambulance. It burst open and the glass in the windows shattered into small fragments which rained onto the road rushing away beneath us. I felt Sidekick's arm come up around my throat and I twisted under it, using his momentum to push him towards the open door and the fleeing road. He realised too late what I was doing and panic twisted his face as he grabbed onto the edge of the rim above the door. He hung there like an enormous spider trying to cling on. I used all the force I had left and kicked him.

His hands gave way, and he dropped back and collapsed in a heap on the wet road. The headlights of the car behind us swerved abruptly and narrowly missed striking him, but in swerving it struck a car going the other way and there was a dreadful crunching bang and the sound of skidding as other cars tried to stop on the wet road.

"What the fuck?" said Fat-Boy. "He was a security guard. You killed him. What the fuck?"

As I pulled the door closed, I saw Sidekick stumble to his feet. The headlights of cars behind him silhouetted his narrow body and cast his shadow towards us through the rain like a monster rising from the deep.

"I didn't kill him," I said. "I should have."

"Who are you?" said Fat-Boy. "Who the fuck are you? How the fuck did you do that?"

I didn't answer him because I felt the tug of the unconscious. I felt no pain, only a nagging regret. It would be some time before I realised the cost of having spared Sidekick's life. I dropped back onto the stretcher, and my consciousness floated up and away.

NINETEEN

R obyn was sitting under a wooden sash window with light coming in at a shallow angle and catching the steam rising from her mug. Her hair was pinned back, and she looked stern. The nurse on duty. She had a book in her lap and both hands around the mug as if she was trying to warm herself up. Like an advert for cocoa, the girl next door relaxing in the mountain hut before a night of unexpected intimacy. Mountain hut because the walls were stone, and the chair was made of natural branches like some kind of DIY craft project. Robyn looked up at me and found my eyes on her. She didn't burst into song or jump up and down with joy. She sat there and looked at me.

"Where are we?" I asked.

"Franschhoek," she replied. "Up the Franschhoek pass." She didn't sound overwhelmingly happy about it. "I'll call Colonel."

The Franschhoek pass ran through the Hottentots Holland Mountains, which formed a protective arc separating the Cape Peninsula from the rest of Africa. We would be about an hour's drive from the city, depending how high up the pass we were. I had just got around to wondering whether I was smelling breakfast or dinner, when Chandler came into the room wiping his hands on a dishcloth with pictures of wildflowers on it.

"You had us worried," he said in an accusatory way.

"I had it under control," I said.

"Sure you did. The bullet ricocheted off the concrete. That guy with the scar can't shoot for shit. Didn't even get all the way through you. The doc pulled it out, and said there was a knife wound too, but I said that was none of our business so he left that."

"Thanks," I said.

Chandler allowed himself a small smile.

"Fat-Boy said you frightened him."

"I'll be sure to apologise."

"Damn right you will. The doc pumped you full of drugs and said it would be eighteen hours before you'd surface." He consulted his watch. "You beat him to it by twelve minutes. Excellent." He beamed another flat-line smile in my direction. "Now get some clothes on and join us on the veranda for supper. That's enough lying around feeling sorry for yourself."

―――――

The little getaway retreat Chandler had rented was snuggled into the folds of the Hottentots Holland Mountain, and from the terrace we had a view over the lush vineyards of Franschhoek where Chandler claimed some of the world's best wines were made. He even had some of that wine for us to drink with the lamb chops he'd cooked on the outside fire, although everyone agreed I shouldn't have any, what with the amount of drugs I had in my system. And although the lamb smelt delicious and Fat-Boy said it was the best he'd ever tasted, I couldn't bring myself to have any. I nibbled on a slice of bread that Chandler called bruschetta because he'd toasted it on the fire, and I wondered whether I should get a second opinion on the fact that my internal organs were undamaged. For all I knew, the 'doc' Chandler kept mentioning could have been his vet.

Chandler placed a bent and stained cardboard file on the table before me.

"Robyn picked it up," he said, "and Fat-Boy cleaned the blood off."

They could see my surprise. I thanked them, but Chandler held up a hand. "Less said about it the better," he said. "But we got something out of the archives after all."

Fat-Boy was chewing a lamb rib. He finished it and put it down. "Not the gold, though," he said, and stared glumly at the clean bones on his plate. "I couldn't breathe. That fucking vest."

"We got out with our lives," said Chandler. "That's what counts."

Fat-Boy looked up at me. "There was a knife," he said. "In the ambulance. When we got you out of it, we found a knife."

"That man didn't intend for us to reach the hospital," I said. Fat-Boy nodded and forced his lazy eye a little wider to get a good look at me.

"You not eating that?" asked Fat-Boy, indicating my untouched lamb. I pushed the plate over to him. He picked up a rib but hesitated before biting into it. "I didn't mean that stuff," he said. "What I said in the ambulance. I couldn't breathe, I was all confused."

I said I understood, and Chandler poured more wine for us. He raised his glass.

"May you have the hindsight to know where you've been," he said, "the foresight to know where you are going, and the insight to know when you have gone too far."

"What the fuck you talking about, Colonel?" said Fat-Boy.

"It means that we're done," said Robyn, whose eyes were smouldering angrily from the dark corner seat.

"It does," said Chandler. "We're going our separate ways as soon as we finish dinner." He turned to me. "That man Lategan has been scanning hospitals and clinics for a man with gunshot and knife wounds. He knows your name, and he's watching your apartment. So you stay here a few days. The doctor insists you need bed rest. Think you can do that?"

I said I thought I could.

"I've asked Robyn to stay on and act the nursemaid. She's agreed." He turned to her for confirmation.

"I have," said Robyn without enthusiasm.

———

Chandler and Fat-Boy left after dinner. Chandler shook my hand and told me not to call him if I had any other hare-brained ideas, and Fat-Boy tried a few new grips on my right hand and said he hoped we'd not meet again. I found Robyn sitting on the terrace gazing out at the vineyards. Puffy clouds were glowing orange underneath, like alien spaceships being heated by the lights of Franschhoek. Robyn was holding a cup of cocoa in both hands and blowing into it like a breathing meditation. She had made me some, and I sat beside her on the cane couch, sighing with relief as the foam cushions supported me and eased the pain.

"You didn't tell the Colonel about the wine," said Robyn, as if we were resuming a conversation, although she had not said more than a few words to me since our disagreement on the roof of the match factory two days earlier. Even now she did not look at me, but kept gazing out at the alien clouds.

"I didn't."

"You should have." Robyn turned to me, and her eyes were full of anger. "We're a team, and that's how it works. You should have told him."

"It didn't affect us. Nothing would have been gained by telling him."

Robyn said nothing, and we sat in silence for a few minutes.

"That last operation," Robyn said suddenly, "on the mines. Brian told you about what we'd decided?"

"Was it something about your wedding?" I said, casting my mind back reluctantly.

"No," said Robyn.

I thought back again. I remembered the night we'd celebrated their decision to marry. The meal at the steakhouse, Brian drinking too much red wine, and Robyn's laughing face lit by candles. A table full of the candles Brian had insisted the management bring in order to better see his bride-to-be.

"We didn't talk about those kinds of things when we were in the field."

"No?" Robyn looked at me with cool eyes through the steam from her cocoa. "What did you talk about?"

I shrugged. "Meaningless things. Things that wouldn't distract. Things we wouldn't find ourselves thinking about when we had an ADF fanatic pointing an AK-47 in our faces."

Robyn sipped her cocoa and nodded. "I remember that. I had to promise never to call or write. Brian was obsessive about keeping his focus."

She put her cocoa aside, and lay back on the couch, her arms folded tightly about her. I could smell the scent that was uniquely hers. The combination of soap and shampoo and freshly washed clothes. It was not so much a smell, but the absence of a smell, a fragrance that sneaked in between breaths.

"What had you decided?" I asked.

"We had decided not to get married. To end it. We had separated."

"I had no idea. He said nothing about it."

Robyn was biting her lip, looking as if there was anger building up inside her.

"I have wondered so often whether Brian told you," she said.

"Why? I mean, why had you decided to split up? I thought ... it sounds trite, but you two were happy."

Robyn turned to me. Her eyes were brimming with tears. One of them ran down her cheek, and I felt a familiar punch of guilt.

"You're such an arsehole, Ben, you know that?"

"You've already told me that part of it."

Robyn's mouth opened and for a moment I thought she was going to shout, but it was a laugh that came out.

"You know why we decided not to marry," she said.

The evening went suddenly quiet. Robyn's face was close to mine, her eyes dancing slightly as she looked from one of my eyes to the other. The silence was filled with a rush of memories. Moments that I had misunderstood, actions I had misinterpreted, foolish mistakes crowding in on me.

"You need to stop doing this to me, Ben," she said.

"Stop what?" I asked, but I wasn't that stupid. I said it so that the moment would linger. Being that close to her, feeling her breath on my lips. But she pulled away and snuggled up to her cocoa mug.

"Brian could see it," she said. "The way you looked at me. The way you avoided us. You stopped coming around. Avoided places we used to hang out. It was Brian who pointed it out. He could see how you felt. You need to stop looking at me like that, Ben. Stop thinking about me like that. Just stop."

"I didn't realise I was that transparent," I said. "Why didn't Brian just tell me to bugger off? I would have done that for him. Travelled to the other side of the world."

"Brian didn't tell you to bugger off because he didn't blame you."

My cocoa was strong and sweet. Robyn had probably put twice the recommended amount of everything into the mug.

"Didn't blame me? Who did he blame? He had nothing to blame *you* for," I said.

"Didn't he?" Robyn turned away from me and her cheek was damp. "Sometimes you seem fairly bright, Ben. Perceptive even. But most of the time you're just dense. It isn't only our actions we're responsible for. Our thoughts and feelings are ours to own as well."

Robyn finished her cocoa and put down her mug. She turned to me.

"You're such a fool, Ben," she said, and rose from the couch and went inside, leaving me to read between the lines and figure out what it all meant.

I didn't sleep that night. Chandler had been right about my having spent enough time lying around, although it was not true that I felt sorry for myself. I sat on the terrace and smoked too many cigarettes and paged through the file we'd stolen from the archives. It answered some of the questions I'd been asking about the death of Lindiwe Dlomo, but it raised many more.

I ran out of cigarettes as the eastern horizon started to glow. That was when an absurd idea occurred to me. One question I had the answer to was the one Du Toit himself had suggested I ask: what personal reason had kept Fehrson away from the operation? The absurd idea came to me because there was something else that was bothering me. And as the sun poked its head above the parapet, it came back to me. Lategan is shouting angrily into his phone after identifying me as the friend of the journalist Johansson. He listens to the response of the person on the other end of the line, says a couple of "yessirs" and "no-sirs", and finally he says what sounds like a name. I am being lifted into the air. Scarface has given me a last kick, and is it my imagination, or does Lategan say "Fehrson"?

TWENTY

A northwesterly wind was blowing over Cape Town the next evening. When that happens, the clouds roll down the front of Table Mountain and spill themselves as soon as they strike the big houses at the top. A little further down, in among some of the older buildings of the city, is a late-night coffee house called Roxy's that charges too much for an Irish coffee, and an outrageous amount for their mud pie. The theme is old movies, and everything that doesn't move is plastered with posters. Vivien Leigh swoons in the corner while Cary Grant watches the exits. I sat at a table next to the big windows and stared out at the rain. Not a gentle apologetic drizzle, but an aggressive, defiant rain. A couple scurried across the square with a coat over their heads, and arrived at the restaurant across from Roxy's, dripping with water. They were swallowed up into the warmth, and the square was deserted again. In Roxy's the music changed from Edith Piaf to a collection of Italian arias and Khanyi arrived, folding an umbrella and hesitating at the door like a frightened buck, her big eyes scanning the room. African print trousers hugged her thighs and splayed out to give breathing space to the four-inch heels of her clogs. A tight-fitting top had a ruff of artificial fur like a lion's mane, which balanced itself precariously on top of her breasts, deceiving the beholder as to the amount of breast she was actually displaying. It all had the desired effect. Eyes followed her as she moved over to my table.

"If I'd known we were dressing up, I would have put on my cowboy suit," I said.

Khanyi showed me two rows of exquisite teeth. She would not spoil the entrance with a scowl.

"And I was going to try to be nice to you," she said with a mock sigh.

A waitress arrived at our table. Khanyi ordered espresso coffee and a glass of ice without looking at the menu, or taking her eyes from me. It was all part of the performance, and I've got to say it was pretty effective.

"You had a question," she said when the waitress had left.

"Is the name Lategan familiar to you?"

Khanyi wrinkled her brow and stared over my shoulder as if the answer was in one of the movie posters.

"Lategan," she repeated. "I don't think so. Should it be?"

"He's a big cheese at the Gold Archives."

"Oh, Gabriel," Khanyi sighed. "You're not still going on about those files in the archives? They don't have them. I told you to drop the whole thing."

"It turns out that this file didn't go missing after all," I said, and placed the battered file on the table between us.

Khanyi frowned at it.

"Is that blood?" she asked. She looked back up at me and tilted her head to the side as if that way she could see me better. "And what's that look on your face? Are you in pain?"

Shifting on my chair to reach for the file had caused the cut in my side to open up. It was bleeding again.

"No," I said. "It's just the look people get when they know it's too late to get out of this dirty business."

"Don't do your big experience thing with me, Gabriel. You're not in this dirty business anymore. Besides, I've studied all this stuff."

That was right; she had. In the brief time that I'd worked for the Department, I'd made things up as I went along, which was how I thought everyone did it. But Khanyi had been doing the training courses. I kept forgetting that.

The waitress arrived with Khanyi's espresso. I took another bite of the mud pie.

"The thing is," I said. "This man Lategan has your boss on speed dial."

"He does?" said Khanyi. She spooned three sugars into her espresso, then poured the coffee into the glass of ice, and used the spoon to stir it vigorously, making a terrific noise of clattering glass. "Why is that a problem? Perhaps they golf together over the weekend?"

"It's more complicated than that. Lategan recognised me as a friend of Johansson, the journalist."

"I thought you said you weren't friends."

"We are now," I said. "But regardless of the status of our relationship, Lategan made a connection between us."

"When you were asking Lategan for this file? After Father explicitly instructed you to leave it alone?"

"Who do you think it was that decided that this file should conveniently go missing?"

"You're a conspiracy theorist, aren't you?" said Khanyi

with derision. "Convinced the world is out to get you. What on earth are you on about, Gabriel?"

"I'm on about Lategan," I said. "And your boss. If Fehrson told him to deny access to this file, then he is protecting someone."

"Someone," said Khanyi scornfully. "You mean the president-elect. Are we back on that one again?"

"Maybe. I would like you to take a look at the file."

"We're back to your big conspiracy, are we? The president-elect is a killer, and Father is complicit in his crime by protecting him. Why don't you just confront Father directly? You want me to hold your hand, Gabriel? Is that it?"

"I wanted you to see the file," I said. "Before I speak to him. Then tell me I'm wrong."

Khanyi said nothing. She blew over the top of her drink and caused a small cloud to rise from the glass. As a screen for her to hide behind it turned out to be inadequate.

"Why?" she asked.

"The first page," I said. "The one that explains why a young black girl in the apartheid years happened to have contacts in military intelligence."

She sipped at her iced coffee and gave me the innocent under-the-eyelashes routine. Then she sighed, placed her glass back into the saucer and opened the file. It didn't take her long. She closed the file and looked back up at me.

"I don't understand," she said.

I explained the crazy idea that had come to me as the sun rose that morning. Khanyi laughed sarcastically and shook her head in dismissal of my idea.

"Come in and talk to Father tomorrow," she said. "Ask him your questions. I'm sure he will answer them."

"When has Father ever answered my questions?" I said

and smiled to show her it was a rhetorical question. But seriously, when had he?

"I know why you came to me," said Khanyi, her head tilted to the side, the better to see my pain.

"Why was that?"

"You want me to hold *Father's* hand, don't you? Not yours. I'm beginning to think you might have a heart after all, Gabriel."

"You have it all wrong," I said and took a mouthful of mud pie.

Khanyi finished her iced espresso and stared across at the *Invaders from Space IX* poster. Three remarkably humanoid figures were firing brightly coloured lasers at some uniformed humans. You knew the ones in uniform were the good guys because they had short-cropped hair, good looking faces, and they were all dying.

———

Fehrson was an angel recently descended from heaven to spread some bad news. His antique desk was arranged so that he had his back to the window, and his white hair was glowing like a halo around his head. His office was crammed so full of antiques that one could hardly move, but there was a comfortable old-world smell about it that always made me feel as if I'd stepped fifty years into the past.

"Thank you for coming in, Ben," Fehrson said to me as if it had been his idea, and he smiled wearily.

"I spoke to you last night, Father," Khanyi piped up to remind us all that she was doing her job.

"Of course you did, my dear, of course you did," Fehrson said vaguely. His eyes drifted past us and alighted on something on the wall behind. He brightened percepti-bly. "Did you notice something?" he asked.

I turned to look. There were seven old clocks on the wall, some of them wheezing so badly they didn't sound like they'd make it to midday.

"A new clock?" I said.

Fehrson glowed with pride. "Picked it up yesterday. Can you believe it? An original Frodsham mantle clock. I didn't think I'd ever lay my hands on one of them. Signed dial, original Earnshaw-type spring detent escapement. It's magnificent."

Of all possible locations in Cape Town, Fehrson's department had its offices one block from an antique market. Sometimes I pitied him. He was frightened to leave the building in case he saw something that he had to buy.

"Does it go?"

"Go?" Fehrson frowned at the irrelevance of the ques-tion, chose to ignore it and switched track suddenly. "Some-thing about telephones. That's what our Khanyisile said. Is that right?"

"It's about a phone call that you received a couple of nights ago," I said. "From Lategan, the man who runs the Gold Archives."

"Oh yes?" said Fehrson vaguely. "Lategan? Do we know a Lategan?"

"We don't," said Khanyi.

"Well then," Fehrson turned to me as if that concluded the matter, and a regretful smile twitched at his lips.

"I went into the Gold Archives," I said. "A few days ago. To get hold of a file on Lindiwe Dlomo."

"Those files went missing," said Fehrson. "I did tell you that."

"Except that they didn't," I said. I placed the file on his

desk. Fehrson's eyes flickered down to it, then back to mine with surprise. "Isn't that why Lategan phoned you?" I asked. "To tell you that something had gone wrong with hiding the files."

The door opened suddenly, and Belinda came in with a tray of three steaming mugs.

"I've given up asking Belinda to knock," said Fehrson, perhaps grateful for the change of subject, but Belinda pretended not to hear. She handed me my mug which said on the side 'Too dumb to work, too poor to quit'.

"I made it strong," she said and gave us all a glare before leaving again.

"Something went wrong," I repeated. Fehrson looked up from the white lumps floating on the top of his coffee.

"You're telling me something went wrong," he said. He pressed the squawker on his desk. "Belinda, come and remove this stuff immediately. It's making me ill." There was only silence in reply. Fehrson sighed.

"Something went wrong at the archives," I persisted. "That's why Lategan called you."

Fehrson tore a small piece of paper from a report on his desk and started trying to soak up the white lumps from the top of his coffee. He said: "Attempted robbery, that's what the man said. He said the whole file thing was a smoke-screen. That the files were just an excuse you used to get into the building. What on earth were you trying to steal from them?" He looked up at me with angry incredulity.

"Lategan called you because it was at your request that the file went missing," I said.

Fehrson tut-tutted, but I think that was because he was discovering the science of menisci the hard way. "Non-sense," he said. "Goodness me! What has happened to you, Gabriel? Using your connections with us to embark upon a life of crime? I had no idea that you had abandoned sanity to this degree."

"And you requested they block access to the files because there is someone you are protecting," I persisted.

"Sheer and utter nonsense," said Fehrson, and then he held up his hand suddenly with an anxious stare at the wall behind me.

"Father, there is something that Gabriel has discovered," said Khanyi. "Something that we feel should be discussed. I was hoping ..." But Fehrson shushed her. He kept his hand up in the air and rose silently from his chair. He moved around the desk and approached one of the clocks behind us, silently so it wouldn't notice. It looked like an old school clock, with a huge, cracked face, faded numbers and a weathered wooden frame. Fehrson held his ear up to the clock, and his face screwed itself up with concentration. The prognosis was obviously not good. His hand dropped to his side, and his eyes opened to contemplate the floor. Khanyi gave an irritated cough to remind him we were there.

"It stopped," he said.

"Well, it's not the fact that it goes that matters surely, is it?" I said. It seemed to me that a moment ago Fehrson had been scornful of the fact that I considered it important. Khanyi had asked me to keep the conversation friendly, and I was doing my best, but sometimes Fehrson could be more than a little trying. He looked at me now through fresh eyes. He'd not realised that I could be so perceptive.

"You're right, of course, you're right," he said and gave a deep sigh, but he didn't move.

"I was hoping," said Khanyi again putting a little more force behind her delivery, "that we might discuss the background to the Lindiwe Dlomo case again. We know how she came to be introduced to the Department."

Fehrson looked up at her. Then his gaze returned to me, and a shadow passed across the blue sky of his eyes. He returned to his seat, sat down heavily and grasped the edge of the desk as if he needed something to hold on to.

"It wasn't the Department," said Fehrson. "Not in those days." But his voice had lost some of its jaunty impatience, and his eyes drooped a little as if he was ageing before us.

"Lindiwe was adopted," I said. "You told me about Lindiwe's domestic-worker mother who had such a kind employer. She encouraged Lindiwe to study along with her own child. That kind employer was Cindy."

Fehrson looked up at me as if I'd thrust a knife into his chest. "Your wife, Cindy," I added stupidly. "It was Cindy who insisted that Lindiwe do her homework at the same table as your son."

Fehrson let go of his desk, and his shoulders sagged. A silence fell on the room. The ticking of the clocks swelled to fill it.

"What if it was?" he asked.

"You didn't mention it," I said.

"Why should I? Her family history wasn't of any interest to you. You wanted to know about what she did with the service. What she did to Mbuyo. I told you."

Fehrson's clear blue eyes held mine, and for a moment, before his anger rushed in to cover it up, I glimpsed the pain.

"Would knowing this have changed anything?" Fehrson sat forward again and his indignation gave him renewed strength. "You came back to us flinging all kinds of accusations about, and I think we've been very patient. Now you have the gall to come back demanding to know details of my personal life. Let me remind you, Ben Gabriel, that you were damaged goods when I took you in. Well-nigh unemployable. And now you're back to dig around in my personal life?"

"I think that you asked the archives to hide those files because you are protecting someone."

"Protecting someone?" cried Fehrson. "You think I would do a single thing to protect that man Mbuyo?"

"No, I don't," I said. "That's the point. You would not protect the man who killed your adopted daughter."

Fehrson looked up at me with his big blue eyes. He took a deep breath and let the rest of his anger out with a sigh. "The word 'adopted' makes it sound cold," he said. "She was a part of our family, not only on paper but ..." He cast about for the right word. A bony hand came up to his chest, and he held it there as if about to take an oath. "Just because some misguided friend of yours dreams up a conspiracy involving her doesn't mean that I'm obliged to tell you about my personal life. Telling you her family history wouldn't bring her back, would it?"

I had no answer for that. We sat in silence for a moment.

"It was not Mbuyo that you were protecting by hiding the files, was it?" I said.

Fehrson's gaze came back to me.

"It is your daughter that you are protecting," I said. "Lindiwe."

"Don't be absurd," said Fehrson. "My daughter's been dead thirty years. Why would I protect her?"

I hesitated. He was right. This was the absurd bit, and I knew Fehrson would deny what I was about to say, but I needed to detect the truth behind the denial.

"Because she hasn't been dead for thirty years," I said.

"Perhaps she isn't dead at all. Is that why none of the files mention the manner of her death? Because she is still alive?"

"That's preposterous," said Fehrson. He turned to Khanyi. "Take this man away will you, Khanyisile? Whatever damage those special forces did to him is obviously irreparable. Take him away."

I could see the flash of anger in Khanyi's eyes as she stood up. I'd overstepped the mark. I also stood.

"Did Lindiwe know anyone with the clan name of Faku?" I asked, careful to pronounce it the way Fat-Boy had, not like Johansson.

Fehrson looked up at me. Behind his anger, his eyes shone with painful regret. "Her name was Mona," he said. "A girlfriend. They used to insist I call her by the clan name so they could have a giggle at my foul mouth."

I moved to the door where Khanyi waited to escort me out. Fehrson looked back to the clock that had caused all the trouble earlier. It was not ticking. He stood up slowly, as if every joint in his body was giving him pain. He walked up to the clock and stood before it, like he was about to engage in a conversation with it. Khanyi's mouth opened as if she wanted to say something, but she thought better of it, and closed the door.

TWENTY-ONE

Khanyi's office was a floor below Fehrson's. It provided a view over the leaking sewerage pipes of the internal courtyard, and with the window open the buzz of flies reached in with the stench.

"You're going to need me," said Khanyi. She opened a bottle of mineral water which was lined up with two glasses on a plastic tray on the old school desk that she used. She poured us both a glass. The tiny room was like a narrow slice of corridor that extended between the window and the door, furnished with cast-offs. One wall was lined with bookshelves of the most tedious books; it was rumoured that Khanyi read history for entertainment. Papers and reports covered the school desk, different coloured folders representing various levels of security. I noticed that, being the good girl she was, there were no red papers on her desk. I sat on the old wooden chair that faced the desk.

"Need you? For what?"

"Who is Mona, of the Faku clan?"

"I thought you would be angry with me," I said. "It didn't go as well as I hoped with Fehrson."

"But you were right about Lindiwe still being alive," said Khanyi. "Who is this Mona?"

"Johansson, the journalist, claimed his source was someone from the Faku clan."

"That's why you need me," said Khanyi. "I can find her."

"I'm not sure there's any point. If Lindiwe is still alive, Mbuyo clearly didn't kill her."

Khanyi smiled. Big even teeth, a whole lot of them, sparkling white against her dark skin.

"You won't shake me off that easily, Gabriel. You're not going to drop this. If there is one thing I know about you, it's that you are no quitter. If you're about to destroy this Department by exposing some big cover-up, I'd like to know about it."

———

The skies darkened with more rain clouds as we waited for Khanyi's contact at the Xhosa heritage museum to provide us with details of all the Monas in the Faku clan. Khanyi transformed her office into a cosy cocoon of orange light by means of desk lamps whose dusty globes provided only the illusion of warmth with the tungsten light they dribbled over her school desk.

"The *iziduko*," said Khanyi, putting a soft click in place at the front of the word so it sounded as if she was tut-tutting to herself, but then turning it into a word, "are like Scottish clans," she said, "only brown. Our clans are like an extended family. Cousins and cousins of cousins, all of whom make up our clan."

Khanyi's phone announced the arrival of a message. There were only three Monas. The second one Khanyi called, Mona Mxolisi of the Faku clan, remembered Lindiwe Dlomo, of course she did. They were the best of friends, weren't they? Was this because of what she'd told that journalist? She would be happy to meet us, and she knew why we wanted to talk about her friend, even though she had been dead for so many years.

"You do?" said Khanyi with a look at me to be sure I'd heard that.

"It's that man, isn't it?" said Mona Mxolisi. "That man they say will be the president."

———

The drive to Khayelitsha took over an hour in the heavy afternoon traffic leaving the city. We wound our way around the foot of the mountain, then turned east onto the highway. Corrugated iron shacks started appearing beside the road, and then they clustered closer and thicker so it felt as if we were driving through a forest of them. We were in my old Fiat because Khanyi was certain that if we took her new Volkswagen, it wouldn't return with all its hubcaps. The clouds coming in off the Atlantic grew steadily darker, and they finally engulfed us as we turned off the N2 highway. My windscreen wiper was missing most of its rubber bits, and so we completed the journey in anxious silence as Khanyi pressed the floor with her brake foot every time I approached the blurry shape of another vehicle in front of us.

Most of the tar on the road leading to Mona Mxolisi's house had disintegrated, and large crevices and pools of water made it into an obstacle course. We were forced to weave from one side of the road to the other, while avoiding oncoming traffic, and being careful not to leave one of our wheels behind in the large water-filled potholes. A cart laden with bundles of chopped kindling slowed things further as the horse pulling it struggled over the terrain. Beside the road a wide strip of dust was being churned into mud, and a stream of huddled pedestrians picked their way along it, heading home from work, or making their way to an evening shift, several with plastic bags held over their heads to protect them from rain. A man carried two chickens, one tucked under each arm, and several of the women carried all manner of things in the traditional African manner: piled on top of their heads. As we moved closer to the old centre of the township, the tin shacks gave way to more established houses. They were small, only two or three rooms to a house, but built of brick and had glass windowpanes.

Mona Mxolisi had been looking out for us, because the door opened as we approached it, and she stood there watching us splash our way up the muddy track that led to the front door.

Her hair was beaded and curled onto her head like a sleeping snake. She wore a loose caftan over her ample figure, and as we approached, she held out a welcoming arm which jingled with bangles and bracelets.

Her house was a warm cave, a comfortable shelter from the rain, the cold, and even the constant presence of poverty outside. It was a tiny two-roomed house. Every surface of the front room held artifacts made from papier mâché, reworked cooldrink cans, even the roots of trees. Mona was a teacher at the local primary school, and the objects were the work of her students, testament to the love they had for her.

A kettle was boiling, and Mona made us strong *Rooibos* tea which she served with lemon.

"I knew I should have kept my mouth shut," she said.

"Should never have said anything to that journalist. When they announced that monster was going to be the president of the country I knew it would not be long before I'd be sitting here explaining myself."

"Monster?" asked Khanyi.

"Oh, yes." Mona smiled and sipped at her tea. "He's a monster, but no one knows it. Isn't that the truth of this world?" Her bangles played a quick melody as she placed her teacup back into its saucer.

"By all accounts he's a hero of the people," I said, trying not to make it sound sarcastic.

"And there's the irony, isn't it? Because he spent time on Robben Island, he is a hero. But because I spend time in the church, does that make me a saint? We are not defined by our location, but by our deeds."

Mona's face was serene, a constant amused expression on it as if everything she saw struck her in some way as being odd. But it was an amusement tinged with regret.

"And his deeds … the things the president-elect did … he did something … monstrous?" asked Khanyi.

Mona nodded. "He did."

"Something to Lindiwe?"

Another nod. Mona sipped her tea.

"It's too late for justice, though," said Mona. "Isn't it?"

"We don't know that it's too late. Some crimes deserve justice no matter how many years have passed."

"I suppose so," said Mona, and her bangles gave another burst of music.

"We wondered whether he might have been responsible for her death," said Khanyi.

"No," said Mona. "The monstrous thing he did was not to kill her."

"Could you tell us what he did?" said Khanyi.

"No one knows about it," said Mona. "That journalist was the only person I told, and I saw that he died in an accident." She pulled a tissue from her brassiere and used it to wipe her eyes. "I'm sorry," she said through the tears that had suddenly sprung there, "it's so foolish of me after all these years."

We sat in silence for a moment as Mona composed herself. The room had a slight haze in the air, and I noticed a stick of incense burning in a holder on the kitchen table.

"I didn't understand where you said you came from," she said when the tears were dry. "You're not with the press are you?"

"We're in the civil service," said Khanyi as if that had some meaning.

"I wouldn't want to talk to the press again. That journalist was a mistake. They drag everything out into the open, and before you know it they've twisted all your words, and you're the one in trouble."

"Not press," said Khanyi, and Mona felt good enough about that to pour her more tea.

"I do have to tell someone," she admitted. "Because there's nobody else who knows about it. They're all dead, aren't they?" She smiled as if that was a good thing and sipped some of her tea.

"All the people who knew what he did to Lindiwe are dead?" I said.

"That's right. All burned." Another sweet smile.

"He did something to her before the fire?"

"It was long before the fire. Must have been two years before. She was only sixteen."

"Could you tell us about it?" I asked.

"I could," said Mona. "And should." She drew a deep breath. "Lindi and Wandile had been an item as we used to say, for only a few months. They were like soul mates. Or what is it they say today? Twin flames. From the moment they laid eyes on each other it was a union that was inevitable. At least it seemed that way to all of us, her friends. A union made in the heavens." A pause, another sip of tea.

"Wandile was the brother of Thulani?" I asked.

Mona nodded. "But Wandile's brother, the monster, he also noticed Lindi's beauty. Did you know she was beautiful? Not the emaciated sticks they put in magazines now, but the kind of beauty that takes your breath away when you're with them, and that stays with you afterwards. I still feel her beauty, here in my heart." Mona placed a hand on her ample bosom. "Because her beauty was not only physical. It was her spirit. It was something that never dies."

Mona stood up abruptly and moved over to the kitchen area where she busied herself filling a kettle with water.

"Then that night," she continued with her hand on the kettle and her gaze directed out of the window at the miserable dusk. "That night she and Wandile were having a night out, and Lindi had me along as chaperone. She and Wandile had kissed, but no more. In those days it was different. It wasn't drugs and alcohol and sex at the age of fourteen. It was holding hands and sending messages to each other on scraps of paper. Or telling a friend to tell their friend, you know the kind of thing." Mona gave the kettle a shake to encourage the water to boil faster.

"It was at the Nyanga Bar on the corner of Street Three. It's gone now, of course, but if I were to go there now, I wouldn't want to approach within a hundred metres of the place. It was a dive. No lights. Most of Khayelitsha had no power back then, it was like one big campsite, and the paraffin lamps ..." Mona emitted a low 'whooo', "so dangerous. But there was enough light from the paraffin lamps in the Nyanga Bar for the monster to see Lindi, and to be reminded of her beauty."

Another shake of the kettle. From the chair on which Mona had been sitting, an orange cushion detached itself and stretched. It was an enormous ginger cat which yawned, stretched again, gave a brief purr like a tractor getting started, then lay down again.

"He saw her and he wanted her for himself," continued Mona. "For himself and his friends. Monsters, all of them. Even the word monster does them no justice. The words *umoya o ngendawo* in Xhosa are better, but that's not a phrase you know. Foul spirits ... You need a word that is so awful you cannot bring yourself to say it.

"They sent Wandile to get them all drinks, then told me he'd need help carrying them. Such a sweet man, Wandile. He didn't know how to get served at the bar. Timid as a mouse. Stood behind the crowd and we waited while he hoped the barman would see him. We were underage, but Wandile was already tall, and so he just stood waiting for the barman to see him. The barman wouldn't bother about our age. There was no 'show me your ID' in those days. In any case the monster brother already had a reputation, and everyone knew him. They all loved him, as the entire country does now. But in those days it was just the locals who knew him. They loved him because he was brash. He was angry and repulsive. They loved him because he was a bully. We needed a bully. That's what they said. Needed a bully to fight the oppressors, stand up for ourselves."

The kettle boiled and Mona refilled the teapot and brought it back to us. Her cheeks were moist, gentle tears rolling down them. She smiled through the tears as she refilled my cup. "Eventually the barman did see poor

Wandile. He looked very much like the monster brother. A skinnier version, but there was a strong likeness, and so Wandile benefited from the love and respect everyone had for the monster. That's something I often wonder, even to this day. Why all the respect, all the love for that man? Am I the only person in this world to see him for the monster he is? How does no one else see it? Of course, Wandile saw it, and he's looking down on me now, I'm sure. Shaking his head and urging me gently to tell the world what a monster his brother is." Mona reached for the tissue again and dabbed at her face. Khanyi sipped her tea noisily.

"Wandile didn't even have to say what he wanted, the barman just handed over the beers. That was all we used to drink back then, Lion beer. He handed Wandile the five beers for the monsters, and then three for us, which I carried.

"By the time we got back to the table where we'd left Lindi, they were all gone. The monsters, Lindi, all of them. It wasn't like it is now, that you go outside to have a smoke. We all just smoked wherever we liked. So we didn't expect to find them gone." Mona noticed the cat beside her and stroked it absently. The cat produced the loud tractor-like purr.

"I saw Wandile begin to panic. He knew his brother, and he didn't like finding them all missing.

"We went out into the street, Wandile and me. It was crowded, young people standing around breaking the law by drinking outside the premises, but who cared about that? The police would cruise around in their yellow Casspirs, but we'd know they were coming long before they got there. I'm thinking to myself: Lindi has come outside with the older boys because she doesn't want to sit at the table alone. We'd taken a long time to get those beers."

"It was cold, bitterly cold, and the breath of all the street drinkers formed little clouds above their heads. I remember that clearly. There was one bright light at the end of the street, and I remember how all the groups had clouds above them that caught the light. We went from one to the next, looking and asking. Wandile's panic built up, and I kept saying it's OK, Wandie, they've gone back home. They've gone to buy weed. They'll be back."

"I don't remember how long we searched. Two, three hours? We went back to Wandie's shack, but there was no one there. We went to the shacks of all his brother's friends. Nothing. Back to my shack where Lindi was staying for the weekend. She lived in the whitey's suburbs, but she would come and stay with me to see Wandile. Nothing."

"Back at the bar later and Wandie can hardly breathe now, he keeps saying 'they've killed her, I know they have'. I stop denying it. What can I say? I follow Wandie back in, and there is the monster! There he is. All the monsters. Back in the bar. He's got a scratch on his face, and a bruised eye that will be bad in the morning. Wandie runs at him. 'Where is she?' The monster laughs. He laughs." Mona stopped and dabbed at her eyes again with the tissue which was beginning to disintegrate in her hands. Khanyi made a sympathetic clucking sound.

"Then Wandie hits him. Good and square in the face and a fight breaks out. They haul him out the door and beat him. I try to stop them, but they lash out at me, and another boy from the school holds me back and pulls me away. It's between the brothers he says, nothing to do with me. They stop the beating when he stops moving, and they leave Wandie lying in the street. I go to him, and he's just groaning with pain. But he's breathing and still moving. I help him up. Then we start looking. Wandie leaning on me so much I have to keep stopping to recover my strength. His face is smashed, his eyes swollen so he can hardly see, and there's a new black hole in his nice white teeth except now they're all covered in blood. We walk around and around, calling and looking.

"All night we do this. The streets go quiet about three in the morning, maybe four. There are no phones. In those days we didn't have little computers in our pockets, or even watches on our wrists. All I know is we're alone in that black night, just the two of us. One foot in front of the other, calling for Lindi.

"Then there's some light. Not much, but there's light in the sky and I can see the bushes beside the road. And then I see Lindi too. She's lying in the ditch next to the road. I drop Wandie right there, and I scramble and fall down the side of the ditch. I know in my heart she's dead, and when I get to her, she doesn't move. Her face is down in the dust, and I grab her shoulder and roll her over. Her face is all blood. But then she groans. She's alive."

Mona sipped some tea and gave the cat another stroke. "I don't know how Wandie and I got her back to my shack. My mother was a nurse, and she had everything. Lindi lay in that bed of mine for three weeks. I phoned the whiteys she lived with. Told them Lindi was ill. They wanted to come and fetch her, but Lindi stayed with us."

Mona sighed as if a great ordeal was over. Her bangles played another merry tune as she reached for her tea and drank.

"They took it in turns," she said. "All five of them. The others held her down and when she struggled they hit her until she passed out."

"She didn't go to the police? Report it?" asked Khanyi.

Mona shook her head. "Not back then. We talked about

it. But what good would it have done? The monster was the leader of the pack, he was destined to be the saviour of our people. Already everyone was saying that. He could have whatever woman he wanted as far as they were concerned. The police were mostly white, they'd point their guns at us and throw tear-gas to keep us inside the fences. But a little domestic squabble? What did they care?"

We sat in silence for a moment and then Mona turned to me. "So you see, the monster did kill her. She died that night."

"And later," I asked. "Two years later. After the fire. What happened then?"

"After the fire she came alive again," said Mona. "For a few days. She came to me and said, did I know that Karma had come to town? That they'd all died in a fire. She was like another person, her eyes full of hope. The monster was dead, and Wandile was badly burned, but he would survive. Her life would come back to her. She said that. But of course it wasn't Wandile who survived the fire. The monster survived. It wasn't karma after all. Sweet Wandie, so gentle and full of love for her, who'd been beaten all his life by his monstrous brother, and had his heart ripped out of him when they raped her. He was the one who died, and the monster survived."

"What happened to her after that?" I said.

"She faded," said Mona. "That's what she did. When she discovered it was not Wandile lying in that hospital bed, the lights went off and she faded."

"The files don't explain how she died. Was there an accident? A crime?"

Mona shook her head. The tears had stopped now, but her eyes were red, and her lips trembled.

"They said they found her body in a ditch, just as I had

found her before. Like a wrinkle of time, as if she had never left that ditch. Said it was suicide, but Lindi was stronger than that, despite everything."

"Is Lindiwe still alive?" I asked.

A silence filled the room. Mona looked at me. She stroked the cat again, fuelling another engine start which was so loud it swelled to fill the room.

"Where did you say you were from?" asked Mona.

"We work for the security policeman who adopted Lindiwe," said Khanyi. "Father Don Fehrson."

"Father?" said Mona.

"He was once a priest."

"I didn't know that," said Mona. "We used to call him the Frightener ... no that's not right ... Fearsome ... that was it. He was a kind man, I remember, but I didn't know he was a priest. Lindi used to say there were good people on the other side, they weren't all oppressors, and he was one of the good ones. Did her adopted father send you to see me then?"

Khanyi opened her mouth to deny it, but I beat her to it.

"Yes," I said. "He told us you were one of Lindiwe's closest friends."

"You should have said he sent you," said Mona. "I wouldn't have wasted so much of your time."

"She is still alive?"

"For thirty years I have kept her secret," said Mona. "But that monster is going to find her now, isn't he? He's going to find her, and finish what he started."

"We would like to prevent that," said Khanyi.

"I will give you an address," said Mona. She heaved herself out of the chair and wrote something on the edge of a page in a notebook which she tore from the book and folded up carefully. She handed Khanyi the folded paper.

"There will be no justice, will there?" said Mona. "I knew that, even when I told that foreign journalist some of the story. I should have told him that the monster had killed her, and I'd seen it with my own eyes. There might have been some justice then, but there will be no justice for the victim of a gang rape."

Khanyi looked regretful, but there was no denying it.

"A bit like that story from Cape Town," said Mona. "I'm sure it's not true, just an urban myth. The woman who phoned the police because there was an intruder in her house, and they told her it would take them half an hour to get a patrol car there, and she should protect herself as best she could. She knew half an hour meant two hours – this is Cape Town after all. So she called them back and said: 'Don't bother, I killed the intruder.' Three minutes later the helicopters arrived."

Mona laughed at her story. The telling of Lindiwe's tragedy had lightened her somehow.

———

The rain was still coming down hard. Khanyi and I were both drenched by the time we had squelched our way through the mud and climbed into my car. Khanyi opened the folded paper while I banged the dashboard in the hopes of getting the heater to work. She unfolded it carefully lest it might disintegrate upon exposure to the daylight.

"KwaZulu-Natal," she said. "Near the Zulu battlefields, my homeland. Let's get to the airport."

"Shouldn't you be getting back to the office?"

"Sometimes, Gabriel, you act as if you are the only person with a moral compass. You're not."

"What will Fehrson say about you disappearing?"

"I'll tell him I'm with you."

"He'll say I'm corrupting your mind. Hasn't he warned you off me? Told you I'm suffering from post-traumatic stress disorder and have obsessive-compulsive tendencies?"

Khanyi laughed. "He would suspect something far worse."

"What could be worse?"

Khanyi's face darkened. She turned away from me to look into the haze of rain. "You know ... a journey to the battlefields ... a bit of time away."

She turned back to me, and I realised she was blushing.

TWENTY-TWO

Our flight to Durban brought us in at the dying end of the day. If Cape Town had been miserable, Durban was suicidal. The thick bank of cloud that had tossed our plane around on final approach went all the way down to three hundred feet, and from there it spat at the earth with such force that I thought our hired car might not ford the river of water running in the channels beside the road. We turned onto the R33, heading into the old Zulu battlefields in the foothills of the Drakensberg mountains.

The address that Mona had given us was a three-hour drive from the airport, a tiny village in the heart of rural Zululand. The road approaching the village looked on the map as if it might be treacherous as it wound its way down the valley and across the Tugela River, particularly in bad weather. Two hours into the journey I spotted a temporary signpost that warned the road was closed for fear of flooding. We were only a few minutes outside the town of Dundee, so we turned back.

The old Central Hotel was a building that dated back

almost to the famous battles of Isandlwana and Rorke's Drift. In grand colonial style it had a wide veranda upon which sat a group of ancient locals surveying the comings and goings of the town. They watched us with interest as we dashed through the downpour, Khanyi in a bright orange raincoat that floated behind her like a superhero cape.

The receptionist explained that horse and cart tours around the town and guided tours of the battlefields would only be possible if the rain stopped by morning. I was more interested in the location of the bar and met Khanyi there an hour later, after she'd refreshed herself. She arrived looking sparkling and fresh, causing the old men on the veranda to lose their false teeth.

The bar was like an English country pub, with dark wood panelling and paintings of historical battles. I'd had the opportunity to go around the room twice and study the etchings from the early 1800s by the time Khanyi joined me.

"It was England's most expensive war to date," said Khanyi, "including the Second World War, the Falklands, Afghanistan ... all of them. Did you know that?"

I admitted I hadn't known it.

"They came here thinking they would quickly deal with the local native problem, but they hadn't accounted for the Zulu warrior spirit." Khanyi sipped at her sparkling mineral water and her eyes glistened with the warrior spirit. "Did you know the Zulus killed almost every member of the force at Isandlwana? It was a massacre."

"I did know that," I said, thinking of the conversation Robyn had with the Zulu waiter. "But the next day the British fought back and evened the score at Rorke's Drift."

"Yes," said Khanyi regretfully. "Everyone knows the Rorke's Drift story because the British won." She peered at an etching of a man on a horse in a field of dead bodies. "That's Lord Chelmsford, the British captain, coming back to his camp to find all his men dead."

"Where had he been?"

"Chelmsford took half the British force out of the camp, chasing what he thought would be a disorganised scattering of Zulus. The Zulus spent the night running from hilltop to hilltop, lighting fires to give the idea that they were spread out, so Chelmsford took his men the next morning to go hunt them. They didn't find a single Zulu. But back at the camp they heard gunfire from the lookouts and found a valley filled with over six thousand Zulus."

"It must have been a nasty shock."

"Even nastier for Chelmsford when he got back to the camp and found all his men dead and disembowelled."

"Disembowelled?"

"It's Zulu tradition. After you kill someone you disembowel them as a sign of respect. It releases their spirit."

"Good to know," I said, and drank a little whisky to keep the demons at bay.

"You judge Father too harshly," said Khanyi, her eyes still on the figure of Chelmsford on his horse. "He's a good man, he is genuinely concerned for the people he works with. Including you. He hasn't warned me about you. In fact he's encouraged me to keep you away from your merry band of thieves."

"My merry band?"

"He's convinced you've started down a spiral that you'll never escape."

"A spiral into?"

Khanyi shrugged. "A criminal life, I suppose. He's not said it in as many words."

A man and woman came into the bar. The man was in his forties, pock-marked skin, a scowl and an evening suit. He nodded his head in surly greeting. The lady had her hair pinned back and was wearing a flowing silk evening dress. Her greeting was a tight smile. The two of them sat at the bar and looked past each other as if they were watching the exits. There was something incongruous about them but I couldn't put my finger on it.

"Father doesn't approve of the way you got hold of that file," said Khanyi.

"Sometimes," I said, "you need to step outside of the law to achieve an outcome that is entirely legal."

Khanyi smiled and raised her glass of mineral water as if making a toast.

"You see," she said. "Now you're justifying it."

"At least we're not still winding up clocks and denying we've heard of anyone called Lindiwe. If I remember correctly that was the official approach."

"You're so stuffy when you get angry," said Khanyi. "I don't mind if you want to go off and do criminal things."

"I hope you'll modernise the Department when they put you in charge."

"In charge? Don't be ridiculous."

"It's what everyone says will happen."

"Everyone says?" said Khanyi, sipping her water. "What do you mean, everyone says?"

"What else do you think they're all talking about when they stand around the water cooler?"

"Nonsense," said Khanyi, and she blushed, sipping at the water to hide her fluster.

"It would be an awful mistake," I said. "I'm sure it won't happen."

"You can be such a jerk, you know, Ben."

"I know. It's been pointed out to me before."

Khanyi regarded me from beneath her heavy black lashes.

"What do you think would happen if we all stepped 'outside the law' as you put it?"

"Anarchy," I said.

"That's what you'd enjoy, I suppose?"

"I've spent most of my life fighting for it."

Khanyi considered that for a moment and her eyes narrowed.

"I'm onto you," she said. "You never say what you mean, do you, Gabriel? Most of what you say is the exact opposite of what you mean. It's pathological."

"It's worked out alright for me so far," I said.

"What do you really think about me heading up the Department?"

"Awful idea," I said and treated her to a rare full-toothed smile.

———

But later that night, as I sneaked a cigarette on the small balcony of my room and looked out over the wet and bedraggled town of Dundee, I wondered about what she had said. The bit about the spiral. I thought of Chandler's fall from grace. Special forces captain to confidence trickster and thief. He'd always told me I was too much of a rebel for the military, and I'd sometimes wondered if it took one to recognise one. I'd not allowed myself to think about it, but

I couldn't deny that what we'd done in the archives had felt … felt what?

It had felt right.

The time I'd spent with Chandler, Fat-Boy and Robyn had been like belonging again. And I hadn't experienced that feeling since parachuting into the scene of a plane wreck in the North Kivu region of the Congo.

TWENTY-THREE

D undee was given a brief reprieve by the rain in the morning. As we left for the village of Masotsheni, the couple I'd seen in the bar the night before were mounting the horse-drawn cart that would take them to all the places where the colonials had been most successful in killing the natives. I waved at them in greeting, and the man waved back.

"Good thing the rain's stopped," he called out in a strong American accent. "Doing a tour of the town, then out to the battlefields."

"Should be a fine day for it," I called back.

"If the weather holds," he said with a doubtful look to the sky.

"You two have a lovely day," added the woman. "Such a lovely place to honeymoon."

"Honeymoon?" said Khanyi from the passenger seat. "Does she think we're on a honeymoon?"

"And later we might take in the live re-enactments," said the man as he climbed into the cart.

"I didn't know they did that," I said.

"Honeymoon?" said Khanyi again, her voice rising.

"Rubber spears, and the bullets are duds," said the man regretfully. "But they say you get the feeling for being right there on the battlefield." The driver of the cart opened a blanket with a flourish, like a magician about to make them vanish. The blanket settled on their laps, and he tucked in the edges to keep them warm.

"But without the fear of being disembowelled," I said.

The man laughed. "Except by the wife," he said and chuckled so much that it turned into a coughing fit.

We didn't wait to see whether he survived that.

"Honeymoon?" said Khanyi again as we turned the corner.

"It's a natural mistake, I wouldn't get hot under the collar about it."

"You should have put them straight," said Khanyi.

"I was working around to it."

"Except for the wife?" she said incredulously. "What sort of people does he think we are, that we would find that funny?"

I shrugged. "Just go with the flow, Khanyi. We can't control what people say to us."

"But we can control what we say back," she said. "I've a mind to get you to turn back and tell him we don't appreciate comments like that. That's the problem today. Everybody assumes you think the way they do. And we don't. Do we?"

"I'm sure we don't," I said.

The Ngwebeni valley is a piece of raw Africa dropped into the heart of modern-day South Africa. When you crest the Impati ridge, you are treated to its breathtaking beauty. And something else: a sense of the reality of life lived off the land. As we descended the hair-raising Noustrop pass, winding in and out of the folds of the Endumeni slopes, we gradually transitioned to the other side of life, leaving the guided tours and trappings of modern life behind. Khanyi kept holding her mobile phone up to ensure she still had a signal and gave disgruntled noises as it faded away.

The road was narrow, the surface broken and potholed. The edges crumbled away into nothing in some areas. As we descended the side of the mountain, there were places where the precipitous slope dropped away from the road so steeply that I had the sensation we were floating above a void. There was no fence or railing in parts, and an error of judgement on the tighter turns would have ended in disaster.

We reached the bottom of the valley and Khanyi spluttered with indignation at the fact that her phone had no signal. Here the road straightened itself out to build courage for crossing the Tugela River, which gushed through its narrow ravine with enthusiasm. The bridge was a rusted iron structure that looked as if it hadn't been designed to last as long as it had. Two great big iron hoops spanned the hundred-metre gap, with spindly cables suspending the precarious platform across which we were expected to drive.

"Get some speed up," advised Khanyi.

"What about the people?" I asked, for the bridge appeared to be a meeting place for the locals who were standing around chatting, a cluster of children showing off by climbing the suspension rods and hanging precariously over the rushing water.

"They'll move," said Khanyi with equanimity.

I chose instead to slow down, and we inched our way across the bridge, which made worrying sounds as the wooden planks that supported us shifted and groaned under the weight of the car.

"You're sure this isn't a pedestrian bridge?" asked Khanyi as the people she had been so confident would move showed no inclination to do so until the front bumper of the car nudged them out of the way.

On the other side of the river we picked our way between tumbledown buildings which formed the commercial centre of Tugela Ferry, then we broke out into open ground. I accelerated up the hill. Our destination was ten minutes ahead.

Khanyi turned to look across the valley, and gasped with surprise. On the precipitous slope beneath the road we had just travelled were the skeletal remains of a dozen cars. Most of them had been reduced by fire or time to their structural frames, but a few more recent ones were still solid, and gave the bizarre impression of vehicles trying to make their way down the slope, some of them on their wheels, others on their backs like beetles struggling to right themselves.

Another few minutes of jostling along the muddy surface of what should have been a road, and we arrived at Masotsheni. More of a hamlet than a village, it was a cluster of houses, small cubes built of brick with rusty iron roofs.

The address on our slip of paper was for a larger house which sat a little distance from the others, higher up the slope of the hill so it looked like a mother duck with a brood of chicks at her feet. It was by no means a grand establishment, but it must have been five times as big as the other houses and had a wide veranda which wrapped around three sides of the house. It had a touch of Cape Dutch style in the high gable and the dirty white of its walls.

On the veranda a figure was standing watching our car

struggle along the path. Someone with short-cropped hair, so that from a distance they cut a slender, manly figure. We abandoned the car a hundred metres from the house and completed the journey on foot. As we approached, the high cheekbones and wide eyes became evident. She was an attractive woman in her early fifties.

At her feet were a trio of small girls, none more than five years old, and about the veranda were other children, some sitting on the dishevelled chairs, one in a homemade hammock, and one of them, the oldest, standing in a proprietorial way at the front door.

"We guessed you were coming for us," said the woman as we approached. "Bongani has been watching your approach." She indicated the older boy who nodded in confirmation of this and held a pair of binoculars up to demonstrate how it had been achieved.

"We are sorry to arrive unannounced," said Khanyi. "We had no number."

The woman laughed, an open-mouthed, friendly laugh. "You needn't worry about that. I have no phone. Now come on children," she clapped her hands. "You should all go inside and make us some lemonade. Our guests don't want to be stared at, they've come to speak to me, not you rabble."

The children moved off reluctantly, herded into the house by the older boy.

"How did you find me?" asked the woman when the last toddler had disappeared.

"Mona Mxolisi." Khanyi said, with the soft 'tsk' click in the surname.

"Mona wrote to me and said someone was stirring the pot," said the woman. "A journalist asking questions. I wrote back that she should send anyone else my way. I knew it was just a matter of time. Are you journalists too?"

"Not journalists," said Khanyi. "We are civil servants. Government employees."

The woman's face flickered with a smile. "Government?" she said.

"We work for a small government department, under Don Fehrson," said Khanyi.

"Ah, you're that kind of civil servant." She studied us calmly with her wide, gentle eyes. "How is my father?" she asked.

"He's well," said Khanyi. "Well enough."

"He and Cindy are good people. They didn't deserve any of this."

A small gust of wind buffeted us as we stood in silence for a moment.

"Why don't you sit down?" Lindiwe suggested. "The children will be ages making the lemonade."

"All yours?" asked Khanyi, and we sat down on a lumpy piece of furniture that might once have been a couch.

"Goodness no. None of them are mine. They're orphans. I have no children of my own."

Lindiwe sat elegantly on the edge of an armchair, her hands clasped on her knees and her back straight like she was holding a yoga pose.

"Have you come to take me back?" asked Lindiwe. "Make me pay for my sins?"

"No," said Khanyi with some confusion. "Not at all."

"That's a pity," said Lindiwe and she turned to look out at the valley which spread itself beneath the house like a tapestry. In the distance clouds were stacking themselves into vast towers which would soon reach the sun. Lindiwe's face still had a simple beauty, but the cheeks were a little too drawn, her big eyes little hollow.

"Endumeni," she said. "That mountain peak there. The

place of thunderstorms. You will see, we'll get another one soon."

"We've come to ask a few questions," I said. "The journalist you mentioned, the one who visited Mona, died in what might be suspicious circumstances."

"Died?" said Lindiwe. "Because of what Mona told him?"

"More likely because of the conclusions he drew from what she told him."

"Which were?"

"We're not entirely sure," I admitted. "He didn't get the chance to express them."

"We made the assumption," said Khanyi, "that he was making incriminating allegations about the circumstances of your death."

"Reports of my demise have been exaggerated," said Lindiwe. She smiled regretfully.

"An erroneous assumption," admitted Khanyi.

"Incriminating who?" asked Lindiwe.

"Thulani Mbuyo," said Khanyi, then added, "The man who is to become president of the country," as if that might remind Lindiwe who he was.

"Oh, that man," said Lindiwe, and she smiled again. "No, my death was all my doing, I can assure you."

"But your need to disappear," I said. "It was driven by a fear of what Mbuyo might do to you?"

Lindiwe's eyes flickered back to me. "Might do to me?" she said.

"After the fire in Khayelitsha," I said. "If Mbuyo knew the part you played in that operation, he might have been driven to take revenge?"

"Oh goodness," said Lindiwe. "There was no operation. Surely you know that?"

"The files are a little confused when it comes to the details of the operation that led up to the fire," I said.

"There was no operation," said Lindiwe. "No operation at all. And Mbuyo knew very well the part I played. He is not seeking revenge for anything."

Lindiwe turned to look out at the valley. "When I saw your car approaching," she said, "I felt a sense of relief. You have no idea what a burden guilt can be. I hoped that the time had come for me to pay for my crimes."

"Your crimes?" I said.

"Oh yes." Lindiwe turned back to me, her eyes filled with tears. "You see, the murderer you are looking for," she said, "is me."

I couldn't find anything to say. Khanyi too was silent.

"But now you say a journalist has been killed?" asked Lindiwe.

"He died," said Khanyi. "We're not sure how or why."

"I can tell you why," said Lindiwe. "But first I want you to know that I killed those men in that hut. I don't deny it. I didn't do it alone, but I did do it. The Khayelitsha massacre. It was a massacre, but it was not political. It was murder. My father and his government department would have everything political. But sometimes killing is simply killing. And I killed those men."

Lindiwe paused, and we waited. She turned abruptly and looked out over the valley again.

"Mona told us what Mbuyo and the others did to you," said Khanyi eventually.

The clouds chose this moment to obscure the sun, and it felt as if someone had switched off the heat. Lindiwe shivered. "I took my revenge," she said. "I killed them all. It is as simple as that."

"But Mbuyo survived the fire," said Khanyi. "Isn't that why you staged your disappearance?"

Lindiwe kept looking out at the valley as if she was waiting for something to happen. She shook her head.

"No, it isn't," she said. "I was not running from the men who raped me. They are all dead, every one of them. Killed in the fire."

"But the man who survived," I said, struggling to fit the pieces of the puzzle back into place. "Who is he?"

"I have not been running from Thulani Mbuyo," said Lindiwe. "I've been running to protect him. And to protect myself. We've both been running from the truth."

"Who is he?" I asked again.

Lindiwe stood up abruptly and moved over to the edge of the veranda where she stood like she was at the prow of a ship.

"Wandile," she said.

We sat for a moment in shocked silence. I said: "The person we know as Thulani Mbuyo is his brother Wandile?"

Lindiwe nodded.

"They would have killed him," she said. "Worse. They would have necklaced him, then hung him from a street-lamp for all to see. They would have come after me, the Fehrsons, my friends, his family. They would have killed us all."

"Are you saying," said Khanyi, "that the man who is becoming president of the country is not Thulani Mbuyo? It is Wandile Mbuyo?"

"It was my idea," said Lindiwe. "I realised he would not survive. I knew we had been deceived."

"Deceived?" I said. "Who deceived you?"

"They called him a man on the ground, or some such

nonsense. He was the man Wandile met with when he had something to tell them."

"And he deceived you?"

"Oh yes," said Lindiwe, and she looked back out at the valley. "He called himself Frans. A student at the university, a member of the youth league, always standing up and shaking his fists at the rallies. Chanting the slogans, waving the flags. But he was a fraud, a government plant."

The door to the veranda opened and two young children emerged, balancing a tray with three glasses and a plate of sandwiches. Behind them four other children followed, their eyes wide with curiosity, and they gathered in a circle to watch us. Khanyi sipped at her lemonade and flinched at the bitter taste.

"Delicious," she said, "did you make this?"

The children nodded in unison.

"So clever," she said. I sipped at mine. It was pure lemon juice as far as I could tell.

Lindiwe's eyes twinkled. "We don't add sugar. So bad for us, isn't it?"

The children murmured their agreement.

"Has something happened to him, mama?" asked one of the five-year-olds as she gave me an accusatory stare.

Lindiwe laughed. "Of course not, angel."

"You've been crying," said the little girl in defence of her argument.

"Well, nothing is wrong."

"Mama has a man," confided the little girl to Khanyi. "A man she loves."

"That's a wonderful thing," said Khanyi.

"But he hasn't visited for a long time," said the girl with a touch of anger.

"Back inside children," said Lindiwe. "I want to see your homework all done when I come in."

They reluctantly moved back in, the talkative girl giving me a particularly intense look as if to commit my face to memory. Just in case I did turn out to have been the bearer of bad news.

"From the mouths of babes," said Lindiwe. "Wandile has not visited us for many months, for obvious reasons. They love him, he is such a kind man. He is no saint though. He wasn't one and isn't one. He killed his own brother. We both did."

"What the brother did to you was unforgivable," said Khanyi.

"Was it? He left me alive, which is more than we did for him. And does it make it any better that Wandile did it out of love for me? If anything, it makes it worse. I live with that every day." Lindiwe finished her lemon juice and winced at the bitter taste of it.

"You know what I think?" She smiled at us. "I think Wandie knew it would be unbearable and had no intention of living to bear that guilt. He wasn't caught in that fire by mistake, which was what I thought at first. He never talks about it, but I think he closed the door of that shack, bolted it behind him and prepared to die with them. It was the final twist of our fate that he was the one that survived. Survived to know that he had killed his own brother out of revenge for what he had done to a woman he loved and would see only occasionally for the rest of his life."

"Could you tell us more about the man called Frans?" I asked.

"I had told Wandile I didn't trust him, but I only realised what he had done when I met with that man Du Toit. After the fire."

"What had Frans done?"

"Frans was one of those good listeners. He heard everything Wandile told him about what had happened to me. The two of them would meet for a drink and Wandile would pass on information about what his brother was up to. Wandile probably drank too much, said too much to Frans. Frans was like the serpent in the grass. He started whispering about what his people would like to have happen to Wandile's brother and his gang."

"So you thought the fire was a state-sanctioned operation?" said Khanyi.

"Yes, we did. But I make no excuses. I did what I did out of hatred. The whispering of that snake was no excuse. He knew what to say, that was his talent. And we wanted to hear it."

"But why?" said Khanyi. "Why did he pretend it was a state-sanctioned operation when it wasn't?"

Lindiwe looked at Khanyi, and her wide eyes were full of kindness.

"He was a weakling," she said. "He did it because he wanted to kill. I could see that in him, could see it in his eyes, and I should have realised. I too wanted to kill. We were all young and dangerous. His whispers offered us the chance, that was all."

"And Wandile?" said Khanyi.

"Wandile did it out of love. For me. But what does that matter? There is no justification for killing. Whether it is for hatred, revenge, love or by permission of the state. It is killing."

Lindiwe's eyes settled on me, and for a moment I had the sensation that her remark was directed at me, as if she knew of the blood on my own hands.

"When you discovered Frans had deceived you," I said,

"you had the idea that Mbuyo should adopt his brother's identity?"

"I met with Du Toit, and he told me there had been no operation. We'd been lied to. Frans had been trying to find me, and I realised why when I met with Du Toit. Frans wanted to kill me. The hospital had mistakenly identified Wandile as Thulani, and I knew that if he revealed the truth Frans would kill him too."

"You persuaded Du Toit to get you in to see Mbuyo on Robben Island?"

Lindiwe nodded. "By then Frans was hunting me. I was on the run. Wandile had disappeared behind the blank screen of the apartheid machine and I knew that he would tell them who he was. That information would get back to Frans. By then I had realised how dangerous Frans was."

"But you told Du Toit it was Mbuyo you were running from?"

"I told everyone it was Mbuyo I was running from. Nobody knows who he is. If I had told Du Toit the man without a face they had sitting on Robben Island was Wandile it would have got straight back to Frans. Du Toit said that Frans had disappeared, but I couldn't trust a word he said. I couldn't trust any of them."

"And Wandile accepted your idea?"

"Not at first," Lindiwe gave a sad smile. "We had half an hour. That was all, with a policeman at the door. Wandile knew that Frans was a maniac. That Frans would get to him. But I think he wanted it. Welcomed it even. He wanted to pay for his crimes, and if that came through the hand of Frans that was okay with him."

"He didn't come clean though. The world knows him as Thulani, not Wandile."

"That is another of my crimes," said Lindiwe. "Perhaps

the greatest of them. When he refused, I asked him to do it for me. Unlike Wandile, I did not want to stand up and pay for what I had done. I wanted to run, and I wanted Wandile to live. I imagined we had a life ahead of us."

In the distance, the clouds produced an experimental roll of thunder. From the veranda we could see the full extent of the valley, see the perilous road descending from the Endumeni ridge, the bridge which from this distance appeared to leap over the deep Tugela ravine, and beyond to where the African grasslands merged into the haze beneath the building thunderstorm.

"And if Mbuyo confesses now, it would destroy him," said Khanyi.

Lindiwe nodded. "It would. And kill him. And kill me. I used to have fantasies of telling the truth myself and reclaiming the life I lost. Not a day has passed that I haven't wondered, could I tell the truth now? But it would expose him as a traitor and a killer. Because make no mistake – that is what he is. A traitor to his people. He might have found his faith over the years, but he betrayed them thirty years ago. He killed his own brother and betrayed his people in the process. And I helped him do it. Thulani Mbuyo was one of the big hopes for the South African people. His death set back the fight for freedom in this country many years. With each passing year I wonder: is it a little more forgivable? What if we tell the truth now? Wandie has done some good things, would he be forgiven now? But I don't think that kind of betrayal fades over time. Or does it?"

"He had his reasons for what he did," said Khanyi as if that mitigating fact might contribute to the fading of the betrayal.

"He did, but what do they count for now?"

From inside the house came the sudden howl of a young

child in pain. Lindiwe was on her feet before I'd even identified the sound. "Let me see what the little devils are up to," she said and disappeared into the house. A few moments later the howling was silenced, to be replaced by strident denials from another child.

"Who was Frans?" asked Khanyi.

"He is not identified in the file," I said. "Du Toit raised warning flags about him. He believed what Lindiwe told him and put it into his report: that their man in the field had fooled Lindiwe and Wandile into thinking they were carrying out an approved action. But Du Toit was laughed at. Mocked for falling for the desperate pleas of a pretty young woman. They refused to identify the man in the field. Everyone claimed not to know who he was."

"That's not unreasonable, they would have had cutouts," said Khanyi. "It was how they worked. Limiting knowledge of the chain. It protected their people in the field."

"And exposed them to megalomaniacs with homicidal tendencies," I said.

From the house came the sounds of a truce, some laughter and excited chatter. I watched the tower of clouds in the distance. The sky here seemed huge, as if our position on the hill above Masotsheni provided us with more sky than normal. The base of the cloud was heavy and dark, resting just above the level of the foothills at the far end of the valley. At the top the cloud became puffy and white like a squashed chef's hat. But the anvil shape of a thunderstorm was forming, and occasionally the entire formation lit up with a flash.

Lindiwe came back out to the veranda. "Their dramas are always so big," she said. "It's comforting sometimes to focus on the little problems in life. Helps to put everything into perspective."

———

We spent another hour on the veranda as the storm built up and moved ever closer. The children treated us to a second dose of lemon juice and they glared at me in case I made Lindiwe cry again, which I didn't.

"Why do you think the journalist died?" I asked Lindiwe as she walked with us back to our car.

"There were three of us," said Lindiwe. "Each of us played our part in killing those men. I am ready to pay for my crimes. I believe Wandile is ready too. But one of the three is not ready. Mona told the journalist the first part of my story only. She has been a faithful friend all these years and kept my secret. But that was enough for him to stir the pot. And one of us didn't want that pot stirred."

"You mean Frans?" said Khanyi.

"Wandile tells me they see each other, isn't that amusing? Frans has done well in business. He's involved in politics too, as so many big businessmen are. It has been Wandile's fate that they have been brought back together. Frans looks at Wandile's broken face and doesn't recognise him. Wandile keeps his mouth closed because he knows Frans is still looking for me. I beg him to tell Frans where I am. Let him come for me, I am ready."

"But Wandile refuses?" I said. "Refuses to tell Frans where you are?"

Lindiwe looked up at the sky as the first heavy drops of rain fell. "Wandile refuses," she said. "But now, with everything that is happening, it will not be long before Frans finds me, and realises who Wandile really is."

"Who is Frans?" I asked.

Lindiwe looked back down at us. "I don't know," she said. "Wandie speaks of him as Frans, when we speak of him at all, which is hardly ever." She smiled. "When your car approached, I thought perhaps my time had come. That Frans had sent you to bring an end to it all."

"He must be stopped," said Khanyi.

Lindiwe shook her head. "You haven't been listening. I want Frans to come. Don't you see? It is time."

"Is there somewhere you could go?" I said. "Just for a few weeks?"

Lindiwe laughed. "With twelve children? Not likely."

"Consider taking some precautions at least. For the sake of your children."

"The children will be fine. Wandile pays for all of this. He's made sure it will continue after we are gone. It's our legacy. One small bit of good we can do, after all."

The storm loomed overhead as Khanyi and I climbed back into the car. I reversed back into the gully that served as a road and watched Lindiwe dash back to the shelter of the veranda. Khanyi shook her phone as if that might help it recover reception.

We struggled down the slippery road in silence, the driving consuming my attention.

"I've been a fool," I said after a few minutes. "'We have nothing to fear from the truth' – that is what he said. Those words exactly. 'We have nothing to fear. But carrying it can become a burden.'"

"You will have to draw me a diagram," said Khanyi. "What are you saying?"

I turned the windscreen wipers up as the storm suddenly engulfed us. The winding track would soon turn to mud, and I was keen to reach the tarmac before we were washed away.

"They are both tired of carrying the burden of their truth. You heard Lindiwe say it. What a relief it would be if Frans came to end it all. For thirty years they have carried their burden, but they have had enough."

"What are you saying? That they are waiting for that man Frans to end it? End it how?"

"By finishing what he started all those years ago."

"We need to stop him. Find him and stop him."

"We do," I agreed. "And there is only one person who can tell us who he is."

———

The moment Khanyi's phone showed a glimmer of connectivity on the perilous climb back out of the valley, she called Fehrson.

"Father," she said, oblivious to the irony of calling him that. "I've got you on speaker. Ben can hear you."

"What on earth do you mean he can hear me?" said Fehrson.

Khanyi explained that her phone had a loudspeaker. Then she explained that we needed an audience with Mbuyo.

"Certainly not," said Fehrson.

"It might be important," said Khanyi.

"Might it? Oh well, in that case," said Fehrson with heavy sarcasm. "I'm sure that he will cancel his address to the nation. Have you forgotten that's tonight?"

I had forgotten. The televised address to the nation before his inauguration as state president.

Fehrson sniffed. "I'll see what I can arrange for next week. You two having a nice time?" he asked archly.

Khanyi gave me a warning look. "Very nice, thank you sir," I said.

"Don't let that man get you into any more trouble, Khanyisile," said Fehrson, and he ended the call.

———

We continued through the storm, which sent squalls of rain across the road like the giant folds of a lace curtain.

"You think the battlefield re-enactments were cancelled?" I asked.

"What do you mean?"

"That couple we spoke to this morning," I said. "The ones watching the exits in the bar last night. They must have changed their plans. We passed them a few minutes ago."

"The Americans?" said Khanyi. "They're just tourists, Gabriel."

"I'm not so sure."

"Father's right about you."

"In what way?"

"You let your paranoia get the better of you."

Another squall hit us, and I slowed down as the visibility reduced. Khanyi went quiet, I gave a non-committal grunt and did my best not to look paranoid as I wondered why the man had been wearing a holster under his jacket that morning when he climbed into the horse-drawn cart. And why his American accent had slipped into flat South African tones on his final "except by the wife".

I pulled off the road, flicked on the hazard lights and waited for a gap in the traffic.

"What are you doing?" said Khanyi.

"They are not American tourists," I said, and swung us around in a tight u-turn, killed the hazard lights and accelerated in pursuit of the small yellow car I had seen pass us.

"For goodness sake, Gabriel," said Khanyi, but she went silent as I negotiated the treacherous pass at a speed that left no margin for error. There were not many cars on the road, and they were all driving in the poor visibility at a sensible crawl. I pushed past them at speed and we had a few worrying moments as the headlights of vehicles travelling in the opposite direction loomed suddenly out of the haze. There were several junctions where side roads joined the road we were on, but I didn't see any yellow cars moving down them. We took the wooden bridge at speed, and arrived again within sight of Lindiwe's house.

There was no yellow car, no fake American tourists with shoulder holsters. The bonnet of our car produced a thin mist of steam as the rain continued to fall. The lights of Lindiwe's house were on, a warm refuge from the cold and rain.

"Happy?" asked Khanyi. "There's nobody here."

A few of the kids were out on the verandah, and I saw Lindiwe come out to call them in. I had been wrong about the couple in the yellow car. Perhaps Khanyi and Fehrson were right and I was simply paranoid.

"We'd better get to the airport," said Khanyi. "And this time could you keep to the speed limit?"

———

We came out on the other side of the storm as we approached the airport. The sun shone benignly, and anxious little gusts of wind were the only sign that the foul weather was doing its best to catch up with us. Khanyi went ahead to get herself a bottle of mineral water while I loitered outside the terminal building with a cigarette.

Bill answered my call with a reluctant grunt. I explained to him what I wanted, and he grunted again, in a not entirely negative manner it seemed, but then he told me he wouldn't do it.

"You still causing trouble for that new president?" he asked.

I admitted that I was, puffed on the cigarette and waited. He sighed heavily.

"I'll call him," said Bill.

"The Nyanga Bar, don't forget. A mutual friend from the Nyanga Bar," I said.

"I've written it down, Gabriel, have a little faith."

I finished my cigarette and watched the ominous wall of cloud approaching from the Drakensberg. One way or another, that weather seemed determined to reach me.

TWENTY-FOUR

Jacob Matlala had been squeezed into a brand-new suit. Dark navy blue with red stitching. It was the kind of suit that befitted a member of parliament, and one could overlook the fact that his physical presence had swelled a little beyond the initial expectations of the haberdashers, because he was now so important that details like that were trivial. His eyes glinted with scorn as I met him in the foyer of the VIP suites of the Green Point Stadium. I wasn't wearing a new suit, and the wound in my side had opened. It left the smear of a bloodstain on my shirt, which because my jacket's zip had broken was displayed to public view as I tried not to limp across the shiny marble floor.

"I don't suppose that you are the mutual acquaintance from Nyanga Bar," said Matlala.

As the Nyanga Bar had closed before I reached an age of double digits there seemed little point in denying it.

Before they ushered me into the presence of their supreme leader, a couple of bodybuilders ran their hands over me, checked the stitching of my hems, then asked me to smile for the security camera. I had the feeling that tensions were mounting.

The president-elect was standing at the glass wall of the VIP suite, gazing out over the floodlit stadium. Matlala instructed me to wait as he approached the dark silhouette of his leader. The stadium beyond them was so bright that it felt as if we were in a cinema, watching a panoramic 3D movie. Mbuyo didn't turn but laid his hand on Matlala's shoulder and whispered something in his ear. Matlala announced to the room that the president would like a few minutes alone. As my eyes grew accustomed to the gloom, I could see small groups of aides clustered around laptops and sitting at the tables in discussion. There was a hum of disgruntled muttering as they gathered their electronics and gave me curious glances on their way out. Eventually only Mbuyo and Matlala remained.

"You too, Jake," said Mbuyo. "Just a few minutes." He still did not turn to face us and missed the furious glare that Matlala directed at me as his new patent leather shoes squeaked past. He closed the door behind himself with a little more force than was necessary.

Mbuyo said nothing for a good minute, and I was selecting one of my prepared openings when his deep bass voice finally spoke.

"They had to import a special vehicle just to change those bulbs, did you know that?"

"It seems a waste," I said. The silhouette of a man could be seen standing in a cage before the floodlights. I guessed the vehicle holding him aloft was the imported one.

Mbuyo nodded, and he turned to me. His scarred face glinted slightly as the smooth skin caught the light.

"Doesn't it?" he said, but his mind was no longer on imported trucks. He studied me carefully.

"I've known this day would come," he said. "In thirty years not a day has passed that I haven't wondered how it would happen. It seems somehow fitting for it to be here, and now. On the eve of my triumph." He turned back and looked out over the stadium as if to imprint the moment on his mind. "She is still beautiful, isn't she?"

"She is."

"In all these years I've never met anyone to match her," he said. The imported truck's cage lifted the man higher so he could reach the top level of lights. "And she told you about the Nyanga Bar? All about it? And all that followed?"

"She might have left a few of the details out."

He nodded and watched the man in the cage give a dead bulb an experimental twist. The bulb was as wide as his chest, and it looked as if it took all his strength to twist it. "It is right that this happens now," said Mbuyo again.

"You haven't thought of bringing it upon yourself?" I asked. "Coming out and saying it?"

"I've thought of little else," he said. "How many times have I considered raising my hand and saying 'I'm not Thulani'?" He turned to me, to assure himself that wasn't a surprise to me, a final confirmation that I knew. I showed no surprise. "I'm Wandile," he said, "The traitor of the people. And I am a killer. I killed my own brother."

I gave a small nod. It seemed the least I could do, given the magnitude of his confession.

He held out a scarred left hand. Two of the fingers were joined and one finger was missing altogether so that the hand resembled a claw.

"You see that?" he said. "That chain around my wrist."

I could see the scar tissue around his wrist, which did resemble a chain.

"That's why they thought I was my brother. That chain

there. It melted into my skin. My brother wore a medical bracelet, had an allergy to penicillin. And in those last moments I took it from him. When we realised we weren't getting out. I took the bracelet from him."

Mbuyo withdrew his hand and pulled a sleeve over the scarred wrist.

"Why did you do that?" I asked.

"I thought if anyone survived, the security police would finish the job on my brother. I still thought we were doing what they wanted you see. And that if we failed, they would simply shoot him and be done with it."

"But why take the bracelet?"

Mbuyo shrugged. "I wanted them to shoot me. The bracelet identified him. I thought if we survived the fire, it should be me they killed."

Mbuyo's face showed no emotion, but his eyes made up for that. They were dark and gentle and seemed to plead with me.

"Are you taking me away?" he said. "Just you? Or is there a team waiting outside?"

"Just me," I said. "But I'm not taking you anywhere."

"Isn't this the end?"

"Who said anything about an end?"

Mbuyo turned his head to one side like a bird trying to hear something.

"You're not here to tell me it's all over?"

"That's not for me to decide. Whether you are who you say you are, whether you are the hero of your people, or a traitor to them is none of my concern."

"You're here to prod my conscience then? Force a confession?"

"I'm not sure I'd recognise a conscience if it slapped me

in the face. No, I'm here to ask you about the man you started the fire with. Who is Frans?"

Mbuyo's head tilted again, and his eyes raised a question.

"He's untouchable," he said. "What do you want with him?"

"He killed a journalist. A friend of mine. And I think he's going to kill again."

"Of course he is," said Mbuyo. "But you'll not stop him. Nobody can stop him."

"I passed two killers on the road today. I could be wrong about them, but I have some experience in that field. I think they were killers biding their time."

"Killers? Where?"

"In Zululand. On the road to Masotsheni. If he is going to do anything," I said. "He will act against both of you. Both you and Lindiwe."

"Act against me?" said Mbuyo and the corner of his scarred mouth twisted into a smile. "You're going to tell me not to go on stage tonight?"

"Step up your security. And ensure that Lindiwe is safe."

"How would I do that? Lindiwe has no security."

"None that I could see," I agreed, thinking of the adolescent boy with the battered binoculars.

"She wants the end to come," said Mbuyo. "You don't understand that." He turned to look out over the stadium. At the far end a stage had been constructed, and men were crawling over the steel girders adjusting lights. In the seating areas a team of policemen were moving along the rows of seats with large Alsatian dogs who were sniffing with enthusiasm in case anyone had been foolish enough to leave any explosives behind.

"She is overwhelmed with regret," said Mbuyo. "As am I." He kept gazing out over the stadium and was silent. "Something starts as a small secret," he said eventually. "The plan of a beautiful woman to survive, and to enable me to survive. A life without each other, but a life none-theless. It was more than I deserved, but I took it. And I regret it. I regret everything. You have no idea what it was like on Robben Island. No idea what it is like to regret your very existence. I regret it all, particularly that fire. Not because it killed my brother. Not because it killed four of his comrades. I regret it because it didn't kill me."

Suddenly a popping sound reverberated around the stadium, and the lights dropped to a dull orange glow and gradually faded into the early evening. The figures that a moment ago had been projected in full Technicolor onto the window in front of us became shadowy shapes without definition. There was a moment of confused silence, and then some figures broke away from the stage area and ran across the field, beams from torches they were carrying bounced across the ground ahead of them.

"Africa," said Mbuyo, and his mouth twisted in the way the country had learned to recognise as a smile. "The only thing that's certain here is that something will go wrong."

"That small secret of yours has become something that other people are dying for," I said.

"Two killers on the road, you said?"

"It looked that way."

Mbuyo gazed out over the dark stadium.

"The man who called himself Frans," I said. "He can be stopped."

"How?" asked Mbuyo. "How do you stop a man like that?"

"I have some experience in the field," I said. "Killing is one of my talents."

He turned back to me. "Are you saying you would do it?"

He hesitated, then raised an objection. "But you don't know who he is."

"Does he have mining interests?" I asked. "His successful business interests have included gold mines?"

Mbuyo nodded.

"Do his friends call him BB?"

Mbuyo nodded again. "They do."

"Riaan Breytenbach was a national serviceman thirty years ago," I said. "He worked for the same small division of military intelligence that Lindiwe's adoptive father worked for. His job was to collate the information passed on to him by the field contact. But when everything went wrong, nobody could find the field contact. They said he disappeared."

"He didn't disappear," said Mbuyo. "He was the contact. They didn't know that?"

"There was a man called Du Toit who had his suspicions. He wrote a report in which he suggested it, but everyone laughed at him and the report was buried."

"They laughed at him? Or did they know what Breytenbach was doing and wanted it kept quiet?"

"That's a question that needs asking," I said.

"He supports the party now," said Mbuyo. In the gloom of the early evening I could see his eyes glint. "A big donor. We sit in meetings together, and he looks at my new face, and he smiles at me. It's been a few years now, and never once has he shown any recognition."

"But if I am right," I said. "That has changed. He knows who you are now. And knows where Lindiwe is."

"He called me," said Mbuyo. "I thought it was odd. A couple of days ago."

"What did he want?"

"To say that he couldn't be here tonight. As a big donor, he would have been here for the show. Wanted to tell me personally. Pledge his support, all that nonsense."

"What reason did he give for not being here?"

"Some garbled story about being robbed. Retreating to a private game farm in Mpumalanga. Couldn't get back here in time. I thought it was odd that he called."

"He often calls you?"

"Never before."

"Where did he get your number?"

"Goodness knows. I asked the team. They had no idea."

"Do you pay the costs of Lindiwe's orphanage?"

"Not in my name. I pay through a trust."

"But your number could be linked to some of those accounts? Even if not your name, there might be a number?"

Mbuyo said nothing.

"If someone with connections in the right places found Lindiwe and her orphanage, is it possible that they might find your number? Might call that number to see who answers?"

Mbuyo still said nothing, but he raised his arms as if we were in an old spaghetti western, the harmonica music had started, and I was pointing a shotgun at him.

"It will be a relief," he said. "You don't understand. Thirty years I have waited for him to finish the job. You should kill me, not him. Allowing me to survive would be nothing short of treasonous. I am the traitor."

The door across the room burst open suddenly, and someone shone a torch into the gloomy interior.

"Power failure," called the man who was wearing the black outfit of the president's guard. "Won't be long, sir." He noticed Mbuyo's posture, and the torch beam shook as he pulled his revolver.

"What's going on?" he asked.

Mbuyo dropped his arms. "Everything's fine," he called. "Leave us."

The man hesitated, but then withdrew.

"This started thirty years ago," said Mbuyo, "and it is time for it to end. I knew it the moment you walked into that lounge at the Waterfront and asked me about Lindiwe. I knew that was the beginning of the end. Now finally, this is the end."

"You have a duty to protect yourself," I said.

"What duty? The people of this country do not need a killer president. I am the wrong person for the job."

Through the window behind Mbuyo I could see the racing outlines of clouds moving in to darken the sky. With the sun about to drop below the sea, the winter evening would be a dark one. The stadium was like a black cardboard cut-out against the shifting greys, but then suddenly the lights sprang on, and a black curtain was drawn over the sky, and the stadium returned to its full Technicolor glory.

"They found the switch for the generators," said Mbuyo, "and the spare diesel because the tanks had probably been drained and the fuel sold for cash. It's Africa, that's the way it's done here."

The door to the suite opened again, and one of the junior aides put his head in.

Mbuyo held up a hand to acknowledge him. "We're done," he called to him, then said to me, "There is no protection for Lindi, and there is none for me. This is a stone that has been waiting to roll for many years. It is too late to stop it now."

Mbuyo reached out with his crippled hand and gripped my shoulder. His face was a mask of scar tissue, his eyes full of kindness.

"Don't kill him," he said. "There has been enough killing."

I thought he was going to say something more, but he gave my shoulder a parting squeeze, released it and looked back to the aide. "Call the circus back in," he said, and his scarred face twisted into a regretful smile.

———

I drove through the descending gloom of the evening towards the beckoning warmth of the cosy retreat where Robyn would be waiting, and the thought of her filled my mind as I struggled along the slippery roads, banging the heater of the car and shivering despite my insulated jacket. I thought of the regrets of the two people who had confessed to me that day that they were killers and I wondered about my own regrets.

It had taken me over an hour to get out of the parking lot at the stadium because of the endless security checks and all the people streaming in to hear the president-to-be speak, so it was two hours before I dropped into the Franschhoek valley. The quaint village greeted me with the warm twinkling lights of its bars and restaurants, and with the smell of wood smoke from the fires keeping their customers warm. The door of a bar burst open, throwing a golden light onto the road ahead of me and a man came running out as if he was being chased. He stood in the road in front of me and waved his hands above his head. I slowed to a halt, and he came around to the window.

"They've killed him," he said in a voice strangled by panic. Rain poured down his face, and he stared at me with wide-eyed challenge as if I might provide an answer. I recognised the signs of shock. "Shot him," he said as I didn't react.

"Shot who?" I asked.

"Fucking idiots," said the man, and he ran off to spread the news further.

Fear crept over me like a suffocating wave. I parked the car and went into the bar the man had emerged from. Everyone was gathered around a TV mounted on the wall. The volume was up, and the only sound in the place was the strained, slightly breathless voice of a news reporter. Mbuyo was on the screen, his hands held up in the gesture of a great orator. Behind him were the members of his new parliament, looking pleased with themselves. The image moved slowly as the news crew made the most of the moment and cranked up the slow motion. Even in slow motion, it happened surprisingly fast. One moment Mbuyo's scarred face was opening its mouth to say something. The next he had fallen out of frame, and in the background other people on stage were suddenly crouched to the ground. Other camera shots showed security men stepping forward, putting themselves into the line of fire. Mbuyo lying sprawled on the stage. Security men clustering around him, and then medics appeared. In the background I could see Matlala crouched low and gazing with horror at the fallen figure of Mbuyo.

There was no movement from Mbuyo.

"A shot to the head," said the news reporter, and the image switched to show a man in a sheepskin jacket outside the stadium, holding a microphone in one hand and an umbrella in the other. Behind him the floodlit stadium looked like some alien witch's cauldron beaming light up into the sky to signal its home planet. No one was being allowed to leave, he explained. The police had a perimeter around the stadium. Still no news on President-elect Mbuyo's condition. "But we have reports coming in of a man who threatened the president-elect earlier this evening. Here at Green Point Stadium. The police are urgently seeking this man."

I returned to my car and was with Robyn within five minutes. She had cooked a lamb stew, and the cottage was warm from the fire she'd had going all day. The rooms were lit with candles, and for a moment I glimpsed another way of life. But we turned the lights on, and I called the Department's emergency number.

TWENTY-FIVE

Not one of the five policemen who searched, x-rayed
and prodded me on my way back into the stadium
seemed to think for a moment that I bore any resemblance
to the blurry image of the man they were urgently searching
for, whose picture was pinned up beside their makeshift
workstations.

Green Point Stadium had the feeling of a disaster relief
camp. The police had decided that the person who pulled
the trigger was still within the stadium, a reasonable
assumption given that there were no outside vantage points
overlooking the stage, and that the police surrounding the
stadium had closed all exits within a minute of the shot
being fired. And so they had decided to record the identity
of every single person leaving the stadium and had called in
the army to help with the processing. Twenty temporary
search and record stations had been set up, and they were
photographing faces and scanning ID cards. By the time I
arrived they had been busy with this for almost three hours
and were a little over halfway through the thirty thousand
people in the stadium. The mood was surprisingly buoyant,

in the way that the survivors of a disaster gather and feel the elation of having survived. The army was tasked with moving the people who had been processed out of the building and into their cars, because most of them loitered and held back, not wanting to leave the embrace of this new community.

"Nothing like disaster to bring us together," agreed the sergeant who escorted me up to the VIP suites.

"How do they know people aren't sneaking through an exit they don't have covered?"

"They'll not have the mark, will they?" The sergeant lifted a hand with his thumb up as if he was making an OK sign. He pulled a pen out of a pocket and pressed a button on it. His thumb glowed brightly in the dim corridor. "Ultraviolet," he said. "Same stuff they use when you vote. Takes a week to wear off. They won't let you out if you don't have one of these."

"How do I get myself one?"

"Show them that entry card on your way out, and they'll do it."

"I have to join the queue?" I asked. "I should cancel my dinner plans."

The sergeant laughed. "No queue. With the entry card, you bypass all that."

———

Fehrson's greeting lacked the enthusiasm of our previous encounters. He rose to his feet and sighed heavily, as if he'd hoped I might not arrive despite his insistence that I should. Khanyi stood obediently beside him and her eyes were no more welcoming.

"Here's your man," said Fehrson to a tall man with a

bald head and bulbous nose in a police uniform. The man looked me up and down as if he wasn't sure that I met expectations, then he thrust out a hand which I shook.

"Major Fehrson tells me you were on official business," he said in a deep bass voice and a tone that made it clear he didn't believe Major Fehrson.

"I was," I said, and Khanyi's lips pursed.

"Mind sharing with me some details of that official business?"

"It is mostly classified, Captain Shiya," said Khanyi before I could say anything.

"Broad strokes then," said the Captain. "Leave out the mostly classified bits."

Khanyi nodded at me as if tacitly granting permission.

"We had been running some background checks for him, and I was reporting back," I said. We watched to see how the Captain would take this quickly improvised fabrication. He didn't take it well.

"Background checks that required you to be alone with him for ten minutes?" said the Captain.

"There were some sensitive aspects," I said. "Women in the past, that kind of thing."

This made more sense to the Captain.

"But you found it necessary to threaten him?" he said.

"That was a misunderstanding. I made no threat. If anything, I was concerned for his safety."

The Captain sucked on his teeth while keeping his eyes fixed on me. We were in a similar VIP suite to the one that I had stood in with Mbuyo. It was occupied by teams of military personnel who had set up an impromptu operations room and they milled about us in a state of frenetic haste.

"We'll need a statement," said the Captain.

"I regret," said Fehrson, clearing his throat with that

regret, "that it is unlikely that we will be able to contribute anything meaningful."

The Captain looked at Fehrson as if trying to remember who he was. "Make it a meaningless statement then," he said in a patronising voice.

Khanyi showed her teeth and applied her charm at full throttle. "We will do our best, Captain Shiya," she said. The Captain's hard face melted a little under the glare.

"Thank you," said the Captain. "Any help that you and your elite team of concerned citizens can provide will be much appreciated." He stepped away from us before the force of Khanyi's charm could do permanent damage.

"Want to tell us what's going on?" asked Fehrson.

"I'm not sure you'd like it," I said.

"I'm sure I won't," he said. "But let me decide that." He turned to Khanyi. "Find us somewhere quiet to talk."

———

Khanyi found us a quiet corner of the room where we could talk undisturbed. The VIP suite was at fever pitch because of their conviction that the shooter was still in the stadium and would soon be forced to make a move. Sure enough, as we settled down in our quiet corner, the room erupted. The sergeant who had escorted me upstairs was talking to the Captain in a high-pitched, anxious voice as if someone was squeezing his voice box. An ambulance had passed through the exit gates a few minutes before. A single driver. With an exit card, but the driver had not matched the photo of the person issued with that card. The Captain spoke into his radio. And then we heard the sirens wailing into the distance as the chase began.

The TVs mounted on the glass walls were displaying

the news and it wasn't long before the helicopter circling the stadium picked up the ambulance travelling at high speed with its lights flashing, and not far behind it the fleet of flickering blue lights giving chase. The Captain was on the radio to the leader of the vehicles, and we could hear them calling distances, and confirming the progress of other vehicles approaching from the opposite direction. As we watched the fleeing ambulance, I wondered about the choice of escape vehicle. And couldn't help wondering whether imitation was indeed the greatest form of flattery.

The ambulance was on the N1 highway now, and the traffic ahead of it was slowing because of the impromptu roadblocks that had been set up further to the north. Traffic heading in the other direction had been stopped, and those lanes were enticingly empty. Further ahead was another fleet of police vehicles, but the driver of the ambulance couldn't see them yet. Each direction of the highway consisted of three lanes, with a ditch between them. A water drain ran through the middle of the ditch and lining the side of the road in both directions was a crash railing. Crossing over to the other lane would not be possible.

As the police vehicles gained on the ambulance, the tension in the room mounted. Then suddenly a policeman shouted out excitedly.

We saw it then. A break in the barrier, and a narrow track linking the two lanes, created for service vehicles and a place for emergency vehicles to change direction. The ambulance wobbled in the road as the driver also noticed the narrow gap

"He'll never make it," said Khanyi. She was right. The track was designed for negotiating at walking speed. The ambulance was travelling at a speed that would have enabled it to get airborne if it had been a little more aerodynamic. But after the initial wobble the driver turned the wheel and hit the brakes hard so that the vehicle looked as if the forward momentum had it sliding along on two wheels. Everyone drew their breath in, a communal gasp, as the ambulance veered towards the narrow gap in the railing.

"He made it," cried one of the policemen as the ambulance spewed sparks against the railings. But it was travelling too fast, and instead of dropping into the ravine, it launched into it like a long-distance ski jumper leaving the ramp. For a breathless moment it sailed across the ravine, but then hit the far side with such force that the back of the vehicle jumped upwards and it performed a cartwheel, landing on its roof in a shower of sparks in the other lane. It slid into the middle of the road like a beetle on its back and burst into flames.

"Poor devil," said Fehrson. No one else in the room spoke. The helicopter circled the burning vehicle and revealed the arrow-shaped cluster of police cars with their flashing blue lights approaching from the north. They skidded to a halt in a defensive formation and figures jumped out and took cover behind their vehicles.

"They need him alive," said Khanyi. "Surely they know that? They need to know who put him up to it."

There was a sudden commotion from the men gathered around the radio station as it crackled anxiously. A policeman pointed at the TV, and as the helicopter came around, we could see a man emerging from the inferno, his clothes on fire, an arm raised up and pointing at the police line. The arm jerked, and the radio crackled again. The man was firing on them.

They let him approach to within twenty metres of the police line, his arm jerking with the recoil of the shots he was firing, and then a sniper fired.

The man dropped, first to his knees, and then he fell forward, and lay face down, his clothes still flickering with flames. The room was silent for a moment. And then suddenly everyone was talking, the Captain was calling for updates on the radio, and others were reaching for their handheld radios and phones. On the screens we saw the first wave of police approach the prone body of the ambulance driver, and fire fighters started spraying foam over the burning vehicle.

"Well, that's that," said Khanyi. "Now we'll never know who tried to kill Mbuyo."

"Tried?" I said.

"It turns out half his skull is steel," said Khanyi. "They put metal plates in after the fire. But his condition is serious. It doesn't look good."

———

Khanyi managed to persuade a policeman to help her insert some coins into a coffee machine, which he did while gazing at her cleavage. Then he took out his frustration on the vending machine with some helpful but unnecessary punches. We settled into the quiet corner of the room, and Fehrson glowered at me.

"That's absurd," he announced after I'd told them that Mbuyo had refused to identify the person they'd called Frans.

"Absurd that he refused?" I said.

"Absurd that you think this attempted assassination has anything to do with what happened all those years ago. There are other political issues at play here. More relevant issues. Current issues."

"Absolutely," I agreed. "An unfortunate coincidence."

Fehrson sniffed and sipped at his coffee as if he enjoyed it. Khanyi's eyes narrowed as she tried to determine the depth of my lie.

"He gave you no idea who that person might be?" she asked.

"No idea," I said.

Khanyi's face radiated her disbelief. Fehrson grunted with approval and placed his coffee cup on the low table between us.

"That brings an end to it then," he said with some satisfaction and he smiled at me.

Khanyi had explained the content of our afternoon discoveries to Fehrson while they waited for my return to the stadium. Discoveries which I suspected he was already working to discredit and bury in the file of absurd speculation.

I agreed that brought an end to it, and Fehrson nodded again and tried to smile his approval. His eyes were drooping with tiredness, and they were rimmed with red. He reached for his coffee again and sipped at it, then repeated how pleased he was that it was all over.

Khanyi walked me to the door. "You can trust Father," she said. "You should know that."

"Of course I know it," I assured her. We looked back at Fehrson, huddled in his armchair in the corner like a man recovering from a disaster. Khanyi turned to me.

"There was another shooting," she said. "Near Dundee, Masotsheni. A woman was killed. I don't know any details. The initial report came in an hour ago."

"You haven't told Fehrson?"

Khanyi shook her head. "Not yet." She looked back at Fehrson and said, "If Mbuyo gave you a name it would be a breach of justice to keep quiet about it."

She turned back to me and I could see the exhaustion in her eyes too. It was an exhaustion I shared, which is probably why I didn't keep my mouth shut.

"What justice?" I said. "The problem, Khanyi, is that some people are beyond justice. The justice system in this country is about hiding the truth and protecting the privileged. Not righting any wrongs."

"You *are* an anarchist, Gabriel," said Khanyi. "I didn't realise it was true."

"And you are better? The man you call Father has spent his life covering up the heinous actions of people who use justice to increase their own privilege."

"You don't understand, Gabriel."

"No, I don't. Justice is not filing a report and then locking it away in some archive. Justice is action, not a neat little written summary of what went wrong."

Khanyi shook her head, but I could see she was too tired to argue. She contented herself with telling me I was a fool. I agreed with her. And I left her and Fehrson to write the report and close the file.

I limped out of the stadium. The cut in my side had opened up again, and I was pretty sure the entry wound from Scarface's bullet was infected. Fortunately, I knew someone who would dress the wounds and feed me some lamb stew. Robyn was a felon, but then so was I. It had just taken me longer to realise it. I was crossing back over Chandler's line, travelling further down Fehrson's spiral, and my rusty old Fiat couldn't get me there fast enough.

TWENTY-SIX

R obyn and I ate dinner well after midnight on the terrace of our Franschhoek hideaway. Robyn had kept the stew warm and chilled the wine to just above frozen which was the way Brian had told me she liked it when I had questioned the slivers of ice in my glass on an evening years before.

"I'm thinking I will just stay here," she said after I had complimented the stew, and asked for a second helping.

"You like it that much?"

"I went into the village today and bought groceries. It's so peaceful and quiet. Beats the city." She sipped her wine. "You could stay on a bit too if you need to. You're less likely to have people coming at you with their knives."

Robyn had dressed my wounds and thrown away the clothes ruined by the bloodstains. Violence was on her mind.

"It would be very cosy," she said, and her dark eyes did that thing which made me feel as if she was about to kiss me, despite the heavy oak table, candles, wine cooler and plates of food between us. I wondered whether the cosy plan included me in a leading role, or whether I was cast as a bit-part player. The latter seemed more likely.

"We could rob the quiet little village bank when we run low," I said, testing sensitive waters.

"Or just when we get bored," said Robyn. "If we have to wait until we run low it might take a while."

"Business with Chandler has been that good?"

Robyn smiled and sipped her wine coyly. "No," she said, but her eyes told the truth.

"I had no idea. I've obviously been playing for the wrong team."

"There's no right team, or wrong team, Ben. You know that. It's every man and woman for themselves."

"When did you and Chandler start this?" I asked.

"After Brian was killed, when you two came back and it had all just happened. We buried Brian and then you went into a hole in the ground because you felt so sorry for yourself. Steven was good to me. He supported me. Nothing inappropriate. You know that, but I have to say it, even if only to myself because I've fallen into that trap before. Doing inappropriate things." She sipped her wine, and I said nothing.

"Anyway, there was nothing inappropriate. Steven is the only man I know that I can say is a real gentleman. And a gentle man." Robyn laughed, and the sound was genuinely uplifting. "Don't look at me with those puppy-dog eyes," she said and took another mouthful, then spoke through it in the way my mother had always said I shouldn't.

"We talked about my time in prison. About the boy I'd been so stupid about. The one they killed. I'm sure Brian told you."

I nodded.

"Steven was trying to put his life together again. What happened in the Congo killed Brian, and it nearly destroyed Steven. It did the same to you. I could see it happening to Steven like an accident playing out in slow motion. He was getting calls from old army buddies. They were doing jobs for security companies, the kind of companies that send people into the nasty parts of Africa and dress them in Armani suits instead of uniforms. Steven did a few of those jobs, but mostly they just depressed him even more. He did some things he didn't like and found himself rubbing shoulders with people he liked even less. Then one day he was complaining about a job he was doing for one of those companies. They'd protected some guy who was carrying a lot of cash, flying into the Congo by private jet. He was convinced it was money for an arms deal, and he said it was all wrong. Why was he protecting the people who were causing the trouble? The money would be for weapons that would be turned against innocent people. All that kind of nonsense. He got into quite a state about it. Ranted on and on. So I said he should just take the money for himself and put it to better use. It was a joke, but all the best things in life start as a joke, don't they?"

"So you put him up to it?"

"I wouldn't say that," she said with false modesty and her eyes did that thing again. "It was just the two of us at first, and it was very clever. It was all his ideas. It did him the world of good. He found himself again. You know how he is now, he's found his balance, or his mojo, or whatever they call it."

"And you?"

"My problems turned out to be harder to fix."

"You couldn't bring Brian back," I said.

"It wasn't that. And you know it. Do I have to remind

you every day, Ben?" Robyn's eyes flashed with anger. "I didn't want Brian back, you know that."

We fell into silence. It had been stupid of me to mention Brian.

"Staying here would be lovely, you should do it," I said in a feeble attempt to clear the air, but the good moment between us was dead. Robyn kept her head down and ate her stew. I felt a sense of regret creep over me. Not since Sandy's disappearance had I allowed myself to feel like this. Not since long before I'd even met Sandy. I'd grown accustomed to my safe bubble of isolation. But Robyn had inadvertently broken that, and it had been so subtle that I'd not noticed it happening. Looking at her now, I realised how deep my feelings for her were. And it wasn't just her beauty, although there was that, no doubt about it. But there was more. It was as Mona had described Lindiwe with that hand on her chest. Not physical beauty, but something that she gave me to carry around in my heart. Robyn looked up as if she'd felt my eyes on her, and she saw something in them.

"Lighten up a little, Ben, it's not that bad." She smiled, and I knew I was done for. You can go through life putting up walls against anything or anyone that could hurt you, but it's the people inside those walls that do the worst damage.

———

We shared a cigarette on the couch with the view after dinner. The candles were still burning on the table, casting a warm glow over my half-full glass of wine. Robyn was making a comfortable nest with her duvet. The moon poked through the clouds and cast a cool light over her marble face as she looked out over the lights of Franschhoek. Then the moon skipped back behind the clouds, and the valley was all ours.

"I still cannot believe Brian said nothing," said Robyn, picking at the wound and bringing back the ghost of our past. "I suppose it was because he was angry with me, and not with you."

"You had a big row about it?"

"Did we ever. But Brian was kind. He was angry but never violent. I know what your squad did, and when he told me it surprised me, because he never showed his anger. I guess the army had taught him to control it. Not control it perhaps, but direct it. I honestly feared that he might take some of that anger out on you."

"He didn't."

Robyn drew on the cigarette and let the smoke drift out of her mouth as if she had stopped breathing.

"Did I kill him, Ben? That thing about focus. No letters from home, all of that."

"Don't be absurd. There was nothing wrong with his focus. His death had nothing to do with you."

"But if I'd waited until you returned from that operation. His mind wouldn't have been clouded by all that anger."

"It wasn't clouded by anything. Believe me, he showed no anger, no lack of focus. He was a good soldier, and no different on that operation."

"But he might have noticed that mine."

"No."

"They wouldn't tell me how he died. Did you know that? 'In the course of active duty', they said. Military procedure prevented them from telling me anything. Why, for fuck's sake, I asked. Why can't I know how it happened? It's not like I will breach national security by knowing how he died."

"It's just how they do things."

"Well, it's ridiculous. Do you know how often I wake up in the night, thinking about that mine? That fucking mine? That was the only word they would give me. One word … it was a mine. Not a bullet, not a grenade, not a bomb, not a terrorist, not an enemy soldier. A mine."

I said nothing. Was every moment that I spent with Robyn going to be marred by the presence of Brian?

"And then you and Steven returned like zombies. Like someone had taken your brains and turned them inside out. You'd seen people killed before, not just the people you killed, but colleagues you knew and loved. I know you had because Brian certainly had. But this was different. And don't tell me it was just because Brian was your close friend. Steven was the same, and Brian wasn't his friend."

"We were unprepared for what happened," I said, and felt the tightening of my chest that came whenever I thought back to it.

"Because it was a plane crash?"

"Not because of that. Because of what happened after the crash."

"Steven said it was a civilian plane. Is that why it was different? Normal people, not soldiers."

"It was a private charter flight that flew over the North Kivu region. There were lots of gooks there, and they used to shoot at the planes that went overhead, but it was like pissing in the rain. The planes were usually so high it was just a waste of their ammo. But this plane was hit. It had engine trouble, and no one knows whether the engine trouble happened first or whether it was shot down. Anyway, it went down late afternoon the thirteenth October. There were forty holiday-makers on board, honeymoon couples, families, pensioners. They'd been on safari in the Okapi, flying back to Jo'burg."

"Why were you there?"

"The plane went down in the Virunga mountains, the heart of the terrorist encampments. We were the closest because we were on the mines in the northwestern corner of Uganda. We were near the end of a rough tour. We were worn out, frazzled, but we were there. The South Africans weren't about to send in their aviation inspectors with their nice linen suits and umbrellas. Someone had to get there to see if there were survivors. We took off at first light on the fourteenth and spent hours flying over the area looking for the wreckage. Back and forth in a grid pattern, guessing how far the plane had travelled since the last radar track. Then Brian saw it, the metal body of the fuselage. The weather was nasty, really turbulent, and high winds. We wouldn't have jumped in normal circumstances, but Chandler didn't hesitate. He had the pilot circle the area and climb to find smoother air, then they dropped us. Honestly, we were lucky we all made it down to the ground. Chandler broke his foot when he came in. There was so much wind we might as well have left the chutes in the plane."

"I remember he was on crutches for months. Or it seemed like it. Were there no survivors of the crash?" Robyn lit us another cigarette. "You don't have to tell me."

"At first we didn't think there were any survivors. It was dead quiet on the ground. The five of us gathered around the fuselage which was twisted and broken into sections. The copilot was still in his seat. Dead. The pilot's seat was empty, but we found him not far away, also dead. There were passengers still in their seats in the body of the plane. I guess about half of them were killed on impact. But there were signs that some had survived, the tracks of people moving away from the craft. Then a woman came out of the bush. In her underwear, streaked with blood and mud. She came rushing at us, and Chandler caught her. She couldn't speak, she was just gasping for air. Couldn't tell us anything, couldn't bring herself to say any words, just pointed into the bush. Chandler settled her and left two men with her. Brian, Chandler and I went looking for the others. Their tracks were clear, but then we found other tracks. People in heavy boots moving back to the plane, roaming over the ground, searching."

"The ADF? Brian told me about the ADF"

"The African Defence Force, yes."

"You don't have to tell me," said Robyn again. "Don't bring it all back." She could probably sense my dread at what was to come. But I'd started on the path into the dark heart of it all, and it was too late for me to stop now. I continued with the story. Robyn lay her head down on my shoulder, and the warmth of her kept me grounded. Perhaps with her the telling of this story would be cathartic, and not just a flagellation of old wounds.

"The tracks led us to a clearing where we found the people who had survived the crash."

Robyn's breath was hot on my cheek. I remembered moving into that clearing. There had been fifteen people in a line, men, women and three children. They had been arranged in that line and had been shot as if by a firing squad. Not single shots, but a hail of them. And then the murderers had fitted bayonets onto their guns and finished their work by stabbing them. The moment that we entered the clearing and saw what they had done to the survivors of that plane crash was the moment my life changed. I'd seen death before. Too often. But never anything like this. It was the surreal transposition of holidaymakers, in their bright colourful clothes, into the setting of a war. Seeing a uniformed soldier lying dead in the bush is one thing. A line of fifteen holidaymakers is another. Holidaymakers who have survived a plane crash, and are trying to find help, wounded and desperate, supporting each other and struggling through the African bush without water or food, leaving behind their dead brothers, parents and children, trying to make their way to find help and escape from the horror of the crash. Only to stumble into a war zone and have their lives taken from them in a brutal massacre.

"They were alive?" asked Robyn, and I realised I'd stopped talking.

"No, they weren't alive."

The three of us had stopped at the entrance of the clearing and it had taken a moment for the scene to imprint itself onto our memories. Brian swore. He took a step forward, but Chandler held him back. Chandler's face was white. He said nothing, just held Brian back. Then we heard the crying.

"The ADF killed them?" asked Robyn because I'd not spoken out loud again.

"There was a young child who was still alive. A four-year-old boy, we learned later. He'd spent the night beside the dead body of his father, his legs trapped under the weight of his father's body. At least that's what we thought when we saw him."

Brian had stepped forward, and the boy's head turned towards us. He'd been shot and probably also stabbed, his face was covered in blood, but he was alive. Chandler called Brian back, ordered him to stop. But the boy was looking at Brian now and begging for help. Brian kept going.

"Brian went to him," I said aloud. They'd found a way

of trapping the boy there, we realised later, because he didn't move. Chandler and I discussed it many weeks later. When our memories had been coaxed back by therapists and drugs. Probably a bayonet through a leg or an arm. I think Brian could see there was no chance that he would live. That is why he stepped up to him, didn't hold back. I heard the click as Brian stepped on a jerry-rigged tripwire. It's a clear, latching kind of click that those homemade tripwires made, like a spring lock finding its home. Brian heard it, and he half turned to us. He looked at me, and at Chandler. Held our eyes. Then he turned back to the boy who was within reaching distance. Brian stooped down and reached out to touch the boy and hold him. Chandler called out to him not to move.

"That's when he stepped on the mine?" asked Robyn.

"Yes, that's when he stepped on the mine."

We were silent for a long time then. Me sitting, half-lying on the couch, and Robyn's hot tears running down my chest and soaking my shirt. Probably some tears of my own too. Eventually she asked, "Did any of them survive?"

"Three escaped the ADF search. We lifted them out the next day." A night spent among the dead, splattered with the blood of my friend, not moving for fear of other booby traps. It had been the longest night of my life.

Robyn sat up and emerged from her duvet cocoon. Her red moist eyes were so close I couldn't focus on them.

"Thank you for telling me," she said. "Now Brian must leave us alone. We've lost him, but we have a friendship that still lives."

She leaned forward and kissed me on the lips. It was like a powerful current passing through my body, as if her mouth was electrically charged. And at that moment, and for some time after that, I believed we really had put Brian behind us.

"Don't go getting any ideas though," she said. "We've been through this, Ben, and you need to stop your shit. Find your journalist. Stop trailing after me like a ghoul. It won't work. You know that."

I wasn't sure that I did know that. Had we been through it? But I didn't say anything. Robyn placed her head back onto my shoulder and we gazed out at the lights and I settled for the memory of the kiss.

―――

"Here's what we're going to do," said Brian on the last night of his life. "We are going to find that underground vault in sunny South Africa, and we're going to take ourselves some of that gold."

"That's called stealing," said our captain. "Common thievery."

"It is," agreed Brian. "And it's what we're going to do."

We were in the messroom of the temporary barracks at the Kigesi Gold mining complex. Bleak prefabricated cardboard walls, which did nothing to mute the snores of our chopper pilot in the next room. The orders had come through for the drop into the Virunga mountains to find survivors of a civilian plane crash, and Brian was feeling irritable. Not because of the orders, which had a sense of purpose about them. Finding civilians who might have survived a plane crash had a touch of the heroic: the possibility of saving lives, not taking them. But that sense of purpose had triggered Brian's discontent. Because of the contrast with the orders we were currently executing, in a posting that we were only two days from completing.

The messroom was where our captain allowed us to speak our minds. Beyond these cardboard walls we obeyed his orders without question, we spoke when spoken to, and were an entity that transcended our individual beings. But in the messroom the converse was true. This compact space was where we were people and not soldiers. And this evening we were exhausted, disgruntled people.

"You're with me aren't you, Benny?" asked Brian.

"You'd be nothing more than common thieves," said the captain.

"Better than being hired killers," said Brian.

There was a silence between us. We'd travelled this conversational path several times this evening, and the captain had tired of insisting that as soldiers of Her Majesty's government we were doing Her honourable work. The duplicitous reasons for our presence here had become clear to us all.

"It's a step up, from hired killer to common thief," said Brian. "And that man Breytenbach will be our proud sponsor. Tell me you're with me, Benny."

I said that I was with him. Brian turned to the captain.

"Captain?"

"I'll not stand in your way," said Captain Chandler. "But it will be a snowy day in hell before I stoop so low as to become a common thief."

TWENTY-SEVEN

Mpumalanga is a region of South Africa that deserves a better name. It sits on the northeastern edge of the country, providing a strip of border with Mozambique, and tucking the independent country of Swaziland under its armpit. It hosts some of the most renowned wildlife parks in the world, and much of it sits up on a high plateau where the air is thin, and the weather unpredictable, fluctuating wildly from bright sunshine to chilling mist in the space of an hour. It was Fat-Boy who told me it deserves a better name because the 'Place of the Rising Sun' is only true for the people who happen to find themselves to the west of Mpumalanga.

"The Zulus," said Fat-Boy elucidating for those of us who were geographically challenged. "They are the only ones who see the sun rising here. For the Swazis it's the place of the setting sun, and for us," he placed a large hand over his heart, "for us Xhosas it's the 'Place of Who the Fuck Cares?'"

"I think it's a beautiful name," said Robyn. "Whether the sun is rising or setting."

"The route is plotted?" asked Chandler, tiring of the banter.

"Almost, Colonel," said Fat-Boy. "I'm running it now." He turned his attention back to his laptop computer where something that looked like a paper aeroplane was travelling along a pink line superimposed over a map.

"If we don't run this test soon it'll be dark," said Chandler, with an edge of irritation.

"Those babies will be airborne in just a few minutes," said Fat-Boy.

We were on the elevated wooden terrace of our Timbavati Lodge chalet. Chandler had booked two on the edges of the fenced area which offered the most secluded bush experience. The chalet was built on stilts in the style of a log cabin, and from the terrace we could see beyond the game fence over the treetops of the low-lying Sabie River valley all the way to the slopes of the Drakensberg range. An evening mist was descending into the cushion of trees, and the sun was dropping some burnt sienna into the wash.

The two Phantom drones were resting like miniature spaceships on a table, and Robyn was checking their battery levels while Fat-Boy uploaded the route to the second one. Their destination was so far away that we needed two so that one could float high and relay joystick commands to the other.

The slowly blinking red light changed to a solid green and Fat-Boy disconnected the cable and gave the drone a pat with his gloved hand. The odds of both drones returning were slim, and we didn't want any incriminating fingerprints on their shiny plastic covers.

"Ready to go," announced Fat-Boy, and we stood to the side as he fired up the motors on the first one. The drone lifted a metre into the air and then wobbled about a bit as

Fat-Boy adjusted the trim on his controls. Then it climbed away from us at an angle and hovered about five metres up.

"You got picture?" asked Fat-Boy.

"Clear as a bell," said Robyn. On the laptop screen we could see an image of the four of us on our terrace. I resisted the temptation to wave.

"Off she goes then," said Fat-Boy, and he switched the controls over to the pre-programmed GPS route. The drone climbed up another twenty metres, then hesitated a moment as if it was choosing a direction, tilted itself and sped off towards the setting sun.

"It's going all the way?" asked Chandler.

"As ordered, Colonel."

"But it stays high?"

"They won't see or hear a thing, Colonel. We're keeping that surprise for the morning."

The second drone was up in the air a few minutes later, and then we settled down in front of the laptop where a split screen showed us the progress of the two drones on a map, beside their camera images.

"What if they go at different speeds?" asked Robyn. "Won't they bump into each other?"

"Different routes, baby," said Fat-Boy. "You think I'm as dumb as I look?"

"You're sure they're high enough?" asked Chandler.

Fat-Boy sighed. He had been sending his new toys out on experimental flights all day. But Chandler had been in the municipal offices of Nelspruit, so he'd missed the painstaking elaborations that Fat-Boy had provided us with.

"They are," said Robyn on his behalf. "He's checked the route."

"And when they get there, the one stays high?"

"So high they won't even know it's there. Esmeralda

goes down low and causes all the trouble, but Shirley stays up high as the relay."

"Esmeralda?" said Chandler.

"He's named them," said Robyn and exchanged a warning glance with Chandler. He didn't pursue it.

"And the low one you can control?"

"To some extent," said Fat-Boy, indicating a joystick attached to the computer. "Through the relay."

That seemed to satisfy Chandler, and the questions dried up. We watched the progress of the two drones as they inched their way across the screen.

"Twelve minutes you say?" asked Chandler.

"Twelve minutes there, twelve minutes back."

"Just about enough time for the wine to breathe. Why doesn't the Angel open the bottles for us?"

Chandler had selected a Merlot to accompany the evening meal. I opened a few of the bottles and added some wood to the fire that was crackling in the hearth. We were at nearly seven thousand feet above sea level, and the evening would be a cold one.

It had not been hard to find Breytenbach's private game reserve. You don't spend the equivalent of five million US dollars on your holiday home without a few people noticing. The difficult part had been figuring out how we would get in, a puzzle that was eventually solved for us by a man called Hannes whose wife had recently left him, and who had a penchant for sweet rum, which tended to loosen his tongue. He had been feeling sorry for himself in the little bar of Welverdiend and had welcomed the opportunity of having his tongue loosened by the friendly man with the white hair and British accent who took such an interest in his job as security adviser to some local resorts.

Breytenbach's residence appeared through the evening

mist as a cluster of twinkling lights. Chandler had been right to push Fat-Boy because the light was failing as our drones arrived in position high above the complex. But there was still enough for us to make out the shapes of the buildings. The large central one was Breytenbach's personal spot, then another building a brief walk through the trees was his guest house. There were three security buildings, one of which was a control centre, one a gatehouse, and the third a barracks for the private army that kept the area secure.

Chandler rolled out the plans he'd printed at the municipality that morning and we matched the buildings with the architect's drawings, while Fat-Boy tested his joystick and had Esmeralda fly slow loops, keeping her high and out of earshot of the sentries that were prowling about the place. The lights of the principal building were all burning, confirming that the master was in residence. Daylight was all but gone when Fat-Boy issued the command to bring the drones home, and Chandler, Robyn and I went inside to see if the Merlot lived up to its five-star rating.

Robyn tested the mobile phone antenna we'd installed, while I put more wood onto the fire and shifted the coals about to get a good flame up. Chandler put on an apron and set about filleting the trout he'd bought from a local fisherman. Fat-Boy sat outside in the cold waiting for his girls to come back.

"He realises the one isn't likely to get back?" asked Chandler.

"It's why he's so tetchy," said Robyn, "you need to give him a bit of space, that's all."

"A bit of space?" said Chandler. "It's a machine, for god's sake. Not a close family member."

"You know what he's like," said Robyn. "Don't wind him up, Steven. We don't need any issues."

"He's a goddamn lunatic is what he is," said Chandler, but he didn't mention the matter again.

———

"He has his own private army," Chandler reminded us as we looked over the plans of the Breytenbach estate after dinner. We'd been over all this at least a dozen times, but none of us questioned Chandler's need for repetition. It was a comforting routine. "It's the army he deploys to the mines," he said, "so it's a big one. Over a thousand men altogether, a small portion of them posted here. And not just men; he's a modern type and has no problem recruiting women as long as they're prepared to pull the trigger when it comes to that."

"This place here," he indicated the barracks block with a silver mechanical pencil, "is where they stay when they're posted here. There are up to fifty of them on site at any time. They use the place as a training ground. Outside the perimeter they do the hard stuff. The endurance courses, sniper training, target practice and so forth. It means they can pretty much do what they like in terms of shaping their soldiers because they're far from prying eyes. And they double up as security for the farm. They're the same security we encountered at the archives, but these ones have something to prove. They've got their training captains watching them."

"Not the usual dozy security team," said Robyn.

"They're not," agreed Chandler. "Highly trained and pumped up. Expect them to be trigger-happy because they're keen to show the boss how good they are."

"Not a walk in the park then," said Fat-Boy, feeling almost jovial now that both his drones had returned from their test flights.

"No, but we have many things to our advantage. They're a mixed bag. Some of them will be green: newbies on their first training. And they have a fast turnover. They do a few weeks here before being shipped back to the mines to look after the rest of BB's gold. So a few new faces will not be headline news. They're used to the constant change. And that's our opportunity."

"Which is why we've got the fancy dress," I said.

"The full kit," confirmed Chandler. "Not the light-weight version we had in the archives."

"And this here," said Fat-Boy placing a sausage of a finger onto a room with a large x marked in red felt-tip pen, "is his private study?"

"It is," said Chandler. "That is the focus of our attention."

"Because we need the alarm."

"That's correct. As Hannes pointed out," a slight grimace at the memory of his long evening listening to the inebriated drivel of the recently cuckolded security adviser, "this is the one room that BB has armed at all times."

"Not even the gold."

"Correct. The place was not designed for high security storage. It is illegal for him to keep this much gold on his premises. Which is why all they have is a big door with an electronic lock and an alarm on it. And two disinterested guards just waiting for a distraction. The extra security is being installed next week."

"And this," said Fat-Boy, shifting the sausage to an adjacent larger square, "is where the big door is, where he's put the gold?"

"Correct. One floor below, the entrance is round the back because the place is built on a slope, you don't even know there's a lower floor until you drive around."

"And we will have only a few minutes," said Robyn.

"Indeed." Chandler stared intently at the plans like they were a chessboard, and he was thinking several moves ahead. The entrance to the underground storage area was a narrow driveway. Not the kind of place you want to get stuck in while members of a small private army demonstrate their sharpshooting skills.

"Timing is critical," said Chandler. "Give me the sequence Fat-Boy."

"We trigger the alarm," said Fat-Boy, "then we blow the power."

"Slow down," said Chandler. "We must make sure that alarm is disabled before you blow the power."

"Roger that, Colonel. We trigger the alarm in the study. They disable it, then we blow the power."

"Good. Then the Angel provides us with a distraction when the alarm is disabled," said Chandler. "Pulls the guards away. The backup generator takes sixty seconds to come on-line. The system will arm automatically when the power comes back."

"Which means you have sixty seconds to open that door," I said.

"We only need ten. It's an electronic lock, Hannes was clear about that. Without power, it's a matter of sliding the door open. They haven't brought in the fancy security yet."

"And the alarm on the storeroom door won't arm if it is already open," said Fat-Boy. "So no alarm when they enable it again."

"By which time they'll be too busy to worry about a storeroom door failing to arm," I said.

Chandler nodded. "The security team don't know what has been stored down there. They won't bother."

"And your B-plan, Colonel," said Robyn. "You will have called the army already?"

"I'll make the call to the military base ahead of time," said Chandler. "Before we go in."

"What happens if they send a police van?" said Robyn. "We can get out, but Ben will be trapped."

"You don't send a police van to deal with a private army," said Chandler. "You send a bigger army. They'll come alright, just a matter of when. Gabriel will be fine."

"And we meet here," said Fat-Boy placing his finger on a small square on the outskirts of the property. "The outdoor sauna and jacuzzi? Why here?"

"It's the last place they'll look," said Chandler. He looked at each of us in turn. "Are we ready then? We have our A-B-C's?"

"I want to be with Ben," said Robyn.

"The Angel will do just fine on his own," said Chandler. "We don't change things now."

Robyn was looking at me with her dark eyes. "We've got our A-B-C's worked out, Colonel, but Ben has no exit. You know he doesn't."

"Gabriel can look after himself," said Chandler.

"It makes sense for me to be with him. One of us is too obvious as a distraction, they won't buy it. It won't give you enough time. It needs to be convincing."

"Gabriel has his reasons for going in there," said Chandler. "You know he does. We've been through this."

"I won't get in his way," said Robyn. "Trust me on this, Colonel. I need to be with him."

Chandler looked at me. I was still watching Robyn, whose dark eyes were holding steady on me. When Robyn decided on something, there was very little anyone could do to change her mind. There was a moment of silence filled by the frogs from the river below the cabin.

"That's okay with me, Colonel," I said. "I'll pair up with Robyn on this."

———

"I know what you're doing," said Robyn as we shared a cigarette on the terrace of our own wooden cabin. "I can read your mind, Ben. Don't you know that? It's why we're so connected."

"I can't read yours," I said. "You're a complete mystery to me."

"Can't you?" Robyn turned her head and considered me at an angle. The sound of Fat-Boy gargling came to us through the still night. Chandler had insisted that we turn in early and get some sleep before the big day. "You like to think of me as a mystery, perhaps," said Robyn. "But I'm not."

"If you know what I'm doing, what is it?"

"You want me to say it? Out loud? That you plan to kill him?"

The light on the terrace of Fat-Boy and Chandler's cabin turned off and the sudden darkness smothered us.

"It's obvious Ben. I know about the history you and the Colonel have with Breytenbach."

Sounds of the frogs in the valley below us built up like a chorus to fill the silence.

"So, having read my mind with regard to my intentions," I said, "you will stop me from fulfilling them. Is that why you wanted Chandler to change the plans?"

"I'm not going to stop you from killing him, Ben. I have a feeling you will need me there with you."

"I will?"

Robyn leaned towards me and kissed me. Not a small kiss. Not a dry, sensible, reserved kiss. She pulled back, and her eyes studied me.

"You will," she said. "Sometimes we need each other."

———

Esmeralda and Shirley departed at oh six hundred hours the next day. Fat-Boy had replaced their batteries, tightened all the screws he could find, applied a little oil to the rotors, and even drawn a smiley face onto Esmeralda with some lipstick he stole from Robyn.

"What the hell you do that for?" asked Chandler.

"She'll go down smiling," said Fat-Boy.

"Clean it off. Poor security."

"They're not going to trace the lipstick," said Fat-Boy, and left the smiley face there. Robyn gave Chandler a stern look as she came out with the hot chocolate.

The twelve-minute flight was uneventful. The two cameras showed us breathtaking images of the mist rising from the trees, and glimpses of wildlife startled by the sound of the motors.

The Breytenbach game farm looked tranquil as it came into view, like a cluster of large sandwiches floating on a cushion of mist in the middle of the bush. Behind the complex the stark sides of a rocky hill rose above it, providing shelter from the wind and a craggy backdrop for the magazine articles. The resemblance to sandwiches came from the vast horizontal slabs of concrete which formed the floor and roof of the primary structure, with floor to ceiling glass squeezed between them. The other buildings in the complex mimicked the principal residence, but in a less extravagant manner. The gatehouse offered a cheeky variation on the theme by looking like someone had accidentally knocked the sandwich off the table and it had stuck at an awkward angle into the ground.

Chandler told me he thought I was being absurd when I mentioned this, and that I shouldn't distract Fat-Boy, who needed to focus. Fat-Boy demonstrated his need to focus by sticking his tongue out and chewing on it as he watched his screen. The drones were settling, and he explained that this could take a few minutes as they adjusted to the wind and balanced themselves. Both cameras were pointing towards the fallen sandwiches, and he zoomed one of them in a little.

We could see the sentries moving around the perimeter. Two of them, dressed in black and carrying semi-automatic Vektor R5 carbines. It would have made more sense for them to have worn camouflage uniforms, but as Chandler said, their priority was looking good to the boss as opposed to being effective in the bush environment.

The drones let Fat-Boy know that they were settled, and he took the joystick in hand, and gently nudged Esmeralda forward. In a few moments we saw the drone appear in the camera view of the other one. Fat-Boy paused and looked up to Chandler.

"On your command, Colonel," he said.

"Have we checked the phone?" Chandler asked Robyn.

"Yessir." Robyn was in military mode, which was coming across a bit overdone. Something about her incongruous beauty made it seem as if she was being disrespectful. She had her hair pulled back, her voice was clipped, and she had a scowl on her face.

"Send her down," said Chandler.

Fat-Boy pressed forward on the joystick and our view of Esmeralda showed her gently descending away from Shirley. Esmeralda's camera showed us the Breytenbach resort, gradually expanding and exposing more of its secrets. The glass walls of the main building glinted the sunrise back to us like a mischievous wink. One of the sliding panels was open and we could see the shape of a man sitting at a table on the balcony.

"There's your man," said Chandler. "An early riser," he added with approval.

The drone continued drifting lower, and Fat-Boy called the height out as it descended.

"Two hundred feet, one hundred, eighty ..."

The sentries continued their slow progress around the perimeter, careful to keep a few metres inside the electrified game fence and keeping the Alsatian dog with them on a tight leash. They were walking away from us now, starting the climb back up to the far side of the property.

"What if they don't notice?" asked Robyn.

"We'll get close enough," said Fat-Boy. "They'll notice alright."

"If we'd had their schedule, we could have timed it better," said Chandler regretfully.

The sentries did notice the drone, but only when Fat-Boy had brought her all the way down below fifty feet. The moment was worth waiting for. One of them stopped and cocked his head to the side and looked up as if he thought a plane was flying overhead. The other one saw the drone and grabbed his partner so hard he almost dropped his R5 carbine.

The dog noticed the drone next and was the first to actually do anything. It raised up on its back legs and lunged forward with its jaws working. Barking presumably, although we had no audio.

"Hold her there," said Chandler. "Let's draw them out."

The sentry not holding the dog's leash spoke into the radio strapped to his shoulder, and then he raised his R5, and it jerked as he pulled the trigger.

"Pull back," said Chandler.

The camera jumped as Fat-Boy pulled back on the joystick and the drone stumbled away from the sentries. From the higher drone we could see the entire complex and the group of five black-clad guards jogging towards the perimeter position with their R5 weapons held loosely ready for action.

Esmeralda recovered her balance and the silently barking dog appeared in view again. The sentry who had fired earlier was taking careful aim and we could see the barrel of the rifle lining up with the lens.

"Take her in," said Chandler.

Fat-Boy's tongue endured an extra assault from his teeth as he swerved his heavy body in an effort to twist the drone. The camera swung round as the drone lurched towards the chief residence. A fleeting image of Breytenbach on the balcony standing at the railing, his hand raised and pointing up as if no one else had noticed the drone. Fat-Boy brought her to within thirty feet, did a loop and headed back out again.

"Back over the fence," said Chandler as if he and Fat-Boy hadn't discussed this in detail.

"Getting there," said Fat-Boy through gritted teeth.

The camera swept over the group of five guards who all had their rifles on their shoulders; the barrels jumping as they fired at the drone.

"Trigger happy," said Robyn under her breath.

The camera view suddenly lurched to the side.

"I'm hit," cried Fat-Boy.

"Over the fence," shouted Chandler. "Get it over the fence."

The camera was pointing directly down now, and the image flickered, then disappeared into a small dot which lingered, then faded altogether. Robyn was at the second laptop and zoomed the camera in to maximum. We could see the black shape of the wounded drone still moving towards the perimeter fence.

"Keep her up," said Chandler. "Nearly there, nearly there."

The black dot reached the fence and stopped moving as it snagged against the wires.

"Lift her," said Chandler.

Fat-Boy pulled the joystick all the way, and a moment later the shape crossed the nearly invisible barrier of the fence.

"Yes, baby!" cried Fat-Boy. The drone continued for about fifty metres, when it suddenly disintegrated and dropped in pieces to the ground. We stood in silence for a moment. Chandler patted Fat-Boy's shoulder.

"Splendid job," he said. "Let's see how long it takes them."

———

We had another hot chocolate each and Chandler was warming the espresso machine when the phone receiver beeped. He picked up the headset and flicked the speaker on.

"Hannes?" said a gruff voice.

"Hannes isn't on today," said Chandler, "can I help you?"

"Not on? What the fuck? Where is he?"

"Hospital," said Chandler, and left it at that. There was a moment's silence.

"Who're you?" asked the voice.

"Colchester," said Chandler. "I'm working with Hannes." He hesitated to add a little gravity. "Over this time."

"Ask him to call me," said the voice. "It's urgent."

"If it's urgent, best I help you," said Chandler. "Where are you calling from?"

"Ashanti."

"There's a problem?"

"We had a drone come over."

"A weaponised drone?"

"We're trying to retrieve it. Went down outside the fence."

Chandler smiled at Robyn and me. Fat-Boy was outside on the terrace cleaning Shirley.

"I've got just the thing for you. Anything approaches within fifty metres it gets fried. I'll come round."

"Hannes not available? You don't know how our boss gets about new people."

"It's all external. Your boss need not know we're there."

There was a thoughtful silence. "OK," said the voice.

"Be there in an hour," said Chandler and ended the call. "Psychology," he announced to us. "Understand their psychology and the rest is child's play."

"We had a lucky break," said Robyn.

"Nonsense. They behaved the way they always have. Hannes told us they were always on the phone to him. Every time they had a scare. Humans are creatures of habit.

What they've done before they will do again. It's the basis of every successful plan."

"Let's hope Hannes doesn't realise it was you who switched his sim card."

"It'll be a few hours before they issue a replacement."

"Well then let's hope a few hours is all we need," said Robyn.

TWENTY-EIGHT

The sandwich that had fallen to the ground and was being used as a gatehouse didn't look so much like a sandwich when we pulled up in front of it at oh eight hundred hours in one of the Ashanti Jeeps. It was a menacing entrance that appeared suddenly as you rounded the bend of the dirt road that approached it. Robyn suggested I only found it menacing because I was approaching with nefarious intentions. She could have been right about that. The two armed guards who came out to greet us also came across as pretty menacing, particularly the way one of them held back and hoisted his weapon up and pointed it in our direction as his colleague approached my window.

Chandler explained that we were there for the installation, and that the electrician in the panel van behind us was needed to plug things in.

The fact that we were driving a black Jeep that matched the vehicles they drove, and were wearing uniforms that matched theirs might have helped ease the tension a little, but we weren't greeted like welcome colleagues. The uniforms were absurd, designed by some fanciful artist. Black from top to toe, with enough pockets and straps to ensure that you could lose things in them for days. But they did have built-in webbing, and the steel-laced Kevlar that stops most pistol bullets before they do too much damage. Despite our fancy dress we were searched, and were required to leave our weapons with them, locked in a safe behind the reception counter. They also searched the vehicles, but the electronic junk we'd picked up in town the day before didn't cause any alarm. Neither did the metal box that exactly matched the boxes that had recently arrived from the Cape cause any alarm. And why should it? Those boxes from the Cape had not arrived with manifests listing their contents, and so the guards probably had no idea what they had locked away in their storeroom.

Stripped of our weaponry, the guards decided that we posed no immediate threat, although they gave Robyn an extra check just to ensure that the bullet-proof vest was fitting as tightly as it seemed. They ushered us through to an empty room with a water cooler and a glossy wooden table upon which were the broken pieces of a large drone. We looked at them with interest. The chief guard, who was made mostly of muscle and had a face of stone and not quite enough blood to fuel the brain as well as all the muscles, swept the pieces of Esmeralda to the side.

"That the drone that caused the trouble?" asked Chandler with interest.

The guard grunted. The red smiley face was still intact and I could see Fat-Boy took some satisfaction in that. Chandler spread the plans he'd brought of the complex on the cleared table.

He explained that we'd have to install our gizmo in the roof, and that we would need to access the power routing, to run a cable to the box. He stabbed a finger at the red lines we'd sketched in the night before, showing where we needed to access the power.

"It will require a bit of drilling," said Chandler, "but we'll keep the disturbance to a minimum."

The chief guard shook his head and tried to think of ways he could be obstructive. He came up with one pretty quickly.

"Not that room," he said, and sat back in his chair to see how Chandler would respond to that.

"What's the problem with that room?" asked Chandler.

"You can put it in the room next to it."

"No can do," said Chandler, and pointed at the symbols Robyn had stencilled over the other rooms around it. "What's the problem? The boss works in there?"

The guard shook his head. "Out of bounds," he said.

"You could post someone with us," suggested Chandler. "Make sure we don't steal the silver."

"It's out of bounds," said the guard again, having reached the limit of his vocabulary on the topic.

"Well," Chandler stared bleakly at the plans. "I suppose we could use this room," he said, indicating a tiny storeroom adjoining the other. "We'd have to do more drilling, though."

"Drill away," said the guard.

"It will take us longer," said Chandler.

"Take all day," said the guard magnanimously. "I won't rush you."

———

And he was true to his word. He didn't rush us. He personally walked ahead of our vehicles to guide us to a convenient parking spot near to where we would be working. I drove the customised Jeep with Chandler, Robyn drove the panel van because she needed the time at the wheel. "Practice, practice, practice," said Chandler as we crawled down the dirt track between the thorn trees. He was getting himself into the zone, I was beginning to recognise the signs. "Marvellous vehicles these," he said in his military British voice which was his chosen character for the day.

"It feels higher," I observed. "It sits higher than it did yesterday."

"Verisimilitude," said Chandler. "I had it fitted with the extra suspension they have on all their vehicles. We have to get the details right."

I nodded. Chandler had delivered several lectures on the subject.

"They can take a load of three tons," said Chandler. "Four-wheel drive, raised air inlet and sealed doors so they can practically drive under water. Veritable monsters."

"Three tons sounds a lot," I said.

"Not when you need to carry loads of that heavy yellow metal around," said Chandler, and his mouth stretched into a smile.

The storeroom that Chandler had reluctantly selected as a compromise was a narrow room that held Fat-Boy and the mortar drill and not much else. It had only one door which let onto the yard outside, where Chandler stood in the early morning sun engaging our chaperone in conversation. I fiddled about on the roof, pretending to fix a dome-shaped plastic box with some wires trailing out of it onto the flat concrete. Robyn moved the Jeep for no apparent reason down to the lower entrance, where she parked it with a group of matching vehicles under the watchful eye of two bored guards. I watched her walking back up the hill to the panel van, her pace measured and purposeful. She was doing her best not to attract attention. She reached the van, climbed into it and settled into the driver's seat to wait.

The guard with Chandler didn't seem to notice anything unusual when Fat-Boy emerged after half an hour of intensive drilling and pulled off his goggles and breathing mask and stood gasping for air at the entrance to the room. He looked like a grey ball onto which someone had sprayed a brown Zorro mask to look like eyes, a round circle for a mouth. The guard didn't mention that it seemed an exorbitant amount of dust for a few holes that would take power cables, but I guessed that he wasn't employed for his deductive reasoning capacity.

The same guard also showed no surprise when I was called down from the roof to help Fat-Boy and the two of us squeezed into the cupboard-sized room and disappeared into the cloud of masonry dust. Fat-Boy used his stage whisper, which I would have thought they could have heard all the way over at the entrance gates. He had connected the circuit breaker and was ready to trip the power. It was time to trigger the alarm.

I squeezed through the hole he had drilled in the wall and between the shelves of the cupboard in the next room. I twisted one arm back to signal to Fat-Boy that I was ready. He fired up the drill again and chose an arbitrary spot on the wall to provide the sound of a drill cutting into the wall. I pushed on the door of the cupboard. Nothing happened. It was locked. I backed out of the narrow gap, found a screwdriver in Fat-Boy's toolbox and squeezed back in. I detached the lock from the inside of the door, keeping the screws in my hand so I could replace them quickly.

With the lock detached, I pushed on the door. It had one of those gentle closing springs, so I had to be careful that it didn't spring open enthusiastically and leave me hanging through an open hole in a room full of invisible laser beams.

Those laser beams had been thoroughly positioned. The door hadn't opened more than a few inches when the alarm triggered. Like some unearthly spirit suddenly discovering a heart-wrenching loss, the wailing filled the room and vibrated in the air.

Fat-Boy stopped the drilling, and I felt him tripping over my legs to get to the door. I let the door spring closed again and replaced the screws on the lock. There was shouting from outside, and I could hear Chandler's voice, steady and calm. I got three of the screws in, then dropped the last one which I abandoned, and pulled myself out from between the shelves. Still the deafening wailing of the alarm continued. Fat-Boy was blocking the door, and I gave him a prod so he knew I was ready, and he stepped forward so I could follow as if I'd been there all along. Not that anyone noticed. The guard with Chandler had his gun raised, and his face was twitching anxiously. Chandler had his hands half raised in a placatory manner, and beyond them a group of three guards came running with their R5 carbines ready to be brought up to the shoulder and be put to use.

The siren stopped its wailing with a final squawk as if someone had it by the throat. The silence was sudden, broken only by the heavy breathing of the guards as they came up to us and raised their guns.

"It must have been the drill," said Chandler loudly. "I was just saying to your colleague here that the vibration on the wall could trigger a sensitive alarm."

The guards didn't respond and kept their guns trained on us. Their radios crackled, and two of them lowered their weapons and moved away reluctantly.

"They will check the room," said the guard who had been in conversation with Chandler.

"Good idea," said Chandler, and he nodded with approval. The tension eased a little, and the guards lowered their guns. It took them a few minutes, but they called the all-clear when they had checked that the master's private study was undisturbed.

"All good then," said Chandler, and he tried to produce a warm smile, but there was a little too much tension in his cheeks. "We're nearly done, but probably best that you disable the alarm. Just until we're done with the drilling."

Chandler's new friend suggested this over his radio to the control room and was rewarded with a scornful, foul-mouthed response. "They'll disable it for a few minutes only," he interpreted for Chandler. The other guards passed by on the way back to their stations, and Chandler called out that we'd try not to do that again, and produced a sound that I think was meant to be a laugh, but sounded more like a cough to me. Mind you, my adrenalin levels were mounting, and my perception was probably distorted. Chandler turned to Fat-Boy and me and barked at us to get the job finished.

He turned and walked towards the panel van, leaving his chaperone undecided as to where he should be concentrating. At the panel van Chandler would discover that what he needed was in the Jeep and he would walk calmly down to that vehicle, and out of sight of the chaperone. We had calculated ninety seconds for that and doubled it for safety. Three minutes was all it would take. Fat-Boy started the countdown timer attached to the circuit breaker and then went back outside, gesturing vaguely to the panel van. Our chaperone did his best to keep an eye on him as he climbed into the van, then glanced back warily towards the dark doorway where I moved some tools around to draw his attention and watched the countdown carefully.

Fat-Boy shed his overalls in the van, climbed through it and exited on the far side where we couldn't see him. I dropped a drill bit, which made a loud clatter, and Fat-Boy used the distraction to follow Chandler down the hill.

We had sixty seconds on the clock.

————

At thirty seconds I heard a fresh voice, one that sounded familiar. Another guard had joined our chaperone. But my time was up, I needed to be clear of the place before the circuit breaker triggered. The sunlight blinded me momentarily as I came out of the room into the yard.

"All done here," I said and held my hand up to my eyes. It took me a moment to recognise the man with his back to me, but when I did the surge of adrenalin was like an explosion in my chest.

He turned to face me. Pale, almost white skin, and cold blue eyes. Then the hard ridge of the red scar running down his cheek came into view.

He recognised me with a shock. He dropped the cigarette he was bringing up to his mouth, and his hands went for his R5. He started to raise it, but I wasn't waiting to see how quick he was on the draw. I dropped into a crouch and leapt straight towards him. I caught him on the chest just as he was swinging the gun around and hit him with enough force to push him over backwards. I kept moving, sprinting the thirty metres to the van, which lurched away from the road edge as I approached, the passenger door swinging open. I grabbed the stanchion and pulled myself in. Robyn was at the wheel and as I hit the seat, she kicked the pedal and the van bucked like a wild horse and kicked up a cloud of dust before shooting forwards and along the track towards the gate.

In the side mirror I could see Scarface and the chaperone firing at us. Our panel van had extra sheets of steel in the panelling to protect us, but a bullet struck the mirror and their two figures splintered into myriad repeated slivers.

The small charge attached to the circuit-breaker sounded like the popping of a cork out of a bottle over the whining engine of the van. The only indication that the complex had lost power was in the strangled wail that came from the manually triggered alarm as it tried to start up but then lost power.

We had two hundred metres to go, and Robyn accelerated all the way, shifting gears like a professional. She sat behind the wheel in a relaxed way, well back against the seat so that her head was not exposed, and she held the wheel loosely, allowing the tyres to bounce on the rough track, but keeping our path steady all the way to the gate.

Breytenbach's private army did all the right things in the eight seconds that it took us to cover the distance to the gate. They didn't stand in front of us. Only complete idiots stand in front of a fleeing vehicle. And they opened the gates for us, which was a relief because I wasn't looking forward to discovering which was stronger, the front of the van or the steel ribbing of the gate. They raised the spikes, and Robyn gunned us over them, doing almost a hundred.

The tyres exploded with sharp bangs and I could see the rubber flying off into the bush at the side of the road. Robyn almost lost control of the van, but she held the wheel steady and let the rims carry us like the blades of ice skates across the rocky surface. She'd stopped accelerating and focused all her attention on bringing us to a smooth stop without rolling. Another series of bangs told us the guards were firing on us and doing their best to take out the rear doors of the van. I was grateful for Chandler's obsession with detail and the three steel plates that were leaning up against the back of our seats.

The van ground to a halt amidst an awful screeching of the metal rims against the rock substrate. Eventually it shuddered, and we were stationary. A cloud of dust caught up with us and billowed past the windows. Robyn turned to me. Her eyes were dancing, and her nostrils were wide.

"Convinced?" she asked.

"More than convincing," I said. "I was regretting not having written my will."

Robyn smiled. I don't think she had ever looked so beautiful. She kissed me, then kicked open her door, and held out a white handkerchief that she'd brought for the purpose. It fluttered in the wind, and the popping sound of the shots being fired into the back of the van slowed reluctantly, then stopped altogether. We waited, then heard a loud voice.

"Step out of the vehicle," it said, finding more syllables in the word 'vehicle' than I would have thought possible. Robyn raised her hands and stepped out. I opened my door and did the same. A team of twelve guards faced us, their guns raised.

"Don't move," called the voice, and then realising that they needed us to move amended that to "Turn and face the vehicle with your hands behind your heads."

I did as instructed and assumed that Robyn did the same. Rough hands searched me, then I was pushed to the ground, and the two men assigned to me gave a few determined kicks to show me how angry they were. Then they rolled me over onto my stomach with their feet, and one of them knelt on my back and used his gun barrel to check that nothing I was carrying was made of metal. He stepped away from me and let me struggle to my feet.

I joined Robyn at the back of the van where the guards were trying to get the rear doors open and having a difficult time of it because of the buckling caused by their gunfire. We waited and watched until eventually one of the doors came away and dropped to the ground with a crash.

The metal box glinted in the sunlight. It had stood up well to the many bullets that had struck it, sustaining only some buckles and dents in the burnished aluminium edges.

"What the fuck?" said the leader of the troop. "What is this?" he demanded of me.

"It's a box," I said, and was rewarded with the butt of his rifle on my jaw.

"What's in it, fucker?"

I shrugged. Not in a defiant way, but in a friendly, we're-all-confused-together kind of way. "We'll have to open it," I said.

The man considered applying the butt of his rifle again, but the inclusive "we" won him over. Instead, he stepped forward to look more closely at the box. He twisted the clasps and confirmed they were locked.

"We'll take it back to the boss," he pronounced.

TWENTY-NINE

The Breytenbach residence was designed to provide the optimum environment for just about every conceivable circumstance. But the one contingency that didn't seem to have been planned for was the necessity for conducting an unfriendly interrogation. There were no rooms with raw concrete and tiled floors for easy cleaning of the blood and no rooms with ceiling-mounted hooks for suspending the guests. This shortcoming bothered the leader of our squadron, who engaged in frustrated conversation over his radio about where we should be taken. He wanted to take us to their barracks, but the boss wouldn't stoop that low and so eventually Robyn and I were ushered into one of the smaller reception rooms like we were weekend guests.

The room had a hunting theme, from the zebra skin rugs on the floor to the old-fashioned shotguns displayed in racks on the walls interspersed with original paintings of wild animals. There was a wall-mounted animal head which was an angular metal sculpture of a surprised deer with gold-plated horns. But the most dominant feature of the room was the wall of glass that looked out over the African bush with not a building, telephone pole or other man-made object in sight.

The two men who had carried the metal box placed it in front of the glass wall like a sparse piece of set dressing, and then we all waited.

Riaan Breytenbach came into the room like a bull being released into the fighting ring. Short and stocky with a reserve of energy that seemed to force him into continuous movement, his legs moving in quick snappy strides. He glared at the two of us in fury, spending a moment on each of our faces. He lingered on my face and nodded to himself as if I'd just answered a question that he had guessed the correct answer to.

"Where are the others?" he asked of the room, in a voice taut with anger.

Nobody said anything and so Breytenbach swung around to the guards, still pointing their R5's at us.

"Find the others," he roared. "There were four of them, you incompetent idiots. The others must be running about the place looking for a way out. Find them. Hunt them down. Kill them if you have to."

The final sentence was a bellow from Breytenbach which gave them the motivation they needed to get moving. A moment after the last one left, another black-clad figure stepped into the room. Tall and emaciated, his face was a familiar one. Black hollows for eyes, sharp ridges as cheeks. It was the man I had last seen getting to his feet off a wet road as our ambulance fled away. In his hand Sidekick was holding a small ring which held a single key. He showed it to Breytenbach, who nodded with approval.

We waited in silence. Breytenbach strode back and forth a bit as if he was waiting for the arrival of our colleagues before starting with the kangaroo court. Then he came to a stop in front of me.

"Your friend's a killing machine, did you know that?" he said, his voice raised to make it clear he was addressing Robyn, even though he was looking at me. "A killing machine," he repeated with admiration. "You dealt with those pesky villagers for me, didn't you? Just killed the lot of them. Fuck … it was a sight to behold." Breytenbach had the polished eloquence of a man used to being quoted in the media, naturally structuring everything he said into convenient sound bites. The profanity was out of place and he knew it, using it for shock effect.

"Killing is clearly your greatest talent. I should have known you scum were making notes and dreaming up ways of taking your cut. But it was only when you walked into my office that I finally cottoned on. All that drivel about the Khayelitsha fire was an excuse. You'd come to get my gold. You've fucked it up though, haven't you?"

Breytenbach stepped up to Robyn and stared at her.

"The real psycho," he said, "was your friend's call-sign leader. Now there was a killer if ever I saw one. Was it him that stepped on a mine after the terrorists shot down that plane? I'm sure I heard some story along those lines. The candle-maker, they called him. And then one day he lit up that candle in a big way." Breytenbach allowed himself an amused smile. "Anyway, a killing machine is what your friend is. Did you know that?"

Robyn said nothing.

I said, "It takes one to know one."

Breytenbach turned back to me with surprise. "You think so?" he said. "You think I'm a killer? Coming from you, I consider that a compliment." He paused as if this had given him something to think about, then said, "Oh, I see what you are saying. It's your justification for stealing from me." He gave me a patronising smile.

"We have no justification," I said. "As you had no justification for killing Lindiwe Dlomo and Wandile Mbuyo."

Breytenbach covered his surprise with a smile that showed us what money can buy in terms of dental work.

"That train has left the station," he said. "Didn't you hear? Mbuyo's lying in a hospital bed with a bullet in his brain. There's not much you can do for him now."

"He told his story before your hired buffoon put that bullet there," I said. "Told me the whole story. All about you helping him light the fire."

Breytenbach gave me another smile.

"And you think I care?"

"No, I don't think you do," I said.

"We were fighting a war," he said. "That's what everyone forgets."

"But you weren't. You personally were not fighting a war, were you? You'd been kept far away from the action, posted to an insignificant section of military intelligence. Did you want to feel the power? Did you create your own action by killing some people you thought nobody would bother too much about?"

Breytenbach turned away from me with a scoffing laugh and stood at the window.

"What are they doing out there?" he asked. "How long can it take to chase down these bungling fools?"

"They are wearing our uniforms," pointed out Sidekick in his surprisingly high-pitched voice.

Breytenbach nodded and looked at Sidekick as if suddenly remembering why we were all here.

"You got yourselves one of my little boxes," he said with another scoffing laugh. "One box ... how pathetic is that?

One little box, and for that I would have hunted you down for the rest of your lives."

"Only for the rest of your life though," I said.

"Is that meant to be a threat?"

"I wouldn't bother to threaten you. You're untouchable, aren't you, Mister Breytenbach? That's why you don't care that Mbuyo told his story to me before you had him shot. You don't care who knows about what you did. Because you have someone looking after your best interests."

Breytenbach gave the smile that I remembered from the mines on Uganda. The conceited look of a man who knew he would win.

"A senior government official is covering for you, isn't he?" I said.

Breytenbach brought his hands up and clapped them together in mock applause.

"Well done, you brave little soldier," he said. "Did you work that all out yourself?"

"Don Fehrson knows your nasty little secret," I said. "And he is making sure that it stays hidden."

Breytenbach's smile grew a little wider and became a smug grimace.

"It's a mutual relationship," he said. "I scratch his back and he scratches mine."

"It must have been a surprise to discover that he'd been lying to you all those years about his daughter. And to learn that he had helped Lindiwe disappear and made it look like she'd died."

"Water under the bridge," said Breytenbach. "It's been so many years, and Don Fehrson's been a wonderful ally, I'll allow him some sentiment."

"You're not worried that killing his daughter has broken his trust?"

Breytenbach shrugged.

"It was either or, wasn't it? He knew that. His son has a drug problem. Killed a man, but the case was dropped. Dropping a case like that takes influence, and a lot of money. Fehrson knew it was either the daughter or the son. I explained that to him."

"You bought his protection by buying his son's freedom?"

"Among other things. Do you think that journalist fell into the sea all on his own? If I wanted I could have your Father Fehrson put away for a long time. Or worse."

"That's the power of the killer, isn't it?" I said. "There is always that ultimate threat."

Breytenbach's smile had grown weary. He let it fade.

"I think you might have made the mistake of underestimating my influence," he said.

"I might," I admitted. "But you have made mistakes too."

Breytenbach gave his scoffing laugh again. "I have? Such as?"

"Such as thinking that we're here for the gold."

Breytenbach's laugh morphed into a mocking snarl.

"There it is," he said, indicating the metal box. "Your one little box of my gold. Why else are you here?"

"Why do you think?" I said.

"You wanted to talk about those people? You wanted to frighten me with your threats?"

I didn't say anything. Robyn did.

"He's here to do what he does best," she said.

Breytenbach's confidence wavered. He turned to the cadaverous Sidekick.

"Open the box," he said.

Sidekick knelt before the box and used his key to unlock

the clasps. It turned easily because we'd rigged the locks to open with any key. Then he lifted the top of the box and moved aside so we could all see what it contained.

A jumble of steel washers, nuts and bolts.

The sight had a dramatic effect on Breytenbach.

His confidence slipped from him like the shedding of a skin. He looked at us in confusion, then back at the scrap metal in the box.

"There's no gold," he complained.

I said nothing. Breytenbach looked at me, and the blood drained from his face.

"You're not armed," he said as if that objection could change the course of events.

"Who needs weapons?" I said.

But Breytenbach clearly did, and he was not going to wait around to see whether his suspicions were well founded. He took action and did so fast. It was our bad luck that the room happened to contain many weapons, hanging invitingly on the walls. He strode over to a side wall and wrenched an antique Winchester shotgun from its bracket. Displayed conveniently below it was a box of cartridges in the original cardboard packaging. He looked up at Sidekick, who was still gazing with confusion at the contents of the box.

"They've come to kill me, you fucking idiot," he screamed with panic in his voice. "Shoot them."

Sidekick was a bit slow on the uptake, but he reached for his handgun and withdrew it from the holster under his arm. Breytenbach cracked the shotgun open.

"Shoot them," he said again, and then shouted with sudden rage, "fucking shoot them."

He was fumbling with the cartridges and dropped one, which clattered off the tiled floor. Sidekick raised his weapon and pointed it at me, then at Robyn. His finger trembled on the trigger, and his eyes were full of confusion. I don't think he would have squeezed the trigger if it had not been for the sudden cracking noise as Breytenbach snapped the barrels of the shotgun back.

The sound of the blast deafened me for a moment and in that silence Robyn collapsed beside me. Her head twisted sharply towards me and she crumpled noiselessly. I dropped to my knees and saw her eyelids flutter as she lost consciousness. It was a head wound. A trickle of blood appeared and made a path across the tiles.

I have been trained to respond to a sudden burst of adrenalin with instinctive, immediate action. I had the hot barrel of Sidekick's Beretta in my right hand as my left arm gripped his skull-like face and twisted. He buckled under the blow to his groin from my right knee, and as his body curled up, I released his head and dislocated his right arm. His fingers released the Beretta, and he dropped to the floor with a howl.

Breytenbach had the Winchester up and pointing at me. I saw the stretched grimace of exertion as he pulled the trigger. I dropped to land with a jolt on the hard tiles beside Robyn.

Suddenly it was raining glass, and I was deaf again from the blast of the old Winchester. I felt the pain from the small pieces of shot that lodged themselves in my legs and back. The edge of the spreading blast had caught me, but only the edge. Breytenbach had loaded a single cartridge, and I glimpsed him struggling to open the gun again. Sound rushed back a moment later, and a siren wailed into life somewhere. I lifted Robyn onto my shoulder and stepped through the shattered remains of the glass wall and onto the thin lip of concrete outside. I glanced back. Breytenbach had the shotgun cracked open and was fitting another cartridge.

There was a four-metre drop into a patch of garden with neatly trimmed ornamental trees. Beyond them was thick scrub, and a dusty path winding into the bush. I could make out the forms of guards in the far distance running towards the alarm. I tucked the Beretta into my empty holster, held Robyn in my arms with her head supported against my shoulder and jumped. I landed badly and felt the anterior ligament in my left leg pop. I stumbled and almost dropped Robyn's limp body, but managed to break her fall and then limped twenty metres away from the approaching guards, with Robyn's feet dragging in the dirt. I laid Robyn down carefully and crouched beside her. Her breathing was shallow but rapid. The blood from the wound was spreading over her face now, and I made sure her nose and mouth were clear.

The guards were still far enough in the distance that I didn't think they had seen us jump, but I heard the sudden shout of alarm from one of them, and through the haze of greenery saw their figures scattering to take cover. Breytenbach had stepped out onto the ledge and had probably mistaken their movement through the trees for his fleeing prey. He brought the shotgun up to his shoulder and fired both barrels towards them. The shot spread wide and kicked up a cloud of dust well clear of the guards, but their confusion was palpable in the silence that followed.

Breytenbach had the sun behind him from where I crouched. I could make out his shadowy form breaking the gun open again and fumbling to insert another two cartridges, little more than a black silhouette against the sun. As he raised the gun to his shoulder, I took careful aim with the Beretta and shot him three times.

The first shot caught him in the arm. He spun around, the shotgun flew from his grasp and dropped onto the ground with a clatter. The second shot went through his leg just above the knee, shattering the femur and passing all the way through. The third shot finally brought him down, catching him in the hip, where the bullet lodged. He gave a surprised gasping cry of pain and then crumpled like a paper bag and dropped into the ornamental garden with a sickening crunch. He lay in a heap only twenty metres from us and didn't move. There was an awed hush for a moment and then the guards rushed over to him.

I knew that it would be a matter of only a minute or two before they found us. Despite their confusion and the focus on their fallen master, they would spread out and start the search. I wouldn't be able to lift Robyn and limp out of sight in time. Her face was mostly covered now with streaks of the blood that was still seeping from the wound on the side of her head. I felt gingerly and found it above her ear. Her eyelids fluttered as she struggled to regain consciousness. It felt like a tear in the skin which meant a surface wound, but there wasn't much hope if we waited for those guards to find us. They would probably shoot us on sight.

However, if I called them over, I might get them to help.

And then, just as I prepared to give ourselves up, I heard the sound of Chandler's B-plan. The churning thump of a chopper's blades. Not one chopper, but three of them. You don't send a police van in to deal with a private army, you send an army.

The guards all looked up at the approaching heli-copters. They recognised the camouflage markings and the distinctive shapes of the air force Denel Rooivalk attack helicopters. The choppers flew low over us to drop their troops onto the helicopter pad on the roof of the main lodge, blowing up a rolling mist of dust. The guards lowered their weapons and their leader called out orders. He posted two men with Breytenbach, and the others turned back to the barracks. It looked like the search for the person who had shot their boss would be postponed. A guard arrived with a field stretcher a minute later, and they loaded Breytenbach onto it. They carried him off, and we were left alone.

I lifted Robyn onto my shoulder. It was only a couple of hundred metres to the outdoor sauna and I limped all the way.

———

We laid Robyn on the slatted wooden terrace between the sauna and the ice pool. She had lost a lot of blood and her face was deathly pale beneath it, her hair a matted tangle.

I cleaned her face while Chandler cut her hair with scissors from the medical kit and gingerly explored the wound. His face was stone, his hands steady. Fat-Boy knelt at her feet, his eyes closed and he muttered under his breath, a prayer or perhaps an African enchantment.

We worked in silence and in haste. The entire lodge seemed to have gone quiet. Chandler's assumption that the search for us would be abandoned when the army arrived was probably correct. The sauna outhouse was also the most unlikely place for us to run to, the furthest building from the main gatehouse, positioned on the edge of the bush not far from the small gate in the game fence used by the morning and evening patrols.

Robyn's breathing was still shallow, but her pulse was steady and Chandler said the signs were good, although he didn't look as if he believed his own words. But after a few minutes he gave a grunt and looked up at me.

"It's a surface wound," he said. "Scraped the side of the skull, gave her a nasty knock, took a few splinters with it. She's concussed. But she'll live."

Fat-Boy stopped his incantation and opened his eyes. He turned away from us before we could see the tears.

I cleaned the wound and Chandler stitched the torn skin with an uneven row of small sutures. I attached a drip to her arm, and we wrapped her in a nano-heat blanket. Chandler worked on cutting the shot out of me and disinfecting the wounds. Fat-Boy used binoculars to watch for the return of the morning patrol. In the distance, we could hear the gentle hum of an approaching helicopter.

"I expect that's BB's ambulance," I said.

From the terrace we were afforded an unimpeded view of the speck of dust that became a white chopper with a red cross on it as it approached over the scrub.

"Ambulance?" said Chandler. "You telling me they didn't call a hearse?"

———

When Chandler was satisfied that Robyn's condition was stable, we moved her into the Jeep, which was roughly camouflaged behind some leafy branches. Then we waited on the terrace for the return of the morning patrol. The army helicopters had been on the ground a good hour, and everything was uncannily peaceful. Somewhere on the other side of the complex Breytenbach's private army was facing the military team, and someone was trying to explain how it had happened that one of the ten wealthiest South Africans had been shot three times and fallen four metres from a terrace of his private estate. And trying to explain how it was that the person who had done the shooting might have been wearing their uniform. I expected they were also wondering why the call to the military base had been made an hour before Breytenbach had been shot.

We looked out over the African bush which stretched away to the distance. High above us the vultures were circling.

"The arm, the leg and hip?" said Chandler. "What were you playing at?"

"I needed to make sure he wasn't going to follow us," I said.

Chandler's eyes narrowed, and he watched me closely.

"You can hit a one pound coin from fifty metres with a blindfold on, Corporal Gabriel. Are you telling me now that you didn't go in there to kill him?"

"I chose not to."

"Chose not to?" said Chandler incredulously.

"Robyn was with me," I said, and lit another cigarette.

Chandler nodded as if that explained it, then decided that he was entitled to deliver some unsolicited advice.

"You need to play it carefully," he said.

"Play what?"

"With Robyn."

"She's a big girl; she can look after herself."

"It's not her I'm worried about," said Chandler. "She's damaged goods and damaged people only pass the damage on."

Before I could respond Fat-Boy called out. A cloud of dust was approaching from the wild side of the fence. The morning patrol was returning.

———

The patrol car threw up a cloud of dust which drifted past us as they spoke into the intercom at the gate. We watched from our leafy shelter as the gate squeaked open, and then they gunned the motor and filled their rear-view mirror with more dust as they headed into the complex. We needn't have worried that they would wait to ensure that the gate closed behind them; they were out of sight before it had completely opened.

"You sure it's not going to close on us?" asked Chandler.

"I did everything you said, Colonel. Cut the camera cable, blocked the sensor. You wait and see."

We sat in our Jeep and watched as the dust settled. The gate didn't close.

"All clear?" asked Fat-Boy.

"All clear," I confirmed.

We rolled forwards and shook off our camouflage branches. Once we were on the far side of the gate Fat-Boy stopped the vehicle and climbed out to enable the sensor again. The gate squeaked closed.

"Shouldn't we go back for Esmeralda?" asked Fat-Boy as he climbed back in.

"Who the hell's Esmeralda?" said Chandler. Then he remembered and his mouth tightened. "Put your foot down on that accelerator, and don't take it off until I tell you to."

I was sitting beside Robyn's head and her eyes flickered open as the Jeep bounced over the rough ground. Her eyes focused on mine, and I could see some clarity return through the cloud of confusion. She groaned and closed her eyes again.

Chandler gave me a tight smile. He was crouched in the back and his arm was resting on an old tarpaulin that covered an uneven pile of boxes.

"Is this car sitting a little lower than it was?" I asked.

"Not much," said Chandler.

"Three tons did you say?"

"We've not loaded half of that," he said and smiled again.

As we drove off down the dusty road into the wild game area, the ambulance chopper flew over us on its way to Nelspruit hospital. Chandler gave me a puzzled look.

"You're a changed man, Corporal Gabriel," he said. "Sending people to the hospital, and not the morgue. Never thought I'd see the day."

THIRTY

"An awful lot of people you come into contact with seem to sustain gun injuries," said Fehrson in his most plaintive tone.

I said nothing.

"Well," Fehrson sniffed. "He's lucky to be alive, although he lost that leg."

"And he blames me?" I said.

"He complained that you tried to kill him."

I didn't say anything, but Fehrson raised a hand as if to stop me.

"I told him that in my experience if you tried to do something, you rarely failed to actually do it. Particularly when it came to killing."

We sat in silence for a moment. The clocks ticked loudly.

"You are no longer employed by the Department," said Khanyi. "We wanted to remind you of that, and also of the fact that you are still bound by the Official Secrets Act."

"You wanted to be sure I would keep quiet," I suggested.

There was another brief silence.

"He's also been kicking up a fuss about some gold that was stolen from him," said Fehrson. "Do you know anything about that?" He looked at me with his innocent blue eyes.

"Was it a lot of gold?" I asked.

"Only a few bars. There are laws about how much he's allowed to hold on private property, and there is something about a register not matching, which is probably why he's being vague."

"It probably is," I said.

"Some of his staff have suggested that it was more than a few bars," said Khanyi.

"Big numbers have been floated," said Fehrson. "US dollars ... millions of US dollars ... tens of millions."

"Goodness," I said, and we sat for a moment in silence.

"We would be grateful to you, Gabriel," said Khanyi. "If you did keep this whole thing quiet. The Lindiwe business, Mbuyo and so forth."

"Yes, of course," said Fehrson as if that had been one of his lines that he kept forgetting. "Very grateful if you left us out of it."

"Very," said Khanyi before I could spend too much time thinking about the specifics of their gratitude. "Father has even been taking a look at those expenses, haven't you, Father?"

"I have," said Fehrson, and he sniffed. There was a pause as he forgot his lines again. "There are one or two we might be able to concede," he added when they came back to him.

"That's very generous of you," I said, and everyone smiled.

There are some days in the beginning of winter when Cape Town sits up and realises that it has had enough of all the moodiness and those temperamental rain clouds. It shrugs them off and provides the weary inhabitants with a clear and sunny day, and we all think winter might have been delayed until we open the front door and feel the bite of the snow from the mountains.

This had been one of those days and as Bill and I sat on his terrace and gazed out to sea, there was not a breath of wind. Bill poured us each a glass of a new Chardonnay he'd discovered. The sea was a solid steel plate across which a fishing boat was etching an elegant arc in the evening light.

"I can hardly believe he's back on his feet," said Bill. "They're swearing him in next month. Is he immortal?"

"He has a steel plate in his head," I said, "which probably amounts to the same thing."

"Matlala's still not convinced it wasn't you who tried to kill Mbuyo."

"Perhaps I did," I said. "Stirring up the past."

"That veal should be ready," said Bill. "Let's eat inside, it's not getting any warmer out here."

He stood, but didn't move towards the house.

"I don't want you to be angry," he said.

"About what?"

"I received an envelope." He placed his wineglass on the table as if he might need his hands to fend me off. He looked at me and drew a deep breath. "Addressed to you, but I opened it. It's about Sandy."

"What about her?"

"Photographs of her. A list of dates and some comments. A report of sorts." Bill picked up his glass and discovered that it was empty. "I shouldn't have opened it. It was addressed to you. Was it someone you hired to find her?"

"No," I said, "it was a journalist."

"That journalist friend of yours who died?"

I nodded and wondered whether my decision to provide the late Johansson with Bill's address had been an arbitrary one. "He was working on a story and came across a photograph of Sandy."

"Several photographs," said Bill. "They're inside." His big face drooped.

"Your veal will be overdone if we're not careful. Let's go and eat and you can show me."

————

There were many photographs in the folder, which I guessed the police had posted to the address I had conveniently written on the front cover. After they had decided the contents had no bearing on Johansson's death.

Close-up photographs of Sandy's vulnerable face. Wider-angle photographs of her walking with a group of men. In one of them she was wearing an elegant ruby suit, the only colour on the bleak, grey streets of Johannesburg. The men were in black suits and sunglasses despite the absence of the sun.

"Trafficking," said Bill. "It says a suspected ring of human traffickers."

He finished his veal and pushed the plate away as if glad to be rid of it. His heavy face was set with gloom.

"She doesn't look as if she's there under duress," he said and looked away from me when I looked up.

"It doesn't look that way," I agreed.

354

"Do you think she's working with them? How can she, Gabriel? It can't be."

"I don't think, Bill," I said, and tried to say it in a kind way. "For the people she left behind, it is best not to think at all."

"Now I've made you angry," said Bill. "I knew it would." He took a large handkerchief out of a pocket and blew his nose noisily.

"You lost a friend," I said. "That is worse than losing a lover."

"But you lost both," he said. "I still ask myself: why did she do it?"

"Maybe we'll find out one day," I said. "In the meantime, get me more of that delicious veal, and let's see if we can finish the bottle of Chardonnay."

———

I placed the folder of photos in the bottom drawer of my desk. Then I stepped out onto the balcony. My sliver of sea was lying calm and polished, syphoning the spilt milk of the moon up to shore in a wobbly line.

"It's your journalist, isn't it? Sandy."

Robyn stood at the door of the balcony, wearing nothing but a sheet from my bed. Her head was shaved and a jagged scar arched over her left ear. It was a look which should have robbed her of her femininity but which somehow only enhanced her appeal.

"Someone photographed her," I said. "Recently, in Johannesburg."

Robyn came to join me and shivered from the cold.

"You'll have to go and find her," she said.

"For what purpose? She doesn't want to be found."

"It's not what she wants, Ben. It's for you. You're trapped by her, don't you see? You need to confront her. Get some closure."

"Closure? Fat-Boy told me you were a psychologist."

"Not just for you, Ben. Do it for me, because we cannot happen, can we? Don't you see that? Not until you've moved on."

She smiled, and I wished for all the world that it wasn't true.

"Besides, I like the City of Gold," she said.

"Chandler warned me about you. Said I should be careful."

"And so you should," said Robyn. "Colonel Steven Chandler knows me better than anyone. Well, almost anyone."

She stood up, dropped the sheet to the ground and walked back to the door.

"It's cold out here, Ben. When you're done punishing yourself and gazing into the distance, come inside and warm up."

ENJOY THIS BOOK?

YOU CAN MAKE A BIG DIFFERENCE

Reviews are the most powerful tools at my disposal when it comes to getting attention for my books. Much as I'd like to, I don't have the financial muscle of a big publishing house. I can't take out full page ads in newspapers or put posters on the subway. (Not yet anyway!)
But I do have something much more powerful and effective than that, and it's something those publishers would kill to get their hands on.

A committed and loyal bunch of readers.

Honest reviews of my books help bring them to the attention of other readers.

If you've enjoyed this book I would be very grateful if you could spend just five minutes leaving a review (it can be as short as you like) on the book's Amazon page, on Good-Reads, BookBub and everywhere else.

Thank you very much!

357

GET EXCLUSIVE GABRIEL MATERIAL

Building a relationship with my readers is the most rewarding part of writing. And I would love to reward you, my reader!

Join my Readers' Club and receive a free Gabriel Series novella eBook, as well as updates about new books in the series and special Readers' Club deals.

Join the club and get your free novella on my website: https://davidhickson.com

I look forward to welcoming you to the club!

ABOUT THE AUTHOR

David Hickson is an award-winning filmmaker and writer from South Africa. His work has included internationally released feature films, television series and live entertainment television shows.

David travelled to Italy in 2010, an adventure that he and his family, including two young troublemakers and an assortment of very spoilt and demanding domestic animals, are still enjoying. He loves walking and cycling in the hills of Italy, drinking the local wine, and telling stories that entertain and stir the emotions of his readers.

For more books and updates:
www.davidhickson.com

ALSO BY DAVID HICKSON

Have you read them all?

Treasonous - *The Gabriel Series - Book One*

A journalist's dead body is pulled from the waters of Cape Town harbour, and disillusioned ex-assassin Ben Gabriel wonders whether he died because of questions he was asking about the new president. Gabriel knows that sometimes it takes one killer to stop another, and will do anything to discover the truth, even if that means stepping outside the law. (You're reading it now!)

Murderous - *The Gabriel Series - Book Two*

When a massacre in a small country church shatters an Afrikaans farming community, the message that this is "only the beginning" sparks the fear of genocide. The Department asks Ben Gabriel to apply his unconventional approach to discover the truth behind the massacre - a task made more difficult by the intensive search to find a large number of gold bars stolen from one of the country's most powerful men.

Vengeful - *The Gabriel Series - Book Three*

A series of prominent members of South African society are being brutally murdered. When the police discover that a certain Ben Gabriel recently visited each of them, he becomes a hunted man. And when Gabriel is linked to a multi-million dollar gold heist, his life becomes even more complicated.

Printed in Great Britain
by Amazon

68192441R00218